An excerpt from *The Secret Heir* by Zuri Day

"I am sorry to disturb you...

"I saw your light was on." Nothing.

Abe stood for a moment, but just as he started to walk away from the door, it opened. He turned to see Reign looking forlorn and sad.

He immediately pulled her into his arms. "Out of all of this beauty," he softly whispered, "you are the most beautiful, valuable and rarest bloom in this room."

His words touched something. He was sure she cried now. Softly, hiding her face from his view.

A few moments passed before she leaned back. "We've got to stop meeting like this."

Her words brought out that feeling again, an overwhelming passion, a possessive streak to have Reign as his own.

She was in his arms, soft and vulnerable, looking like sunshine, smelling like paradise. Without thought he reacted, pressed his lips against hers. She opened up and welcomed him in...and her mouth felt like home.

An excerpt from *After Hours Agenda* by Kianna Alexander

"The entire city of Atlanta is now waiting on the results of our little collaboration."

She said nothing, instead picking up her flute and finishing the small amount of champagne inside. "It's very bold of you to flirt with me like this, in the middle of an event and in front of my family."

He sensed the eyes of her brother on him and smiled. "I won't stay much longer. I'm sure the Woodson men won't stand to have you accosted. And that's as it should be." He took a step back and offered a bow. "I'll see you soon then, Nia."

A small smile showed on her face. "Go on back to your table, Pierce Hamilton."

He turned and walked away, well aware of the teasing tone of her dismissal.

She's not quite as frosty as she'd like me to believe.

Working with her should be very, very entertaining.

ZURI DAY
&
KIANNA ALEXANDER

THE SECRET HEIR
&
AFTER HOURS AGENDA

Recycling programs
for this product may
not exist in your area.

ISBN-13: 978-1-335-45753-0

The Secret Heir & After Hours Agenda

Copyright © 2023 by Harlequin Enterprises ULC

The Secret Heir
Copyright © 2023 by Zuri Day

After Hours Agenda
Copyright © 2023 by Eboni Manning

For questions and comments about the quality of this book,
please contact us at CustomerService@Harlequin.com.

Harlequin Enterprises ULC
22 Adelaide St. West, 41st Floor
Toronto, Ontario M5H 4E3, Canada
www.Harlequin.com

Printed in U.S.A.

Zuri Day is the award-winning, nationally bestselling author of a slew of novels translated into almost a dozen languages. When not writing or enjoying the adventures of international travel, she can be found in the weeds, literally, engaged in gardening, her latest passion, or in the kitchen whipping up tasty vegan and vegetarian dishes while being a chef in her own mind! Check out her bookshelf and become a part of her beautiful day by signing up for her newsletter at zuriday.com.

Books by Zuri Day

Harlequin Desire

The Eddington Heirs

Inconvenient Attraction
The Nanny Game
Two Rivals, One Bed
A Game of Secrets
The Secret Heir

Sin City Secrets

Sin City Vows
Ready for the Rancher
Sin City Seduction
The Last Little Secret

Visit the Author Profile page
at Harlequin.com for more titles.

You can also find Zuri Day on Facebook,
along with other Harlequin Desire authors,
at Facebook.com/HarlequinDesireAuthors!

Dear Reader,

You beautiful Daydreamer!

Have you seen the movie *Coming to America*? This last installment of The Eddington Heirs series, detailing Reign and Abe's story, is a loving nod to the late '80s romantic comedy featuring Eddie Murphy, Arsenio Hall and a star-studded cast that became an instant classic. Similar to in the movie, my hero, Aldric "Abe" Baiden, leaves an African paradise, the fictional Kingdom of Kutoka, to spend a year in America before honoring his duty to marry, continue the Baiden lineage and take his place in the family's corporate empire. Abe's parents think he's taking the trip to "sow his wild oats." Abe has other plans. He hopes to meet someone who will love him without knowledge of his wealth and royal connections. Abe wants to marry for love.

To do so, he'll have to convince Chicagoan Reign Eddington that the lowly blue-collar worker he's portraying is worthy of her wealthy, successful, high-society heart. Not an easy task. Reign has pressures of her own. As the youngest in a family of overachievers—Cayden Barker, Desmond, Maeve and Jake—Reign has something to prove. Can she make her mark and find love, too? Grab a glass of goodness, settle into a comfy chair, turn the page and let's find out!

Zuri

THE SECRET HEIR

Zuri Day

Rebels are sexy, unafraid to break rules
Living life on their own terms and nobody's fool.
With nothing to lose and everything to gain
Chances are taken and eventually love reigns.

out adding distance to the mix. Being with a superstar player, one whose popularity transcended basketball into A-list celebrity status, was an even harder, sometimes impossible, relationship to navigate. Their first year of dating had proved that. All the travel—forty-plus away games. All the components that made up his lucrative empire—shoe deals, corporate sponsorships, the investment portfolio her brother Jake managed. All the women, groupies, barracudas, hangers-on. All the haters. The unnecessary BS.

There had been more than one incident where she'd questioned his loyalty. The last was eight months ago when pictures of him cozied up with a certain famous, alluring pop star had been splashed all over the web. Blatant honesty had saved him. There had been almost constant arguments leading up to the affair. Jealousy, insecurities, mistrust on both sides. He'd accused her of flirting with a teammate. She'd admittedly been a bit too friendly with one of Jake's clients but had quickly reminded Trenton that she was only guilty of playful teasing while he'd done much worse and more often.

They'd been on an unofficial break when he'd slipped up with the busty brunette, and had stayed apart for two months. They'd not been technically exclusive when he'd cheated, and Reign hadn't been completely innocent, either, but through the whole sordid situation she'd had a realization. She wanted monogamy. It had taken a slew of extravagant gifts, almost nightly phone conversations, several heart-to-hearts and an ironclad commitment to exclusivity for Trenton to win her back. But her return had come with a warning: "Cheat again and I'm gone for good."

Since then, he'd been on his best behavior. There'd even been hints of forever, so much so that when Cupid shot his bow next month, she wouldn't be surprised to see an engagement ring attached. Having a relationship with a man that every other woman wanted hadn't been easy, but it was worth it.

That was why tonight was going to be super special. Company business had taken her to New York with her father, Derrick, and sister, Maeve. She hadn't been sure she'd be back in time to make the party. Trenton hadn't been happy, but he'd understood. Business came first. Especially when said business involved a family empire. When the lavish, deal-closing dinner she'd thought would take four hours finished in two, Reign couldn't believe her luck. She'd headed to the airport, calling Trenton along the way. After repeatedly getting voice mail, she'd finally sent a text just before the company plane had taken off for Chicago.

As if celebrating her boyfriend's good fortune wasn't enough, there was one more reason Reign was excited about tonight. The celebration would officially kick off her personal business. After years of dreaming about an online presence as a lifestyle influencer, she'd taken Jake's advice, followed his business model, and re-vamped her desire into an area not only closer aligned to a proved skill set, but also closer to something that complemented the family business. Something she was already known for and very good at. She'd created a branding business—Make It Reign—to expand her marketing and public relations expertise outside the finance arena.

Everything about tonight—from the balloons, table-cloths, napkins and invites to the complimentary ball caps and shot glasses for the men and crystal-studded wineglasses and tees for the ladies—would bear his unique logo. An artistic rendition of Trenton's profile with his short trademark twists, sexy scowl and one hand fluidly releasing a basketball, transposed over the letters TC in a commanding font. The photographer she'd hired would capture the action, along with a slew of media outlets covering the festive aftermath of Trenton's good news.

By morning, pictures of her TC branding would be seen everywhere, worn by some of America's favorite A-listers. A line of merchandise—more hats, tees and a signature shoe—courtesy of Ace Montgomery, her best friend London's internationally known, award-winning, designer husband, would follow the rollout. With his management team and the front office fully behind her ideas, this would not only be a stellar launch for Make It Reign, but sales created from tonight's publicity alone would potentially add tens of millions to Trenton's already overflowing coffers.

The flight landed early. A stretch limo sat idling on the tarmac to whisk her directly to Verve, Chicago's latest nightlife sensation. Still no text from Trenton, but she wasn't worried. He was no doubt being pulled in a thousand directions while basking in a sea of congratulations from adoring fans.

On the drive to the club, she went from day to eve-

ning by replacing the conservative pinstriped suitcoat
worn over a little black dress with a blinged-out, one-of-
a-kind version of the T-shirt each specially invited guest
received. She'd just released her hair from its clasp,
spruced up her makeup and traded comfortable pumps
for a pair of sexy stilettos when the driver arrived at the
entrance. He placed the car in Park and hurried around
to get her door. She settled a black faux mink around her
shoulders then pulled a crisp bill touting Ben Franklin's
picture from her clutch and tipped the driver.

"Have a beautiful evening, Ms. Eddington."

Reign thought about the barely there Fifth Avenue
purchase to be worn during her and Trenton's private
after-party and smiled.

"That's exactly the kind I have planned."

A slew of cameras went off immediately, one from
the photographer of a Point du Sable television reporter
she recognized. She bypassed the line and walked to
the door. The manager recognized her and ushered her
inside. Reign wasn't unaware of the looks and whispers
as she glided past at least a hundred people hoping for
a chance to get inside. The glares and comments from
the women. The stares and compliments from the men.

She was a beautiful woman who'd inherited the best
traits from parents Derrick and Mona. She was a member of a family recognized as Illinois royalty, especially
in the township of Point du Sable where the Eddingtons
lived. She was smart, gifted, drew in people with her
magnetism. Yet she wasn't conceited. She didn't always
see what others saw. Her siblings had set the bar for the
baby of the family very high. Reign felt she was always

trying to reach it and sometimes fell short. In her mind, Make It Reign would close the gap and help make her feel as talented and successful as her sister and brothers.

She stepped into an establishment pulsating with life. The music was loud and lively, a steady bass beat fairly shaking the walls. Everybody was dancing, conversing, fully engaged. She recognized several faces while being escorted to the elevator leading to the third floor's private VIP section where, much like in an arena, Trenton would be holding court. VIP was as turned up as the crowd downstairs. Her TC logo was everywhere—guys sporting the hats, women wearing the tees. Myriad conversations went on at once. She smiled, taking in the joyous atmosphere. All of this for her baby and what he'd accomplished. A Chicago Bull for five more years!

Reign strolled to the plush booths that lined the back wall. A pair of long legs stretched out from the last one. Her strides increased, effortlessly walking like a runway model in five-inch heels.

"Hey, ba—"

Screech! The scene she took in stopped all movement. The legs belonged to Trenton. He wasn't alone. His lips were moving, but he wasn't talking. He, or more specifically, his tongue, was engaged in a rather serious get-to-know with the scantily clad woman sitting on his lap. The tableau paralyzed Reign, but not for long. Noting an open bottle of Dom on the table, she envisioned a champagne shower over their heads and took a step to make it happen. Less than a yard away from completing the mission, a strong hand clamped her arm.

"Let me go!"

She yanked away from the determined grip, whipped around and came face-to-face with Donald, the photographer she'd hired to document Trenton's celebration and her business launch.

"Cameras are everywhere," he hastily whispered. "Remember the brand."

The caustic words she'd ironically shared with him just weeks before brought her out of the haze of anger temporarily clouding her good sense. Aware of cameras now capturing her moves, she looked up and saw that either her outburst or an observant friend had helped Trenton get the memo. His girlfriend, the one who was supposed to be exclusive, had arrived. He pushed the woman off his lap and stood in one motion.

"Reign!"

Like a ballerina in a jewelry box, she spun around on the heel of one stiletto and quickly retraced her steps. Trenton's voice grew louder.

"Baby, wait!"

So, now I'm your baby? Reign walked faster.

She reached the elevator, tapped her VIP card on the scanner and willed the doors to open.

Trenton reached her in less than a dozen long strides. "Reign!" He placed a hand on her shoulder.

She jumped as though scalded. "Don't! Touch! Me!"

The elevator doors opened. Thank God, it was empty. She stepped inside. Trenton followed.

"Get out, Trenton."

"No," he all but slurred.

Drunk. It figured. Obviously, the Dom she'd seen on the table hadn't been his first bottle.

"Let me explain."

"I don't want to hear it."

Someone on another floor pushed the elevator button, causing the doors to close. Reign stepped back and hugged the wall, glaring at the man she'd devoted head and heart to for the past eighteen months.

"How could you?" She managed to push the words past the lump in her throat. "This night is everything!"

"Baby, I thought…" He ran both hands over his head and along his face. Reign imagined the move was to help sober him up.

Good luck with that. She shook her head, disgusted.

"Why didn't…how… I thought you were in New York."

"Clearly, I wasn't expected."

"Why didn't you call me?"

Missed calls and voice mails showed up on phones. He'd get that reality check later.

"You knew how important this night was for me, for my business. You didn't care!"

"I did. I do! Everybody loves your stuff, baby, they—"

Reign choked out a laugh as the elevator doors opened. She pushed through a group waiting to get on. Accolades for Trenton followed them as the argument continued.

"Save it, Trenton. Hope the logo works out for you." She yanked her phone from her purse and texted the driver. "Don't expect me to follow through with the rest of the plan though. You'll get my bill for the design in the mail."

"C'mon, Reign. Don't be like that. Those girls mean nothing to me."

"Oh, girls. As in plural."

"No, those, that…you know what I mean."

"Sadly, I think I do."

Reign hurried toward the main entrance but, remembering the long line of fans, changed course and made a beeline for a side door. More fans noticed Trenton and yelled his name as he fell into step beside her.

"Stop following me!" She spoke quietly and through clenched teeth, aware of the eyes turned in their direction and cell phones snapping shots.

Trenton ignored her demand and easily kept pace. "Why are you so mad? That girl was just a fan congratulating me on the deal."

"Oh, is that what you call it? I'd think it would be kind of hard to convey that with your tongue down her throat."

"We weren't—"

"You were!"

"Sweetheart…"

Reign tried to tune out his excuses. She checked her phone. No response from the driver, whom she'd relieved for the night and, for all she knew, could be halfway back to the Point. She sent another message anyway and attached a 9-1-1. Thankfully, he answered.

Be there in five.

She yanked open the side door, not at all minding the frigid air that kept her from internally combusting.

Trenton continued to follow her. "Sweetheart, it was nothing. Please don't leave. This night's celebration is for you too."

"Trenton, I do not want to talk to you."

"Come on, Reign," he pleaded, his intoxicated tongue making her name sound like Wayne. "This is our night! This is the moment we envisioned, why we worked so hard."

"This is harassment. Leave me alone."

Trenton tried to embrace her. She shimmied away and turned to leave. He caught her arm.

"Stop it!" She struggled to free herself. Trenton's hold tightened.

"You heard the lady."

A slight scuffle followed that voice of authority. "Your presence is no longer desired."

A stranger now had Trenton's arm tucked behind his back, the other pinned to his side.

They'd both been startled by the man who'd quietly walked up and intervened. Reign couldn't believe someone had dared mess with Trenton. She didn't speak, but gratitude and curiosity shone in her eyes.

"Man, get off me!" Trenton shouted while trying to free himself from what appeared to Reign to be an ironlike grip.

"Only if your anger has been contained and you kindly give her the space she has requested."

"I'm okay," Reign said, her voice a shaky mixture of anger, embarrassment and the pain of a heart breaking in real time.

The stranger didn't appear to believe her words but released his hold on Trenton.

Six-foot-five Trenton rubbed his arm while turning to more fully take in a man Reign guessed to be around five-eleven. In the moment, the difference was negligible. Power exuded from his compact body. Reign didn't know who he was, but the guy sounded like someone used to having his orders followed.

"Who the hell are you?" Trenton asked.

"At the moment, I'm this woman's defender."

Someone must have heard the commotion. A few lookie-loos came around the corner. Seeing what would surely become a growing crowd, Trenton managed a chuckle.

"Where are you from, Wakanda? Back off and mind your business."

The expression on the stranger's face didn't change, nor did his soft tone. Shifting away from the onlookers, he said, "I am also someone who you do not wish to make angry. Please, leave her be."

Trenton took a step forward and stumbled. The stranger righted him even as he moved to become a barrier between Trenton and Reign. Her attention shifted from the horrible betrayal she'd witnessed inside the club to the heroic scenario playing out now.

Who is this guy?

A staredown ensued. More phones were pulled out. Reign watched the stranger step into the shadow to avoid being photographed. She did, too. The side door burst open. Trenton's friend, Luke the one who'd spotted her inside the club, bounded down the walk, her photographer, Donald, and two of Trenton's bodyguards close behind.

"Is there a problem?" a burly guard asked, glancing from Trenton to the stranger and back.

Luke spoke up. "Trenton! Let's go back in the club before a fight and not your new contract becomes front-page news."

Trenton glared at the stranger still watching their exchange. "You're lucky I'm in a celebratory mood and we have an audience. Next time will be different."

"There won't be a next time," the stranger calmly responded. His eyes remained on Trenton as the men reentered the building then slowly shifted to Reign. She felt a wave of something warm and protective from his gaze.

"Are you sure you're okay?"

She wasn't but nodded anyway, feeling his eyes still on her. *Mesmerizing*, Reign decided when she looked up and met his gaze. That was the best way to describe his eyes. Under the outside lighting, they were dark brown, almost obsidian. They held a sparkle. He wasn't handsome in the classical sense, yet there was something breathtaking about him. Another time, another place, Reign might be interested. Not now.

Her limo turned the corner and stopped right behind a car that had pulled to the curb, the man inside urging the stranger to get in. It was an older model vehicle that didn't at all match the aura of the man in front of her. She'd imagined the fashionably dressed stranger in a high-end sports car or luxury sedan. He turned, his eyes narrowing slightly as he looked back at her.

"What's your name?"

"Reign."

He smiled, a move that seemed to wrap around her like an intimate hug. Not only his gentle, caring expression, but the commanding energy that emanated from the man behind it.

"I like the name."

The man inside the idling car rolled down the passenger window. "Come on, man, we've got to go!"

"Are you sure you're okay?" the stranger repeated. "Do you have a ride? Do you need a taxi?"

"I'm fine, really. Go on with your friend."

"It is a pleasure to meet you, Reign."

"What's your name?"

He hesitated before saying, "It's not important. I'm just a good Samaritan glad I could help."

"All right, then. Take it easy."

The man gave a slight bow before striding over and getting into the car and a brief wave before it eased away from the curb and down the street.

Reign watched the taillights until the car reached the traffic light at the end of the next block and turned right.

She felt a certain void, an emptiness, and not just from seeing her boyfriend with some random girl. No, it was that guy. The stranger. Showing up as a knight in shining armor. Too bad that just moments before she'd learned that knights like that didn't exist.

Two

"Aldric!" His cousin Nolan eased from the curb and stepped on the gas. "What in the heck do you think you were you doing back there?"

"The same as I would have done at home," he calmly responded, checking the time on his rare Aboagye watch. "And while here in Chicago, my name is Abe. I don't want the competition to know that I'm here. It is imperative you remember that."

Meanwhile, Nolan's eyes bulged like he was about to implode. "You're not at home, Abe!" He all but spat out the nickname his cousin sometimes used when wanting to remain incognito.

They reached a red light. Nolan stayed silent until it turned green. "This isn't the Kingdom of Kutoka. In your homeland, your uncle is the king. Your family is distinguished. You are safe everywhere. Here in Chicago, you could get hurt for much less than that confrontation…or worse."

"I am not worried about dying."

"I'm not worried about you dying either. I'm only thinking of my aunt's and uncle's reaction when I tell them you're dead."

"I understand. They'd surely kill the messenger of that news."

"Exactly." The two shared a laugh.

Nolan shook his head and sighed again, louder this time.

"I'm not their only son," Abe reminded. "Nor their favorite."

"Maybe not. But you're still in line to head up that huge-ass company your grandfather started and your dad helped build. Your brother will most likely be Ghana's next president. Your cousin, and best friend, is next in line for the Kutoka throne. Compared to most people, your life is a dream."

Abe scowled. Remained silent. He understood why his cousin felt that way. Nolan wasn't aware of the challenges Abe faced. The pressure from his mother to marry and settle down. The tension that existed between him and his dad. Deciding to play professional soccer instead of joining the company after graduating college had caused a rift between them that had lasted for years. Only now that he'd retired from the sport, joined the company full-time, and offered an extended trip abroad to help expand their American inter-

ests, had the glacial friction between him and his dad
begun to thaw.

Having an older brother who did everything right
didn't help. Danso had worked for Kutoka Global from
the age of thirteen, leaving nearly two decades later to
become a successful politician, a move that had deeply
strengthened the bonds between Danso and his wife
Felicia's influential, politically well-connected Ghanian family. Even with his meteoric political rise in
the Ghanian government, he remained a member of
the company's board and an active contributor to its
future direction. These moves made the older son his
father's clear favorite. That he'd married strategically
thrilled both parents. He'd followed all their unwritten
but clearly defined rules.

Abe was different. Both personally and professionally, he'd gone against tradition. At almost thirty years
of age, he was still paying the price.

"How long are you staying here in America?" Nolan
asked.

Abe shrugged. "Not sure yet. Three to six months,
maybe longer."

Definitely longer, if he had his way. Getting back in
his father's good graces wasn't the only reason Abe had
suggested an extended visit in the US of A.

Returning to Kutoka and joining the company full-
time had amped up his mother's expectations for him
to marry, and soon. Preferably to someone from a family she knew and approved of. Women who married for
status and, in Abe's experience, were often superficial
and materialistic, more interested in what someone did

and had than in his character. Abe wasn't necessarily against marriage. But he wasn't in a hurry. When he decided to tie the knot, it would be him, not his mama, deciding who would be his wife.

"If most of that time is going to be spent in Chicago," Nolan continued, "I'm going to have to school you on some things."

"Like what?"

"Like not jumping into situations that are none of your business."

"I appreciate your concern, cousin, but I can take care of myself."

"Look, dude, I'm not trying to step on your swagger. But like I said earlier, this isn't Kutoka. Do something like that in my neighborhood and you might not live to tell the tale."

"I've been to where you live. It's…not terrible."

Nolan chuckled. "Not great either. I see you haven't been back."

Abe didn't answer. Nolan looked over with a gleam in his eye. "Face it, cousin. You and I grew up different. Every neighborhood comes with its own sets of rules. In mine, we help each other out if we can. But when it comes to personal situations, we stay in our lane."

"I've lived in London and traveled the world. Plus, the village where my maternal grandmother still lives is very rustic, very basic. I would have no problem navigating your neighborhood. I could live there."

"You couldn't do what I do or live where I live."

"No offense, cousin, but you clean buildings. It's not rocket science. As for your neighborhood? Yes, it's a low-income community. But that doesn't matter. I can live anywhere."

Nolan laughed again, louder this time.

Abe crossed his arms, more than a little chagrined. "You think I can't handle a rough neighborhood?"

"Or a vacuum cleaner."

"I could handle both," Abe said. "As long as the cleaner came with clear instructions," he added under his breath.

Nolan heard him. "You wouldn't last a day."

"I'd last much longer than that."

The conversation stilled. Each man deep in thought.

"Prove it," Nolan finally said.

Abe tsked.

"Uh-huh. Just as I figured. All talk and no action."

Nolan's words were like a gauntlet thrown down, one that Abe immediately picked up.

"Okay, I'll do it."

"You'll do what?"

"Move into your place."

"With those bougie clients you're trying to impress? How's that gonna work?"

"Most of my initial meetings are being held remotely right now. Where I live doesn't matter."

"We're swapping? I can stay at your place?"

Abe shrugged. "If you'd like."

"Shit," Nolan responded, dragging out the word as though it had several syllables. "I'd love it. More than that, my girl would love it."

Abe scowled at the feeling he'd been set up. "How long? A week?"

"It'll take me that long to teach you how to run all our equipment."

"What are you talking about now?"

"Cleaning, Mr. Corporate. The challenge was to live in my apartment and do my job." Nolan smiled broadly.

"Glad to see you enjoying yourself." Abe's frown deepened.

"I am. Immensely. But I'll lighten up." He paused, slowing to take the exit. In Chicago winters, errant ice could be anywhere. "Two weeks. You'll live in my apartment and work for the Clean Up Crew. Make it the two weeks and I'll owe you a hundred. Lose, and owe me a grand."

"What's fair about that?"

"Adjusting for net worth, man!" Nolan paused. "Never mind."

"What?"

"You can't work for me. Background checks are required. You don't want anyone to know Aldric Baiden lives here."

Abe reached for his satellite phone. "I'll handle that."

"You can get ID with Abe printed on it?"

"When you know the right people, you can get anything."

Abe sent a text to a childhood best friend now living and working in Washington, D.C. Within minutes, he received a thumbs up.

"Okay, that's settled. When do I start?"

"Once your paperwork is in order. Your pay is going to take a hit, though. I can only pay you minimum wage."

"You don't have to pay me at all. Because I'm going to

win the bet. And when I do…" Abe thoughtfully stroked his chin. "You're going to introduce me to Reign."

"Sounds like you already know her. How'd that happen?"

"Simple. I asked her. I wasn't so caught up in chivalry as to not recognize her beauty. I'd like a proper introduction."

"Said as though every Chicagoan knows each other. We don't. This is a big place." Nolan eased through an intersection as a yellow light turned red. "I do know her, though."

"Why didn't you just say so?"

"Because I like messing with you. I don't really know her know her, but I'm familiar with her family. They are as big-time here as yours is back home."

"What do they do?"

"Own and operate an international financial services company. She's one of the execs. But lately she's most recognized as Trenton Carpenter's girlfriend."

"The basketball player?"

Nolan nodded.

"I thought he looked familiar."

"It was Chicago's golden boy and the world's basketball star that you almost fought tonight."

"There would have been no fight. A quick and slight pressure applied to a certain nerve at his wrist would have rendered him more harmless than the amount of liquor he seemed to have consumed."

"He may have been tipsy but his guards weren't drunk. And they were probably packing."

"Packing?"

"Armed. Gunfights have replaced fistfights around here. Keeping that in mind might keep you alive."

They reached the mansion where Abe had lived for all of the five days he'd been in town. Nolan pulled into the circular drive, continuing to talk as the car idled.

"Reign's brother's wife is one of my customers."

"For the office cleaning company?"

"No, for the FBI." Nolan chuckled. "I said my customer, didn't I?"

"Is this woman also in corporate America?"

"Ivy founded and runs a private school about twenty miles from here in a town more closely resembling your bougie kingdom. It's called Point du Sable."

Abe stroked a newly grown beard as he pondered this information. An idea began to form. "What does your cleaning service do for them exactly?"

"What we do for all of our customers—clean their establishments until they sparkle from top to bottom." Nolan took in his cousin's confused expression. "Sweep, mop, vacuum, dust, polish the floors, windows, and everything in between."

"And this happens daily?"

"Monday through Friday for most of our customers. On the weekends for businesses with smaller budgets or facilities."

"I see." Abe's mental wheel kept turning. "And you've seen Reign there?"

"Only once or twice."

After a few minutes, a slow smile split Abe's face. "That's it!"

"What?" Nolan looked over and caught the excited

expression. "Aldric—I mean Abe—don't get any stupid ideas."

"Not stupid. Genius." Abe turned to Nolan and spoke with authority. "I will help clean the school."

"Didn't you hear what I just said about not being stupid? Ivy is an important client who demands perfection. I was thinking you could work at The Haven."

"What's that? A restaurant?"

"A nursing home."

Abe opened his door, welcoming in a blast of frigid air. "Guess you don't want to stay here after all."

"Aldric, wait! Let's talk this out."

Abe eyed his cousin as he calmly closed the door. "There's nothing to discuss. I will live in your apartment and work for your company. In return, you'll ensure I meet Reign."

"How can I do that?" Nolan asked. "I have no control over her schedule!"

"I'll give it a month. If I haven't met her by then, the bet is over. I'll move back here, hop in my Maybach, and meet another princess. This is a big city. Reigns gorgeous, but I'm sure not the only one."

Nolan shook his head. "I don't know, Abe. Ivy is a very important client. Point du Sable is a small town. If something goes wrong, word will spread quickly."

"What can go wrong?"

"Plenty! You've never cleaned anything a day in your life. You wouldn't know a mop's head from its handle."

"I can learn," Abe replied. "Working at the school is not only a way for our paths to possibly cross again, but it is a way for me to test what kind of person she is—a spoiled brat or a woman of substance. Whether she'll like me for who I am, not what I have."

"Who says she'll like you at all?"

"She will like me. We made a connection."

"While you were threatening to beat up her boy-friend?"

"While I was offering my protection."

Abe's excitement grew. "If not Reign, I can meet other women while living like a regular chap. Ones who will get to know Abe the Janitor, a simple man with no money or status. If they fall in love with that man, I will know their feelings are pure."

"You're well known all over the world where soccer is popular," Nolan continued, "and in Kutoka you're like royalty. Chicago is a major entry point for international travel. How do you know you won't be recognized?"

"This," Abe replied, pointing to his scraggly beard. "And by keeping a low profile, like being part of the cleaning crew for a private school in a small town out-side of this metropolis."

Nolan grunted. Minutes ticked by as resignation set in. "If I let you do this, you'll take the time to learn how to run the equipment and professionally clean an office building?"

"Of course."

"You're not afraid of getting your hands dirty?"

Abe gave him a look. "I started playing football when I was two."

"You keep calling it football."

"It's played with the feet."

"Americans call it soccer."

"Whatever. I've been dirty plenty of times. If Reign sees me cleaning a floor and still joins me for coffee, it will be a sign of her character, proof that she's not judging me from an exterior perspective."

"I hate to break it to you, bro, but a woman like Reign doesn't go out with guys who clean office buildings for a living. It's not personal. It's just not happening."

"We will see."

"I'll hire you," Nolan grumbled. "For the record, I'm doing so against my better judgment."

Abe smiled broadly. "Thank you, dear cousin."

Nolan tsked and shook his head. "Don't 'dear cousin' me. Something tells me this isn't going to end well."

Abe's satellite phone rang. His mother, Veliane. In the States for less than a week and already she was urging him to come home.

"Your mother again?"

Abe sighed. "She's called every day. I haven't always answered. But I'd better before she hops on a plane." He tapped an app on his phone to unlock the front door of the mansion then got out of the car. "Let's talk tomorrow, Nolan."

"I'll come over. With suitcases. Be ready to relinquish those keys!"

A myriad of thoughts clamored for attention as Abe entered the opulent two-story foyer of the glamorous home his family's Realtor had secured for his stay.

Why had he had to assuage his stupid ego and take Nolan up on his bet? He already had enough on his plate. Becoming a contributing team player to impress his father. Dodging the constant stream of women his mother lined up to wed. Both parents hoping for a strategic, profitable union and perfect heirs.

Abe respected his parents' wishes but would live life on his terms. Possibly beginning with a beautiful stranger who, with a mere look, had made his heartbeat increase. His jaw set along with his resolve. He was going to learn more about this woman he could see spending a lifetime protecting. A beautiful woman named Reign.

Three

A week had passed since Reign had arrived at Verve ready to surprise Trenton only to find out the surprise was on her. The press had been relentless, blowing the incident out of proportion. Darkness and poor lighting had prevented good photos from being taken outside, but a few from when they'd crossed the lobby had gone viral. Her yelling at Trenton. Him in hot pursuit. The intervention of a person "unnamed." Trenton's public betrayal had cut to the core, too deep to be healed by "I'm sorry." The only bright spot from that dark night had been the infamous introduction of Make It Reign. Stories of Trenton's party had included photos of the logo she'd created and mention of her newly formed company. Some believed that all publicity was good publicity. She'd find out.

Trenton had left long apology messages and texts. She'd responded only once before blocking his number. There was no point to further communication. She'd clearly warned him that one more time caught cheating and they would be done. He'd promised to not let it happen again. He hadn't kept his word. She would.

Keeping her mind off what was likely the ending to what she'd thought could be a fairy-tale relationship was difficult but thankfully Eddington Enterprise and her own branding company kept her busy. Another Friday approached. She didn't feel quite as thankful. Her plans were to hibernate for the weekend, sit in the pain of what had happened, and figure out how to be single for the first time in almost.

two years.

She arrived at the east wing of the Eddington Estate to unexpected, unwanted company. Her sister Maeve and sisters-in-law, known as "sisters-in-love," Ivy, Sasha and Avery were at her door.

"Hi, guys."

They returned the greeting and followed Reign as she walked into the elaborately appointed living space, plopped on the couch and removed high-heeled boots.

"Y'all look ready to go out. I wish you'd called before coming over. I don't feel like socializing."

"Exactly why we didn't phone you," Maeve said. "Reign, we've all been where you are. We're not minimizing his actions, your pain, or how what he did sucks. The media has been relentless. It's awful. We get it. But we can't let you bury your head in the corporate sand or hide away from the world. From us."

"You've done a great job maintaining a professional exterior," Ivy added. "But we know you're hurting. Which is why we want you to join us for dinner. Take some time to get out of your head."

"Thanks, guys. I know you mean well and appreciate the thought. I haven't taken the time to process what happened or afforded myself the chance to sit and have a good cry. All week I've distracted myself with work. I need time to decompress...from everything."

"Ah, sis. I understand." Maeve joined Reign on the couch and placed an arm around her. "My breakup was brutal. You know. You were there. You absolutely need time to process what happened. Just try not to focus on it for too long."

"I won't," Reign replied while not being sure if that was true.

"I've often found my pain lessens when in service to others," Ivy offered. "When I'm thinking about someone else's well-being and peace of mind instead of my own."

"That's a good idea," Reign said.

"Glad you think so! I need your help."

"I walked right into that one."

Their laughter helped lighten the mood.

"We've recently started a new school program. On Mondays, we have a special lunch called Mentorship Monday. It's where professionals from various occupations eat lunch with the girls, answer questions and give advice about everything from clothing to careers."

"The setting is informal and nonthreatening," Maeve added, "allowing the students an up-close-and-personal interaction with success and, in turn, begin to dream bigger dreams for themselves."

"It's only an hour," Ivy continued despite the pout that appeared on Reign's face. "Think about bringing sunshine to a little girl's life when it's raining in yours."

The girls went to dinner without her.

When they'd left, Reign had had no plans to join them for Mentorship Monday. But after a whole day on Sunday of her big sister's gentle prodding, Reign agreed to join her and several other ladies for the mentorship luncheon.

Monday morning arrived and was busier than usual, with a surprising amount of time spent responding to emails requesting more information on Make It Reign and the services offered. Time flew. Reign felt like she'd drank a coffee, blinked, and it was past noon. The luncheon started at twelve thirty and went for one hour. It was almost that time when she whipped her Bentley Continental Speedster into a reserved parking lot and rushed up the walk as though she weren't wearing five-inch pumps and there wasn't snow on the ground.

Entering the school, she pulled out her phone to re-read the text Ivy had sent her. She knew they were meeting in the lunchroom but wasn't sure where that was. She neared an intersection.

Should I go right or left?

Right, Reign decided. She reached the end of the hall while still reading the text, turned the corner and hit a wall. Or so she'd thought until a pair of strong arms reached out to prevent her from falling. That's when she looked up and realized that the wall had been the very hard chest of a good-looking man with…those eyes. The stranger who'd rescued her at the nightclub was here at Ivy's school? What were the chances? Why was he here?

"Careful!"

"I'm sorry," Reign gasped, breathless from running into a manly mass of muscle. A tad embarrassed, too, as she reached down to retrieve the items that had fallen out of her tote.

"Are you all right?" he asked, bending to help her at the same time.

They bumped heads.

"Ow!" Reign flinched, placing a hand on the spot where they'd collided.

The stranger sucked in his breath, rubbed his own head even as he reached out a hand to steady her.

Their eyes met. He smiled. Her heart skipped a beat. It was definitely her knight in shining armor, the one with the melodious accent who'd manhandled Trenton into leaving her alone. His eyes shone with the same compassion as the other night. The same sparkle, too. The face was the same, but his vibe was different from the cosmopolitan stranger she'd seen that Friday night. She remembered that man wearing an expensive-looking coat. The jumpsuit he now wore was decidedly ordinary and ill-fitting. It looked out of place on a body obviously familiar with a weight room or two. He looked out of place in a uniform, and at the school.

"I'm running late for the mentor's lunch."

"Ah, that is what's happening. I saw a group of women head into the lunchroom." The kind stranger pointed toward a set of double doors at the end of the hall.

"Thank you." Reign threw the words over her shoulder as she walked in that direction.

"You're welcome." A pause and then, "My name is Abe!"

Reign reached the doors where he'd pointed. She gave a backward wave without turning around and went inside the room.

Thankfully, the lunchroom was organized chaos. Conversations echoed from every table, the girls excitedly chatting with mentors while dining on a spinach and arugula salad, roasted mushroom lasagna and freshly baked bread.

Ivy waved her over and immediately paired her with a girl named Lilah. The child was quiet, almost withdrawn. Her answers were short to the questions Reign asked, but when a comment about the lasagna turned the talk to one about food, the girl opened up. She used to help her "Big Mama" cook and liked it. Reign told her about her good friend Quinn who owned a restaurant. From there, conversation flowed.

For the first time since it had happened, neither work nor the breakup was the topic. Ivy had been right about needing a distraction. Reign was surprised to have such a good time. When a bell sounded, signaling the end of lunch, Reign encouraged Lilah to follow her dreams of becoming a chef and thanked her for the opportunity to have a great chat. Heading toward the exit, she spotted Ivy and walked over.

"Sorry for being late," she said, giving her in-love a one-armed hug.

"No worries," Ivy said. "You have a lot going on. How was it with Lilah?"

"I think it went well. She seemed shy and reserved until the conversation turned to food and I mentioned Quinn's restaurant. She became more engaged after that."

"I'm surprised she talked at all. Six months ago, a tragedy struck their family. Her beloved great-grandmother died."

"Big Mama?"

"That is what everyone called her, the family's matriarch. Lilah was her favorite. I understand theirs was a special bond. Since then, we've tried different things to pull her out of that shell of sadness. Her love of cooking just might be it."

"Maybe I can take her to Tasty Vegan one weekend, introduce her to Quinn, and maybe let her see how a professional kitchen operates. We could both go. Have lunch. Maybe afterward, take in a movie."

"I won't be able to join you, but I'll speak with her parents. From what you've told me, I think Lilah would be thrilled."

Reign looked at her watch. "Thanks for suggesting this. It was fun." She leaned over to hug Ivy. "Love you."

"Love you too."

Reign pulled out her phone to check messages. This time, she kept one eye on where she was going. She'd reached the double doors leading outside and had just pushed one open when she heard her name.

"Reign!"

She turned around. Her knight. Abe. She wondered whether his full name was Abraham, and why her belly had the nerve to do a little flip-flop as he awkwardly pushed a broom down the hall. She stepped back inside the doors, away from the cold wind that slipped through the opening.

He reached into his pocket as he neared her. "I think this is yours."

He held out a thin, gold bangle adorned with positive symbols; one of her favorites.

"Yes, thank you." She accepted the bracelet. "It must have fallen out of the pocket on my briefcase. Again, I apologize for running into you."

"Accidents happen."

And again, that smile. Reign saw a dimple wink at her from behind his growing beard, along with a fleeting flash of the confident man she'd encountered at the club. There was something mesmerizing about him even while her heart reminded her of its recent tearing and she reminded herself of the subsequent dating break.

"What are you doing here?"

"Working." He made a sweeping gesture with his arm.

"You're a janitor?"

His back straightened. His tone became clipped. "According to my contract, I'm a custodial technician."

Reign placed a faux flummoxed hand on her heart. "I stand corrected."

They laughed.

"I like your accent. Where are you from?"

A slight pause and then, "Ghana."

"What brought you here?"

He motioned with the broom. "I needed a job."

Reign's brow raised.

"The cleaning company is owned by my cousin. It's a new business. I came over to help him out."

"That's generous of you," Reign replied in a way that suggested she was only half convinced. Her message indicator dinged. She checked her phone. Unknown number. Probably Trenton. She slipped the phone into her tote.

"You're here for another mentor's lunch?"

"Yes."

"What is your profession, if I may ask?"

Reign smirked at the obvious play for information then remembered he wasn't from there. "Marketing and PR," she said, purposefully vague.

"Sounds interesting."

"It can be."

"I would like to know more. Would you be willing to further this discussion, over dinner perhaps?"

"Excuse me?" Reign asked, attitude reflecting in her voice while noting the stranger's surprise.

"Oh, please, forgive me if that question was inappropriate. I didn't mean to offend."

His bowed head and slumped shoulders brought out Reign's compassionate side. A rarity. "I accept your apology but am not interested in dinner, or dating. Nothing personal."

Abe gave a careless shrug. "I thought my suggestion an innocuous one. It may be different here in your country, but in mine, everyone has to eat."

Reign chuckled, relaxed her guard. His accent was adorable. His face and body weren't bad either.

"I appreciate that, Abe, but, no thanks." Reign noticed it had begun snowing again. She pulled up the hood on her leather jacket and once again, turned toward the exit.

Abe quickly fell into step beside her. "Allow me to get the door." He placed the broom aside and opened it.

"Thanks." Her smile was sincere. "'Bye."

Abe stepped outside. "Where are you parked? Allow me to get the car door as well."

His comment brought on a burst of laughter. "Thanks," Reign said, touched by his chivalry. "But I've got it from here."

Abe smiled too. "Be safe, Reign. Goodbye for now."

Reign thought about Abe all the way back to Point du Sable. He was a study in contrasts. A man of opposites. The night they'd met, he'd worn an expensive-looking leather coat and watch, but had gotten into a car that looked old and beat up. Today, he was dressed as an average guy yet spoke with the intelligence of someone well-bred.

Despite her self-imposed dating hiatus, Reign was surprised to find herself attracted to Abe. He wasn't like the type of men she normally dated, nothing at all like the one who'd just broken her heart. She entertained the thought of accepting Abe's dinner invitation. Explaining the ins and outs of marketing was, to use his word *innocuous*, a safe and comfortable topic that had nothing to do with pain.

By the time she arrived back at Eddington Enter-

Four

"She turned me down!" Abe exclaimed, pacing the small space of his cousin's apartment that served as both living and dining room. They'd switched residences the previous Sunday. Nolan had come over to collect a few additional items and now served as Abe's sounding board. "I cannot believe it!"

Nolan laughed heartily, something that happened often during his chagrined cousin's retelling of the literal run-in with Reign.

Abe didn't find anything funny, a sentiment that showed on his face. "Do you know how rarely that has happened?"

"Sounds like you're harassing the clients, Aldric."

"Abe."

"Exactly what I told you not to do. You're lucky I don't fire you immediately, like right now."

"Reign wasn't a client, but a visitor to the school."

"Same difference."

Abe's scowl deepened.

"Don't act like you've never been turned down before."

"It's happened, but not lately."

"Until today." Nolan smiled broadly as he playfully elbowed Abe.

"I find no humor in what I have shared."

"Hey, man. This is what it feels like to be a regular guy. For the next month, you're Abe Wetherbee, the janitor."

"Custodial technician," Abe reminded with a touch of dry humor and no response to the full use of his pseudo name. It wasn't a new moniker. It had been created years ago, during the height of his soccer fame, to allow for a less recognizable social media presence.

Nolan ignored him. "Reign is like her name suggests—a princess. Chicago royalty. Much like yourself back home in Kutoka. She might give Aldric Baiden a shot, but she's way out of Abe the Janitor's league. Women like her don't date guys like you and me."

"All rich women don't exclusively date rich men."

"Women like Reign Eddington do."

"Eddington." Abe placed his cell phone on the coffee table, his interest piqued. "As in Eddington Enterprise?"

"Ah, so you already know them."

"I know about them. My accountant uses one of their apps."

The plot had thickened. Not only did he think Reign would be a great date, but she might have valuable connections in the corporate world that could help him expand Kutoka Global's American interest.

He retrieved his phone. Went to the search engine. "What more do you know about them?"

"What do you want to know?" Nolan went into the bedroom and returned with a stuffed, leather duffel bag that he tossed toward the door before heading into the kitchen.

Abe joined him there, leaned against the counter and watched Nolan make a sandwich. "How long have Reign and the ball player been together?"

"A year, maybe longer."

"From what I saw the other night, that situation is over." Something about that possibility made Abe smile.

Nolan caught it. "Don't even think about it."

"Think about what?"

"I've seen that smile. Your mind is working overtime."

"You don't know what I'm thinking."

Nolan smirked. "From what I hear, her and Trenton are practically engaged."

Abe laughed. Busted.

"Was I right?" Nolan gleefully asked.

"Guilty as charged." Again, Reign's face wafted into his mind. "You can't blame me. She's a beautiful woman. Working at Eddington Enterprise tells me she's smart as well."

"Obviously. She turned you down."

Abe ignored Nolan's dig. "It will only take her getting to know me. Then she and I will become great friends. I am sure of it."

"I think you should set your sights a little lower, my friend."

"Reign is the woman who's captured my eye. I simply want to get to know her."

"I hear you, man, but she's not the only beautiful woman in town." Nolan placed lettuce, tomato and sliced turkey on mayo-slathered bread, then placed a bag of chips on the bar counter before sitting down.

"Tell you what. One of the local artists is having a release party on Saturday night. At Verve, the same spot you met Reign, and invitation only. I'm invited. You should come. The honeys will be there. Take your pick and improve your chances of being hit on as an ordinary guy."

"Did you know that she works in marketing and PR?"

"I tell you about a potential smorgasbord of sweet things and you're still talking about Reign?"

Abe was sure he'd left just such a smorgasbord back on the Continent. And another in Europe. And more on a Caribbean island or two. His mother had a list of at least half a dozen that she swore were perfect wife material. He'd fled to America partly to get away from a "smorgasbord of sweet things," otherwise known as potential brides.

"Reign is the one currently holding my interest."

Nolan snorted. "Obviously, and yeah, I know she's in PR."

"What else can you tell me about her?"

"I know she's close to her family."

"Tell me about them."

"Her dad is a big shot. Brothers, too. They're always in the limelight for one reason or another."

How many brothers does she have?"

"Two. Desmond and Jake. And before you ask, yes, they work for the company, along with Reign's sister, Maeve, who's as beautiful as Reign. Unfortunately, she's no longer on the market. Married this rich hot-shot lawyer dude named Victor Cortez. There's another guy, Cayden, who's not related but is treated like family and works there, too."

"You know a great deal about their family."

"All easily accessible public information. Plus, I've researched several companies in Point du Sable."

"Why?"

"Why else? Looking for more business, more buildings to clean."

Nolan became quiet, focusing on his sandwich and chips.

"What aren't you telling me?" Abe finally asked.

"What do you mean?"

"I'm an expert interpreter of body language. Yours suggests there is more to this story."

Nolan reached for a napkin. "I don't know what you're talking about."

Abe didn't believe that comment for a second. His ringing satellite phone saved Nolan from continued interrogation. The call from home was from his father this time.

"You haven't called with an update," Daniel intoned without a proper greeting.

"Dad, I've barely been here a week."

Abe looked up as Nolan went to the door, slung the duffel bag that he'd placed there over his shoulder and nodded a silent goodbye.

"You're on a business trip, not an extended vacation," his father continued. "Keep that in mind."

"How could I not? The trip was my idea."

"Mind your tongue, Aldric. I will not tolerate disrespect."

Abe took a deep breath, clenching his teeth to hold back a slew of sarcastic responses. "I have several meetings lined up with our stateside affiliates. I'm also researching a few startups we may be able to buy out. I will send a biweekly update, as stated in my report."

His father remained silent. Abe wanted to get off the phone. While he'd indeed set up a few conference calls, his father's comment made him realize that he'd been distracted from the main reason he was in the US. A beautiful, tempting distraction, but one that had taken his focus nonetheless.

"If that is all, Father—"

"It is not."

Abe gripped the phone, containing his aggravation as he walked into the kitchen and awaited the next condescending topic his father had planned.

"It's *Kbaba*."

Abe straightened, on instant alert. He adored his grandfather. When Abe had been torn between his duty to join the company and his dream of playing soccer professionally, it had been his grandfather who'd encouraged him toward the latter. Something in his father's tone suggested the news regarding the family patriarch was not good.

"How is Grandfather?" No longer able to stand quietly, he began to pace the room.

"The cancer is back."

The news caused a physical pain in Abe's heart.

"He is being treated, but this time the doctors are not as hopeful as before."

"Should I return home?"

He heard his father sigh. Imagined him leaning back in the well-worn, deep burgundy leather chair in the home office that smelled of cigars and success.

"Son, you should take care to establish yourself as a valuable member of Kutoka Global, then return home and choose a bride. Quickly. Your inheritance depends on both being achieved before Kbaba passes."

The call ended with Abe feeling more pressure than ever. First from his parents. Now from the potential loss of his beloved grandfather. He'd given himself up to a year to increase the profits of existing interests and generate new ones. Now he felt an urgency to move much faster. If he wasn't successful in those endeavors, or his grandfather took a sudden turn for the worse, he'd be back where he started. Back home, single, in Kutoka, and forced to quickly choose a bride…before one was chosen for him.

February blew in on a snowstorm that blanketed the city. Even through college and playing soccer in London, Abe had never experienced such cold. Running and other outdoor activities he preferred were not options.

Not a fan of public gyms yet determined to stay in shape, and keep his mind off his troubles, he arrived at PDS Prep that Monday carrying a newly purchased soccer ball, one he'd picked up after browsing a thrift store for "regular" clothes and paying cash for a used Ford Explorer. The school's physical education director had offered him use of the gym and weight room after-hours. Since his shift didn't start until classes had ended, Abe intended to take full advantage.

Arriving at the school safely and still in one piece proved to Abe that angels existed. He rushed from the SUV to the school entrance and a welcomed blast of heat. On his way to the storeroom to hang his coat and store the ball, he ran into Ivy. Instead of being unapproachable, as his cousin had suggested, she'd introduced herself on his first day at work and been pleasant when meeting since then.

"Good evening, Mrs. Eddington."

"Hey there, Abe. It's Ivy, remember? We staff aren't that formal around here."

"Okay, Ivy. Thank you."

"Nolan had mentioned to me he'd be hiring more workers. How's everything going with you so far?"

"Work is going fine. I have no complaints." Well, he had one, trying to get close to the woman's in-law But he thought it best to not mention that.

Ivy nodded at the ball. "You're a soccer player?"

Abe worked to maintain a neutral expression. "I play around."

"Are you any good?" she teased.

"I do okay."

"We've talked about adding soccer to the athletic program. I'll have to introduce you to Phil."

"The physical education director."

"You've met him?"

"Briefly. He saw me eyeing the gym last week and said I could use it after-hours. When on break," he quickly added, lest he be labeled a slacker.

"He's absolutely correct. Does he know you play soccer?"

Abe surely hoped not. "We didn't discuss that."

"You should. Depending on how well you know the game, you might qualify as an assistant coach."

"No." The firm answer flew out before he could stop it. "I mean I appreciate the offer and could perhaps be of some help, but I couldn't accept a teaching assignment."

Being involved in sports in a professional capacity was the last type of attention that Abe needed. Under the glare of public scrutiny, his high-level skills would quickly show. They were second nature and, except for short periods, would be hard to turn off.

"Are you sure? Don't worry about needing a certain level of education. In some instances, skill and experience can be substituted for a college degree."

Abe hid a smile. With double masters in international marketing and political science, and a minor in Chinese languages, he was very much overqualified to both teach and coach at Ivy's school.

"I appreciate the interest, but I'm here to help my cousin, and for only several months."

"Nolan is your cousin?"

"Yes."

"I'm not surprised at how quickly his business is growing. He has an impeccable reputation and résumé. You guys do great work."

"We try."

"I get that you don't want a job here, but if you don't mind, I'd still like to mention you to Phil. Perhaps you can at least help him get the program started, and who knows? Maybe you'll change your mind and agree to help him, even part-time."

"Okay," was Abe's reluctant answer.

"May I pass along your phone number?"

"Sure." Although secretly Abe wished she wouldn't. He felt it best not to be contacted by Phil or anyone else even remotely connected to his former pro sport.

"I could get it from Nolan or look in the files, but can I get your number now?"

"Sure."

She pulled out her phone. Abe rattled off his number.

"Don't be surprised to get a call more sooner than later. The new semester just started. If we move quickly, we can fit the new sport into the spring curriculum."

That night Phil called, much to Abe's chagrin. Despite playing down his knowledge and skills, Phil offered Abe a part-time coaching job. He didn't want to accept it, but didn't want to disappoint Ivy, someone who may prove beneficial in his getting closer to Reign. He compromised by agreeing to help Phil set up the program and to revisit the coaching opportunity at a later date.

Just when he'd given up on it happening anytime soon, Abe saw the object of his desire walk through the school's main entrance. It was Friday, late, almost six o'clock. He wondered what had brought her to the school at that hour but, after watching how she sashayed down the hall, determined why she was there didn't matter. He knew he should pay her no mind and continue buffing the floors, but that was impossible.

He stood transfixed as she glided along the hall, something that seemed impossible to do while wearing what resembled stilts the fashion industry tagged as high heels. She looked casually sleek in an off-white leather jacket, black skinny jeans and knee-high zebra-printed boots. His heart swelled. Despite Nolan's warning about acting too friendly, he stood motionless, watching her close the distance between them. Her attention glued to the phone that seemed an ever-present extension, his perusal had gone unnoticed. He wanted to pull her in for a big hug and kiss but feigned being busy just as she raised her eyes, wrapping up the buffer cord to calm his rapid heartbeat and prevent his lower head from getting harder than the stone tile he'd just cleaned.

"Oh, hi, Abe!"

He looked up, pseudo shocked. "Hello, Reign. You remembered my name."

"It's an easy one to remember."

"I thought it was because of my amazing talents with a buffer."

Reign smiled. Abe's heart skittered across his chest. His lower head bobbed and weaved like Tyson in a prizefight. Abe was reminded that hit had been more than a month since the last time he'd had sex. Good thing the company jumpsuits were loose-fitting. Otherwise, his attraction to Reign would have been made public. Not a good look.

"The floors do look pristine."

He poked out his chest in exaggerated fashion. "I'm told I have skills." The comment got the laugh he'd aimed for and made him want to be the cause of that happening again and again. "I thought the mentor's meeting happened on Monday."

"It does, but since I wasn't able to attend this week, I promised one of the girls that we'd do something special today."

"So, you are as kind on the inside as you are beautiful on the outside." Abe's words were spoken sincerely with no hint of flirtation.

"I don't know about that, but thank you."

"You're welcome."

A slightly overweight young girl exited Ivy's office and walked toward them. She was wearing a variation of the school's uniform—a black wool sweater over a starched, white blouse and a pair of printed slacks with a customized design. Her posture was that of someone timid and unsure of herself.

Ace watched Reign wave enthusiastically at the student and offer a smile bigger smile than the one she'd given him.

"Hi, Lilah!"

Lilah's eyes turned downcast as she offered a shy half smile. "Hi."

Reign gave her a quick one-armed hug. "Hope you're ready to cook up some orders."

Lilah lifted her head. "Your friend is going to let me cook?"

"I think the correct term is 'prepping' for what we'll be doing. After that, we'll try dishes from what we've prepared. Does that sound like a plan?"

Lilah nodded. Abe noted that in Reign's presence a bit of the little girl's hesitance seemed to fade away. Yep, his queen was special all right.

Queen? His? Slow your roll, buddy, Abe inwardly chided. To use a popular American phrase based on one of their favorite pastimes, he'd not yet gotten to first base.

Lilah's eyes shifted from Reign to Abe. "You play soccer."

Abe swallowed *oh shit* and *what the hell* in one big gulp. Was a quiet, unsure eleven year-old going to blow his carefully crafted plan?

He recovered quickly and asked, "Who told you that?"

"I overheard Miss Ivy talking to Mr. Phil."

"I see." Sensing the child might be nervous, he smiled and held out his hand. "My name is Abe."

"Lilah," she all but whispered, shy once again as they shook hands.

"That's a beautiful name. Do you play soccer?"

Her eyes widened as she vigorously shook her head. "Oh, no. I couldn't do that."

"Why not?"

"Because I'm fat, and not good at sports."

"Weight is something that changes with exercise,

and no one is good at anything until they try, and are taught."

"Not me."

"Yes, you. Definitely you, young lady. With enough practice and determination, one can achieve anything."

He spoke to Lilah but the statement was more to himself about Reign, who, he noted, was now looking at him with something resembling admiration.

Hot diggity dog! He kept talking. If working with her charge would give him brownie points with Reign, he might do a little coaching after all.

"Perhaps one day we can practice, just you and me. And Reign, of course," he skillfully added. "Would you like that?"

Lilah shrugged.

"I think you should do it," Reign said with a subtle wink at Abe.

"Do you play?" he asked her.

"Me? Oh, no. I'm not into sports like that."

"All the more reason for you to join Lilah. The two of you could learn together."

"We should do it, Reign," Lilah said, now warming to the idea.

"I'll think about it." Reign looked at her watch. "Come on, Lilah. We should go before Friday-night traffic heats up. You'll want to put on your coat though. It's cold outside."

Lilah removed the down coat from over her arm and put it on.

"Thank you, Abe," Reign said with a nod at Lilah.

"We'll see you later." She took a step and added, "Don't worry, we can get the door."

She not only remembered his name but their last humorous exchange? Abe felt like he was on a roll. He didn't care how discouraging his cousin had tried to be about it, he was confident that at the very least he and Reign were going to be great friends.

"I wouldn't think of it," he answered, already moving toward the doors. He held one open and made a sweeping motion with his arm. "Ladies…"

Reign chuckled. "Lilah, take note. This is how a man is supposed to treat you." And then to him with another one of those dazzling smiles, she said, "Goodbye, Abe."

"Goodbye, Reign. Goodbye, Lilah. Enjoy your evening."

Abe watched Reign and Lilah walked to a car he immediately recognized. The gleaming black Bentley was the newest model of a white one he'd driven years ago. When the brake lights lit up, he forced himself away from the door and jogged toward the gymnasium. It was time for a workout to release the pent-up sexual energy that Reign's presence had stirred. Nolan's voice trailed after him.

She's way out of Abe the janitor's league… Women like her don't date guys like you.

Abe tried to remain optimistic but remembering his cousin's ominous words brought a cloud over the sunshine Reign's smile had left behind. He didn't want to think his queen was like many of the women he'd met, ones more interested in what a man had or what he did than in who he was. But as a series of images flashed through his mind—the upscale bar where he'd met her, the expensive clothing she wore, the luxury vehicle, her family's upper-class status, Trenton's movie-star looks compared to his less distinct ones—Abe couldn't ignore the obvious. The scales weren't tipped in a regular man's favor.

Then other memories forced themselves into his mind. His grandfather's illness. His mother's daughter-in-law wish list. The inescapable reality of his need to please his father by gainfully contributing to the family legacy. Despite his determination to stay positive about his chances with Reign, he secretly admitted that when it came to Reign being out of his league, Nolan just might be right.

Five

Reign dreaded the week ahead. No doubt it would bring back everything she both loved and now hated about what used to be one of her favorite holidays. Trenton was to blame. Last year on Valentine's Day, he'd whisked her away to David Copperfield's private island, Musha Cay, Bahamas, for what was indeed a magical night; one that had ended with a custard desert surrounded by a ten-carat-diamond bracelet. Three days later, a wannabe Instagram star had felt the need to send Reign a pic of the gift Trenton had given her. It was of a beautiful, diamond bracelet—exactly like the one that dangled from Reign's arm. That cheating evidence had led to their biggest ever argument, longest separation and the ultimatum that had her now single and dreading the end of the week.

She'd been working around-the-clock to keep her mind off the memories. Make It Reign had benefitted from her distress. In the past three days, she'd secured ten clients, including a national bestselling author, a life coach, and a surprise request from Quinn, Tasty Vegan's owner and chef. That she had no professional athletes as clients was no accident.

Several family members had called to include her in their plans. Maeve had invited her to join her and Victor for a quick trip to Costa Rica. Jake had thought it would be cool for Reign to join him and his wife Sasha and head to Hawaii for a day of zip-lining, balloon riding, or both. Desmond was in the middle of the next cryptocurrency offering and wouldn't be going anywhere, though Ivy would most likely put the kids to bed early and put together an intimate dinner. She knew what her siblings were trying to do and loved them for it.

When her phone rang and Ivy's name showed up, she answered with her decline. "No thank you, Ivy."

"I haven't even asked you anything," Ivy laughed. "I could have been getting ready to ask if you wanted a million dollars!"

"My answer is still no." She paused. "I want two million."

"You're a mess. What did you think I was going to ask?"

"If I wanted to be a third wheel at something you and Des have planned. My answer is the same as the one I gave Maeve and Jake."

"I love you, sis, but I wasn't going to invite you to

the sexy dinner I have planned for my man. I have been thinking about you though. This can't be an easy time."

Reign relaxed against the back of her chair. "No, it isn't."

"Is he still trying to reach you?"

"Yeah, he's tried. Unknown or private numbers. One of the guards even saw his car near our gates."

"Do you think you'll ever talk to him?"

"And say what, Ivy? I told him it was the last time, the last time he cheated."

"Hey, I get it. I just want you to be okay. Believe it or not, though, that's not why I called. The Mentorship Monday sessions are going so well that I'm thinking about expanding the more successful interactions to include activities outside of school. The Friday evening you spent with Lilah further spurred the idea. Think you'd be interested?"

"Are you sure this call isn't about my ex?"

"Not at all, though staying busy can't be a bad thing. You've done such a great job with Lilah. There's a sparkle back in her eyes."

"What will this extra time entail exactly?"

"I don't know. Just got the idea and need to brainstorm. Can you help me?"

"When?"

"I'd love to start today."

Reign almost asked Ivy what was the rush but didn't think she'd get a completely true answer. Ivy loved her students and went above and beyond to set them up for success, but Reign had no doubt that the urgency of the

planning session happening now was to give her something else to fill her thoughts on heart day.

Reign spent the next few hours on a company cam-
paign, then wrapped up around six and took the short
drive over to PDS Prep. She pulled into the reserved
parking spot nearest the door and rushed inside to
escape the cold air. Inside, her heels clicked smartly
against the colorfully tiled hallway. She reached Ivy's
opened door and tapped it lightly before stepping inside.

"Hey, girl."

"Hey, yourself." Ivy stood, came around her desk
and gave Reign a brief hug. "Thanks for making time
for me today."

"I always have time for family." Reign followed Ivy
to a brightly colored love seat covered in various smiling emojis and sat down. "Speaking of, how are my
babies?"

"Trying to mimic bad seeds," Ivy teased. "Desiree
has decided to extend the terrible twos stage into the
temper tantrum threes."

"Independent, with a mind of her own. Just like
mama and daddy."

Ivy let out an exasperated breath. "I can't disagree.
I'm afraid baby brother Iden is taking notes. He wants
to do everything she does."

"Good Lord."

"Keep sending those prayers up, honey. We're going
to need them!" The office phone rang. Ivy stood. "That's
probably the nanny now. Excuse me a moment."

She walked over and answered the phone. While chatting with the caller, Ivy looked up and motioned for someone walking past to enter. Reign followed the move.

Abe entered the office wearing the Clean Up Crew company uniform, a baggy jumpsuit. The way her body reacted surprised her. Nipples pebbled. Noni clenched. Was she missing regular sex that badly? Clearly, the answer was yes.

Abe stood quietly just inside the door. Noticing Reign, a smile appeared. He nodded a greeting but remained where he stood until Ivy finished the call.

"Come on in, Abe." She returned to the love seat and gestured to a nearby chair. "Have a seat. You remember Reign?"

"Of course. How are you, Reign?"

"I'm okay. And you?"

"Considering their new contract," Ivy interrupted, "I'm sure he's doing excellent." Her attention shifted back to Abe. "Congratulations."

"Forgive my ignorance, but we've been so busy that I wasn't aware of a new contract with your school. I'm sure Nolan intended to tell me the next time we spoke. It's wonderful news."

"We'll definitely renew the Clean Up Crew contract next year. But I'm speaking of the one for Reign's building, the one that houses Eddington Enterprise. Several stories high and a ton of businesses. He says it's your biggest so far."

"That is great news," Reign added, trying to ignore the fact that her first thought after hearing Ivy's announcement was hoping a new contract might get Abe to stick around Point du Sable longer than he'd planned.

This thought surprised her more than her body's reaction. Valentine's Day approaching had her all jacked up!

"Ivy says you're a great worker," Reign said. "Maybe you can gain more hours by cleaning our offices too."

"It would be my pleasure."

Said sincerely, without flirting. Reign told herself she wasn't disappointed. After the way she'd acted when he'd asked her out to dinner, she was lucky he talked to her at all. Something she couldn't explain and didn't try to figure out made her want to change that. Even though she was on a break from dating, she could be nice. Besides, Abe was not only ruggedly attractive, he seemed like a genuinely good guy.

"Do you think it's possible that you'll be moved to that crew?" she asked.

He shrugged. "That'll be up to the boss."

"No, I'm keeping Abe," Ivy teased. "He's a good and patient teacher, and all the girls think he's cute. We're hoping he works here long enough to fall in love with the students, change his plans about returning to Africa, and agree to coach soccer."

"Is that a possibility?" Reign asked, secretly agreeing with the girls that their good and patient teacher was indeed cute too.

Abe shook his head. "My visa expires in December. I'll return home at least by then."

"Where's home?" Ivy asked.

"Ghana," Reign spontaneously replied, receiving curious looks from both Ivy and Abe for her trouble. They weren't the only ones who found her answer unexpected. In remembering what he'd shared with Trenton, Reign had surprised herself.

"My ex asked where you were from during our infamous first meeting. Do you remember that?"

"Honestly, I've tried to forget that night, especially the guy who needs a lesson on how to treat women."

"That makes two of us," Reign said then, seeing Ivy's confused expression, added, "I'll explain later."

"Abe, if you interested in getting a green card," Ivy continued, "gaining full-time employment will greatly help your chances."

"Thank you but no. As I've stated, I will return home."

"You're adamant about that timeline," Ivy joked. "Sounds like you might have someone there waiting for you."

Reign all but leaned forward to catch his response. When he simply smiled without answering, she boldly prodded, "Is there a girlfriend?"

"There are friends, but no one steady."

He'd paused before saying this, as if carefully choosing his words. His hesitation led Reign to assume that, like Trenton and most other men, even hardworking, kind men like Abe could be dogs. Was any man capable of being faithful? Reign's recently betrayed mind served up a resounding no, followed immediately by thoughts of her father and brothers to prove that thought wasn't true.

"Then we may need to make you an offer that you can't refuse."

Abe delivered a shy, lopsided smile that Reign determined looked quite tasty, in spite of the canine category she'd just put him in.

"Seriously," Ivy said. "You have a way with young children that cannot be taught. And it's obvious you grew up playing soccer."

"I love kids, and the sport."

"It shows."

He eyed the clock on the wall. "If you have nothing further, Ivy, I must get back to work."

"Of course. I didn't mean to keep you from your responsibilities. That kind of work ethic is why you guys snagged that latest contract and why demand for the Clean Up Crew's services grows more every day."

He stood. "I appreciate that and will share your kind words with Nolan." He turned and gave a slight bow. "Reign, it is a pleasure seeing you again."

Why did his comment cause goose bumps? Sure, he was cute, but she didn't find him *that* attractive, did she? Enough to go out with him despite her self-imposed vow? No, of course not. Had to be the forced celibacy of the past few weeks. She responded in a tone that was almost dismissive.

"Thanks, Abe. See you later."

Both ladies watched him walk out the door. Ivy got up and closed it. "Okay, what's this about you and Abe meeting before?"

"He broke up me and Trenton's last argument."

Reign gave Ivy a quick recap of that fateful night at Verve. "Most guys wouldn't have interfered, especially with someone like Trenton."

"Or anyone else," Ivy said. "These days, instead of intervening, people pull out their phones."

"Isn't that crazy? Anyway, he swept in like a knight in shining armor. I was surprised, impressed, and absolutely sure that I'd never see him again. When I came here for the luncheon and saw him working, I couldn't believe it."

"Interesting." Ivy said the word slowly, a certain gleam in her eye.

"No."

"I didn't say anything!"

"I heard what you were thinking."

"I know he isn't your usual type but he is kinda adorable."

Reign shrugged. "I'll give him that."

"He's only here temporarily. You wouldn't have to worry about always seeing him around."

"Why would I worry about that?" Reign knew why exactly.

Ivy's smile widened. "You know what they say about heartbreak. The fastest way to get over one man is to get under another one."

"On that note, why don't we talk about this mentorship event planning so important that it had to start today."

"It probably could have waited until later," Ivy admitted. "That was Maisie who called. Desiree has a slight fever."

"Isn't your nanny also a registered nurse?"

"Yes, and an excellent one. But it's late. You're probably tired. We can do this some other time."

"I appreciate your thoughtfulness," Reign slyly replied, "but I'm here now."

"So am I."

Both women started at the deep voice coming from the door's entrance.

Reign stood on instinct. "Trenton!"

"Hello, Reign."

"Why are you here?"

"Who let you into the building?" Ivy's body language appeared calm though her eyes were alert.

"Calm down, Ivy. You know the guards love me. I'm practically family." He continued into the office.

Ivy took a step toward the phone on her desk.

Reign stopped her. "Ivy, it's okay. He won't be here long."

"Are you sure?"

Trenton's demeanor was casual, relaxed. "She'll be fine."

Ivy gave Trenton a long look as she walked to the door. "I need to have a talk with security."

Trenton strode over to where Reign was standing. She crossed her arms with an expression that dared him to touch her. He got the message and walked past her to the love seat. Reign couldn't help but notice his handsome face, the sweatshirt with the TC logo she'd designed, and the smell of the cologne she'd purchased for his birthday that trailed as he walked by. She was also aware that the goose bumps seeing him used to cause were nowhere in sight. Those seemed to be reserved for a certain scraggly-bearded, baggy-jumpsuit-wearing janitor. Thinking of Abe brought a strange peace of mind.

"What do you want, Trenton?"

"Come on, baby. Sit down. Let's talk. You know I've been trying to reach you."

"That you haven't should have told you something."

Lowered voices could be heard from a nearby hallway. Reign recognized Ivy's and assumed the deeper one was the older man who served as security, a man who, in a town as safe as Point du Sable, was there mostly for show.

Trenton looked from them to Reign. "Can we go somewhere private?"

"No."

"At least close the door?"

"No, Trenton." Reign looked at her watch. "You've got five minutes."

Trenton sighed audibly, giving her a look that at one time she thought sexy as hell. Now it made her almost throw up.

"It's simple. I miss you. Things aren't the same without you around."

"You should have thought about that before doing what you did."

"We were all celebrating. She got a little too excited. Reign, it meant nothing! She means nothing to me."

"Neither did our promise to be exclusive."

"Ah, come on, baby. You know how it is."

"You're right. I do. Which is why you and I are over. This time, I'm not changing my mind."

"I didn't cheat though. After you left, I had that girl tossed out of the club."

Reign cocked a brow. "And the ones who've come around since then?"

Trenton didn't answer.

"I don't hate you, Trenton. Really, I don't. I no longer wish to be a part of your...entourage."

"You know how crazy women can be trying to get at us players. But the only one I'm trying to be with is you."

Reign glared at him. "Both of us know that's a lie."

The sound of a high-powered vacuum cleaner cut through the tense atmosphere. It grew louder as it neared, passed the door and then abruptly turned off. Both Reign and Trenton watched as Abe strolled confidently into the room.

"Excuse me, Reign. Is everything okay?"

Trenton's posture went from relaxed to rigid. "Who in the hell are you? Get the fuck outta here."

Abe held his ground, his focus solely on Reign. "I apologize for interrupting. While passing by the door just now, I couldn't help but notice the strain on your face."

"It's all right," Reign said, moving to stand next to Abe. "He was just leaving."

Trenton stood, or rather uncoiled, to his full height. He neared them, frowning. "Aren't you that Wakanda joker from the other night?"

"I am."

"I thought you looked familiar."

Abe offered the merest of smiles. "Glad that our first

meeting left an impression. I want no trouble from you,
Trenton. Only for no harm to come to Reign."

Trenton looked aghast. "Are you seeing this dude?"

"Who I am seeing is none of your concern."

"You've gone from the Turn Around Jumper to a
broke-down janitor? I didn't know times were that hard
for getting a man." He shook his head slowly. "That's
a damned shame."

Reign had had enough. "Goodbye, Trenton."

"Look, baby…" He took a step toward her.

Abe took a step toward him.

Ivy and the security guard entered the room.

Trenton held up his hands. "No need for drama. I'm
leaving." He walked to the door.

Reign watched Abe meet Trenton's threatening stare
with a cool, collected one. He stepped aside to let Trenton pass, never breaking eye contact.

"That's the second time you've interfered in a situation that wasn't your business. Don't let there be a
third time."

"I won't if you won't."

Trenton stopped. "What did you say?"

"You heard me. Don't harass the lady and there will
be no need for my interference."

Just then the PE director, Phil, appeared in the
hallway. "Ivy, if you have a minute, I… Trenton Carpenter?" He continued in with his hand outstretched,
completely unaware of the land mines he was dodging.
"What a pleasure to meet you! I'm a huge fan."

"Good," Ivy said. "Trenton was just leaving. Please
do me a favor and see him safely outside."

She watched Phil and Trenton walk toward the exit. In her peripheral vision, she noted Abe walk toward the vacuum. She thought to call after him, or to follow, or both. It was important that he knew she and Trenton were over. Why, exactly, she couldn't have answered if asked.

"Hey, Reign!" Trenton called over his shoulder. "We're off on Thursday. Leave the night open. I'll make special plans."

Ivy marched over, shut the office door and turned the lock, then became mama bear. "I'm so sorry that happened." She followed Reign to where she stood by a window, reached up and squeezed her shoulder. "Are you okay?"

"Yes, I actually am." Reign was surprised that she meant it.

"Looks like your knight was ready to save you again. You might want to keep him around."

Reign's emotions were too frazzled to respond to Ivy's suggestion, but a rational space somewhere deep inside her was thinking the very same thing.

Six

Abe's grandfather, *kbaba*, as he was called in the Kgo language of Kutoka, was a very wise man and, aside from Abe's parents, his greatest teacher. His lessons had been simple and life-lasting. As a child, when Abe had become excited and started stuttering, his grandfather would say, "Take a breath. Quiet your mind. There are too many words trying to get through to your mouth!" Later, in school, this same tool had helped him to focus on his studies and make excellent grades. On the soccer field, in extremely tense moments, Abe would become quiet in his mind until tens of thousands of fans disappeared, along with the men on the field, until there was only him, the ball and the goal. Within that tunnel of concentration, miracles had happened time and again. That one lesson alone had proved golden in Abe's life.

Leaving Reign's office, he returned to that practice to handle the bundles of words bouncing around in his head and the feelings that flowed everywhere else. He'd been hit with one surprise after another, all pivotal in becoming Reign's friend.

Nolan had gotten a major contract and hadn't shared the news. And not just any contract but one with Eddington Enterprise, a development that could place Abe near Reign every day. Reign had called Trenton an ex, yet he dared to continue coming around. Was this the dance of two people not quite uncoupled? Perhaps they'd broken up and gotten back together many times; it was the way of some of the friends that he knew. Reign had been understandably hurt by the betrayal. In her head, she believed herself over Trenton. Was her heart finished as well?

Abe wasn't a violent man. Except for the soccer field, he abhorred confrontation. Yet seeing Trenton with Reign had unleashed a raw, almost primal desire to protect her. He'd left the office because, in the face of Trenton's cockiness, he hadn't been quite sure he could continue with gentleman-like behavior.

After work, his first stop was the mansion where Nolan now resided. This conversation with his cousin had to be face-to-face. He'd likely balk at the notion of Abe working at the Eddington Enterprise building. He was ready for debate. But another came first. Five minutes from the house, his mother called.

"Hello, Mother! How are you?"

"Missing my youngest son," she gleefully answered before switching to their native language. "Dela and

Rachel are missing you, too. And there are other suitable brides, as you are aware. Iya has just returned from her culinary travels. She hopes to start a members only supper club, something I think would match perfectly with being your wife."

"I could be in Chicago for a year, Mother."

"Daniel told you about your *kbaba*?"

"Yes."

"Then you know that time is of the essence. Your priority should be to find a mate and settle down. Losing him before you marry and fully integrate into the company could be life-changing. Not only for your future, but that of your seed. Please take it seriously."

"I am taking it most seriously, Mother. And who knows? I might find a wife here in Chicago."

His mother gasped. "Aldric! You wouldn't. You couldn't."

Abe suppressed a chuckle, even while being glad to be testing these waters. When one married in Kutoka, one wed the whole family.

"If I meet the love of my life, why not?"

"Because she wouldn't be one of our people. She would not be a Kutokan, that's why."

"But she'd be my people, someone I marry not for legacy, inheritance or to build key alliances, but because I choose her."

"Oh, Aldric, don't be silly. One marries exactly for the matters you mentioned." A moment and then, "Please tell me you're not dating anyone seriously."

Abe was glad he could be honest. "No, Mother, I'm not."

"Thank you, Jesus," she said, relief clearly apparent. "Your father and I don't mind you having fun in America. But when you return and join the company full-time and settle down, it will be with a bride from Kutoka. And remember, Aldric, if you haven't found a bride by the time you are thirty..."

"Then one will be arranged. Thanks for the reminder, Mother, and the ultimatum." Abe reverted back to English. "No pressure, right?"

"None at all. You have your choice of the cream of the crop. Some of the finest ladies from the most prestigious of our nation's families are willing and ready to become Mrs. Baiden. Look at how happy Danso is with his family. You are risking everything, your inheritance and more, just to be defiant."

"Not purposely. Danso married the love of his life."

"From a family we've known for decades."

There was no winning this conversation. Time to change the subject. "How is *Kbaba?*"

"About the same. Nothing that a wedding and more grandchildren couldn't cure."

"Seriously, Mother."

He heard her sigh. "About the same. We fly to Switzerland next week. Some of the best specialists and most progressive treatments are there. Hopefully, they'll give us good news."

"I hope so, too." Abe reached the house. "I have to go, Mother, but we'll talk later. I love you."

"I love you too."

The conversation with Vallienne firmed up his resolve. His grandfather was ailing and the clock on Abe's freedom kept ticking away. He wasn't sure why, but getting to better know Reign was feeling more and more important. He wasn't looking for a wife, but if he found one, and it was her, he didn't think he'd be disappointed.

"What happened?" Was Nolan's annoyed greeting. "Did you lose both phones?"

"I won't be long."

"Good. And call next time."

"I hear congratulations are in order," he said, following Nolan through the home's grand foyer and into an airy, two-story, open-concept space.

Nolan managed a sheepish grin. "Who told you?"

"Ivy. Why the secrecy?"

"It wasn't a secret. I was going to tell you eventually."

"A contract that huge? A client that important? Why wait?"

"You know why. As you said, this is a huge contract, an important client. I can't take any chances on it getting messed up."

"How could telling me do that?"

"Because you'd asked to be put on that detail and I'd have to tell you no. I don't want to have to do that."

"Of course, I'm going to work at Reign's offices. When does the contract start?"

Nolan didn't answer.

"You're working there already. That's why you've been so busy lately. I give you access to all this—" Abe waved a hand around the opulence "—in exchange for a job without pay. And this is the thanks I get?"

"Seriously, bro, you're beginning to sound like a stalker."

Abe almost told Nolan about his encounter with Trenton, and his need to not only protect Reign but to be the reason behind her magnificent smile, but decided against sharing something that would cause Nolan to hesitate even more.

"From the moment of our first encounter, I've wanted to spend more time with her. You should thank me for that contract. I believe it is this desire that secured the deal for you."

"That would be a negative, soldier. I've been working on this contract for years. I was networking and making myself known to Derrick when this company was just a thought in my head."

"I will begin work there tomorrow."

"Can't do it, man."

"Fine." Abe took a couple steps toward the stairs. "Your party is about to end early. I want my home back."

Nolan's jaw dropped. "Tonight?" he asked, his voice raised a notch.

"Right now," Abe replied. He looked beyond him, took in the low-burning candles and the soft music wafting down from upstairs. "Or I can begin cleaning the Eddington Enterprise building tomorrow and leave you to your…company."

"The bet was for one month!" Nolan shouted. Abe raised a brow. "This is extortion!"

Abe responded by taking another step toward the stairs.

"All right, all right. I'll put you there one or two days a week. I still need you at PDS Prep until I hire more guys."

"I am happy to work at both places, as I've promised Ivy and her athletic director that I will help set up a soccer program at their school."

"Oh, so they know Aldric Baiden, the star soccer player."

"Of course not."

Abe saw a light flash in his cousin's eye. "Don't even think about it. To them and Reign, I am still Abe the Janitor. That is how it will remain."

"Or what?"

"Trust me, cousin, you do not want to find out."

"You'd better be glad I love you, man."

Abe chuckled in relief.

The next day, after trading the rest of his week's shifts with a coworker, Nolan's right-hand man Charles gave Abe a grand tour of the Eddington Enterprise office building and put him to work.

Reign's company took up the building's top two floors. While mopping, sweeping, buffing and dusting, Abe pondered what if anything he'd do if he saw Reign tomorrow—Valentine's Day. Would she even still be at work after-hours? Or would she be somewhere with the beanstalk, being romanticized and hearing lies. He thought of purchasing a gift, something thoughtful or funny. Or slipping a card beneath her office door asking that she be his Valentine.

The next day arrived. Abe came to work on time and empty-handed. He'd taken extra care with his appearance, trimmed up his beard, had his jumpsuit dry-cleaned and allowed himself a spritz of his favorite cologne. He'd decided against purchasing a gift for

Reign, something he was sure Nolan would view as inappropriate.

In his country, some had embraced the holiday that had begun as a Christian feast honoring two martyrs and evolved to a day the world celebrated love, but his family hadn't traditionally participated. In their clan, love wasn't celebrated on one certain day but ideally practiced twenty-four-seven, three sixty-five.

Abe had bought his share of Valentine gifts but mostly out of what felt like obligation. With Reign, being less than truthful about his identity was inorganic enough. Whatever he shared or gave to her would have to be real, not some knickknack bought at the last moment. It would have to be something as valuable as she was somehow becoming to him, even though they'd not yet kissed. Whatever it was, it couldn't possibly be bought by someone on his present salary. The gift he gave would be superficial at best, unless he gave her the truth, or as close as he could come right now.

And what was that? What was it about the woman who had him so enthralled? While mixing the solution to begin the night's cleaning, Abe pondered the question. As he turned the corner and entered the hall housing her office, a slither of light shone from beneath her closed door. Without giving himself more time to think or, worse, talk himself out of acting, he walked resolutely to her door and lightly tapped on it.

He waited. Silence. He tapped again. "Reign?"

He turned and was about to leave when a sound stopped him. A sniffle, barely audible but clearly identified. Again, acting purely on instinct, he reached for

the knob and opened the door. The scent of fresh orchids assailed him along with that of hyacinth, roses
and other fragrant buds. Her office looked like a flower
shop. Every table held a vase of flowers. Others had
been set on the floor. Apology presents from Trenton,
he guessed. He could have sent a semitruckful and more
would have been needed. Betrayal was a hard stench
to cover.

"Reign? It's me, Abe."

He looked around and did not see her. Then he noticed a closed door at the short end of the L-shaped
room. He walked over and knocked gently.

"Reign. It's Abe. I am sorry to disturb you. I saw
your light and heard a noise. Reign?"

Nothing.

He stood there, not sure of what to do. After a moment, he decided to mind his own business. If she
wanted her privacy, he should give it to her. He walked
away from the door then heard a click as it opened. He
turned to see Reign looking forlorn. He wasn't sure if
she'd been crying, but she looked sad nonetheless.

He immediately walked to her and pulled her into
his arms. "Out of all of this beauty," he softly whispered, "you are the most beautiful, valuable and rarest
bloom in this room."

His words touched something. He was sure she cried
now. Softly, hiding her face from his view. He held her,
gently rubbed her back.

A few moments passed before she leaned back and
with a tearstained face told him, "We've got to stop
meeting like this."

Her words brought out that feeling again; an over-whelming passion, a possessive streak to have Reign as his own. She was in his arms, soft and vulnerable, looking like sunshine, smelling like paradise. Her next move was unexpected. She lifted her head and kissed him, lightly, on the lips. Without thought, he reacted and returned the favor, pressed his lips against hers and tightened his embrace. She opened her mouth to deepen the kiss. Her mouth felt like home, her tongue the per-fect greeting. She wore a silky, wine-colored suit dress that embraced her curves as his hands did now, before stopping midthigh. In the high heels she always wore, they were almost eye level to each other. Their bodies fit perfectly. In the moment, everything felt right.

Reign moaned, pulled her arms from around his neck and broke the kiss. "Sorry. I don't know what came over me," she explained, stepping back. "Those words were beautiful. I needed to hear them tonight."

Abe took her hand and walked them to a nearby sofa. He reached for a tissue in a holder on a floating shelf and gave it to her before they sat down. She blew her nose, wiped her eyes and grabbed another tissue.

"It appears you're always rescuing me. Like yes-terday. I couldn't' believe Trenton showed up at the school."

"I couldn't either. Seeing him there with you… I charged in without thinking. If it was wrong of me, I apologize."

"I was glad to see you." Reign ran a hand through her hair. "Believe it or not, I'm not usually this fragile."

"Trenton did not call you today as promised?"

Reign all but snorted. "I didn't expect to hear from him. He knew I wouldn't take the call. Which I'm sure is why he did all this." She looked around at the room full of flowers.

"He believes he can win you back. Is he right?"

Reign shook her head. "I will never date him again, or any professional athlete."

Abe almost flinched. He felt guilty as hell. Though doing so for what he felt the right reasons, not telling Reign who he really was felt like its own betrayal. She deserved the truth. He should tell her. ASAP.

"Reign, I—"

"You kiss good."

He swallowed the near confession. He would ask her out, determine her feelings. If what appeared to be a mutual attraction was sure and not just a rebound emotion, if she was truly interested in getting to know Abe the Janitor, he'd come clean and tell her everything. For now, he would stay in the moment and allow the evening to unfold.

"I have forever wanted to taste those lips."

"Were they all that you thought they'd be?" she teased.

"They were that and so much more."

Reign leaned against the seat back. "Relationships suck."

"They can get pretty dicey."

"How do you know? Have you ever been in love?"

Abe sat back too, mindful that he should be working and at the same time knowing that where he was was where he needed to be.

"My first heartbreak came early."

"How old were you?"

"Eleven."

Reign laughed, though her eyes were sad. "Puppy love doesn't count."

"At the time, it was all that mattered Her name was Haniah and she was beautiful, with long, thick braids and crooked white teeth. It had taken me the whole school year to ask her to be my girlfriend. Just before spring recess I got up the nerve. She said yes! I was delighted. Our love lasted a whole twenty-four hours until the next day at school when someone else asked her and she broke up with me and said yes to them."

"How long did it take you to get over her?"

"A whole weekend!"

Reign chuckled.

"Why are you laughing? My love ran deep."

He was glad Reign was laughing and that he'd been the one to put a smile on her face.

"If only grown-up love could be healed as easily."

"The deeper the investment, the more painful the withdrawal. But finding the one is worth all that we go through."

"Still thinking about Haniah?"

He shook his head. "I'm thinking about a grownup heartbreak from a woman who treated me the way Trenton did you."

"Please, do me a favor and don't keep mentioning his name. His actions proved he never cared about me."

Abe would do all he could to help her forget the man ever existed, but he didn't tell her that.

"He seems to have cared, at least a little. Look at all these flowers."

"It may have been his idea to send them but most likely his personal assistant Ralph did the work. They'll be gone within the hour, distributed to hospitals, shelters and other organizations around the city housing clients and patients needing beauty in their lives. That's the only reason I'm still here, waiting for the driver."

"And after that?"

Abe watched as she shrugged while trying valiantly to fight back tears. "Home, I guess."

"Anyone there to keep you company, a roommate or relative to keep you from spending the evening alone?"

"My sister and brothers are all married. Ivy and Desmond have a quiet dinner planned. Jake and his wife made me welcome to hang out with them, but who wants to be a third wheel? I'm not sure what Maeve and Victor are doing—Maeve is my older sister—but it's probably something that would make me feel like an interloper. I'm sure Mom and Dad would welcome me into their evening, but something about spending Valentine's Day with your parents…"

"Yeah, I get it. No explanation needed there."

Reign shifted to the edge of the sofa and prepared to get up.

"It's a poor substitute," he interjected, "but we can go out for coffee. I would have suggested dinner but that might be out of line."

"Then I'll do it. Abe, would you like to have dinner with me?"

"Seriously? You know I'd love to, except I'm still at work for two more hours."

"I don't mind a late night," Reign told him. "Getting a table anywhere might be tricky. The restaurants are probably filled with people in love or at least acting happy. On second thought, eating out tonight is probably not the best idea."

"You're welcome to come to my place if you'd like. It's a humble abode, far less than you're used to, but it's clean and I make a mean martini."

She reared back. "I'd never guess you for a martini man."

"I tended bar for about five minutes while living in London."

"You lived in London?"

Tricky territory, Abe belatedly realized. "For a while, when attending school."

A knock interrupted. For the delivery man's timing, Abe could have tipped him a one-hundred-dollar bill. He had several in his pocket and would have, except such cash in a cleaning man's possession might have caused suspicion from Reign.

"That's the man here to pick up the flowers. Can you direct him? They're all to be taken. I need to use the bathroom and freshen up. I'm sure I look a mess."

"Your mascara is smeared a bit, but you're still lovely, and yes, I'm happy to help."

"Thanks, Abe." She leaned over and gave him a quick peck on the lips then turned toward the bathroom. "Oh, and I'll take you up on that martini. What time do you get off work?"

In about five minutes, Abe thought as he maintained his composure and reached for his phone to text Nolan. His cousin, or somebody, needed to relieve him of the rest of this shift. The night was going better than he'd dared to imagine. He took back everything he'd thought about the "frivolous" holiday and sent a prayer of thanks up to St. Valentine. His special day held a bit of magic and had brought Abe together with his desire after all.

Seven

While waiting for Abe to get off work, and her office fully rid of flowers, Reign walked to the closet where she kept a spare wardrobe and got comfortable. She changed into Fenty jeans, a pink, oversized sweater and black-and-pink hi-tops she'd purchased on her last trip back east. She sat at her desk scrolling through her partially done website, trying not to think much about the evening ahead. She didn't really know Abe, but her gut gave the green light. He wouldn't be working at Ivy's prep school if anything in his background could cause a red flag. More than that, she liked him, plain and simple. After dealing with Trenton's huge ego, Abe was a breath of fresh air. Surprisingly, she wasn't missing the lifestyle she thought that she would or the exclusive trips and private parties she'd enjoyed with her ex. Having to always be "on," impeccably dressed to outshine the constant competition between the girlfriends and wives. Reign was popular in her right, but with Trenton, her star rose higher. She hadn't realized the pressure of maintaining the relationship. She'd had no idea of the weight she'd carried until it was gone. She looked forward to visiting Abe's humble apartment, having a martini and who knew? Maybe sharing something more.

The thought of having sex with Abe had barely formed in her head before she began talking herself out of it. What if he grew too attached as a result of being intimate, or what if he was horrible in bed? Dodging such awkwardness was one of the reasons that Reign never dated colleagues or, since high school, anyone in the town's tight social circle. It was why she'd never had a one-night stand. Before Trenton, she'd spent several years with a guy from the west coast that she'd met in college. After their breakup, he gotten a job and moved to Seattle, much to Reign's relief.

"You changed," Abe said, startling her from her musings. "I like that outfit more than the dress."

"Good. Are you ready?"

"Just wrapped up."

"If you text me your address, I'll meet you there."

"I just remembered my fridge is fairly empty. Should I stop and grab something to go with our drinks?"

"There's a place not far from here that makes a killer pizza. If that sounds good to you, I'll pick one up on the way. My treat."

"That sounds fine."

"Any topping you hate, so I can be sure and get it? Just kidding," she added when she saw how he frowned.

"I eat everything," he responded. His expression transformed into the most tender look. "Thank you, Reign, for buying our dinner and for spending the evening with me. I know this night is hard for you. I hope not spending it alone makes you feel a little bit better."

"You offered a shoulder to cry on and helped get rid of the flowers. My night is better already."

"Okay, then. I'm leaving."

"I'll see you soon."

The pizza place was crowded. It took thirty minutes to get her "loaded spicy" to go. While waiting, she received a thoughtful text from Abe.

Call when you get here. I don't want you walking at night alone.

Being cared for in this thoughtful way was something Reign could get used to. She texted back with thumbs-up and smiley emojis and rethought her decision not to occupy Abe's bed.

Traffic was fairly light, making her commute easy. She drove past downtown Chicago with its skyscrapers and spaghetti overpasses, past strip malls, and took the Martin Luther King Drive exit into an area of the city known as Washington Park. She couldn't recall ever having been in this part of town, one that seemed on the verge of gentrification. Nearing Abe's block, she was thankful he'd suggested coming out to meet her, and that she'd driven one of the plainer company cars. She pulled over and quickly sent a text.

I'm here.

He came out seconds later and looked around. She honked and waved him over. He got into the black Kia sedan.

"Where's the Bentley?"

"Still parked at work. I decided to drive one of our company cars."

"Smart woman." He pointed. "That car's leaving. Park there."

He balanced the large, deep-dish pizza with one hand and grabbed her hand with the other. "Did the GPS give you any problems in finding the place?" he asked.

"I'm familiar with the neighborhood."

"Really?"

"Yes," she said, laughing at his reaction. "I come down from my fortified glass tower every once in a while."

They walked along in companionable silence. Soon, they were inside Abe's modest apartment. He'd not been lying when describing its condition. The place was plain yet pristine.

"I guess it would be weird for a man who cleans to have a dirty apartment."

"Not really. My cousin once lived here. He was a slob."

"Nolan?" Abe nodded. "Where is he now?"

"He moved to a…larger residence." He reached for the pizza. "I'll take that while you get comfortable. There's room in the closet for your coat."

She rejoined him at the counter that separated the kitchen from the larger space. "It's simple but I like it," she said, looking around. A brown leather sofa and two matching side tables took up one wall across from a TV that was at least sixty inches. An autographed Walter Peyton jersey filled a black-lacquer frame hung beside it, the only hanging on the dull, beige walls. *Sports Illustrated* and other manly magazines were strewed across an ottoman that served as the room's coffee table. Reign noticed there were no personal pictures, none of family or a significant other. Unless he'd hid them, which she doubted. Abe didn't strike her as a man who kept secrets. With him, she thought that what one saw was exactly what one got.

She walked over to where he'd lined up martini fixings on the counter. "How long have you lived here?"

"A few months. Dry or sweet, your martini?"

"Definitely sweet," she purred, unable to keep herself from flirting. Abe had changed from his baggy Clean Up Crew uniform to jeans and a black turtleneck sweater. The combo made him look sexy, with a bod that appeared as firm as it had felt when she'd had the good fortune of running into it. The idea to not have sex with him was losing ground quickly. If she didn't hold herself to a couple drinks, all bets might be off.

"The stereo is hooked up to a music streaming service. You can pick a station or turn on the TV if you'd like."

"After my crazy day, I'm actually enjoying the quiet."

"Me too," he answered, smiling. "Though my day's been good so far. He poured liquids into a stainless-steel container and rattled it firmly. Reign watched the muscles ripple beneath the wool fabric as he delivered a drink shaken, not stirred. He poured the frothy yellow liquid into two small glasses.

"Here, taste it."

"First, let's make a toast."

"To Valentine's Day," he offered. "And to you, Ms. Reign Eddington."

"To you, Mr.... What's your last name?"

"Wetherbee."

"To you, Mr. Abe Wetherbee, a custodial technician who cleans up more types of messes than office buildings produce."

"Ah, I like that." They clinked glasses. "Cheers."

Reign took a drink. Her eyes widened. "Wow, what is this?"

"It's called a French martini. Pineapple and cranberry are the juices. I didn't have the liqueur needed to finish it off correctly."

"Which is...?"

"Chambord. It's raspberry flavored."

"I can't imagine this tasting better." She enjoyed another tentative sip. "It's delicious."

"I'm glad you like it, though I hope you don't mind if I grab a beer."

"I could have drunk a beer and saved you the trouble."

"Fixing a drink that you enjoy is my pleasure. Plus, it helps me keep my bartending skills sharp should I ever need them again."

"You think that might happen once you return to your country?"

"No." He walked over and pulled a bottle of beer out of the fridge. "Shall we down this with slices of pizza?"

"Absolutely, I'm starved."

While chowing down on a pizza covered in a variety of meats, vegetables and spicy peppers, Reign and Abe traded details about their lives. She shared the challenges and triumphs of both growing up and working with family, which came with the benefit of knowing someone always had your back. Reign got the feeling that Abe was more private. While mentioning two siblings and stating that they, too, were close, he was less forthcoming about the work he'd done before arriving in America, his college experience or what he hoped to do once back home.

What Reign did observe was the ease with which they kept talking. The silences were comfortable, the laughter often. Abe was a good listener, who seemed to genuinely care about what she was saying. She didn't want to think about Trenton, but it was hard to not compare them. With Abe, she did more of the talking and was the focus, while with her ex, most conversations had been all about him.

With dinner over, they moved to the living room. Abe picked up the remote and began surfing the channels. They continued to talk.

"It sounds like you come from such a great family," he said. "How did you get mixed up with someone like Trenton?"

"Interesting that you bring him up. You two couldn't be more different."

"What do you mean?"

Reign pulled her legs up on the couch, rested her chin on her palm, and thought. "He's loud. You're quiet. He's self-centered. You seem genuinely interested in my life. He's a professional athlete. You're not.

"He's not a bad guy," she finished, allowing herself to remember the good times in between the arguments and infidelities. "Just a spoiled one. While not excusing his behavior, I understand how difficult it must be for a young, viral man to resist temptation when it's thrown at you from everywhere."

"You don't regret dating him?"

"No regrets, but I don't want to do it again."

Reign hadn't planned to talk about Trenton but was keenly aware of how much lighter it felt to have unloaded her feelings. Ordinarily, she would have been embarrassed, but with Abe, it somehow felt okay.

Reign sometimes felt insecure but sharing her true feelings with Abe felt natural. He felt safe. It also helped that they were within the confines of his apartment and not in public, where the paparazzi were still after blood. It would have been unrealistic to think the masses wouldn't be as interested in her and Trenton's breakup as they were in their dating process. With the intimate photo of him and "the fan" circulating through the world's web, there would be no reconciliation. There would be no further public outbursts either. She and Trenton Carpenter had mutually decided to go their separate ways. Period. End of story. Beyond that, she hoped the public would respect her request for privacy.

She looked at Abe, appreciating his presence during this turbulent time. "Thanks for having dinner with me."

"When necessary, I can be determined to get what I want."

Something about the way he said that caused goose bumps to ripple across Reign's lower lips. Casual yet firmly confident. Soft but powerful. And, generalities aside, something about the energy permeating from this man was at odds with the personality of Abe, the carefree janitor.

"It was good to get out my feelings. I feel better."

"I'm glad."

"It probably wouldn't be a bad idea to make an appointment with my therapist."

"Speaking feelings out loud can be very healing, especially with someone trained to break down the emotions surrounding those thoughts. That can be a very healthy move."

"Was that said from personal experience?"

"I've not been to counseling, but if the need arose, I wouldn't hesitate."

Reign shifted until she sat close to Abe. "You're a pretty good therapist yourself."

"A good listener, perhaps," he answered. "Sometimes that's all you need."

"True." Reign put down her glass and scooted even closer to Abe. "And sometimes you need more."

Abe tried to shift away from her but sitting at the end of the couch, he couldn't go far. "What are you doing?"

Reign placed a hand on his muscular biceps, ran a

finger down the length of his arm. "What does it look like I'm doing?"

He stood up. "It looks like I made your drink too strong."

"I'm sorry," she coyly replied. "Didn't mean to scare you."

"I'm not afraid of you," he replied.

"Prove it." She patted the couch. "Please, sit back down. I won't bite…yet."

The remarks had their desired effect. If having older brothers had taught her anything, it was that men and their egos rarely parted.

He sat, his eyes unreadable as they bore into her. "Happy now?"

"I'd be happier if you'd kiss me again. And, for the record," she hurried on, "my desire has nothing to do with alcohol. I'm completely sober."

"And on the rebound."

"Perhaps."

"I don't want you to do something you'll regret."

"Dang! Are you that bad in bed?"

The unintended comment caught them both off guard. Abe burst out laughing, to Reign's relief. The mood lightened. She was glad of that too.

"You know what I mean."

"I do, and I appreciate you considering my feelings. Given the same situation, it's more than most men would have done."

"It's not only that, Reign. It's work. I'm totally focused. I'm not interested in or ready for a serious relationship."

"Good. Neither am I." She turned more fully toward

him, placed a hand on his thigh. "Your being genuine, kind, compassionate, are all what I find attractive about you. The way you care. It makes me feel special and valued. And it's very, very sexy."

"You don't know anything about me." Said even as his eyes shifted to her lips.

"I know you're a good kisser." She leaned over, tentatively, and when he didn't recoil, gently touched her lips to his. "Makes me wonder what else you're good at."

"I can be very disciplined, but only to a point. I'm a man of principle. Not one made of steel."

"I can tell." She kissed him again, lightly. "No man." *Kiss*. "With lips this soft." *Kiss*. "Could be made of metal."

Her statement seemed to ignite a spark in Abe. One minute, he was calm and collected. The next, he'd secured her in his arms and was ravishing her with a focused, skilled tongue. The move was powerful, commanding. She loved it. A take-charge man like that turned her on.

All the nights without intimacy, the unleashed sexual energy built up since her breakup, it all pooled at the center of her core and spiraled down to her pussy. When it came to sex, Reign had never been shy. Tonight was no exception. She positioned herself to lie down and pulled on Abe's shirt to bring him down with her. He didn't resist. Couldn't, what with the way he continued to kiss her lips and face, then her neck and the creamy exposed portion of her weighty globes. His touch brought her nipples to pebbled peaks, made her hot. And wet. And wanting to feel him inside her.

Shaking fingers fumbled to unbutton his shirt.

"Come on," she all but whimpered. "Let's get out of these clothes."

Abe caught her wrist to still her. "Reign. Let's think about this. Are you sure?"

"I know what I want." She maneuvered herself away enough to reach the hem of her sweater and pull it over her head. She watched Abe's eyes sweep across her body and, for additional incentive, quickly undid the front-clasp bra. Her full breasts swung freely, nipples like headlights aimed at Abe's chest. He sucked in a breath then slowly, almost reverently, reached out to touch them. One and then the other. He rubbed a thumb over the hard nub, causing a ripple of pleasure. Leaned down and pulled one into his mouth.

Reign groaned. Her eyes closed. Her hips began to gyrate against him in a slow, lusty grind. Suddenly, he stopped and lifted himself off her. She felt bereft and almost complained…until she saw that he'd stood only to remove his shirt and jeans.

She swung her legs to the floor. Took off her sneakers and shimmied out of her jeans. Looking up, she caught Abe staring, his hooded eyes telegraphing desire, a feeling further evidenced by the sizable bulge beneath pristine-white Calvin Kleins. Why had he hidden such a superbly sculpted body inside a baggy jumpsuit? Now, no part of him looked like an average janitor. Everything screamed power. Confidence. Control.

"Come here."

His voice was low yet filled the room. Reign's body felt weak. She almost began shaking. Wearing nothing but the lacy thong that matched her black bra, she sidled up to a body designed by the gods, a deep, rich brown that looked good enough to eat.

Don't mind if I do.

Emboldened by the decadent thoughts swirling within her, she walked over and placed a hand on his crotch.

"Thought you weren't made of steel," she murmured, rubbing her hand along the length of his hard, thick dick before giving it a squeeze.

He said nothing.

Then…

She got on her knees.

What else could she do? The bulge fairly beckoned. Begging to be kissed, sucked, nipped, licked.

Slowly, gently, she tugged at the briefs, generating a peekaboo show for her eyes only. The band on the shorts gave way to reveal a thick thatch of tightly curled black hair that spread from his lower waist to his groin.

She looked up. Smiling. Teasing. Prolonging the inevitable.

"Keep going."

Said like a man used to giving orders and having them followed. She eased the briefs over his hips. And lower. Until his penis sprang from the confines of cotton like a snake ready to strike. His dick was perfection. Long, thick and weighty in her hands. She placed her nose against it. He smelled of soap and sex. Her kitty purred, throbbed with anticipation. She leaned forward and flicked her tongue against its tip. Heard him hiss as she opened her mouth and pulled him in, slid her tongue around the mushroom tip then along the length of him. She palmed his sac, readied her tongue to take the same journey up that it had taken down. Halfway there, he pulled away. Before she could consider why she was being lifted as though she weighed nothing, she instinctively wrapped her legs around his waist.

Had he planned this move?

Must have, because before she could catch her breath, he'd eased a long middle finger deep inside her heat, swirling it in sync with the tongue now rhythmically moving in her mouth. He found places inside her Reign swore had never been touched. Still christening her core and beyond, he carried them the short distance to the bed then continued the delicious assault. Something began to unfurl inside her, a flicker of a flame that began at her navel and spiraled down to her heat. By the time it arrived, she exploded. The orgasm of her life…

She didn't have time to catch her breath. Abe wasn't talking. He also wasn't done. After retrieving a condom from the dresser, he shielded himself and began making love. For Reign, it felt as though something missing from her soul had come home. He didn't have sex with her. He made love. Slowly, completely, until everything but the feel of Abe's beam of steel inside her faded away and disappeared.

Somewhere between her final orgasm and falling asleep nestled beside Abe's hard body, Reign had a thought. Today had started out as one she was dreading. Once again, her knight had stepped up and saved the day. Reign had no idea how she'd feel about her actions tomorrow. Tonight, though, Abe was her perfect Valentine.

Eight

The sun had just begun to peek over the horizon. Its bursts of oranges, reds, pinks and purples glistened across the dark hue of the ocean as waves gently ebbed and flowed against warm white sand. Abe walked along the water's edge, white-linen cargo pants rolled up to his shins, a matching white shirt unbuttoned and floating behind him, his bare feet massaged by hundreds, thousands, of ancient, tiny warm grains. Here, at the ocean that served as the backyard to his uncle's palace, sunrise and sunset were his favorite times of day. He reached down, picked up a shell. Saw a smooth, red stone and stooped to pick it up too. As he straightened to continue his morning stroll, he saw a figure in the distance. A female, he imagined, judging by the long, white dress that fluttered in the gentle morning breeze around caramel-colored legs, but was in stark contrast to the whipping of long, curly black hair around the stranger's face dancing along the wind.

There was something enchanting about the way she moved toward him... Something both sensual and angelic at once. Something that made his strides lengthen and quicken, that caused his heart to beat an energized rhythm across his hard chest. It struck him that they were both dressed in white and had both chosen this time of morning to rise and greet the first rays of the sun. She looked familiar, though long, silky strands of hair made a peekaboo game of seeing her face. Still, he could feel her; an essence that made his heart sing.

Without knowing why, he started to run toward her. At the same time, she smiled and began doing the same. They grew closer. He held out his arms, creating an open embrace for her, then stopped to provide a firm foundation for when she flew into his arms. Thirty feet away. No, couldn't be. Twenty feet away. The wind died down. Her hair blew back. He saw her face clearly. Ten feet away. He couldn't believe it. His queen was here in the Kingdom of Kutoka. She stopped directly in front of him.

Reign.

"You came," he whispered, afraid that, like a phantom, she would evaporate into the ocean.

"Of course I did," she answered, breathless both from the run and the energy flowing between them.

Once again, he held out his arms. She took one step and then another. Just before their fingers touched—

The bed shifted. He frowned in near sleep. For a moment, confusion mixed with grogginess. Where was he and who was in his bed? His eyes flew open. He turned toward quiet movement and saw her. The events of last night and early morning flooded his consciousness. He was in an apartment in Chicago. He wasn't alone. Reign was there. They'd made intense, wildly passionate love. Memories of her glistening body swirled. Abe's heart smiled. Still, he worried about how Reign felt about last night, and the possible consequences.

"Good morning," he rasped, his voice gravelly with sleep. "Everything okay?"

She jumped. "Oh, sorry," she said, easing into the jeans from last night and sitting on the bed to pull on her sneakers. "I was trying to be quiet. I didn't mean to wake you."

"It's okay." Through a yawn he asked her, "How are you feeling?"

"After last night, thanks to you…" She came over for a quick kiss. "Amazing."

"Glad I could help."

She smirked at him.

Abe relaxed. "What time is it?"

"A little after six."

He groaned. "My God, woman. Why are you up at the crack of dawn?" Dawn. As in the dream. "Oh, wow. This dream. You were…"

Later, he'd swear the warm breeze he'd suddenly felt move across his face had been real. With it came a warning whispered inside his head. *Don't tell her that part. Not yet.*

She reached for her other shoe. "You had a dream?"

"Yeah, I was back home. Even my subconscious misses the sunshine."

"I rarely remember mine," Reign said before going into the adjoining bathroom.

He eased out of bed and slipped on a pair of loose jogging pants, then quickly padded barefoot over to the dresser and pulled out a sweatshirt to cover his cold, bare chest.

"I don't know how people live in such cold," he mumbled, pulling on a thick pair of tube socks and slipping his feet into fur-lined slippers.

He walked out to the living room and turned up the thermostat, then into the kitchen to boil water for tea. Since being in Chicago, he'd become the typical bachelor living on takeout food, but he usually kept the place stocked with essentials. Working both the Eddington Enterprise and prep school locations, and handling video conference calls in between, Abe's increased hours had left little time for shopping. As a result, his cupboards were bare. Opening the fridge yielded the same result. If Reign was hungry, he hoped she liked leftover pizza because this morning that was her singular breakfast choice.

He turned on the oven, arranged four slices of pizza on a sheet pan and placed them inside. With breakfast heating, he walked over to the window, opened the curtains, and got the shock of his life.

"Wow."

"What is it?" Reign said, walking out of the bedroom and over to the closet where she retrieved her coat. She continued to the door. "Hate to run on you like this, but

I need to dash by my house and pick up some things before work."

Abe turned to her with a sober expression. "I don't think you're going anywhere."

Reign laughed. "Let me guess, a little snow on the ground?"

"No. Ice." Abe's gaze went back to the window. "A neighbor is working hard to chip it off his windshield. He's not having much luck. Looks like the block is frozen."

"It's probably not that bad," she said, walking over. "I'll just let my car heat up and... Oh. My. Goodness. What in the heck happened last night?"

Abe walked over to where the remote sat on the ottoman. He turned on the TV, tapped the guide and scrolled to a weather channel. On the way, he passed a local channel with a "breaking news" banner beneath a reporter shivering beside a tree covered in ice. He stopped and turned up the volume.

"...hasn't seen an ice storm this catastrophic since January 1965. There are reports of power outages throughout the area, as well as toppled trees and downed power lines that may be live. There has been at least one report of a pedestrian being injured after falling and breaking their arm.

"The governor has declared a state of emergency. A travel ban has been issued for all interstate and local highways, in effect until three p.m. Folks, this is serious. Except for emergency and law enforcement vehicles, travel is temporarily prohibited. All schools, public facilities and businesses have been strongly encouraged to close for the day. Street crews are out and temperatures have risen. We're hoping the ban can be lifted this afternoon. Until then, we'll keep you posted. Cicely Timon reporting live for Channel 4 News. Mark, back to you."

"Thanks for that report, Cicely. As you heard, a major ice storm unexpectedly began around ten o'clock last night and…"

Reign had heard enough. "This is unbelievable." She reached into her bag, grabbed her phone and dialed. "Maeve, it's me," she said, tapping the speaker button as she walked back to the window.

"Reign! Thank goodness. Where in the heck are you?"

"I came to Chicago for dinner and ended up spending the night."

"At the condo?"

"No."

"Please don't tell me you got back with Trenton."

"I won't because it's not true. That bridge has burned down."

A quick smile in his direction made Abe want to turn a backflip.

"Where are you?"

"We'll talk later."

Abe signaled that he'd go into the bedroom. Reign held out a hand as she walked to the sofa, signaling him to join her. He walked over and sat down.

"At least tell me you're safe, and warm."

"Yes on both counts." Reign snuggled up against Abe, who placed an arm around her shoulders.

"How are things over there?"

"Not as bad as Chicago," Maeve said, "thanks to the city's backup generators and emergency equipment from the bill that Daddy helped push through two years ago. All the people who accused him of wasting tax-payer dollars will now have to eat their words."

"They should get fed blocks of ice."

The sisters enjoyed a laugh. Their camaraderie felt like the kind he shared with Danso, and reminded him to give his brother a call later that day. Even invited, he felt like an interloper. He tried not to listen to the conversation. Hard to do when the soft, fragrant body of the one talking on the phone was pressed against his chest.

"Are the offices open?"

"You must not have checked your emails yet. A memo went out this morning. The building is closed. All meetings and other activities have either been canceled, rescheduled, or changed to virtual settings. I don't think I saw anything urgent for marketing..."

"There wasn't. Which is why I was looking forward to going in and having a day of playing around with mockups for the app's brochure and full-page ad layout. Digital is amazing and allows for faster changes but nothing beats being able to see the stuff in real time."

"Sorry, sis. You'll have to settle for digital. At least until three o'clock."

"I can't believe this."

"The whole city is shocked. Snow and ice was forecasted, but nothing this serious. The news said most of the hard stuff fell between midnight and five this morning, which is how it caught so many off guard. It also wasn't a hailstorm, so fell mostly in silence. The city hasn't seen ice this bad since—"

"Nineteen sixty-five," they said together.

"So you've caught the news already."

"Enough to know that for now I'm on lockdown."

"Again," the sisters simultaneously said.

Abe heard his satellite phone ring in the bedroom. He motioned to Reign before easing off the couch and retrieving his phone. It was Jeffrey, his business colleague. He quietly closed the door and spoke in French when greeting his long-time friend.

"Are you all right over there?" Jeffrey asked. "I just saw news from Chicago. Is the city really buried in ice?"

"It's pretty bad," Abe admitted. "But I'm okay. The roads are closed, not that I'd be going out even if that were possible. For all intents and purposes, the city is shut down."

"What about the affiliates? Any success there?"

"I've held several conference calls and am awash in reports. I should have my own to send over shortly."

"Daniel will be pleased."

"Has Dad said anything to you?"

"Not directly, but I've taken the temperature. A financial win right about now would bode well for you. Which, aside from the weather, is why I'm calling. Any chance you can fly to New York?"

"If cars can't be driven, I doubt planes can fly. Why, what's going on there?"

"Possibly, a new acquisition."

Abe perked up. The timing of this news couldn't be better. Next to getting married, becoming a contributing member of the company he founded was Abe's grandfather's fondest wish. Securing a lucrative asset, especially one with an international reach, would grant him leverage and quite possibly help secure his inheritance without an immediate need to walk down the aisle.

"What's the product?"

"An energy drink."

"To sit next to the other dozens on the market?" Abe's enthusiasm waned.

"No, Abe. This one is different. It's one-hundred-percent natural, no sugars or artificial flavorings, and it's naturally caffeinated."

"A green tea?"

"Kola nuts. They sent me a sample and, Abe, the stuff's amazing. After drinking it, I had more energy, felt more alert, and did so for hours. The best part is not only was there no crash later, as sugar can do, but no jitters and no problems falling asleep. I've never heard of anything quite like it."

"Sounds revolutionary."

"It could be, especially in the sports world, your domain."

"So, this would be promoted as a drink for athletes?"

"No, but I think initially that should be the focus. The number-one sports drink commands almost fifty percent of that market with average annual sales of over two-hundred million. I think with the right marketing, packaging and sales force, we could own the other half. With popular faces touting it in America, and you being the face in places where soccer is king, we could even cut into the competition's profits. Add other healthy alternatives to the line and I think a goal of five-hundred million annually is not far-fetched."

Abe immediately remembered Reign's words. *I will never date...a professional athlete.* He ignored them and said, "Tell me more."

They spoke for thirty minutes. In his excitement, Abe forgot all about Reign being just steps away. He'd spoken quietly but the apartment was small. Was it possible that she'd heard him? If so, he prayed that she didn't speak French.

"Let me check out their website and the information you sent me. I'll keep an eye on the weather and make plans to fly out as soon as the airport reopens."

He'd also have to find someone to cover his shifts and reschedule the planning meeting with Phil at PDS Prep. The weight of being someone other than who he was seemed especially bulky this morning. Yet he felt he'd found a special woman who was attracted to a man she thought was a janitor. There had been no snide comments when she'd come into his place. No grimacing at the lack of conveniences she probably took for granted. They'd eaten a simple meal of pizza and chips. She'd seemed comfortable and happy, had did as he'd suggested and made herself at home.

"Abe?"

He switched to English. "Jeffrey, this is exciting. Let's talk more later. I've got to run."

A knock sounded on the door. He strolled over to answer it.

"Hey, sorry about leaving you. That was a call

from…home." He led them back into the living area. "What do you need?"

"I didn't know pizza was in the oven."

"Oh, no!" Abe rushed into the kitchen to find the oven off and the pan on the stove.

"Thanks, Reign. I became engrossed in that phone call and forgot all about it."

"No problem. I thought I kept smelling pepperoni and spices, and finally figured it out." She sat at the counter while he walked to a far cabinet.

Pulling out plates, he said, "Would you do me the pleasure of joining me for breakfast?"

"I'd be delighted," she said with a generic accent.

He set the plates next to the stove. "My apologies that this morning's selection bears a striking resemblance to what served as dinner last night."

"Good thing it's from one of my favorite restaurants."

Reign slid off her barstool and came into the kitchen. Abe watched as, without being asked, she peered into the refrigerator and pulled out a carton of orange juice. She seemed as comfortable in his cousin's shabby apartment as he imagined she did on the estate where she lived. Soon, he'd be able to tell her everything. Abe was sure of it.

She pulled two glasses from a dish rack and began pouring the juice. "Did I hear you speaking French?"

"Yes," he answered, way more casually than he felt. "Do you speak it?" He asked the question and held his breath while awaiting the answer.

"I took a class in high school but rarely used it, which means over time I forgot much of what I'd learned."

Thank goodness.

"Where did you learn it?"

"Many relatives and friends are from French-speaking nations. It was always spoken in our home."

Out of napkins, Abe tore two paper towels off the roll, the best he could do for a place setting. He set the piping-hot pizza slices next to the orange juice Reign had poured and joined her at the bar counter.

Reign groaned as she took a bite of last night's pizza, which Abe determined tasted even better the second time around.

"So…how many languages do you speak?"

"A few." Abe realized they were swimming toward tricky conversational waters. Time to backstroke in another direction.

"What new product is your company offering? I heard you speaking with your sister about a new brochure."

"Good try, Abe, but last night was all about me and my work. This morning it should be about you."

Not only beautiful and smart, but a good chess player. He would have to be careful. Reign was nobody's fool. They'd just happened on the beginnings of at least a beautiful friendship and possibly more. He didn't want to mess it up. He took a big bite of pizza to buy himself time.

"Abe…."

He pointed to his mouth full of food, his jaw moving slowly, like he was trying to follow the rule suggesting that for the best digestion each bite be chewed twenty times before being swallowed.

Reign rested her chin in the palm of her hand, totally on to his weak delay game. "Take your time," she said sweetly, eyes smiling as she sipped her juice. "I'm not going anywhere until at least three o'clock."

He finished the bite and took a drink himself. "Now, what was the question?"

"Heck, I don't even remember it now." They both found that funny. "Come on, stop being mysterious. Just who is Abe Wetherbee?"

"You already know. I came from Africa to help my cousin's new business. After that, I'll go home."

"Something tells me there's more," Reign said, eyes narrowing as she studied his face. "You seem too... I don't know...cultured, intelligent to just be a janitor. Nothing against janitors," she'd hastily added. "Your wardrobe was different the first time I saw you. Even in my distress, I noticed the coat you were wearing. It reminded me of one out of designer Ace Montgomery's line. I know, because my brother has one."

Abe shrugged, very aware that the coat she spoke of was in the same closet where she'd retrieved hers from moments before. The coat now tossed across an arm of the sofa. He wanted to hang it up and remove any reason for her to return to the closet, but such an action would probably make her conduct an extended search instead.

He forced his attention away from it and back on a face he now noticed looked even prettier in its natural state.

"Borrowed from a friend," he said casually. "What else?"

"You speak several languages."

"Not unusual, where I'm from."

She reached for his hand, turned it over in hers. "These calluses are fresh." Hers eyes looked at him with a question he didn't answer. "Not the hands of a man used to manual labor."

He shrugged as though it were no big deal. "During summers on school break, I did office work back home."

"What type of office work?"

The question was general enough that Abe could answer somewhat truthfully. It also gave him a chance to digress into the difference in office atmospheres between American companies and those in other parts of the world.

Once they finished eating, Abe decided to change courses once again. He took Reign's hand, pulled her from the barstool, picked up his orange juice and led her toward the sofa.

"What are you doing?" she asked with a hint of attitude and no attempt to resist.

"Taking up where we left off last night," he replied as one hand slid down her back and cupped her ass. "Let's see if this orange juice tastes as good on your lips as it does on mine."

They spent a leisurely morning conducting treasure hunts on each other.

Abe was as surprised as he was thrilled to find a woman who matched his sexual stamina. In first seeing Reign at the nightclub, his instincts had been spot-on. He'd been immediately attracted, not just to her looks but to a quality that couldn't quite be defined. When speaking with his mother about finding a wife in America, Abe had been largely joking. saying what he felt would somewhat appease. After spending time with Reign, however, Abe would give the prospect more serious thought. Because truthfully, it could be possible to find a wife in America. Someone passionate, smart, beautiful, successful in her own right.

Someone like Reign.

Nine

The citywide mandatory lockdown ended at three, but it was after eight before all the damage from the freak ice storm had been cleared with highways and interstates reopened. Holed up in Abe's clean but cramped apartment—the one she'd called cozy when he'd apologized for the lack of space—the day had gone surprisingly well. After an hour of long, drawn-out kisses, exploring bodies, and another explosive orgasm, and after being chivalrous enough to chip away ice and retrieve the tote containing her tablet from the trunk of her car, Abe had retreated to the bedroom to chat with friends and family while Reign had gotten comfortable at the bar counter and settled in to work. Abe had even managed to make a great suggestion regarding the brochure she and her team were designing. He'd come out midmorning to find her staring at the screen.

As she neared her exit for Point du Sable, she reflected on the conversation.

"Want some water?" Abe squeezed Reign's shoulder as he passed her on the way to the fridge. "Whoa, baby, you're tight. Stressed?"

"A little bit."

He'd pulled two bottles of water from the fridge, unscrewed both caps and set one in front of her.

"Thanks." Reign's eyes never left the screen.

Abe drank, set his bottle on the counter and began kneading Reign's neck and shoulders. After a few moments, she stopped trying to focus on the screen to enjoy the expert fingers working on her tight muscles.

"Um, that feels good."

He kissed the top of her head. "What are you working on?"

"A pamphlet for a new product we're about to roll out."

"What is the product?"

"An app that helps customers keep track of various cryptocurrencies, including ours, of course, and also gauge the market for the right times to buy and sell." She turned to him. "Do you own any crypto?"

"A little." His strong fingers continued to perform their magic. "It seems to be the way of the future."

"We think so. Financial experts believe that we'll be a completely cashless society in less than ten years."

"I can't imagine there not being money. It will change the world as we know it."

"Won't be the first time. People used to pay for stuff with salt." Reign reached up and placed her hands on Abe's. "Thanks, babe. That felt great, but I need to get back to work and figure this out. I'm trying to send over a new mockup by noon."

Abe leaned in to look at her computer. "What's wrong with that one?"

"Too crowded. Too busy." She leaned toward the screen. "And I'm not sure I like this font."

"It definitely should be bigger."

Said with so much authority, it caused Reign to look back at him. "Oh, really?"

He shrugged, giving her one of those crooked smiles that she decided wouldn't hurt to soak up every day.

"I think so. Like you said, it looks a little crowded. Why not make it bigger?"

"We're hoping to fit all the information in one tri-fold, two-sided design."

"Let me see the second page."

Reign laughed. "Why? Are you thinking about putting down the broom and picking up graphic design?"

"Maybe. My old boss once told me I had a good eye."

Reign figured she had nothing to lose. She'd rearranged the material a dozen times and still wasn't satisfied. She scrolled down to the second page then sat back with her arms crossed while Abe, head cocked to the side, perused the document.

Reign reached for her phone, deciding to spend a couple minutes checking her email. When several had gone by and he was still studying the document, she said, "What you're reading is confidential information. Do I need to have you sign an NDA?"

He glanced at her a bit strangely before asking, "What's that?"

"A nondisclosure agreement."

"You don't have to worry about me. I'm looking less at the actual wording and more at the copy and image juxtaposition."

The professional-sounding statement could have been made by someone on her team. Her head snapped around. "What do you know about copy and image? Who are you?"

He laughed and mussed her hair, hugging her from behind. "Have you thought about taking the fold horizontal?"

"Huh?"

"You know, having the folds go this way—" he used his hands to indicate a downward motion "—instead of this way." He moved his hands to the right.

Reign's eyes narrowed as she studied him. She turned to her computer and looked at the mockup with fresh eyes.

"No, I hadn't," she murmured.

"Might want to try that." He kissed her temple and let her go. She immediately missed his arms around her. "Wouldn't hurt."

She admired his tight ass as he strolled into the bedroom. Then turning her attention back to the screen, she clicked a few buttons, changed the dimensions and began playing around with how the images were positioned. An hour later, she emailed the new layout to the team and received feedback almost immediately.

Wow! This looks good, Reign. That note was from Cayden, Jake's best friend and company executive who'd designed the app.

I like how you flipped the idea on its head. Different, but nice. So said the director, her boss.

She'd replied with the appropriate thank-you while feeling a bit like a fraud. She'd jokingly asked Abe who he was, but the more she thought about it, the more she seriously wanted the question answered. He seemed to possess so many talents, ones she admired, almost too good to be true. He'd showed no fear when confronting Trenton, though her ex'd had him by at least five inches. Ivy was clearly impressed with Abe's cleaning skills, and he was obviously good enough at soccer that she wanted him on staff. His fingers had proved magical both last night and this morning. His tongue... Reign squirmed. He possessed enough skill with his tongue for it to be protected under some kind of law. Just thinking about how it would be to feel him inside her was almost enough to make her orgasm. Was there anything her knight couldn't do?

By the time Reign had swung by the office to reclaim her Bentley and pulled up to the Eddington Estate's elaborate security-system gates, the camera of which recognized said sports car, her original plans regarding Abe had changed.

When she'd promised Maeve they'd talk later, she'd had no plans to reveal who she'd spent the night with, or to tell anybody about their...what was it, exactly? Having had her kitty cat deliciously eaten took his title beyond mere friendship. Yet they weren't exactly lovers, or even friends with benefits, though his skillful tongue and magical fingers had benefitted her very well.

They were acquaintances, she decided, getting to know each other better. When speaking with her sister that's how she'd describe it. She definitely wanted to talk to Maeve, get some big-sister advice. There was something about Abe that had her curious, parts of the whole of him that didn't add up. Maeve had an analytical mind, perfect for being an attorney. She paid attention to detail, thought outside the box. For all Reign knew, Abe could be a serial killer running from the law. If there was anything bad or sinister about him, Maeve Eddington-Cortez could find out.

Reign reached a fork in the road and instead of veering right and climbing the winding road that led to the main house, she veered left to where Maeve and Victor had built their grand spread. Anyone seeing it would find it hard to believe that a little more than a year ago the half acre their spread occupied was completely empty and covered with trees. Together, her sis and bro-in-love had built an architecturally stunning abode, with the best materials, workers and designers that money could buy. She pulled into the part of the driveway closest to the front entrance and pulled out her phone.

"Did you make it back okay?" was Maeve's greeting.

"Yes, in fact I'm in front of your home. Are you guys busy?"

"Not at all. You're just in time to join us for a cocktail. Come on in."

Reign texted Abe that she'd made it home safely then hurried out of the frigid temperatures into the warmth of Victor and Maeve's living room. She would have rather gotten down to investigative business directly but having been raised with impeccable manners, she dutifully accepted a glass of bordeaux and engaged in small talk with them, mostly about the unusual ice storm, one they'd mistaken as rain turning to snow when returning home from their date.

She managed to get through half of her drink before she could wait no longer. "Mind if I borrow your wife for a minute, for a little sister-sister chat?"

"Not at all," Victor said, rising from the leather wingback chair he'd occupied. "You just saved me from having to invent a reason to leave and go see my other girl."

"Hey, don't bring out my jealous side." Said in mock harshness, Reign could feel the love flow from Maeve's eyes to her husband. He kissed both ladies on the cheek. "Give Cutie a hug for me!"

Reign took another sip of wine and reached for the bottle. "Why did y'all name that ugly dog Cutie?"

Maeve shot her a look of warning. "Do you want to get thrown out my house?"

"I love your four-legged babies, but I'm sorry. That pug is ugh."

"Moving from four-legged dogs to two-legged ones, who were you with last night?"

"Ooh, girl. You are wrong for that!"

"You know I'm teasing. That would have only been true had you been with Trenton."

Reign took another, bigger, fortifying sip.

"Well...who was it?"

"Abe."

Maeve frowned. "Abe who?"

"Abe Wetherbee. He works at Ivy's school"

"A teacher?"

"Not exactly. He's a...custodial technician."

"A janitor?"

Reign nodded.

Maeve's face could have won her a poker game. "I'm not judging, but a janitor doesn't seem like your type."

"He's not your average janitor."

"Tell me more."

Reign gave the *Reader's Digest* version of her time with Abe from their introduction on the sidewalk outside Verve to their interaction at the office and her spending Valentine's night at his place.

"He sounds pretty amazing," Maeve said when she'd finished. "Where's the 'but'?" She used air quotes for emphasis.

"I'm not sure." Reign pulled her knees to her chest, reached for a silk-covered throw pillow and crushed it to her chest. "It's like the inside doesn't match the outside. The intelligence that it almost feels he tries not to show. He seems to know a little about a lot. He speaks several languages, but came here to help his cousin clean floors? It just sounds...weird."

Maeve thought for a bit. "Is it possible that you're

simply overthinking? And looking at life from an American point of view?"

"What do you mean?"

"We're a capitalistic society. Part of what makes this country great is anyone with a lot of drive and a little luck can succeed. Having money and material pleasures is often touted as the American dream. And there's nothing wrong with that," she quickly added.

"Look at our family," Reign said.

"We're the poster kids!"

"All countries or cultures aren't like that. When we visit Victor's extended family in Puerto Limon, it's a much different experience than what I grew up in. The houses are plain, the food is simple but delicious. Some of the women couldn't care less about their clothing or hair. With them, it's characteristics that money can't buy. Love. Laughter. Loyalty. Life. They live for the moment and in the moment. If Abe comes from a similar culture, if asked, I could totally see him dropping everything to help his cousin mop floors.

"That being said," Maeve continued with an impish look in her eyes. "We need to find out all we can about him."

She set down the tablet and reached for her phone.

"Who are you calling?"

"Ivy," Maeve said as Ivy answered, giving Reign a wink. "Reign and I are here talking and need a favor. We'll explain more later—"

"Or not!" Reign loudly interjected.

"It's regarding Abe Wetherbee, one of the guys who cleans at your school."

"And the Enterprise offices," Ivy replied. "Don't know what information I'd have that you don't, but I'll help if I can."

"We probably have the same files but asking you instead of HR is more discreet."

"What type of info are you looking for exactly?"

"The personal kind," Maeve said.

"As you know, those files are confidential—"

"Reign slept with him."

Ivy squealed. "I knew I felt something between them!"

Reign gave Maeve a playful shove. "Thanks for sharing my business, *sister*." Then she leaned closer to the speaker on Maeve's iPhone and loudly whispered, "Sometimes sisters can be such a pain."

"That's why you love us, darling," Ivy said, laughing. "Besides, I can understand why you were with him. He definitely blesses that company jumpsuit.

"Regarding personal info, I can say this. Background checks are performed on everyone who works here. We wouldn't hire anyone with a negative history or criminal record."

"Thanks, Ivy. We'll talk later."

Bolstered by news that he wasn't a known criminal, Maeve picked up her tablet and sat next to Reign. She entered "Abe Wetherbee" into a search engine. His internet footprint was meager at best. A Facebook page with a beach scene as the profile picture, was set to only be viewed by friends. Nothing on IG, Twitter, TicTok or other similar apps she enjoyed. That in itself wasn't enough to condemn him.

Though billions of people logged on to them daily, Reign had to look no further than her own family to find people who guarded their privacy and didn't find joy in posting every moment of their lives online. Desmond had a presence on social media, but they were sites one of his assistants created and maintained. Ivy mainly posted news about her school and students. There were others she knew who only used the sites to network and promote. The mystery deepened, just like her feelings. Against all odds, and with Trenton still lurking, Reign felt herself beginning to fall for Abe. But who in the heck was he?

Ten

Being with Reign had been all that he'd imagined it would be and more, but Abe had mixed feelings about it. His plan sounded good in theory but playing it out had a huge downside. He was being less than honest with a woman he really, really, liked. Someone he could see settling down with. As crucial a fact as that was, revealing himself totally to Reign was far from the only factor. There was the grandfather whose wealth had helped found Kutoka Global and whose ultimatum with a ticking time clock had landed him in Chicago, and whose declining health had his mother thinking of arranged marriages, a waning practice Abe knew about but never thought he'd have to do. There was his position as heir apparent to a billion-dollar company, one of the reasons his father, the current president, had agreed to his request. There was the reason he couldn't allow Reign to give herself to him fully, the ghost of a past love and present pain, someone who, in Abe's opinion, was a midget of a man, but who'd somehow captured a heart of gold with no idea how to handle it. There was the not-so-subtle pressure from his mother that he marry one of the women she approved of, one from a familiar family, someone from the Kingdom of Kutoka. He wanted to honor his family, but when it came to whomever he spent his life with, he'd do the choosing, thank you very much.

For now, he was going to focus on duties that, due to his cousin's dare and the Reign distraction, he'd neglected. He'd make travel plans to visit the company's affiliates and write the update his father had demanded, something he'd planned to do all along.

That evening the ice had melted enough for the citywide travel ban to be lifted, but businesses were strongly encouraged to remain closed and residents to stay home if possible. It had taken Reign over an hour for a trip that would normally take twenty minutes.

Around ten o'clock, Abe had received a company memo from Nolan cutting back hours and utilizing only a skeleton crew. Abe had unexpectedly received two days off. With the call from Jeffrey yesterday, the timing couldn't have been better.

Today, he'd gotten up at just past six and by noon had studied the information Jeffrey had sent along with every bit of information on the website of the New York company Kutoka Global might acquire. In addition to detailed research and studying intellectual property, Abe had made successful decisions based on his gut.

Something about the ingenuity of their invention felt exciting and progressive. Harnessing the sun's energy and leaving a lighter footprint on the planet aligned perfectly with the mission and direction of their business. Plus, he liked that it was a small company founded by twins not yet twenty-five.

After an hour-long video chat with Jeffrey and the team back home, followed by an introductory one with the brothers Edward and Elliott, Abe booked a flight to New York for the following morning, returning that same day.

He spent the rest of the day reading reports and handling overseas phone calls. Being back in his comfort zone had been exhilarating. Working with Reign on her pamphlet had been tricky, and perhaps a bit reckless, but getting those creative juices flowing felt good. Until then he hadn't realized just how much he'd missed his old life, how much his work wasn't just what he did but part of who he was. When he finished the last call and checked his watch, he was shocked twelve hours had passed. Knowing there was nothing in the fridge and starting to get cabin fever, he decided to face his fears of driving on ice and head to the mall down the street. On the way, he called Reign.

"Hello, lovely."

"Hey, handsome. How was your day?"

"Surprisingly relaxing, but I got some work done. How was yours?"

"Work? I thought most businesses were closed."

Abe heard the surprise in her voice. Once again, when it came to living between two worlds, he was skating on thin ice. Pun intended.

He swallowed a mouthful of conscience and asked for forgiveness for lies by omission. "Work around the apartment," he explained. "And calls to the folk back home. Since coming here, I've been remiss with my friendships and spent the day catching up with friends."

"What are you doing now?"

"On my way to the mall to grab a bite."

"You're driving?"

"Ha! I know, right? I am, and very slowly. If you'll remember, my cupboards were nearly bare. Thankfully, the mall is only one street over and three or four blocks away. It's a pity that the weather is still misbehaving. I'd love to see you tonight."

"Hmm," was all Reign said, but Abe imagined her smiling. "Tell me about your friends."

Abe stifled a groan, feeling the ditch of half-truths that he'd dug getting deeper. Words of wisdom from his grandmother rang in his ear.

Best to be honest in all you do. If you tell one lie, you'll have to tell two.

"They're guys I've worked with and known a long time, filling me in on all the goings on in Kutoka and around the continent. One of my buddies just got engaged."

That was true, though Abe hadn't spoken with this friend directly. Jeffrey had passed on the news.

"One of your buddies, huh?" Reign asked, intrigue in her voice. "What about the girlfriends you left back home?"

"I dated back home, but I don't have a girlfriend."

"Then tell me something else about you."

"Like what?"

"Abe, you're a great listener, and as a result know a lot about me, but I can't say the same. What's your story?"

"Story?" he croaked.

"Yes, Abe, your story." The words were said as though speaking with a two-year old, enunciating each syllable in a slightly raised voice. "I want to know more about you."

A learned man who spoke five languages seemed to suddenly lose all notions of English. Hearing Reign clear her throat suggested he needed to regain it, and quickly.

"Honestly—" Had he dared to actually use that word? "—Reign, there isn't much to tell."

"Really?"

Abe pulled into a space in front of the near-empty mall, and kept the engine idling. "I'm just an ordinary guy—" *not!* "—working a simple job." *More accurately, one I could play on TV.*

"A job you crossed continents to take."

"My cousin wanted someone working for him that he could trust."

"Is your cousin from Africa, too?"

"No, he grew up here."

"What's his name?"

Abe sighed. Reign was determined to conduct this interrogation. Given how much he knew about her, he couldn't say he blamed her.

"Nolan."

"Does he have siblings?"

"Four half siblings from his father's second marriage. He grew up in a single household, just him and his mom."

"What about you?"

"I have an older brother and a younger sister."

"Have they moved abroad or are they still in Ghana?"

"They are back home."

Abe's heart sank a little with each white lie. What he said was like Reign saying she lived in Chicago, when actually hers was a much different life in Point du Sable.

Though just outside Ghana, the Kingdom of Kutoka was its own small nation, one Abe loved. He wanted to tell her about its progressive politics, smart infrastructure, free education and medical services, and how there was virtually no poverty or crime. More than tell her, he wanted to show her. Introduce her to his parents and siblings, his coworkers and friends. He wanted Reign to get to know Aldric as she was getting to know Abe.

Then why don't you tell her?

Abe promised himself he would. As soon as the ground beneath them shifted from friendship to something deeper, he'd tell her everything.

"You remind me of my brother," Reign was saying. "Even though the internet has made it impossible, Desmond zealously guards what privacy he's able to maintain."

"I am a private person, yes."

"Who probably feels like he's being cross-examined. I'm sorry. Clearly, you're an asset to your cousin."

In the moment, Abe felt less like an asset and more like an ass. His tongue almost tripped over the carefully crafted words. He realized the danger in asking too many questions. The tables could get turned. He realized something else. He hated lying. Wasn't very good at it. Hadn't had to do it often. It felt wrong, and unfair, given the truth he knew about Reign and at least one of her relationships.

"It was very noble of you to leave your life in Africa to help him."

The real reasons Abe was in America pressed against his lips, circled around his tongue and begged to come out. He figured Reign would be able to relate to a demanding father and, at the very least, empathize with being viewed as a prize. She might provide valuable insight on how to handle his mother, given she had two brothers who appeared to have successful marriages. He wondered about those siblings, and Ivy, married to Reign's oldest brother, Desmond. Suddenly, he wanted to spill his heart to her, to tell her everything. But that would defeat the whole reason he'd lied in the first place—to see if someone like Reign could love someone she thought an ordinary guy.

"Reign, I made it. I'm at the mall. Can I call you later?"

"Sure. Thanks to Mother Nature, I won't be far from my phone."

Abe returned to his apartment without incident, but a call from his father that lasted more than two hours had kept him from calling Reign back that night. The next morning at just after 6:00 a.m., he boarded a private jet bound for New York. He considered sending Reign a text then decided against it. The forecast had called for warmer temperatures all weekend. What if Reign wanted to come over or to meet him somewhere?

Abe couldn't chance it. He couldn't keep lying to her either. When he returned from New York, he'd tell her everything and let the chips fall where they may.

Once that decision had been made, it felt like a weight lifted. The customized Gulfstream jet Kutoka Global had rented reached cruising altitude and raced across the sky. Abe reclined the soft leather seat, stretched long legs rippling with muscles before him and gratefully accepted a double espresso latte from the flight attendant whose flirtations he ignored.

What just a few months ago would have been a routine business trip, today had him excited. He loved playing in the high-stakes world of buying and selling, corporate takeovers, strategy and competition that had turned his grandfather's initial investment into a billion-dollar, international powerhouse, one that dabbled in everything from technology to diamonds and gold. Since arriving in America, he'd let his team do the heavy lifting. He was ready to get back in the game.

He adjusted an Ace Montgomery limited edition silk tie, flicked imaginary lint from exquisitely tailored wool slacks. Looking out the window, his fingers methodically rubbed the beard he'd trimmed and shaped that morning, hair that still felt like foreign matter on his face. His thoughts went to where they often did… Reign. She was special. One of a kind. He could hardly believe he'd come to Chicago and found exactly what he hadn't known he was looking for. As crazy as that sounded, it's how he felt right now. Reign was attracted to a man, not the rich, well-known soccer star turned businessman mogul known back home. He had no idea how Reign would react later this weekend when he told her the truth. Hopefully, nothing about their budding romance would change. But everything might.

As the plane neared New York's familiar skyline, his satellite phone rang.

"Good morning, Jeffrey. Or rather, good evening there."

"Are you in New York yet?"

"Just beginning our descent."

"Sounds good. I just heard from the twins. Instead of a service, they're picking you up."

"Why?"

"Excited about your visit, I'm guessing. Even though you'll be there less than forty-eight hours, they've got a full itinerary planned."

"I'm looking forward to it."

"You know, Aldric, once this deal goes through, you'll have to come out of hiding."

"Who says I'm hiding?"

"What would you call it, laying low? Just when you start to play a role in the company, you run off to America. And not just for an extended business trip, but for months! I don't get it."

"You're not supposed to. It's personal, brother, but I can understand your frustration."

Jeffrey sighed. "I sure hope she's worth it."

"Now you're fishing without a pole," Abe said with a smile. "I'll call you later with the details on how the meeting went."

"Ha! The way you dodged that question confirms my suspicion. There's definitely a woman involved."

The New York trip went great, much better than Abe

expected. The twins had indeed lined up a complete itinerary that included all of the usual sites and others known
only to natives. Considering the important decision he'd
recently made, he only wanted to return to Chicago.

After spending the day at the twin's small facility in
Brooklyn, he was wined and dined with five-star this
and Michelin-star-cooked that before enjoying a popular
Broadway show. More adventurous plans awaited him
the following day, but he politely declined them and,
after a private visit with and purchase from a world-re-
nowned jeweler, left the city midmorning. On the way
to the airport, he retrieved his stateside phone from the
briefcase resting on the seat beside him and called Reign.

He got voice mail and left a message. "Reign, it's Abe.
I know the weather is still a bit messy but I'm calling to
see if you'd like to get together tonight, go out for a casual dinner somewhere near my place. Sorry, but I'm not
confident enough with winter driving skills to risk a trip
to your side of town. Okay, let me know. See you later."

He sat back and looked at the sun shining into the
cabin and the clouds hiding it from the world below him.
Somehow the scene reminded him of the direction his
friendship with Reign might take once she knew the
truth about the janitor Abe Wetherbee being the soccer star/mogul Aldric Baiden. The sun of a love affair
could begin shining between them, or a storm could
quench its smoldering fire.

Eleven

Reign stepped out of a leisurely shower where she'd spent a considerable time scrubbing every inch of skin with a new vegan, organic and silicone-free concoction she was in love with. According to the jar, the coffee it contained helped increase blood flow while the shea butter and essential oils improved her skin's overall health. She'd been using it less than a month and had gone online to add hers to a long list of rave reviews. After showering, she'd shampooed and conditioned her hair, and since her favorite spa wouldn't reopen until Monday, she gave herself a bikini wax. The end result wasn't bad, but on her next appointment with Helga, her esthetician, she'd definitely double the tip.

After forty-five minutes, head and body wrapped in towels, Reign exited the en suite bath and walked into her massive closet where she donned a comfy pair of wide-legged yoga pants, a fluffy wool sweater and a pair of kid-leather boots. She returned to the bathroom, did a quick semidry on her long, curly locks and, after adding simple gold jewelry to her funky ensemble, decided to head into the main house in search of a satisfying meal.

On the way, she picked up her phone from the coffee table and saw a missed call. Abe. She smiled. While listening to the voice mail, that smile widened. Funny enough, she'd been thinking of him while pampering her body, had thought a lot about their easy interaction while locked down at his place. Somewhere between then and now, she'd come to terms with a lot of things, starting with her ex. She didn't lie to herself. Feelings remained there. It had been a two-year wild but rocky ride. The highs had been amazing. The lows, though, devastating. And while admitting that she still loved him, she knew there was no going back to that relationship. She was no longer in love. Big difference.

Without knowing it, Abe had given her a different perspective on the type of man she liked. All of her boyfriends had been wealthy, connected, a couple famous like Trenton. They'd all showered her with amazing gifts, taken her to the finest restaurants and hotels, given her expensive everything. It's what she was used to; their acts appreciated.

But with Abe, she'd discovered that more than anything they could buy, it was the simple actions that touched her heart in ways unexpected. His courteous and chivalrous manners. How he insisted on walking her to the car and opening her door. The way he'd gotten up and prepared their pizza breakfast. His interest and assistance with her project, a man with a great eye and attention to detail that would most likely carry over into other areas of life.

If she were honest, she'd probably add that all of those attributes together didn't equal the skill of the man's appendages and tongue! Maybe it was the unplanned drought of the past two months following a very active sex life, but the way her body responded to Abe's attention had been unlike anything she'd felt before. It wasn't just the above-average sexual skill set. It was that she could actually feel his attention and care. Abe didn't have sex with her. He made love. Her needs came first and he took his time making sure to address each and every one.

Those thoughts undoubtedly impacted the thoughts that continued as she walked from her wing to the mansion's main house. She wasn't going to fret over what she did or didn't know about Abe. It wasn't like she was planning to marry him or to include him in a confidential enterprise. It was enough to know that he wasn't a criminal, as the background check would have uncovered, didn't have a girlfriend, at least not in the States, and wasn't an athlete.

Jake had tried to warn her about Trenton, but she hadn't listened. Experience was indeed the best teacher. Other ladies could have the ballers. She'd been there, done that, and had the T-shirt as proof. That lesson learned, it was time to move on from her heartbreak. Ivy was right. The best way to get over one man was to get under another one. Reign was glad she'd taken her sister's advice.

The main dining room and casual breakfast nook were empty. There was no hint of her mom and dad. She continued to the solarium and finally saw signs of family life. Sneaking up behind Jake, she whispered, "Boo." He jumped. She laughed and took a seat at the table across from him.

"Good afternoon, brother!" she sang, reaching over and plucking a cherry tomato from his salad. "What's for lunch?"

After giving her a stern look, he answered, "Whatever your options, they're not on my plate."

"Is Sasha on her way down?"

Jake finished a mouthful of food. "She's over at Val's."

"That girl sure loves her godmother."

"I do too. She's the reason Sasha moved here."

"Now it's time for y'all to start a family."

"Don't get carried away."

"Where's John?" Reign asked, amused by Jake's comment. She looked around for the family's chef. "I'm starved. She reached for a pitcher of fresh-squeezed juice and poured herself a glass. "Yum! Were these pineapples picked fresh just this morning? This juice is delicious."

Jake raised a brow. "Somebody is certainly in a chipper mood."

"Thought I'd bring some sunshine to the dismal day outside."

They both looked out the window. "The temperatures have warmed up, which is a good thing. I hope it doesn't snow."

"They've cleared the roads, right?" Reign asked after greeting John and taking the menu he offered.

"Why, are you thinking of going someplace?"

"Maybe later."

"I hope it isn't to see…you know who."

"Trenton? No, brother, I'm done with him."

"Good."

"You told me so."

"I wasn't going to say that."

"I did so you wouldn't have to."

"I wasn't trying to block your love game, sis, I was just trying to protect you based on my experience of working with athletes. There are one or two of them out there who are faithful but, for the most part, the temptation of beautiful, willing, aggressive women is too much to fight."

"I agree."

"Speaking of willing women, did you see the latest?" he asked, his brow creased.

Reign shook her head.

"It's probably best."

"Why, what happened?"

"According to the latest rumors, your man and the fan have started dating."

John returned with Jake's medium-rare steak and eggs. Reign decided on a veggie frittata with hash brown waffles and accepted the small salad he'd prepared for her.

"How do you feel about that?" Jake prodded.

"About what?"

"That girl after your leftovers."

"The one Trenton swore didn't mean anything?" Reign shrugged. "As long as she doesn't mind publicly shared peen, she'll be fine."

"You know that'll bring back the paparazzi."

"They never left."

That was true. Even though the announcement of a pregnancy between two famous rappers had shifted the spotlight, speculation about Reign's breakup was still selling tabloids.

"I'm proud of how you're handling all this, sis. You're stronger than I thought."

After enjoying a leisurely lunch and spending time with her brother, Reign stopped in to see her parents, Derrick and Mona, before leaving the main house and driving the short distance to Desmond's and Ivy's to spoil her niece and nephew. She told Ivy about taking her advice to move on from Trenton. Ivy probed whether or not that man would continue to be Abe, but Reign decided to keep that most likely reality confidential.

It was just before five that she returned to her place and realized she'd not heard back from Abe. Grabbing an overnight bag from her closet, she stopped and gave him a call.

"I was just about to call you," is how he answered.

"Sure you were."

"No, seriously, I just now returned to the apartment."

"Out shopping again?"

"No, I was at Nolan's, helping with a cleanup project.

Portions of a wooden canopy over his patio fell after being weighed down by a slab of ice."

"Sorry to hear that his place sustained damage. Most of us here in the Point were fortunate. Except for a few downed trees and intermittent power outages, we came through the storm unscathed."

"I'm glad to hear that. Are you calling to accept my dinner invitation?"

"Yes, and just so you know, this wouldn't be considered a date."

"Not at all. Everyone's got to eat. We'll just be two people…assuaging our appetites."

Was it her imagination or did Abe purposely say that as a double entendre? Was he thinking as she was about a hunger that had nothing to do with food?

"I'd love to join you for dinner."

"Great. I was hoping you would. Any particular place you'd like to go?"

Reign thought about the conversation with Jake and the news of Trenton's now-public new romance. Jake was right. She'd likely be hunted for comments or pics. Not the type of evening she wanted, and she definitely didn't want to drag Abe into her mess.

"Yes," Reign said, a plan continuing to come together in real time. "I've got the perfect place in mind. Don't worry about driving, I'll pick you up."

Though she would never admit to consciously planning a seduction, Reign threw toiletries, sexy lingerie and a change of casual clothes into an oversized tote. In case of another once-in-several-decades ice storm, is what she told herself.

She bypassed rows of five-inch stilettos and settled on a pair of designer high-top sneakers with two-inch heels. She loved not being overly concerned with what she wore while spending time with Abe. Reign loved fashion and dressed to impress herself most of all. But dating a high-profile guy in demand with the ladies, one who, with the likelihood of being photographed each time they went out, always wanted her runway-model ready, brought its own type of pressure. There were a lot of things about dating Trenton she didn't miss, the man himself topping that list.

After placing a to-go order at an upscale Chicago restaurant and grabbing two bottles of stellar wine from the home's well-stocked cellar, she headed into the city. Thankfully, the street crew had done its job. The weather was cold, but the highways were clear. Twenty minutes later, she pulled up in front of Abe's apartment in her gleaming white Bentley. It was time to give her ordinary man a ride on the luxurious side.

He must have been looking out the window. Before she could finish texting that she was in front, he was walking toward the car, bundled up as though they were walking to their destination.

"Hi," he said a bit uncomfortably as he got in.

"Are you warm enough," she asked, laughing.

"It's freezing out here."

"It warmed up twenty degrees today."

Abe briskly rubbed his hands together. "I can't tell."

"Ha!" She eased away from the curb and headed toward a discreet condo in a much wealthier part of town.

Abe ran his hand along the car's modernistic dash. "This is very nice."

"Thanks. Ever been in one before?"

"A Bentley? Yes."

Reign was curious as to the circumstances, but when he didn't offer further explanation, she decided not to pry. Chicago's weekend traffic was lighter than usual. Before long, she pulled up to a towering condo building just off Chicago's famous Lakeshore Drive and parked directly in front of the awning.

Abe leaned forward to gaze at the building. "The restaurant is in here?"

"I've brought the restaurant to us. Come on, let's get inside. Our food should be here shortly."

A doorman opened the door and greeted them warmly. She gave him her car keys and received a retrieval ticket, then walked to the trunk and pulled out her tote.

Abe looked and shook his head. "I'll never understand why women carry such large purses."

"We're like the Girl Scouts, always prepared."

"Girl Scouts?"

"Never mind. Come on, let's go."

They rushed inside, crossed the elegant lobby and went directly into an open elevator car. She pulled a card from her purse and tapped a small screen. The doors closed and the elevator began a fast ascent to one of the building's high floors.

Abe remained silent as they entered a hallway with thick carpeting and textured walls. She stopped in front of a unit and used the same card she'd used on the elevator to open the condo's front door. With a wink at Abe, she opened the door and continued down the hallway into an elegant living room with sweeping views of Lake Michigan and the city's downtown.

Reign dropped her tote on one of two sofas and watched as Abe took in the room. He walked to the window. Once there, he placed a hand on the glass and peered out at the view. The gray, overcast sky didn't dim its magnificence as lights twinkled from myriad buildings that surrounded them and the lake, dark and foreboding, snaked along the city's edge.

She joined him at the window, noticed his troubled expression and placed a hand on his shoulder. "Abe, is everything okay?"

"I thought you lived in Point du Sable," he said without looking her way.

"I do."

"This your place too?"

"My brother-in-law Victor lived here before he and Maeve got married and built their house. It's a great piece of real estate, so he kept it as an investment. It's convenient when the family needs to stay overnight in the city. He also sometimes rents it out, mostly to foreign businessmen."

Abe's serious expression continued. She loosened his arms and wrapped them around her, forcing an embrace. "Relax," she whispered, kissing the lips that had been on her mind for two days. "No one is going to kick us out."

The doorbell rang.

"That's dinner. I hope you're hungry." She kissed

him again then placed both hands on his butt. "As for me, I'm starving, and you feel delicious."

The doorbell rang a second time. She left Abe by the window to accept the delivery. He seemed unnerved by the surroundings, but Reign wasn't bothered. If she had her way they'd soon both be naked, engaging in a myriad of acts and positions that would leave then both feeling totally satiated and completely satisfied.

Twelve

Abe let out a long, troubled breath, glad for the brief reprieve from Reign that the delivery had afforded. His thoughts were all over the place, one battling against the next. This isn't the setting he'd imagined telling Reign his secret. He'd imagined a quiet but public place where she'd be forced to take the news calmly and not cause a scene. Not a place like this; elegant, private, a virtual lover's den. There was no doubt that sex was on her mind. It was definitely on his. But before that could happen, there was a much more important matter to discuss. The truth.

"Abe! Come help set the table."

He turned to see Reign carrying two large bags into the dining room. About the same time, a wonderful smell wafted over to greet him as he met her and took one of the bags.

"It feels like you have enough food to feed the building."

"It's said to never order when you're hungry. I might have gone overboard. Plates are in the cabinet," she continued, motioning with her head toward the kitchen. "You'll have to look to see which one. Same with the silverware. Make yourself at home!"

As he helped prepare for dinner, he tried to relax. Imagining a worse-case scenario wasn't productive. Reign could turn out to be completely understanding, especially when he revealed that his plan had paid off and that she was the prize. He had all night to come clean and be one-hundred-percent transparent, but dinner was waiting and the night was young. Being in such a beautiful atmosphere might work to his advantage. Plus, for all of his talk about being "regular," it felt good to continue another night living in the style of which he was accustomed, the way he'd felt in midtown New York at the Baccarat Hotel. With those thoughts in mind, he reentered the dining room ready to go with the flow and enjoy this beautiful evening Reign had so thoughtfully prepared.

Reaching the table, he hugged Reign from behind. "This is very nice, babe. Sorry if earlier I acted a bit weird."

"Good, because I was wondering…" She turned in his arms and placed hers around his neck.

This time, he was the aggressor. After soaking up the scent of her in his arms, he planted kisses on her temple, cheek and neck before moving his lips across soft, silky skin and claiming her delectable mouth. Her bulky sweater wasn't thick enough to hide nipples that quickly protruded. If the kiss continued, the same would soon be true for his hardening sword. Not wanting the fireworks to come prematurely, he placed one final peck on the tip of her nose and broke away.

"Everything smells delicious."

"It's from a pretty cool restaurant I discovered through attending a business luncheon. They combine Italian and Creole cooking. The results is mouth-watering, at least for the dish I tasted."

She opened one of several containers. "I think it's this one. Yes, this is it, Shrimp Hennessy Scampi. I also got their seafood trio of lobster, shrimp and crab. There's wine in my tote on the sofa. Can you grab it and pour us both a glass?"

"Sure." Abe retrieved a bottle of wine from a vineyard he'd not heard of—Drake Wines Resort & Spa in Temecula, CA. He walked to the built-in bar, removed a wine opener and aerator, and prepared their drinks. Once done, he rejoined her at a table now covered with a smorgasbord of choices that included grilled Caesar salad, salmon egg rolls and warm slices of thick-cut bread.

After filling their plates, they decided to forgo the dining room's formality and eat in front of a fireplace that now roared with the flip of a switch. Before sitting down, Reign walked over to a console deftly hidden behind a panel placed seamlessly into the wall. Soon, the light sounds of neo-soul warmed the atmosphere. Within minutes, so did the wine.

For a while, conversation was replaced by forks meeting mouths, save for words like "Um" and "Wow" and "This is delicious." Once he'd enjoyed healthy samples of all of the offerings, he put down his plate, picked up his wineglass and watched Reign assuage the hunger she'd mentioned before.

"What?" she asked once she caught him staring.

"I think your name is very fitting."

"Thank you."

"I'd imagine there's a story behind it."

"You imagine correctly." Reign reached for glass and took a sip. "It was my grandmother's idea. Her name is Myrna. My mom's name is Mona. My sister's name is Maeve. I was supposed to be Monica, after a singer my mom loved at the time."

"What happened?"

"The night following that conversation, my grandmother had a dream. The next day she told my mother about seeing me all grown up and wearing a tiara. She thought it a sign that Mom should break with tradition and go with something different. She wanted to name me Princess. Mom told Dad, who nixed the idea and came up with Reign."

"Creativity obviously runs in the family."

They went back for seconds and, afterward, for the moment, were too full for dessert. They refilled their glasses and settled on the sofa, Abe's legs stretched out on a black quartz table, Reign's in his lap.

"Did I thank you for inviting me over and setting up all this?"

"I think so, but it doesn't hurt to thank me again."

He removed a plush, fluffy sock from her foot and

began to massage it. "Thank you, Reign. You're an amazing woman. I enjoy your company very much."

"I like you too."

A companionable silence as they sipped wine and bobbed their heads to the music. Abe finished massaged one foot and attended the other. When almost done, Reign surprised him by sliding her foot from his hand and slowly rubbing it across his groin. He shifted to allow it and reached for his wine.

"Let's talk about your love life."

"Not much to talk about," he said with a shrug, even as the faces of half a dozen of his mother's bride choices danced in his head. "Nolan has kept me too busy working to think about that."

"What about back home?"

"I dated casually but am not committed to anyone."

"I bet there's a lady or two who wishes you were."

Or twenty, Abe thought.

"With those eyes and that smile, you probably left broken hearts all over Ghana."

In answer, he took another sip of the deep-bodied merlot. On top of feeling cornered and being aroused, he was getting tipsy. Not good, considering how "a drunk tongue" often spoke "a sober mind."

"It makes sense that you're not into a serious relationship. Not many of us would cosign our man leaving home for months on end, whatever the reason."

"You're probably right about that."

"How old are you?"

"Twenty-eight."

"Men have it so easy. You guys can stay single until you're fifty, sixty, and still have a family."

Some men but not him, Abe wanted to add but instead said, "I would hate to be that old still looking for a wife."

"Yeah, that could be a bleak scenario. Have you ever been in a serious relationship?"

"I dated the same girl through my undergrad years."

"What happened, and yes I'm being nosy."

"She was ready to settle down and have a family with someone who could fully support her. I wasn't sure about my career path. She didn't want to wait around while I figured life out."

"Is she married?"

Abe nodded. "To a guy she met a week after our breakup. They live in London and have three kids."

"Do you regret not marrying her?"

"I sometimes wonder about it," was Abe's honest answer. "But in my late teens and early twenties, I wasn't ready for marriage."

"And now?"

"For the right woman, I'd walk down the aisle."

The look that accompanied his answer sent a shiver of heat down Reign's spine. Something about the intensity, the sincerity in his eyes, made her imagine being that right woman that he met at the altar. Just as quickly, she dismissed the thought. She'd only recently gotten out of a bad relationship and while ready to jump into another man's bed, she wasn't looking to get serious. Not right now.

She turned so that her body was snuggled against him. He adjusted and placed his arms around her.

"What kind of woman attracts you?"

"Someone like you." The look of surprise was Reign's confirmation that he'd thought it but not meant to say it out loud.

"I didn't mean that to sound like an invitation but... I admire what I know of you so far."

"'So far' being the operative phrase. You know very little about me."

"I know that you're smart and beautiful."

"I like that you said smart first."

"You are passionate and outgoing. You care for others."

"How do you know that?"

"Because of your work with Lilah."

"Oh. Right." She sat back, reached for her drink. "You're very observant."

"I like studying people. What about you?" he asked after a pause. "What type of man attracts you?"

"I'm not looking for a relationship," Reign said before running a hand over Abe's hard chest. "But to answer your question, I like a guy who's fit, takes care of himself. Someone confident yet kind, understanding. Smart, focused, financially secure," she added a bit self-consciously. "Someone not looking to take advantage, but who loves me for who I am."

"Someone to love you for who you are and not what you have?" Abe asked.

Reign nodded.

"I feel that way exactly."

Again, the urge to blurt out the truth overwhelmed him. Fear kept him quiet. He believed the attraction he felt for Reign was mutual. Would that change if she knew the truth about him? Not because of something he did but due to another guy who had hurt her? He hated being less than truthful but assured himself that once Reign fell in love with him and he told her everything, she'd understand. She was smart and, like him, rich and successful. She'd be able to relate to why he'd behaved as he had.

"I'm sorry he hurt you so badly," Abe finally said. "Not all professional athletes treat women unkindly."

"I know a couple, but they are far and few between. But you don't have anything to worry about. My aversion to guys in sports doesn't extend to janitors, excuse me, custodial technicians, who teach soccer to little girls."

Abe tightened his embrace as he kissed the top of her head, hiding the dilemma that was etched on his face.

"That's good."

"Your beard tickles. I meant to tell you that the other night when you were…when we…you know."

His hand automatically went to the hair on his face. He'd been ready to shave it off since the week it had grown out.

"You know, you're not a bad-looking man."

"Gee, thanks."

"If you shaved off the beard, it would highlight your eyes and sexy lips. You'd be a true panty whisperer."

"If the other night was any indication, I'm not doing so bad now."

She delivered a playful swat. "No, and I'd love to help

you get better." She sat up and pulled off her sweater, revealing juicy orbs of creamy skin behind a white lacy bra.

"Reign…there's something you should know."

"What? That you're a serial killer?" she asked, undoing the clasp.

"No." Her breasts were perfect and, before he knew it, they were cupped in his hands.

"A bank robber?"

He shook his head.

"And you don't play sports."

"I don't now, but…"

"No buts." She stood, pulled off her pants then turned and shook a delicious-looking ass peeking out from a barely-there thong before sitting back down. "Grade school soccer doesn't count. I know you weren't sure the other night but… I want you."

"Reign."

She looked directly into his eyes, reached for his pant zipper, pulled it down and placed her hand on his crotch.

"Ah, baby, you're driving me crazy."

"I'm a grown woman who knows what she's doing. I know that you're only here temporarily, and that what we're doing can't go past being a casual affair. To be honest, it's liberating. I don't have to worry about expectations, or to keep running into you once this is over because we live in the same small town. I like you. The growing bulge beneath me suggests you like me too. You're off the hook for commitment, or a long-term relationship. Now let's use those lips for something besides talking."

Reign reached over to stroke Abe's hardening dick. He stilled her hand and took the lead. Easing off the couch, he took one of Reign's feet in his hand. He began to massage the left one, slowly, gently, before doing the same to the right foot.

Adjusting herself more comfortably, Reign purred, "Abe, that feels so good."

His ministrations continued—shins, thighs, stomach, breasts, neck—without a word. When he spoke, the command was simple.

"Turn over."

Something about the authoritative way he directed Reign turned her all the way on. She complied without argument, grabbed a throw pillow and placed it beneath her arms. For several seconds, nothing happened. Reign imagined Abe eyeing her booty. Goose bumps broke out at the thought of being ogled so brazenly. She heard movement, then felt him kiss her ass cheek. More kisses followed. Then long, slow licks down her backside's crease. Reign was sexually uninhibited and loved the naughty, nasty moves. She wriggled her booty. Two strong hands contained her movement, but not for long. He spread her cheeks and kissed her there. His tongue was like a runner's gun. She exploded.

While still shaking from the aftermath, Abe removed her thong, picked her up to face him, and slid himself inside her. He set the rhythm and the pace. Reign wrapped her arms around Abe's neck and reveled in his pounded thrusts, in the way he possessed her. She swirled her hips against his shaft while initiating a deep, sloppy kiss, the kind given when one's body neared lack of control.

They moved to the bedroom, experimented with positions. All the while, Abe's dick remained rock hard, his focus unwavering while moving deeper and deeper beside her. Finally, the thrusts shortened, the pace increased. A long moan preceded Abe's shuddering release. He fell against the soft sheets and pulled Reign alongside him.

"Did you enjoy that type of conversation?" he asked once their breathing returned to normal.

"What conversation?"

"You asked that I use my lips for something besides talking. How did I do?"

Reign's soft laugh was like music to his ears as she turned and offered a quick kiss on the lips.

"Let me think about it," she said, pulling his arm more firmly around her.

Abe lay flat on his back, stroking Reign's hair as he stared at the ceiling. He'd wanted to get to know this beautiful woman better, but how had she so quickly ended up in his arms? Why did she feel so right being there? What would happen when he told her the truth?

The one thing he knew for sure was that he had to tell her. He was the very type of man she'd sworn to never again date—a professional athlete. He was retired. Would that make a difference?

Abe was a strong man who didn't fear much. But he dreaded the truthful conversation Reign deserved. The result might be Reign deciding not to see him again. As crazy as it sounded given the short time he'd known her and their relationship's casual status, Abe didn't want to consider a world without her in it. His dream of a fling could quickly become a nightmare.

Sleep didn't come easy that night.

Thirteen

Abe was an amazing lover. Reign would never be accused of rating the few lovers she'd had, but if she did, he'd pretty much be at the top of the heap. There were a lot of rumors and stories out there about pro athletes and their prowess, fanned by the way they moved on the courts and their alpha swagger off it. Abe wasn't a pro baller, but he had the same type of unwavering confidence. He was considerate, a giver, paid attention to detail. She'd sworn off dating and vowed that if she did get involved, it would only be for casual romps. She hadn't planned on developing feelings, wasn't ready to admit that she had. Yet something told her that men like Abe didn't come along every day. Everything pointed to him wanting to take the relationship further. To not at least give the possibility consideration would be less than smart. That was why today, a week after their date at Victor's condo, she'd gathered the sisters for a chat.

"Guys, I really like him," Reign whispered somewhat incredulously, looking between Avery, Sasha and Maeve as they relaxed Friday night after work in a booth at the PDS Country Club.

"I know it's crazy. He's from another country. I don't really know him. He's nothing like anyone else I've dated. We're not dating," she corrected.

"You're not dating." Maeve didn't sound convinced.

"I don't want to call it dating, but if I were to be honest…"

"Please be honest," Avery encouraged.

"From the moment he appeared in my life, he's been nothing less than impressive. He's a blue-collar worker, a janitor, yet he carries himself with so much pride and class. Not saying that the men I dated before were bad guys. Well, for the most part. But meeting him at the same time as discovering Trenton is an asshole has brought inevitable comparisons. Abe has given me a completely new definition for how a real man behaves"

"Careful, girl…" Maeve began, choosing a crisp asparagus from their charcuterie tray and running it through a bleu cheese sauce before bringing it to her lips. "You're about to sound like someone flirting with the L-word and we all know it's way too soon to have feelings like that."

"Nobody wants a rebound romance," Sasha added.

"I'm not saying I'm in love with the guy, but honestly, feelings are involved. I'm attracted. I can't help it. I want to keep seeing him and see where it goes."

"At the end of the day," Maeve said, "it's your life. You're over twenty-one. We all have our opinion, but seriously, little sister, do what makes you feel good."

Over the next month, Reign did just that. She loosened up and decided to live in the moment. *Carpe diem!* More than once, Abe tried to take her into a serious conversation, wanted to open up, as she'd pushed him to do at the start. That need to know his entire life story was no longer there. What had happened before her didn't matter. She told him that unless he was running from the law or was somebody's husband, she simply wasn't interested in dissecting his personal life.

Some of the most fun she'd had was showing Abe around Chicago. She'd grown up in its shadow yet, like many who'd been raised there had taken for granted much of what was in her backyard.

She would have argued with anyone suggesting it, but Reign realized that her world was much more insular than she'd realized. She and those of her ilk lived in a society bubble inhabited by the very rich, the well connected, the highly educated and the stars. Her social calendar had always been full. Dating Abe magnified how life for them was lived on another level. Sure, she'd gone to professional football and basketball games but was always in floor seats or suites. Concerts were enjoyed from the front row with backstage passes. The same with theater, dance, fashion shows. Reign had been privy to the best and had taken that world for granted. Abe didn't want or need all that; in fact, whenever she tried to pull him into her world, he resisted.

"I like our simple life," he'd tell her. "You're all the glamour and excitement I need."

Reign had discovered a whole new Chicago, seen the city at ground level. Five-dollar matinees and Second City comedy for just ten bucks. Museum and art galleries. Auto shows and "restaurant week on the cheap," offering everything from the city's diverse ethnicities—African, American, Mexican, Greek, Indian, Italian, Polish. Reign swore that at the end of the week she'd gained ten pounds. Abe conquered a fear of extreme heights by stepping on to the glass platform at the Willis Tower, over one thousand feet in the air! Reign was blown away by the beauty and varied offerings at the Garfield Park Conservatory, an outing that was practically free! At night, they recounted their local adventures, ending the evening by making love.

Two months into their hanging out, the cloud of Trenton's betrayal lifted. Life felt good. Reign could smile and laugh again, and backed off her insane work hours. She didn't mind admitting that Abe was a large part of the reason. She told herself that anything more than what they had right now wasn't likely. That it was just an affair for the moment, in the moment. It couldn't be anything more. They were from different worlds. But her heart spoke differently. And so did his, it seemed. They enjoyed each other. Liked being together. For now, beyond that, Reign couldn't imagine. She tried not to think about it. She lived in the moment, loving the feel of the man's arm now around her. Even his beard had grown on her. At her suggestion, he'd trimmed it into a respectful goatee.

"Good morning, my queen," Abe whispered. Reign smiled with her eyes still closed and snuggled up against him.

"Good morning, my king." She giggled with joy, feeling like a teenager experiencing her first love. When young, even though no one really teased her, she used to dislike the name her grandmother had given her, wanted something simple and more common like Tiffany or Dee. Abe was the first person to make the name sound special, as if she could really be a member of royalty.

She puckered her lips. He kissed her temple.

"What are we going to do today?"

She felt Abe settle his body more comfortably against hers. It was a Saturday, the first one where they'd both been able to sleep late since he'd reluctantly started helping coach soccer part-time. The early morning hours had brought with it a round of heart-stopping lovemaking, followed by another forty-five minutes of sleep. Outside, a bright sun reflected off fresh snowfall, as unexpected in March as the ice storm had been in February. It was cold outside. Inside, Abe felt warm, safe, and sexy behind her. His arms tightened as she rubbed her body against him. As busy as her schedule had been, she'd be totally fine doing nothing but making love and chilling all day.

"Last week we tried roller skating, with me mostly rolling on the floor. So that's out." Abe joined Reign laughing at the memory. He didn't mind being the joke.

"For someone's first time, you were pretty amazing. It's that athletic body," she added, turning to face him and rub her hands over the physique of which she spoke.

"I've always had good balance."

"You're a great athlete," Reign said. "You probably could have played pro sports."

Trenton's face came to mind. Reign sighed, thankful Abe wasn't a professional athlete, that he didn't know what it was like to have to survive in that veritable meat market, a supercompetitive, dog-eat-dog world.

"It's still too cold to do anything outside," Abe said.

"Maybe next month," Reign agreed. "You still haven't attended our family's Sunday brunch. They're curious to meet you and starting to get suspicious."

"I'll come tomorrow."

"You will?"

He nodded. "If that is your wish."

"Hmm. Will you grant me anything I wish?"

She watched as his eyes seemed to bore a hole through her. "Anything within my power," he finally replied.

The next day, it was a typical Sunday at the Eddington Estate. Reign joined family and friends for the weekly brunch in the solarium, her mother Mona's favorite room in the opulently grand house. The atmosphere was festive despite the large, fluffy snowflakes steadily falling. She appreciated sitting at the table with Avery and Willow, who worked with Avery, her chef and restaurant owner friend, Quinn, and a few other guests. The constant chatter kept Reign's thoughts from straying to Abe, who'd still not arrived. Had he changed his mind despite the earlier text confirming that he'd be there?

Reign sipped a glass of fresh orange juice and thought

about Abe. She still viewed him as somewhat of an
enigma and couldn't quite figure out what it was about
him that kept him on her mind. He was cute. She'd give
him that. And kind, it seemed. Smart, too.

But Reign's world was full of decent men, ones who
could grace the cover of men's magazines. She'd dated
some of the finest manly specimens on the planet, Trenton among them. What was it about this Abe fellow that
kept her mind occupied with thoughts of him? Reign
didn't know, and she didn't plan to waste much time
finding out. She wasn't interested in him long-term. She
wasn't trying to get into a committed relationship. She'd
just gotten out of one. Reign had decided to relax and go
with the flow. Live in the now and focus on being hap-
pily single, work, Make It Reign, and mentoring. And
the occasional romp with the cute African. Nothing else.

Moments after coming to this conclusion, Abe arrived. His posture was confident despite his being
simply dressed and, Reign guessed, given his living
situation, feeling slightly out of place in such opulent
surroundings. That may have been the way he felt. Yet
wearing a casual ensemble—pair of jeans and wool
sweater over a button-down shirt—he looked as though
he belonged. She ignored the pitter-patter of her heart
when he smiled, and quickly rose to greet him.

"You made it!"

"I did." Abe answered while taking in the swanky
room. "That snow is a beast. This home is fantastic."

"Thank you. Any problem with the guard?"

"No, thanks to you. He accepted my visa ID, no
problem."

"And your passport."

Abe shook his head. "That has been temporarily misplaced. But since you'd spoken with him, my visa sufficed."

"Good." Reign threaded her arm through his and began walking toward a table. "Hope you're hungry," she said, happier than she should have been at the sight of a casual friend. "John, our chef, outdid himself today."

Not wanting Abe to endure the third degree from the women's table, once he'd fixed a sizable plate, she steered them to a smaller table with a woman he recognized.

"Hello, Ivy," he said once he'd sat down.

"Hello, Abe. Good to see you. This is my husband, Desmond."

The two men exchanged greetings.

"Desmond is my oldest brother," Reign explained. "He's a VP in our company, handling the newer offerings of our industry, such as cryptocurrency and the digital wallets to contain it all. His star rose a few years ago when he created our company's cryptocurrency, E-Squared. Do you dabble in that?"

"Cryptocurrency? A bit."

"Des, you'll have to introduce him to our app."

"I'm not sure I'm ready for that," Abe said.

"Sure you are," Desmond replied, reaching for a napkin and cleaning his hands. "As little as a hundred dollars can get you in the E-Squared game. Have Reign set up a meeting in our offices and I'll give you the rundown."

Reign had always admired her brother, and now was no different. She wasn't surprised that he treated a potential hundred-dollar client the same as he would one with a hundred thousand dollars. Though privileged, they'd grown up with their feet firmly planted in the real world. One of the earliest sayings of her father she remembered was, "A man can make money, but money can't make the man."

"He actually works at our offices," Reign offered. "He's with the Clean Up Crew, the newly contracted company keeping our offices so fresh, so clean."

Reign did a little shoulder bounce in her tribute to the popular song. Soon, they were joined by Reign's other brother, Jake, and Jake's best friend and Avery's husband, Cayden. The men became engrossed in sports talk while the ladies discussed Mentorship Movement, the expanded program Ivy planned to launch that summer. Reign was happy about Lilah's continued improvement, and chimed in here and there, but honestly her attention was on Abe interacting with her brothers.

As with her, he listened more than talked, but seemed comfortable around her family. Not that it mattered, she reminded herself. He was casual, not commitment, and had only been invited to brunch because…well, that's what happened at the Eddington Estate on Sunday. People came and ate.

"You look familiar," she heard Jake say as Abe finished eating and pushed away his plate.

"Who does he look like?" she asked.

"I can't place it, but I never forget a face. I've seen you before."

Abe shrugged. "They say everyone has a twin."

"He works with the crew that cleans the school and your building," Ivy said. "You may have seen him there."

"Maybe," Jake said, his eyes narrowing as he continued to check Abe out.

Reign noticed Abe's discomfort and stepped in.

"Geez, Jake," Reign said, swatting her brother's arm. "Quit staring like the guy's on display."

"My bad, man. Didn't mean to be rude. So, tell me, where are you from?"

"Ghana."

"I was there years ago," Jake said. "Cool place."

Reign watched Abe relax as he spoke of his homeland and the worry lines from a scrunched brow disappear. People began mingling around the dessert and coffee stations. Reign introduced Abe to her parents and Maeve. He was courteous through the introductions, but shortly afterward told Reign that he had something to do and needed to go. She walked him to a set of double doors, the solarium's outside entrance.

"Thank you for coming."

"Thank you for inviting me."

"I hope Jake didn't make you too nervous. That's just how he is."

"He is the same type of protective brother that I am to my sister Rhianna."

"I'd love to meet your family. Maybe I'll visit when you return home."

Abe offered a smile and a hug then left rather quickly.

Reign felt a sense of melancholy watching him leave,

and a plethora of other emotions. Abe was a good guy who would make someone a great husband. Reign shook the thought from her mind before it could settle. She wasn't looking for one of those.

Fourteen

Abe left the Eddington mansion with one thing on his mind. Tell Reign the truth. Now. When Jake had said he looked familiar, Abe had thought he'd been busted. It had taken everything not to squirm under his gaze. Her brother handled athletes. Pro sports was his business. Soccer wasn't as popular in America as in other countries, but with basketball's growing worldwide popularity, someone like Jake probably kept a finger on the international pulse. Abe had retired less than two years ago. It was very possible that Jake could have seen him before. What would he have done if Jake had asked him outright about how he could have known him, or if he played sports? No way could he have lied to Reign's family. He would have had to come clean, a situation that would have been uncomfortable for everyone. With

Jake's interest piqued, and the likelihood of becoming one of the faces of a global sports drink, he had to tell her. Hopefully, she'd understand.

With the falling snow and Abe's inexperience with winter driving, the trek back to Chicago was a slow one. He didn't mind. Cocooned in his modest Ford Explorer while fluffy white flakes fell, he could almost forget the major life choices and changes swirling around him. He turned up the light classical music, his mother's favorite genre, and tried to relax. Just as the tightness began to leave his shoulders, his satellite phone rang.

Instead of his mother, as he'd assumed would be calling, it was his brother.

"Big brother," he answered in his native tongue.

"Little brother," Danso replied.

Abe smiled at the greeting they'd shared for a decade at least. Though only three years older, Danso was what his folk called an "old soul" who'd always viewed Abe with an almost fatherly affection, and when needed, fatherly critiquing as well. Growing up, they hadn't been exceptionally close. Danso was a traditionalist who did what was expected and colored within the lines. Abe was a rebel who made his own rules. Still, Abe admired his older brother. Danso was a brilliant strategist, a principled man, practical and fair, which is why Abe believed he would win the Ghanian election and make a great president. Even more important, Abe had no doubt that, whenever needed, Danso would have his back.

"How's life in America?"

"Different," Abe honestly replied.

"I don't fully understand your reasoning for the extended trip, but I won't harp on you about it. I'm sure you're getting enough of that from Mom and Dad."

"You know they're not happy unless running our lives. I haven't heard from either of them, though, in the past couple days. Perhaps they've figured out I'm an adult."

"Our parents decided to be spontaneous, something highly unlike them. They decided to go on a short holiday and will be back next week."

"You are right. That is highly unlike them, especially Dad. And especially with *Kbaba*'s illness. How is he, brother? The truth."

Danso paused before responding. "It doesn't look good."

Both men became silent then. Their grandfather was not only their hero, but a living treasure of the kingdom.

"Should I come home?"

"And do what? Worry along with the rest of us? What our grandfather could use right now is good news. Proving yourself as a company executive and getting married. And not necessarily in that order."

"Where did they go?" Abe asked, eager to change the subject.

"I didn't speak to them directly. Rhianna told me and I don't think she exactly knows. If it's Dad's choice, they're probably skiing in Switzerland. If Mama had her way, they're in Paris, shopping until they drop along the Champs-élysées."

"At least that's something to occupy her. The busier

she is with her own life the less time she has to meddle in mine."

"Indeed," Danso said with a chuckle. "Your affiliate report was impressive. A couple of the companies are doing better than expected. The energy drink sounds like a good fit. Dad didn't say so exactly, but I believe he is beginning to see your worth beyond that of a football star."

"That's good to hear."

"Don't think your attempt to steer away the conversation from yourself was entirely successful, little brother. I hear you're open to finding an American bride."

"How'd you know about that?"

"Do you think it's a secret? Mom is beside herself with the possibility. Even tried to enlist me to nudge you along a more traditional route. *Kbaba* won't live forever. Given that you must be married to receive your share of the inheritance, and that unless you're engaged by the end of the year your marriage will be arranged, I'd think you'd be shopping for some young lady's ring."

"If Mom had her way, I'd be married already. Anticipating my inability to find my own wife, she's already picked out several Kutokan women, as if choosing a bride is like choosing an outfit."

"There are similarities…"

Abe was on the verge of being offended then heard the humor in Danso's voice.

"I've met a woman," he blurted. An outburst he hadn't planned and immediately regretted. Abe's mother's reaction when mentioning a potential American love interest hadn't been good. He expected the same from his brother.

"An American?"

"Yes."

"Tell me about her."

Against his better judgment, Abe found himself telling Danso everything—from the near altercation that led to his and Reign's meeting, to the dilemma of having to tell her the truth of his identity. "She isn't Kutokan, but she is a very special woman. I think she could be the one."

"Then you must do what is right, little brother. The sooner, the better. You must end this lie you've perpetuated, and pray she'll accept who you truly are."

"I'm an ex-professional football player, the type of man she's sworn to not date again."

"That is unfortunate but may not be your biggest hurdle."

"I believe it is my only one. Could there be others?"

"Sure. You say she is attracted to this alter ego you've created. A lowly janitor well below her station. What if, like you, she wants to marry against expectations, and would rather have someone like the person you're pretending to be instead of the wealthy, successful, ex-football star you are?"

It was a good question and a perspective Abe hadn't considered. "This has gotten entirely more complicated than I intended."

"There is no problem that cannot be solved. This correction begins with the truth."

"I've tried to tell her."

"What stopped you?"

"She wants to keep what we have casual and, outside of something illegal or immoral, didn't think it necessary to know more about my life."

"But you know differently, don't you, Aldric? It is not only necessary but imperative that you tell that woman the truth. Listen, I have work to finish up before leaving the office."

"You're still at work? At this hour?"

"Yes, and I'm sure the wife is waiting with a good scolding."

"Then get back to work so that you can go home. Give her my love and kiss my beautiful niece."

Abe reached the apartment and luckily found a parking space near the building, one that didn't require parallel parking, impossible for him in the snow. Instead of cutting off the engine, he turned down the radio and called Reign.

"Hey, Abe! Jake and I were just talking about you."

"All good I hope," he managed to quip around a mouthful of fear.

"He finally thought of the guy that you remind him of, an English club soccer star named Alden or Allen or something. He showed me a picture and I've got to tell you, he's right. The resemblance is uncanny. You definitely have a twin. You love soccer. Do you know the guy I'm talking about?"

"Yes." Abe closed his eyes and swallowed. "His name is Aldric Baiden."

"Aldric! That's it. In places where soccer is popular, he's a pretty big deal. His family is from a tiny kingdom

I'd never heard of. But you probably know all of this, already, with you living in Ghana, which I understand is right next door to his country."

"It sounds like you and Jake had quite the conversation."

"Once he remembered the name, he began googling information. He can't get over how much the two of you look alike."

With each word, Abe's heart sank lower. Reign knew the truth and he hadn't been the one to tell her. He only hoped it wasn't too late to tell her now.

"Reign, my love, what are you doing?"

"Ooh, 'my love,' huh? Sounds like someone's missing me, and I'm coming over."

"If you could, I'd like that very much."

"Are you okay, Abe? You sound sad."

"I spoke with my brother Danso today. My grandfather is quite ill. We're all hoping that he will get better, but right now, it doesn't look good."

Neither did his prospects for Reign understanding when he told her the truth. That while not lying outright, he'd not been completely honest. A fact she already knew, thanks to her brother. An already complicated secret just got harder. It was time to stem the flow of deception before it reached the point of no return.

"I'm sorry to hear about your grandfather," Reign said. "Several years ago, our grandmother was hospitalized. For almost a week, we were all a wreck, wondering if she'd pull through. She did, and we're grateful. But for that week, we were lost, completely miserable.

So I understand. I'll be sending good thoughts your way."

"I appreciate that."

"Is there something I can bring you? Dinner? A movie? Would you like to go out and get your mind off your troubles, even for a little while?"

"That's kind of you, but no…we need to… I'd rather spend a quiet evening with you."

"Say no more. I'm on my way, ready to offer up a perfect distraction."

Abe's smile was bittersweet as he hung up the phone. He had an idea what Reign had in mind to take his mind off of what was happening back in Kutoka. He only hoped that after learning what he had to tell her, she would still feel like making love—and not war.

Fifteen

After speaking to Abe, Reign threw a couple changes of clothing in an oversized tote and, within minutes, literally, was on her way. She'd been thinking about him since brunch, and not just because of Jake finding his twin. Desmond was a man of great character, and while noting that at times Abe seemed uneasy, he believed him to be sincere. Jake liked that he was from Africa and most likely knew the names of the hottest soccer stars. Perhaps they could even do business together. Taking on the world of immensely wealthy soccer stars would not only do wonders for Eddington Enterprise but for Jake's personal bank account as well. Her mom had commented on his manners. Maeve and Ivy had teased that seeing him in jeans instead of the loose-fitting jumpsuit made his hunk meter soar. All in all, his family liked him. A fact that made Reign happier than she cared to admit.

By the time she reached Chicago, the snowfall had stopped. She thought about texting Abe that she had arrived but seeing a parking space not far from where his Ford Explorer was parked, decided to save him from having to put on outerwear just to walk her less than fifty feet to the gate.

Abe wasn't happy with her decision. "You should have called me," was his greeting after buzzing her in.

Reign placed her tote on a barstool and shrugged off her coat. "Stop fussing and kiss me."

Instead of the long lip-lock she'd expected, Abe offered a quick hug and a peck on the cheek. "We need to talk." He reached for her hand and led her to the sofa.

"What's the matter? You sound serious."

Abe took a deep breath.

"Did somebody die?" she asked. "What's going on?"

She watched him visibly swallow before saying, "I am Aldric Baiden."

A second passed. A couple more. Then Reign cracked up laughing.

"Good try, Abe! But I'm not falling for that game." She laughed more. "I gotta admit, if you tried to impersonate the guy, you could be successful. One picture looked so much like you, I saved it. Let me get my phone."

She rose to get it from her purse on the counter. Abe stopped her.

"Reign, please. This is very difficult for me. I am not

joking. Your brother has a keen eye. He was right. I'm not Aldric Baiden's twin. I am Aldric Baiden."

"The multimillionaire soccer star."

"Yes."

"Whose family is part of a kingdom in Africa."

"The Kingdom of Kutoka."

Reign slowly pulled her hand from his. "You've been lying this whole time?"

He dropped his head. "I've been less than truthful, but for a very good reason."

"What reason is ever good enough to fool someone— no, a whole community of people, with a lie?"

Suddenly, Trenton's face swam into her conscience. The last man who'd lied to her, who'd betrayed her trust. Reign jumped off the couch. The man she couldn't wait to see, the body she'd been longing to touch, now gave her the heebie-jeebies.

"What kind of game are you playing?"

"Please, Reign. I know this is a lot to take in—"

"You think?" Followed by an angry snort.

"I've been meaning to, wanting to tell you. I've tried before." He stood but didn't try to come near her. "Please, if you will only allow me to share my story, at least you will know that there was no ill intent. You may still be angry, but you will be upset with the truth."

"Fine." Reign all but stomped over to the barstool and plunked down on it. "I'm sitting. Talk."

"Would you care for something to drink?"

Reign crossed her arms. "Only the truth."

Abe walked back to the sofa, sat and looked at her directly. "My name is Aldric Baiden."

"Got that part."

Abe nodded solemnly, took a breath. "What you gleaned from the internet is true. I am an ex-soccer player who represented England for seven years, after graduating near the top of my class from one of that country's top colleges. My family, the Baidens, are members of Kutoka's founding families, and have existed as long as the kingdom."

"So you're royalty."

"I am related through bloodline. My uncle is presently the ruling monarch. It is quite a pedigree and with it comes a lot of responsibilities and expectations. Again, something I believe you understand.

"I was expected to attend college, marry well, contribute to the family coffers and live an exemplary life. I love learning, was always a bright kid, and had no problem attending college. Becoming a professional soccer player threw somewhat of a curveball into the life that had been planned out for me. The decision drove a wedge between me and my father that has not yet fully mended. It disappointed my grandfather and set me at odds with the clan. My choice didn't fit into the staid format of my ancestors, yet it was a sport that not only was I gifted and excelled at, but that I truly loved. As you know, being a sports star has its privileges."

Reign couldn't help but roll her eyes.

"Everywhere soccer is popular, the Baiden name is recognized. I was esteemed everywhere except in my own family. They hold professional sports in low esteem. For them, sports is something done by lesser men who cannot excel in more honorable careers such as medicine, business, politics and law. They liken professional players to that of gladiators—placed in an arena for the enjoyment of members of a higher echelon. Eventually, my brother Danso supported my decision. He loves sports and recognizes that I was a true talent. My sister Rhianna supported me, too. Her husband was a fan. But neither my parents nor my grandfather ever saw me play. To this day, though the internet is filled with video highlights of my career, I don't think they've seen one kick of a ball.

"Once I retired from soccer, it was expected of me to return to the established format that my brother had followed. I was to become an executive within the family conglomerate, and marry strategically, in a way that benefitted not only myself but the clan."

"But you didn't want your marriage to be a business deal," Reign suggested, her anger now mixing with compassion, a rare dance partner.

"No." Later, she'd swear she could physically feel the intent of his gaze. "I have always considered myself the master of my own destiny, including who I choose for a bride."

He got off the couch and moved to the window. The sun was setting and it had begun snowing again. Reign was tempted to get up and offer him comfort. Then she remembered something important. He'd lied to her. No matter his story, that clear fact remained.

"At the close of last year, the pressure increased. My grandfather, my *kbaba* as he is called in our language, became ill. Cancer. My family brought in the best specialists, gave him the best treatment that money could buy. For a time, the disease went into remission. We were hopeful that it would remain that way. Recently, however, it has returned.

"I stand to inherit a fortune, but only if I can become a contributing member and prove my worth to the company, and if I am married before he leaves this earth. My mother became desperate for me to marry and began lining up potential brides. My father's perspective was more practical, wanting a union beneficial to the overall Baiden legacy, similar to that of my brother, Danso, who married the daughter of a high-ranking Ghanian official with familial ties to Kutoka."

"There are worse problems to have," Reign offered.

"Indeed. There is war, hunger, racism, disease. In the face of any of these Herculean realities, my desire seems frivolous. But a dare from my cousin Nolan changed everything."

"A dare?"

"Yes." Abe told Reign about swapping apartments with Nolan to prove he could survive outside of the insulated world in which he'd grown up and lived.

"All my life I've been known as the Baiden boy— rich, privileged, a great catch—a situation only magnified when I became a football star. Yet I was not always the self-assured young man I became. At one time, I was merely a scared little boy living in his strong, big brother's shadow. When women began flocking, I was confused. I never knew whether they were attracted to me or to my pedigree. To the professional athlete. To the kingdom heir.

"When Nolan dared me to move into his low-income

neighborhood and work for his company, living in a city where nobody knew me, where I could be seen as a man without material trappings, I found the possibility intriguing. I wanted to see what kind of woman I would attract with nothing more than who I am as a person."

He turned and walked slowly toward Reign, stopping when less than a foot away. "Mere days after accepting Nolan's challenge and moving into his apartment, I met you."

Abe reached up and brushed a tear from Reign's cheek. Until then she hadn't realized she was crying.

"I hate you right now," she whispered as she slid off the barstool and into his arms. "And at the same time, I love you for your honesty."

"Thank you," he replied, his voice raspy with emotion. "The most that I hoped for is that you would listen, and that there would be a place in your heart for you to understand."

"It is a story that I can more than relate to, but it still doesn't take away from the fact that you lied to me." She crossed over to the couch and sat down.

"I was always going to tell you," he countered, claiming the barstool she'd vacated. "Especially once we became lovers. From the moment we met, and our eyes touched, I felt a connection. I was waiting to see if you felt that connection before telling you the truth. Remember that first night we slept together? When we fully made love? Reign, do you remember?"

"How could I forget?"

Reign remembered all too well. That night and

each touch experienced in those moments were forever etched on her body and heart.

"That night, I stated there was something I wanted to tell you. Yes, it was early in our relationship, or whatever you call what we're doing, but I wanted you to know. You asked if I were married, or a criminal. When I said no, you shut down the conversation and said that since ours was a casual liaison, that was all you needed to know."

"So the continued deception is my fault? Give me a break."

"None of anything is your fault. The guilt lies solely with me. I should have forced you to listen, refused to continue seeing you until you knew the truth. But, honestly, I was afraid that if I told you, I'd lose you. I am a professional athlete, albeit retired, the type of man that more than once you said you'd never date again. Me and your ex are two completely different men, but I felt your hurt too great to be able to see it. And since I, too, have been dishonest, it may be too great to see it now."

Reign sat back and looked out the window. Her emotions were roiling, anger simmering once again. She heard Abe's words but what she felt was Trenton's betrayal. The lies were spun from different motives but they'd come too close together. It was difficult to separate them with objective reasoning. Her head understood it, but her heart couldn't be bothered.

For several minutes, the two said nothing. Abe quietly brought her a bottle of sparkling water. She nodded her thanks and sipped in silence, grabbing her phone and scrolling through the pictures of Aldric Baiden.

Even without knowing what she now knew, there was a clear difference between Aldric and Trenton, even in the pictures online. Trenton's pics were of someone larger than life, often surrounded by hangers-on, with a model-type draped on his arm. In contrast, most of Abe's pictures were of him alone, or with a group of his teammates, or with people who looked like his parents, his family. In his pictures, the superstar ex-athlete looked very much like the down-to-earth janitor she'd met months ago.

Reign and Abe returned to the sofa. Over the next two hours, he answered all of her questions and bridged the gap between Abe Wetherbee and Aldric Baiden. She learned details of his childhood and of the Kingdom of Kutoka, his time spent in England and his lofty education.

"No wonder you were such an expert in brochure design," she teased, recalling what happened after the ice storm. "It was accepted, by the way. The team loved it. And no, you're not getting paid."

"I enjoyed helping you and would do so again…for free."

"Do you have a girlfriend?" she asked him when all other subject matters had been exhausted.

"No, but if I could make the choice in having one, it would be you."

"I'm not ready for anything serious," she gently reminded, her anger continuing to dissipate.

"I get it. But until you do, can we have wild, mad, passionate sex?"

"You owe me that much."

For the rest of the night, that's just what they did. Wildly. Passionately. Madly.

The next morning, Reign awoke early. She shifted just enough to take in Abe's sleeping profile, the man she now knew had a whole other name and life. As crazy as it was, she truly understood why he'd done what he had, could even admire it, in a way. The average person would be more than happy to create a mutually profitable union, wouldn't dare risk losing an inheritance to stand by his convictions and be his own man. In a way, he reminded her of Desmond, who'd married Ivy even though she wasn't of the upper-crust crowd. Or Cayden, Avery's husband and Jake's best friend, whom she loved like a brother, even though his background was less than pristine. In the quiet moments of the waking dawn, she forgave Abe. In this moment as she gazed at him, she felt something close to love.

She kissed his cheek.

He opened an eye. "Good morning."

"It is good, isn't it? It would be even better if today weren't Monday and I didn't have to get up and go to work."

"What are you talking about? Your father owns the company."

"If you knew Derrick, you'd know that's even more of a reason for me to not only get there, but to be on time."

He pulled her into an embrace. She welcomed his arms around her.

"Do you work today?" she asked him.

"Not until six."

"At our building, or PDS Prep?"

"Both."

"Is that why you're only coaching the girls part-time?"

"I didn't want to start a job that I knew would end eventually."

"Is that part of your family's expectation—that you'll return home?"

"Not only expectation, but obligation. I am an executive at Kutoka Global. I am expected to marry, and soon. I only hope the woman beside me is not only the best of those available, but the one I truly want to be with for the rest of my life."

He pulled back the cover and kissed an exposed nipple.

"Ooh, it's cold!" Reign wrestled the comforter back over her naked frame. "I need to take a shower, but I'm afraid of freezing between here and the tub."

"Would you like me to warm your water, darling?" he asked with mock British accent.

"Why, that would be most gentlemanly of you, indeed," she sweetly replied.

Abe rolled out of bed in all of his naked glory. He walked into the small yet functional bathroom. Reign admired his tight ass below a set of dimples that winked from his lower back. His legs looked as powerful as they felt when hovering over her or pushing from behind. She heard the shower flip switch, followed by spraying water. She imagined him adjusting the temperature.

"Okay, baby. It's ready."

"I'm coming!"

Reign hurried into the warmth of a steamy shower. Aldric followed right behind. She turned her face to the water, scrubbing her skin and cleansing her mouth. Aldric did the same. Reign used her loofah to create a cascade of bubbles that Aldric traced with his tongue. She ran her hands down the length of his smooth hardness, grinding her hips when she stopped to squeeze his tight ass.

"Don't start nothing you can't finish," Aldric whispered.

"I'm ready to finish everything."

Reign reached between them and stroked his dick. He used his skillful tongue to tease a nipple into hardness. He was just about to turn her around and enter her when there was a banging on the door. Reign looked at Aldric. He looked at Reign.

"Who's that?" she asked.

He shrugged. "I have no idea." Abe stepped out of the shower and wrapped a towel around him. Loud knocks rang out again, followed by the doorbell ringing.

Reign got out, too.

"Stay in the room," he demanded, scurrying into a pair of sweats he grabbed from the floor and jerking on a T-shirt. "It's probably Nolan. He has a key but probably forgot it."

"Grab my tote off the sofa, so I can get dressed."

He winked, his eyes roaming over her body. His lopsided smile turned her all the way on.

He tossed her tote onto the bed and returned to the living room.

Reign walked into the bedroom, glad for the wrinkle-free sweater dress she'd chosen to pack, which would go well with any number of boots she kept at the office.

Just before pulling on a matching bra and panty set, she heard voices. One sounded high-pitched, decidedly female. She almost grabbed the towel she'd discarded and went out to investigate. On second thought, though, she reached for a matching bra and panty set and began pulling them on. Abe had spilled his heart last night, and she'd decided to trust him. Besides, if she was going to get into a catfight, she might as well be dressed.

Sixteen

Abe reached the door, peeked through the hole and was both surprised and relieved to see Nolan standing on the other side. If his cousin's forgetfulness was the only problem he had to contend with, it was going to be a good day. He flipped back the lock as a sarcastic remark tickled his lips and opened the door.

"Did you need GPS to…"

Too late, he read the message of warning flashing from Nolan's eyes. His cousin wasn't alone. Behind him were the last two people on earth he'd either expected or wanted to see right now. His parents. In Chicago. Standing in all of their opulent glory at his cousin's front door. Abe imagined there was some type of luxury limo parked at the curb and a Town car of security behind it. Now, everything from the past week made sense. His parent's rare, spontaneous vacation. Rhianna not being able to provide details, which kept Danso in the dark as well. While trying to connect with them in Africa, his parents had been on their way to America. Now, they were here.

Seeing his parents obliterated the Abe persona completely. His janitor days were over. Aldric was busted. He was shocked speechless. His body, known for its fluid motion on the field, in the boardroom and the bedroom, was paralyzed.

His father Daniel's booming voice broke through the stillness. "Aldric! Stand back so that your mother and I may enter."

"Sure. Of course."

Aldric's mother pulled an enormous fur coat around her and waltzed into the room.

"Mother," he began, attempting to kiss the cheek that rapidly passed by him.

Villianne turned, a swirl of mink, finely spun wool and leather. "Don't 'mother' me, Aldric. Why are you here in this dreadful apartment? What in the world is going on?"

A thousand thoughts exploded in Aldric's mind, several simultaneously. When had his parents arrived in the States? How long had they been in Chicago? They'd obviously been by the mansion and discovered Nolan living there. How much had Nolan told them?

Thinking of his cousin, he turned toward the door still standing ajar. Nolan was nowhere in sight. Aldric didn't blame him but inwardly cursed anyway. Had the roles been reversed, he, too, might have vanished. His eyes shifted to the bedroom door he'd left open. It was now closed.

Reign.

"Mother, let me take your coat."

"We will not be staying, and neither will you."

"This may not have been what you were expecting, but please give me a moment to explain."

Villianne kept her coat but eased it down her shoulders. After a quick search around the room, she sat on a dining room chair. Aldric sat on the sofa. His father continued to stand.

"It's good to see you," Aldric said as if over tea. He decided going on the offense might be his best defense. "What brings you to Chicago, Dad? The sports drink deal—"

"You think we're here to answer your questions?" his father interrupted, incredulous. "Son, your mother and I will ask the questions. You'd better have darn good answers. Now, what are you doing in this place?"

"I live here."

His mother gasped. "In this ghetto? The slums?"

Aldric's eyes slid toward his beautiful, proud mother, a woman who could easily pass for being in her forties though just last year she'd celebrated her fifty-fifth birthday. A woman who'd lived a life of privilege and knew nothing of how the ninety-eight percent lived. Nor did she want to know. Aldric realized explaining himself was going to be a harder sell than he thought. He willed strength into his spine. His back straightened.

"It's a little rough around the edges, but the people are nice. We look out for each other."

"It appears that you'd have to. People living above and below you, and all sides, too. This place feels like a prison, Aldric and not at all safe. I cannot believe you'd call such a place your residence."

His father's lip curved with contempt as he took in his modest, less-than-pristine surroundings. Like Villianne, he'd grown up in the Kingdom of Kutoka, leaving the cushy municipality only to attend prestigious universities and enjoy the best life had to offer while taking Kutoka Global from the multimillion-dollar company Aldric's grandfather had established to the billion-dollar conglomerate that it was today. Oh, and being the successful younger brother of a king.

"Why is Nolan staying in an affluent, respectable area while you live in this dump?"

"He started a successful cleaning service," Aldric said, dodging the question. "I've been helping him out."

"Is that why you've been largely unavailable the past week, and not returning my calls?"

"I have stayed abreast of every project and in contact with New York so that the purchase of the energy drink company can go smoothly. The report was sent, with favorable responses. As for calling, I planned to do so this weekend."

"By then your grandfather could be dead."

The harsh statement from his father brought Aldric to his feet. "What's happening with *Kbaba*?"

Villianne walked over to Aldric and gave his arm a sympathetic squeeze. "It's not good news, son. The doctors have said they've done all they could do. They've labeled his cancer as terminal and given him six months to live."

The news was like a physical punch in the gut. Aldric's legs became wobbly. He returned to the sofa and plopped down.

Villianne sat beside him. "Son, we're sorry to break the news this way. But you left us few choices."

Daniel came closer, but rather than sit, he continued beyond them to the window. "You have always been smart, Aldric. This trip proves you have what it takes to make a fine executive. It's time for you to fully immerse yourself in those duties, and in those of your heritage.

"Which means you no longer have the option of waiting to get married, or time to look for a suitable wife," Villianne said. "We must move forward with an arranged marriage, one that will take place early next year."

Aldric glanced at the closed bedroom door. Fortunately, his parents were too busy fussing to notice.

As Villianne continued, her volume increased. "There are several Kutokan women willing and waiting to become your wife. We are well acquainted with their families. It is time that you return and make your choice from one of them."

"Your mother is correct," Daniel said. "Your *kbaba* must see you wed. You are welcome to continue building our American portfolio. That can only bode well for the boardroom. But when you enter the bedroom, it must be a proper woman who welcomes you there."

Villianne's words overrode Aldric's sadness and brought him once again to his feet. "Do I not get a say in my own affairs? Father, once my football career ended, I did exactly as you wanted. I joined the company even though honestly doing so was not my first choice. There were a myriad of offers in various careers from all over the world. But I returned home. Now you're asking that I do the same in my personal life—put obligations to duty before my free will."

His mother sighed. "Oh, don't be so dramatic, Aldric. You sound like a character in a Shakespearean play."

"At times I feel like one. Mother, Father, the two of you were lucky. You married for love and for country. Danso, too. I've always wondered about the women I dated, whether their love was because I played soccer or because I was rich. I wanted to know what it was like to meet someone who didn't know anything about me and begin dating out of a mutual attraction—nothing else."

Daniel frowned. "Nolan tells me you think you've found such a woman."

"That can't be true," Villianne said, surprised. "I'm sure whatever American pastures in which you've romped cannot compare to those in Kutoka."

"Actually, Mother, that's not true. I've met a woman and—" he spoke louder "—I think she's wonderful."

Villianne crossed her arms. "Does she know about your situation? That you must be married to inherit, and that an arranged marriage was possible, even likely?"

"No." Three pairs of eyes looked over as Reign emerged from the bedroom. "I had no idea Abe was engaged, or arranged, or whatever the setup."

"Abe?" his mother demanded, indignant.

"And even with last night's heart-to-heart conversation," Reign continued, "it appears I don't know Abe, excuse me, Aldric at all."

Seventeen

Reign hadn't planned on making an entrance. She'd decided to wait until the parents left before having the confrontation. Then the next thing she knew, after hearing "proper women" and "Kutokan choices," she bolted out of hiding and was standing in the living room with Abe's parents. The awkwardness clashing against her anger was not a good mix.

She watched as a flurry of emotions played across Aldric's face, likely the same ones skittering like butterflies in her own stomach. He took a step toward her.

"Don't," she commanded. She watched his eyes widen as he took in the tote hanging on her shoulder. "I was just leaving."

She managed to retrieve her coat and leave the apartment with a modicum of dignity. She was too hurt to

feel anything. Too stunned to cry. She'd taken another
chance on love. It hadn't paid off. She was a fool to be
so foolish. It wouldn't happen again.

During the twenty minutes from Chicago to Point du
Sable, Reign's mind was blank. She couldn't think. As
she took the exit toward the town's main street, however, a plan began to form.

When Trenton had betrayed her, she'd lost it. Broke
down. It had taken her weeks even for the initial recov-
ery, months before she felt she'd moved on with her life.
That wasn't going to be what happened this time. She
was going to handle this situation like an Eddington,
like a boss. That determined, she called her assistant,
told her she'd be there in an hour, and turned her car
toward PDS Prep. Ivy would need to look for a new
janitor, and someone else to help with soccer. Because
in just about five minutes, Abe, now rightly known as
Aldric, was going to be out of a job.

She reached Ivy's office. The door was open. Ivy
was speaking with someone, but when she saw Reign,
she waved her in.

"Let me know if you have any more problems," she
said to the woman wearing a colorful outfit, playful
jewelry, and clutching a stack of papers. "But I think
with our new provider, our internet speed will be back
to norm."

"I appreciate it," the woman said, greeting Reign as
she passed her.

Reign followed her to the door and closed it.

"Sorry for coming by without notice," she said, returning to sit in front of the desk Ivy occupied. "But do you have five minutes?"

She watched as Ivy took in her stern expression. "For you, I can spare ten to fifteen."

"Abe and I are over. Excuse me, Aldric—that's his real name."

"Okay, wait. Start over. You're moving too fast for me to keep up."

"I don't have time for the sad, drawn-out story, but the short of it is that the man we've known as Abe Wetherbee is really a multimillion-dollar retired soccer star named Aldric Baiden."

"What?"

"Oh, there's more. He's not from Ghana, exactly, but from a nearby kingdom called Kutoka, where his family is a part of the ruling empire."

Ivy sat back as though her wind had been knocked out. "You've got to be kidding, Reign."

"I wish that I were."

"The man who cleans our floors is from some royal clan? Why in the heck would he leave that to come here?"

"In his words, partly 'to not be desired for his money but to marry the woman he chose'." Air quotes accompanied the frown on Reign's face.

"It takes some kind of man to be that determined."

"Wrong answer. You're supposed to hate him right now."

"Oh, honey. I'm so sorry he tricked you. How did you find out?"

"At brunch yesterday, Jake thought he looked familiar. Later on, he remembered where he'd seen his face. I thought he'd found the twin that it is said we all have. When I went over to his place, he told me the truth. Abe is Aldric. And he and I are done."

The explanation had taken less than five minutes, but Reign was drained. "Can you fire him today? I can't return until he is barred from the premises."

"Technically, no, I cannot. Our contract is with the company, who in turn hires employees. I will, however, speak with Nolan, his supervisor. Under these...unusual circumstances, I'm sure he'll be able to be replaced."

"Good." Reign stood. "I'm headed to work to have the same conversation with our building supervisor. Once he's no longer a part of our cleaning detail, I won't ever have to see him again."

Eighteen

After risking his health to chase Reign barefoot, only to reach her car as it peeled from the curb, Aldric went back inside and confronted his parents. A huge argument ensued. Turned out Nolan was "hiding out," he'd later termed it, giving them privacy, at a next door neighbor's. But when he'd heard the shouting, he'd come back to referee. Once tempers had gotten under control, Aldric and his parents went to the suite at the Ritz where his parents were staying. There, he gave a brief rundown of who Reign was and why he loved her. Finding out she was an Eddington pacified his father. His mother, however, wasn't impressed. She wasn't from Kutoka or a neighboring kingdom, which meant she wasn't good enough. They'd tried to force him home to Africa immediately, but Aldric had stood his ground.

He would make a trip to see his grandfather, then return and complete the business he'd started. He was sure that was what his *kbaba* would want him to do. And as much as he wanted to please his grandfather, securing the energy drink company purchase for Kutoka Global wasn't the only reason. A few more months in America would mean more chances with Reign. Time to hopefully change her mind. Get her to listen and understand that what she thought she'd heard was not as it seemed. His mother was moving ahead with plans for an arranged marriage. Abe had just a few months to get Reign to fall in love, as he now realized was happening to him, and to have a chance at the love he desired rather than one he'd have to settle for.

It wouldn't be easy, he found out.

Reign had shut him out of her life. Instantly. Completely. He didn't blame her. In fact, he understood. She was being betrayed when he'd met her. He'd stepped in to defend and protect her, then basically done the same thing. He deserved her outrage and bitterness. That didn't mean he'd give up.

Aldric wasn't used to not getting his way.

Apparently, she wasn't either. Despite the text and voice messages —before she'd blocked his number— and lone attempt to visit her office—before Nolan had permanently removed him from Eddington Enterprise's cleaning detail—Reign hadn't given an inch on her angrily delivered request to never see him again. Still, he'd asked his cousin that, if the opportunity every arose, to convey the message again and better. One meeting. One conversation to more clearly explain how he'd justified doing what he'd done. When she heard the whole story, if she still wanted him gone, he'd be on the next plane out of the country.

Hearing Nolan's key in the lock caused Aldric to rise from the couch.

"Did you see her?" was his greeting.

"Yes," Nolan said with a sigh.

"Did you get a chance to speak with her?"

"Against my better judgment, I did as you asked."

"And?"

"She doesn't want to talk to you, Aldric. Period."

Aldric shot daggers at his cousin as though Reign not speaking to him was Nolan's fault.

"I revealed my identity!" he snapped.

"But not that you had to get married, Nolan calmly replied.

"I never planned for an arranged marriage. Were Kbaba not dying, we wouldn't be speaking of it now."

"But the issue is now on the table, Aldric. That's the hard, cold fact."

Aldric couldn't disagree. He also couldn't blame Reign for cutting ties with him. Didn't make him feel any better. Images of that morning's magic flooded his mind. They'd been so happy. Had experienced pure bliss. Were about to do it again in the shower before their personal paradise of peace had been shattered by a firm knock at the door. That the intruders might be his parents had been the furthest thought from his mind. For days, everything that had happened after seeing them at the door had played like a movie scene on loop inside his head.

"You didn't mean for it to happen. But Reign was blindsided by hearing that you had to get married, and soon. That your mom has potential brides already lined up. She probably doesn't know what she's feeling right now."

"She knows that she doesn't want to talk to me," Aldric answered.

"She definitely knows that."

Aldric paced the length of the room and turned. "What happened tonight? How did the two of you get talking?"

"Ran into her in the hallway. Did what you asked."

"What did you say exactly?"

"That you'd been trying to reach her and for her to give you a call."

"How do you know she doesn't want to talk to me."

"Because she mentioned something about hell freezing over before that happened."

"Oh."

Around three in the morning, Jeffrey called. Again. He'd blown up Aldric's phone all day but having not been able to reach the twins regarding the energy drink and with nothing new to report, Aldric hadn't felt like talking. He didn't feel like it now either but it beat tossing and turning, unable to sleep.

"Hello?"

"Aldric, good morning."

"It's not morning yet."

"Maybe not, but the sun is shining. Did you hear any of my messages?"

"No."

"You should have listened. I have a very good reason for calling."

Aldric yawned and perched on an elbow. "I'll be the judge of that."

"We got the deal."

This comment sat Aldric straight up. "What deal?"

"Brooklyn. The energy drink. You nailed it. They've agreed to our terms."

Aldric swung his legs over and sat up. "The terms in the preliminary proposal we sent over just to get the ball rolling?"

"Exactly."

"I called their offices several times but hadn't heard back."

"That's because they're here, in Kutoka."

"You're kidding me."

"They told me the travel to Africa was regarding a personal matter, but I think they need the cash and felt that a visit to corporate headquarters might speed up the process."

"I thought the deal might be dead."

"If it was, someone revived it."

"With fifty-fifty ownership?"

"Even better. Sixty-forty. When we upped our percentage, they didn't argue. Which is why I think they're financially strapped."

"Something's going on. Deals like this usually take much longer."

"None of us expected this to move so quickly. But if we move now, we can be highlighted at the next Olympics celebration. Our brand will be known all over the world."

Abe stood slowly, his mind awhirl with thoughts. He'd figured months would pass before any movement happened on the energy drink proposal. That he had time to win Reign back before becoming the face of a product likely to be known worldwide. In that moment, he made a decision. For him and for Reign, the Abe Wetherbee façade was already a thing of the past. It was now time to introduce Chicago and Point du Sable to Aldric Baiden—sports star, royal clan member and the soon-to-be face of an energy drink that would sweep the entire world.

That Friday, Aldric stepped out of the grand leased mansion's marble shower and entered the master suite. A few days earlier, he'd moved out of Nolan's apartment and back into the place more reflective of who he truly was. He'd offered his cousin the use of the home until the lease was up, but Nolan's business had increased to the point where he was able to put a down payment on a sizable two-bed, two-bath condo in a trendy up-and-coming neighborhood. The Realtor had assured him that with the chic coffee shops and restaurants scheduled to move into the area, the home's value would more than double in less than two years. Nolan was already packing up and would move at the end of the month. For Aldric, the short swap with his cousin had ended up being a blessing. Still, he was glad to see his cousin snag his own piece of real estate and move up in the world.

Aldric took care with his appearance. Familiar with

enclaves like Point du Sable, he knew how important it was to make a good first impression. The way he was perceived would impact future business and strategic relationships. He planned to make a good one.

After donning a stark white shirt, a tailored black Brunello Cucinelli suit paired with gold-tipped, spiked loafers, a gold-, black-and-white-striped tie and simple gold accessories, he splashed on a generous amount of his favorite cologne and headed for the Maybach that for the past few months had sat idle.

On the drive over, he pondered the upcoming evening. He was sure the PR and marketing departments had done their job, and that he'd be well received by the business community. He also knew that these dinners were ones the Eddington family usually attended. He imagined Reign would be there but couldn't be sure. Even if not, his plan would be successful. She'd know that he'd shed the Abe persona and was once again living in his true identity. No more faking. No more hiding. Abe Wetherbee was forever dead and buried. He only hoped that any chance to have a relationship with Reign hadn't also given up the ghost.

Aldric arrived at the chamber of commerce's dining facility just before the program was set to begin. Clearly, he'd been expected. Within seconds of giving his name to the host, an attractive woman he guessed to be in her forties approached him.

"Mr. Baiden! My name is Gloria Morgan, the chamber's vice president. We're delighted to have you join us."

"I'm excited to be here. Please, call me Aldric."

"Of course," she purred, while threading her arm through his, a possessive move that he didn't appreciate. He casually disconnected them and straightened his tie to cover the subtle message that conveyed he wasn't interested—or owned.

If she noticed, it didn't show. "My son Liam is a huge soccer fan," she said, directing him away from the registration table and into the main room. "He told me all about your history as a star of the sport."

"That Liam is a fan speaks to his good taste," Aldric easily teased. "But that part of my life is over. Now, I'm solely focused on further expanding our company brand into North America. I'm hopeful tonight will move that goal along."

"With your looks, personality and business savvy, I'm sure you'll have no problem." They reached the raised platform where he would sit until after introductions. "And did I hear correctly that you're single?"

Aldric's face remained placid. "That is correct."

Gloria offered a teasing smile. "Then…if you choose to extend your business dealings in the Point, you'll have no problems in your personal life as well."

The evening began with the introduction of potential new businesses to the area near the top of the program. For all of Gloria's inappropriate flirting, she did an excellent job of offering a succinct portrait of Aldric's background as a college standout, an ex-football star and now an executive of Kutoka Global.

"Ladies and gentlemen," Gloria concluded, "please help me give a warm welcome to Mr. Aldric Baiden!"

Aldric strode confidently toward the podium. Press

conferences and endless interviews as a soccer star had made him very comfortable in front of a crowd.

"Good evening. Ms. Morgan, thank you for that kind and warm introduction. I am delighted to be here. As was stated, I am a former football standout, a sport called soccer here, a description that the rest of the world can't fathom for the life of us."

He smiled to show he was joking, and waited until the laughter died down. "I am equally proud of my position with Kutoka Global, an enterprising company with a diverse portfolio that was started by my grandfather with a few thousand dollars, big dreams, and—pardon me, ladies—equally large *cajones.*

"Our company now spans the African continent and has several offices in more than a dozen European countries. In the next five years, we plan to expand into Asia and gain a bigger footprint into North and South America. That's why I'm here. Several companies that we've acquired have grown exponentially, enough to warrant an office in the States. Big coastal cities such as Los Angeles, San Francisco, New York and Washington, DC, are obvious choices. But my team and I are thinking more progressively and are including southern and Midwest cities in our list of choices. Cities like the sprawling metropolis of Chicago and smaller yet forward-thinking, pro-business, affluent townships such as Point du Sable."

The room erupted in applause. Clearly, the business owners were impressed with what Aldric had to offer.

Once off the podium, he was immediately surrounded by business owners, the city's mayor and a few council members, and more than a few well-heeled females eager to make his acquaintance. Aldric was polite, but focused. There was only one woman he wanted to talk to tonight. Fortunately, he'd been seated at the special guest table, which was next to where Reign and several business owners sat. When one of them got up to mingle, Aldric quickly excused himself from the Realtor trying to sell him a mansion, and walked over to the next table.

"May I sit?"

"The seat's occupied," Reign replied. She did not look up.

"Terrence went to the bar," the woman in the chair next to the empty one offered. "He'll likely be gone for a while."

"Thank you." Aldric sat down.

"Gayle Jones," the woman immediately offered. "My family owns Jones Mortuary, the largest funeral service in the Midwest."

Deadly business, Abe thought. "A pleasure to meet you," he said.

"While in Chicago for seventy-five years, I, too, am new to Point du Sable. We've just opened a top-of-the-line facility here. It would be nice to have a fellow newcomer to help navigate the town's tricky social scene."

Aldric nodded but didn't respond. He shifted his body more fully toward Reign. "Good evening, Ms. Eddington," he said, loud enough to force an answer.

"Good evening, Mr. Baiden." Formally stated, with no emotion at all.

"You look amazing."

"Thank you."

He leaned closer and lowered his voice. "I've missed you."

The servers delivered salads to the table. Reign busied herself choosing a dressing from the carousel of offerings, opened the individual serving bottle and poured the balsamic selection onto a bunch of mixed salad greens.

"I don't blame you for being mad at me," he continued, undaunted. "I'm hoping that with time there can be room for forgiveness."

Reign turned to the man sitting on the other side of her and asked him to pass the basket of rolls.

Aldric sighed inwardly and sat back in his chair. He wasn't always the most patient man, but in certain circumstances, when there was something he wanted, he could have the patience of Job. Clearly, he'd have to channel the biblical figure tonight. Building the bridge back into Reign's good graces would be harder than he'd thought. He hadn't underestimated the difficulty. In fact, he'd imagined it would be harder than hell.

Unfortunately for Aldric, he'd been correct.

Nineteen

Seeing Aldric at the chamber meeting gave Reign a
dual sensation—like reuniting with a soul mate and
meeting a stranger for the first time. Besides being completely surprised at her lover being the night's special
guest, watching him approach the podium did all kinds
of crazy things to her insides. He looked even better
than that last memorable image—his glistening naked
body before covering it to go answer the door and welcome unexpected parents from across the pond. A searing memory. He looked hotter tonight.

Reign wanted to be upset at Aldric's bold move, ac-
costing her in public where she wouldn't run and hide
or cause a scene was genius. But she couldn't. Had the
tables been reversed, it was something she might have
done. Something she'd considered right after Trenton's

treachery, when she'd almost risked her pride to go and confront both him and the fan-turned-girlfriend. And if she were to be honest, which she wouldn't because it might highlight her weak flesh, Reign would admit that it felt damned good to see him again. That's how her heart felt, but she made sure her face didn't show it.

"Reign, did you hear me?"

She hadn't. All of her energy was going into not squirming at his nearness, at quelling the fire gathering at the juncture of her thighs. She was trying to remember the bad stuff, most of which had occurred in a torturous hour where she'd been trapped in a bedroom while Aldric's parents discussed how an arranged marriage was now imminent, and how it would be to a Kutokan woman.

There it was. The anger. Anger was good.

"No, Aldric," she said, emphasizing what she now knew was his real name, "I didn't hear you. What did you say?"

"I'm hoping that in time there can be forgiveness. I ask that even as I understand your anger. I'd be upset, too, if you'd lied to me."

Reign looked beyond Aldric to see Gayle Jones trying hard to act as though she wasn't listening. Reign wasn't fooled. She knew how these social circles worked. If they continued the conversation at the table, it would be broadcast all over Point du Sable before the ten o'clock news.

"Let's go grab a drink at the bar."

They got up from the table and walked in that direction. Reign passed it, however, and continued down a short hallway. Once out of the public view, she dropped her civil façade.

"I don't appreciate being publicly accosted."

"I had to do something. What we shared was too special to be left unfinished."

"To the contrary, Aldric. We're done. And since you understand my feelings, I'm hoping that after tonight you will leave me alone."

"I will do that, Reign, but only if you agree to have dinner with me."

"No."

"One evening, one dinner, so that I can fully explain the context of what you heard from my mother."

"An explanation or your justification?"

The smile that used to melt her heart crossed his face. "A little of both?"

"You lied to me, Aldric. There's no justification for that."

"You are right. What I did was inexcusable. Do you think there is any way you could ever forgive me?"

"I don't know. I don't think so."

"One night. One dinner."

Reign hesitated. He looked so handsome tonight, so sincere. But then again, so had Abe when he'd spoken of being a janitor, and the contentment of simple apartment living.

"I don't hate you, Aldric" she said, remembering that not too long ago similar words had been said to her ex. "But I no longer want to continue the...friendship...or whatever you want to call what we had going on. I just endured a breakup fueled by betrayal. Your reasons for being dishonest may have been noble, but for me, the end result feels the same.

"I actually think you're a good guy who will make some woman happy. But what was done can't be undone. So that woman isn't me."

"But, Reign—"

"Good luck with your business endeavors, Aldric." She stepped forward and kissed his cheek. "Goodbye."

When they returned to the main dining room, they stopped at the bar and then each went back to their assigned table. Reign tried to get back in the flow of things, making small talk with Cornelius, an attorney friend of Maeve's who Reign had known for years. From time to time, she felt Aldric's eyes on her.

He left before dessert was served. Without his presence, the room felt less bright. She told herself she'd done the right thing. That nipping their fling in the bud was the best for everybody, especially with what he'd announced tonight. That he was considering the Point for a business location. If they were going to be navigating the same business and social circles, it was best to put what they'd shared behind them. The sex had been outstanding, so it wouldn't be easy. Reign refused to let that fact sway her. This time she'd think with her head instead of her heart.

As had happened a few months ago, she dove headfirst into work and let busyness save her. She spent more time with Lilah. She also took the lead on Ivy's idea of expanding the Mentorship Monday program, reaching out to other professional women with the idea to set up a twelve-week summer program that would not only deepen mentor/mentee relationships, but would also expose the girls to success, support, and life outside the perimeters of their neighborhoods.

Make It Reign continued to grow. After turning down a couple dozen requests, she finally took on her first professional athlete as a client. The up-and-coming golfer was the exact opposite of Trenton. He was quiet, humble, and more focused on serving others than bringing attention to himself. A refreshing change from the big egos she was used to, one that ironically helped Reign lose her disdain for anyone pro-sports-related, and once again believe goodness could be found in every arena, even one connected to professional sports.

Spring gave way to the beginnings of summer. June came in with near triple-digit heat. Like Reign's emotions, the weather was all over the place. Reign had been putting in ten-hour days at the office but this particular Friday she prepared to leave early. She was actually looking forward to a special date—taking Lilah and Lilah's best friend on a weekend trip where they'd drive to Gary, Indiana, spend the night, take a train to Cleveland the following morning and return to Chicago on Sunday night.

The trip had been spurred by Reign's shock after learning her sweet little charges had never heard of the iconic R&B group, the Jackson 5. The girls had also never been on a train. That had settled it. A road trip was born. They'd visit the family childhood home in Gary, then travel on to the Rock & Roll Hall of Fame in Cleveland, Ohio, and visit a westside market featured on the Food Network. Reign would have liked all of this activity to rid her mind of thoughts of Abe/Aldric. But if she said that was true, she'd be a big fat liar.

After placing her laptop and several reports in a tote, Reign left her office and headed for the parking garage.

She'd just stepped out of the elevator and crossed the garage lobby when she heard a door slam, looked over, and saw a familiar logo—Clean Up Crew—splashed across a white van. Aldric's face swam into her mind, unbidden. At the same time, Nolan looked over and waved. No option. She had to stop. No way could she act like she hadn't seen him.

"Hey, Reign."

"Hi, Nolan."

Okay, she'd been polite. Now on to her car and the escape route from the memories she was trying to forget.

"Reign! Do you have a minute?"

No, she didn't. But he'd already begun walking toward her.

"How are you?" he asked, wiping his hands on a towel.

"Fine, and you?"

"I'm good. Thanks to your company's references, business is booming. I just secured a contract with the PDS Country Club."

"Congratulations."

"I talked to Aldric recently. He asked about you."

"How is he?" Reign asked casually, out of obligation, but found herself really wanting to know.

"He's good."

"Still living at the apartment, I take it?"

Nolan shook his head. "He's back in Africa."

"Oh." Why did this news cause a knot in Reign's stomach? She didn't care where he was, where he lived, did she?

"He went over there to see his grandfather, who's very ill. He's planning to come back, though. Says he has some unfinished business to handle."

"Checking out possible business locations, most likely."

"Actually, Reign, I'm pretty sure he was talking about you."

Reign checked her watch. "I've got to go." She turned to leave.

"I think he's in love with you."

Those words were like a tether, stopping her in her tracks. They rained over her like a warm, summer shower. Wrapped around her like a grandmother's quilt. She remained where she was, a couple steps from Nolan, but didn't turn around.

"I don't agree with what he did," Nolan said, walking around to face her. "And I swore I wouldn't get involved. But I'm partly to blame for why you met Abe and not Aldric."

Reign knew about the dare but remained quiet.

"I made a dare. I told him that there was no way he'd come down off his high horse and live how I did—simple apartment. Challenging neighborhood. I further badgered his ego by saying there was no way he could do my job. I dared him to swap places and become one of my employees. Told him he couldn't last a day, let alone a month. Looking back, it was stupid, especially because of how well I know my cousin. I knew there was no way he'd let what I said go unchallenged. It's hard for a man like Aldric to be proved wrong."

"Aldric told me about that and, you're right, Nolan. That was pretty stupid. And it doesn't explain why Abe—Aldric—at some point didn't tell me the truth, especially about the potential brides waiting back home."

"He always planned to find his own wife."

"Then why didn't he?"

"That's not a question I can answer. Like I said, I really don't want to be involved. There is a clear line between me and my customers. I try not to cross it. Aldric can be an asshole, but at the end of the day, he's my cousin. I love him. He's a good man. And he's hurting. He feels awful about how everything between y'all went down."

"He should feel awful about what happened. What am I supposed to do about it?"

Nolan shrugged. "Hear him out, maybe?"

Reign was conflicted. On one hand, a conversation with Aldric was the last thing she wanted because, on the other hand, being with him had been heavily on her mind. To do so wouldn't take much convincing. But she didn't want to get hurt again.

"Did he tell you he was in love with me?"

Nolan managed a laugh. "Men like us don't admit stuff like that straight-out. But trust me when I tell you, his feelings run deep. The way he talks about you is different than how he's discussed other women he's dated."

Nolan's phone rang. He answered it. "Yeah, man. I'm here. Come on down and get this buffer." He hung up. "Time to get to work. You have a nice weekend."

Reign got in her car, feeling all kinds of conflicted. She would have a weekend all right. She was no longer sure how nice it would be.

Another month went by. Reign heard through the grapevine that Aldric had returned and been given a membership into the country club at Point du Sable. She knew then that seeing him again would only be a mat-

Get up to 4
FREE FABULOUS BOOKS
in your welcome box!

To thank you for being a loyal reader we'd like to send you up to 4 FREE BOOKS, absolutely free when you try the Harlequin Reader Service.

Just write "YES" on the Loyal Reader Voucher and we'll send you your welcome box with 2 free books from each series you choose plus free mystery gifts! Each welcome box is worth over $20.

Try **Harlequin® Desire** and get 2 books featuring the worlds of the American elite with juicy plot twists, delicious sensuality and intriguing scandal.

Try **Harlequin Presents® Larger-Print** and get 2 books featuring the glamourous lives of royals and billionaires in a world of exotic locations, where passion knows no bounds.

Or **TRY BOTH** and get 2 books from each series!

Your welcome box is completely free, even the shipping! If you continue with your subscription, you can look forward to curated monthly shipments of brand-new books from your selected series, always at a discount off the cover price! Plus you can cancel any time.

So don't miss out, return your Loyal Readers Voucher today to get your Free Welcome Box.

Pam Powers

LOYAL READER
FREE BOOKS VOUCHER
WELCOME BOX

YES! I Love Reading, please send me a welcome box with up to 4 FREE BOOKS and Free Mystery Gifts from the series I select.

Just write in "YES" on the dotted line below then return this card today and we'll send your welcome box asap!

➡ YES ⬅

Which do you prefer?

☐ **Harlequin Desire®**
225/326 HDL GRA4

☐ **Harlequin Presents® Larger-Print**
176/376 HDL GRA4

☐ **BOTH**
225/326 & 176/376 HDL GRCG

FIRST NAME

LAST NAME

ADDRESS

APT.#

CITY

STATE/PROV.

ZIP/POSTAL CODE

EMAIL ☐ Please check this box if you would like to receive newsletters and promotional emails from Harlequin Enterprises ULC and its affiliates. You can unsubscribe anytime.

HD/HP-622-LR_LRV22

It was a week later, to be exact, in the coun-
...gar lounge. She'd entered the dark paneled,
...nated room to drop off a file her father had
...That he'd not been alone was not the surprise.
...adn't expected was who shared his table—
...en…and Aldric.

...quared her shoulders as she walked toward
...could do this. She was a strong, confident
...his was her town. Her domain. She wouldn't
...shrinking violet just because the man who'd
...he best sex of her life, and more, was sitting
...ther and brothers.

...hed them and put on a dazzling smile. "Good
... everyone. Dad, here's the folder from work
...sted, plus one that the assistant said might
...eded."

Her father reached for the folders. "Thanks, Reign.
I appreciate you bringing these over."

"No problem."

She lightly punched Cayden in the middle of lighting a stogie. "I thought Avery told me you'd stopped
smoking those things."

"I did, so don't tell her," he replied, eyes twinkling.

"He doesn't smoke around the little ones," Jake explained.

"But you're here," Reign teased.

"Oh, you're calling me a kid now."

Reign relaxed amid the sibling banter. "Just *kidding*,"
she replied.

"You're looking lovely, as always," Aldric said, his

beautiful brown eyes staring into her soul. "It's wonderful to see you again."

"I ran into Nolan," Reign replied, neatly sidestepping the compliments. "He tells me you went to see your grandfather. How is he?"

"Physically weak but mentally alert. I visited daily until he threatened to ban me forever unless I returned to more important things, like helping run the company he founded."

"Sounds like a man after my own heart," Derrick said.

Aldric nodded. "He's as good as they come."

"What is his illness?" Jake said. "If you don't mind me asking."

"Cancer."

Cayden chimed in. "My mother is a nurse who works at PDS Medical. They have one of the best cancer treatment centers in the world."

"Really?"

He nodded. "Indeed. Many who've been given a terminal diagnosis are brought there and defy the odds. I'd be happy to arrange for you to speak with my mom and the specialists."

"That's very thoughtful, Cayden. Thank you. I would definitely love to speak with your mother. I'd also very much like for your sister here to join me for dinner. What do you say, Reign? I've been invited to eat with these gentlemen but, no offense—" he looked around the table "—I'd much rather take this opportunity and spend a bit of time with you."

"Thanks, Aldric, but I really don't—"

"Oh, stop playing hard to get," Jake interjected, "and have dinner with the man."

"Mind your business," Reign warned.

"He told us what happened," Cayden offered.

"He lied and, yes, that was messed up," Jake said. "But he said he was sorry."

Reign crossed her arms, her anger apparent. "What is this? The Aldric amen corner?"

"Ah, stop acting mad, sis. You know you want to. You've been Patty Pouter and Debby Downer since y'all stopped going out."

"You're such a liar," Reign snippily replied but with a laugh she couldn't resist, especially when she took in Abe's confused expression.

"Patty Pouter?"

"I'll explain later," Jake said. "After Reign leaves. She's too scared to share a steak with you, man. That hot sauce they serve with it might melt some of the ice she's placed around her heart."

"I know what you're trying to do, Jake," Reign said. "I'm not taking the bait. Enjoy your meal, gentlemen," she said with syrupy sweetness. "And make sure you cut up yours into small pieces," she added, squeezing Jake's shoulders, "so that you don't choke."

She bopped his head and heard their laughter as she walked out of the room. Head high. Heart intact. And the ice that Jake had so accurately described beginning the slightest thaw.

Twenty

The following Friday morning, Reign called him. "Is that dinner invite still open?" she asked.

"Absolutely."

They met at the country club later that evening, where she'd reserved a private room.

"Thanks for agreeing to have dinner with me," he told her after they shared a light hug. "I hope it's because of what you genuinely desire and not from your brother's teasing."

"You're giving him way too much credit," she replied. "I've borne the brunt of his teasing my entire life."

"I can relate. Remember, I have one of those."

"An older brother."

"Exactly."

The conversation continued around family. Abe

shared the news about his *kbaba*. How he'd indeed spoken with Tami, Cayden's mother, who then connected the team of specialists at PDS Medical with those in Switzerland who'd been treating his grandfather.

"My parents are considering bringing him over. But the treatments the center here offers are alternative and unconventional. They're still not totally convinced."

They spoke of Danso, whose main opponent for the presidency of Ghana was now involved in a major scandal, almost fully ensuring Aldric's brother's win.

Reign talked about Make It Reign. Aldric told her about the energy drink and showed pictures from the photo shoot that would be used in the commercial rollout. Conversation was easy through the first and second courses, and half a bottle of wine. Along with tackling the mammoth Porterhouse the server placed before him, Aldric decided to also cut through the elephant in the room.

"Is there any chance we can get back our friendship?" he asked.

"Aren't we having a friendly evening right now?"

"I'm referring to a connection that moves beyond mere conversation. I want to spend quality time, learn more about each other. I want to know your goals and dreams, your fears and failures. I want to make love to you all night long, and then again the following morning."

"We did have great sex. I can't deny that."

"Is that all it was for you? Pure animalistic desire?"

"That's what we agreed on. Keeping it casual. Remember?"

"My mind remembered that but my heart seems to have forgotten. I… I've developed feelings that go past the casual definition. I'd very much like for you to become my woman, for me to be your man. I'd like us to become a couple, and see if there is enough in common to sustain a more permanent future."

"You ask a lot," Reign softly replied. "Especially when a marriage is being arranged."

"Only if I can't produce a bride of my choosing. Reign, my beautiful queen, I choose you."

After a prolonged silence, Aldric asked, "Will you at least think about it?"

It seemed time stood still before she answered.

"I'll think about it," she finally said.

Four months later, on a warm evening in September, just before sunset, the Bombardier Global 5000 carrying its sole, somber passenger began its descent into the Kingdom of Kutoka. The scenery was spectacular—lush land meticulously landscaped, exotic flowers and tropical trees that went on for miles and miles, hugged up against some of the whitest sand and bluest water on the planet.

It was a landing Aldric normally relished as most times it signaled the end of a successful business trip or weekend tryst. Tonight, it marked the end of much more. Specifically, his will to chart his own course romantically, and any chance to spend a lifetime with Reign. Following the dinner, they had spent time together. Gone to concerts, and museums, and a few trips out of town. They'd returned to an intimacy more heightened than when it was first experienced. He'd finally broken down and told her he loved her.

She hadn't said it back.

As the plane drifted toward earth, Aldric resigned himself to getting married. Not to his first choice, but a suitable second. It was time to face the harsh reality that not being honest had cost him the most precious possession. Lying had cost him true love.

Losing Reign was what happened. That was his past. He was arriving back home, to his present and future. Despite what he'd shared about the medical breakthroughs offered at PDS Medical, his grandfather had declined a trip abroad to prolong his life. He'd enjoyed every one of his ninety-one years. When the Good Lord called, his *kbaba* was ready to answer. That forced an answer on Aldric as well. He would fulfill his obligations and he would do so with honor.

In him ran the blood of kings, royal ancestors, thousands of years chiseled in honor and duty. To maintain honor and duty was also love. Aldric settled against the seat, his chin raised, his thoughts resolute. He squared his jaw and peered into the distance, his uncle's golden palace and surrounding grounds shimmering against the red-orange sunset. He thought of the upcoming holiday season, and the celebrations planned to honor his brother's presidential election. During this season, he would also choose a wife from the families his parents had sanctioned, and get married.

For the first time since seeing Reign outside of the Verve nightclub, he pondered the women who'd spent the past year enjoying their own sense of adventure while awaiting his decision. Each had been given the opportunity for one last selfish indulgence before possibly stepping into the high profile of becoming a member of the

Baiden family as Aldric's wife. Iya had spent the year traveling culinary meccas throughout Asia and the West. His second option, Rachel, was an architectural engineer who'd laid the groundwork for a foundation that would offer free, off-grid, tiny housing all over the world. Dela, the one to whom he felt closest and had known the longest, had remained in the Kingdom of Kutoka.

Less than a month after returning home, he'd made his decision. It was time to announce his choice. The walk from his parents' quarters to where he'd meet his arranged bride was the longest one Aldric had ever taken. Longer than a soccer field. Longer than a hundred strung together. He'd accepted his fate, made peace with it, and was surprised with how hard it still was to walk toward an arranged destiny. At least he'd only be meeting with Dela, and not all three of the women his parents and family had approved, as had been custom with other unmarried males.

This past week, to save all of them a bit of dignity, he'd reached out to the other two women and met with them privately. Briefly. The meetings were difficult and uncomfortable but handled with compassion. Any man would be beyond lucky to have either of them, or Dela, the woman he felt came closest to who he could see as a wife. Their families had known one another for generations. The two had played as children then reconnected in their college years. He'd been consumed with the life of a soccer star. She had been making great strides as an organic biologist. She was as smart as she was beautiful. She was witty, cultured, with all of the grace and charm necessary for a man in his position. He'd always liked Dela. He loved her. He wasn't in love with her.

He was in love with Reign.

Aldric slowed his stride and let that thought sink in. He wouldn't run from it. Rather, he'd continue to face how he felt about the soulful American who'd captured his heart, until the ache of thinking about it went away and only joy and wonderful memories remained. There would always be a place in his heart for Reign Eddington.

When he approached the double doors at the end of the hall, however, and walked through them, he would be doing so with a one-hundred-percent commitment to Dela, to being the best husband, father, partner, everything she deserved. He'd spent a lifetime enjoying the privilege of being near royalty. Time to carry his share of the duty. He reached for the door. Placing his hand on the knob, he took a breath, squared his shoulders and tried to smile. Dela was a wonderful woman. She deserved the best he could give her.

He opened the door.

Dimmed recess lighting and the light from a waning sun were the room's only illumination. Aldric squinted his eyes to adjust to the light. Dela stood across the room, in silhouette. Her back was to him. She wore a fitted gown that flared into a ballroom style, giving her more of an hourglass shape than usual.

"Dela."

"I'm here," the woman whispered.

She's more nervous than I am. Aldric's steps lengthened as he relaxed a bit. This was not only his soon-to-be bride but a long-time friend and an amazing woman. He could do this.

He came to within a few feet of her and stopped. "Hello, Dela."

As the woman began to turn around, Aldric's stomach flip-flopped. Gooseflesh broke out. He felt as though he was having an out-of-body experience. It couldn't be.

But it was...

"Reign?"

"Aldric."

They stood there, pouring love, respect and deep affection into each other's eyes. They looked deep into the past year, and into future lifetimes. Beyond the challenges behind them and the ones they'd likely face.

Aldric came out of a haze. He tried to talk, swallowed, tried again. "What are you... I can't believe..."

"I know. Me either." She reached for his hand.

He took both of hers in his then leaned forward to give her the most reverent of kisses.

"You're here." He kissed her right cheek.

"Yes," she answered, allowing him to kiss her left.

"Does that mean...?"

"Yes. I choose you, too."

"I love you." He kissed her forehead. "I want to spend my life loving you." He kissed her ear and neck.

"I love you, Aldric," Reign said before pressing her lips against his and beginning the dance.

He gently swiped her mouth with his tongue. As if he had to ask. Her arms came up and around his neck, welcoming the kiss. He squeezed her against him—deepening the exchange, telling himself that the soft voluptuousness he was feeling was real and not a dream.

Twenty-One

Reign stirred as fragments of a fantastical dream flitted around her. In it, she was a princess in a faraway land being swept away into a life of unimaginable luxury by a most admirable suitor. She smiled, shifted, and rubbed her hands over a spread of finely spun silk. Her eyes opened, revealing the twenty-foot, gold-plated ceiling of her bedchambers and the mammoth chandelier casting off rainbow colors. She wasn't dreaming. Reign sat up against the cushioned headboard and remembered that everything that had happened in the past seventy-two hours was all too real and happening to her!

A soft bell rang. She looked around. "Hello?"

"Good morning. We are your ladies-in-waiting. May we enter to help start your morning?"

Ladies-in-waiting? *Start my morning*? Reign looked

at the clock and was surprised to see that it was already past nine. She threw back the covers, slipped her feet into jeweled slippers, hastily donned a colorful robe gifted from the night before, and glided to the door. She opened it slightly and peeked outside. Three pairs of kind, beautiful brown eyes stared back at her.

A small curtsy before the first woman said, "The royal breakfast begins in one hour, m'lady. We are to have you ready and delivered no later than ten till the hour. If you'd like help with your bath…"

"Oh, no. I'm fine. What is your name?"

"I am Cynthia ma'am." She motioned to the two other ladies. "This is Elizabeth. And this is Nobi."

"Nice meeting all of you." She ignored their slightly confused expressions, one Reign imagined came from not being used to formal greetings. "Cynthia, I'll take a quick shower and be out in ten minutes."

"It's our job, ma'am."

"I'll take the blame."

The woman's expression quickly changed from joy to crestfallen.

"Tell you what. Step into the hallway while I shower, then you can help me dress."

One of the younger ladies gasped. "A shower, m'lady. No bath?"

Reign winked at the girl who appeared barely out of her teens. "I promise to scrub myself clean." She refocused. "Once I'm finished and slip into my undies, you ladies can help me pick out the best dress."

Relief showed on the older woman's face. "We'll be only a whisper away."

* * *

Reign walked into a large bathroom. She bypassed the urge to lounge in a tub big enough for a party of six and stepped into a solid marble shower stall with six rain heads instead. She set the temperature and turned on the water, a spray of warm, soft water against her flesh. After making quick work of her ablutions, she stepped out of the shower, grabbed fluffy white towels and wrapped her hair and bod. Once clothed in her undies, she stepped to the door and held it slightly ajar, standing back to prevent exposure.

"Cynthia, ladies, I'm ready for you."

She turned back toward the dressing room and heard, "Are you sure about that?"

It was Reign's turn to gasp and scream as five of her favorite women in all the world burst into the room. Maeve, Sasha, Ivy, Avery and Mona, her mom, swept her up into a group hug.

"Oh, my gosh! What are you doing here?"

"We heard you might need our help getting dressed."

"But where's…how… I can't…what are you doing here!"

"Aldric," was Maeve's one-word explanation. "Your guy called and afterward made arrangements for us to be flown over."

"Aldric did this?" Reign was beyond amazed. "When? How?"

She watched as Maeve looked beyond her right shoulder. "The stylists are waiting. Let's talk while you get pretty."

The rest of the day passed by in a blur and later that

evening Reign entered the ballroom to find Aldric, his clan, and her entire family waiting. The families had obviously taken the time—and the wine—to get to know one another.

Derrick, her brothers and Cayden chatted comfortably with Daniel and Danso.

Mona and Villianne engaged in animated conversation, laughing and gesturing animatedly like lifetime friends.

Maeve, Ivy, Avery, Sasha and Aldric's sister, Rhianna, all sat at one table, along with other relatives and longtime family friends.

Aldric only had eyes for her. And vice versa. He greeted with a warm hug, and chaste kiss, and never left her side.

The band started up. Lively African music. Reign's jaw almost dropped as she watched her father walk over, speak to Aldric's mom and then head out to the dance floor. Not far behind them, Mona and Daniel. Soon the entire dance floor was filled with Eddingtons, Baidens and the elite of Kutoka.

Looked like Aldric's parents had gotten their strategic union after all!

Reign and Aldric danced the night away but out of respect for his parent's conservatism, retired to their own suites. Early the next morning, just as the sun kissed the eastern horizon, Reign awakened. She yawned, stretched and eased out of bed. She'd only be in the magnificent Kingdom of Kutoka for another five days and wanted to enjoy every minute.

Remembering yesterday's temperatures, well into the

eighties before noon, she pulled a loose-fitting white maxi over a one-piece, slipped into a pair of white leather sandals and, after sending a group text to her sisters, walked the short distance from her guest chambers to the beach.

The sun had just begun to peek over the horizon. It's bursts of oranges, reds, pinks and purples glistened across the dark hue of the ocean as waves gently ebbed and flowed against warm, white sand. She walked along the ocean's edge, holding her sandals, her bare feet massaged by hundreds, thousands, of tiny warm grains. Here, at the ocean's edge in Kutoka, she'd decided sunrise and sunset were her favorite times of day. She reached down, picked up a shell. Saw a smooth, red stone, and stooped to pick it up, too. As she straightened to continue her morning stroll, she saw a figure in the distance. A man, she imagined, judging from the white linen cargo pants rolled up to his shins and the matching white shirt unbuttoned and floating behind him.

There was something enchanting about the way he moved. Something both sensual and angelic at once. Something familiar, too. Something that made her strides lengthen and quicken, that caused her heart to beat an energized rhythm and a squiggle to tickle her core. It struck her that they were both dressed in white and had both chosen this time of morning to rise and greet the first rays of the sun. Her body told her who it was, though long, silky strands of hair made a peeka-boo game of seeing his face. Still, she could feel him, an essence that made her heart sing. Without knowing why, she began to run toward him. At the same time, he smiled and began doing the same. They grew closer. He held out his arms, creating an open embrace for her, then stopped to provide a firm foundation for when she flew into his embrace. When less than ten feet away, she stopped abruptly.

"Good morning, Aldric," she whispered, afraid that like a phantom he would evaporate into the ocean and she'd have to accept that none of this was real.

"Good morning, my love," he answered, closing the distance between them and pulling her into his arms. He kissed her passionately, endlessly, a move left them both breathless, their fire temporarily doused by the waves lapping over their feet. Silently, they began walking.

"I believe last night was successful," he said after they'd watched a large bird glide effortlessly across the sky.

"That's an understatement. It was fabulous, as if our families had known each for decades instead of a day."

"Indeed. Danso called me last night. He says your father invited him to Chicago, has some DC connections that he'd like him to meet."

"That's crazy because I overheard our mothers discussing fashion. They love some of the same designers. I believe a mutual shopping trip is somewhere in their near future."

"Or two," he said with a laugh.

"Rhianna's fiancé being an attorney couldn't be more perfect. He, Maeve and Victor spent the night chatting away."

"When they weren't dancing."

"Thank you so much, Aldric, for inviting my family over. It was one of the best nights of my life."

"It was only fitting that your family be there. It was necessary to get proper approval from the woman I plan to marry."

"Aldric…"

"Don't worry, the wedding isn't happening this quickly."

"Whew, thank goodness."

"They're still designing the ring."

"Aldric!" She pushed him. He stumbled, grabbing her as they both ended up in the water. "Oh, the water's so warm. It's absolutely amazing."

"Kutoka is special, a heaven on earth. Can't you see yourself spending all of your time here?"

"Maybe half of my time…" she conceded.

"Good!" He swooped her up and began to run. "Let's go tell the family."

"Put me down!" she said, laughing. "Go tell them what?"

"That we're getting married, now, without the ring."

"I can't do that! I don't have a dress."

"I can fly in the designer of your choosing. We can marry as soon as it's done."

Any announcement would have to wait. Aldric took Reign's hand and led them to a private, secluded stretch of beach where they used their bodies to physically declare love to each other. Aldric with his American Princess. Reign with her Prince Charming.

Later, she'd be tempted to pinch herself to make sure she wasn't dreaming. Who would have believed the janitor who cleaned Ivy's school would turn out to be an opulent kingdom's secret heir? Not Reign, that's for sure. She never would have guessed it. But now that she knew, now that the truth was out, she wouldn't change one moment of how they'd come together.

Working through the pain of Aldric's dishonesty had brought them closer, made them stronger, set up healthy boundaries for authenticity moving forward. His true identity pleased her family immensely. That she was basically American royalty set his family at ease. Reign had fallen in love with a janitor but was marrying a member of African royalty. It almost hadn't happened. Fear and past hurts almost caused her to miss out on an incredible kind of love. Thank goodness that hadn't happened. Thank goodness that in the end, love reigns.

* * * * *

Kianna Alexander wears many hats: doting mother, advice-dispensing sister and voracious reader. The author of more than twenty novels, she currently lives in her home state of North Carolina.

Books by Kianna Alexander

Harlequin Desire

404 Sound

After Hours Redemption
After Hours Attraction
After Hours Temptation
What Happens After Hours
After Hours Agenda

Visit the Author Profile page
at Harlequin.com for more titles.

You can also find Kianna Alexander on Facebook,
along with other Harlequin Desire authors,
at Facebook.com/HarlequinDesireAuthors!

Dear Reader,

Hey there! Welcome to the fifth and final installment in my 404 Sound series. Now it's time for Nia, the serious and responsible eldest sibling, to have her world shaken up by love. Do you think she's ready?

The long-awaited thirty-fifth anniversary gala is finally here, and last-minute planning is in high gear. The last thing Nia needs is distraction. But getting paired with her ultimate rival, Pierce Hamilton, for a special project is about the greatest distraction she could face. What will happen when their worlds collide?

Thanks for coming along with me as I've explored Atlanta and Southern hip hop culture. I truly hope you've enjoyed the journey of this series.

Happy reading,

Kianna

AFTER HOURS AGENDA

Kianna Alexander

For my father, Eric Mckinnon, Sr.,
whose love of hip hop I inherited.

One

Standing near the crystal punch bowl, Nia Woodson used the matching ladle to dole out the bright pink liquid into her paper cup. Taking a sip, she smiled as the cold strawberry lemonade concoction washed down her throat.

She was in the family room of the palatial home her younger brother Blaine shared with his wife, Eden. Laughter and conversation flowed all around Nia as her relatives gathered around her very pregnant sister-in-law. Eden was due to deliver the very first Woodson grandchild within the next few weeks, and the excitement in the room was off the charts.

The space was a sea of pink, in celebration of the bouncing baby girl due to make her entrance soon. Mindful of the slight chill of early November, Nia had chosen a soft, long-sleeved pink sweaterdress. The slim-fitting garment was paired with flat-soled brown boots that matched the thin leather belt encircling her waist.

As she stood off to the side, lost in her own thoughts, she couldn't help but be reminded that she was now the last single Woodson sibling. Even her youngest brother, Miles, whom she'd expected to practice lifelong bachelorhood, had married the previous week. He and his platinum-selling singer wife, Cambria Harding-Woodson, were currently enjoying their honeymoon in the Maldives.

But I'm the oldest. And the CEO. Whatever slack there is, no matter the area or department, I'm the one who always picks it up. She knew her role within her family: she was the serious one, the organized one, the one who always had it together. And that always applied, whether in business or in family matters.

Up until recently, marriage hadn't been something she'd given much thought to. *I'm in charge of 404... Work is life. Who has time to build the kind of connections that lead to these long-term, committed relationships? Everyone else but me, apparently.*

"You okay, sis?"

Nia returned to reality and nodded in response to her sister's question. "Yeah, Teagan. I'm fine. Just gathering wool, as Granny used to say."

"Mmm-hmm." The baby girl of the Woodson clan seemed less than convinced of her elder sister's honesty. "If you say so. Come on back over with the rest of us. We're about to play a game."

"I'm coming." She reluctantly followed Teagan and

took a seat in the cream leather armchair positioned across from the matching sectional sofa. Watching as Eden's cousin, Ainsley, brought out a tray of baby bottles filled with a mysterious purple liquid, Nia cringed. *Ugh. These shower games are so corny.*

Teagan giggled as she took a bottle from the tray. "If Mom were here, she'd be eating this up."

"You're right, she would," Gage chuckled as he accepted a bottle from his wife. "Thanks, Ains."

Ainsley pecked Gage on the forehead and moved on with the tray.

"When is Mom coming back from Aunt Laurie's place in Charlotte?" Blaine, wearing a pink T-shirt emblazoned with the words Fatherhood Loading, directed the question at Nia.

She shrugged. "I'm not sure. She just said she'd be back in town in time for the gala."

Circling a hand over her round belly, Eden remarked, "She sent me the largest spa gift basket I've ever seen, plus some adorable things for the baby." Eden looked put together yet comfortable in her pink floral empire-waist dress. A simple crown fashioned of pink roses sat nestled atop her curls.

"And I'm sure there's more to come." Caleb, who'd been sitting in sullen silence in the recliner near the dining room entrance, shook his head. "Addy is incandescent with excitement over her first grandchild. The fact that she's not here speaks to just how angry she must still be with me."

Nia swallowed. This was the first time her father had spoken in the last hour or so, and his words only served as a reminder of the giant rift between her mother and father and the scandal that had caused it. Before leaving town, Addy had depended on Nia heavily for emotional support, and while she missed her mother, Nia was somewhat grateful for the break.

Ever the ray of sunshine, Teagan said, "Let's not dwell on that, Dad. Let's see who's gonna dominate at this game." She held up her baby bottle and gave it a shake.

Nia took the last bottle from the tray and eyed the liquid inside. "Ainsley, what's even in here?"

Ainsley laughed. "It's just cran-grape juice."

Slightly comforted by that knowledge, she nodded.

"Alright, y'all know the drill." Ainsley held up her hand. "We're gonna see who can finish the bottle fastest. No cheating by taking off the lid or biting a bigger hole in the nipple, either." Ainsley glanced around the room. "Okay, bottles up, folks. Ready...set...go!"

Nia felt ridiculous drinking from the baby bottle, but since silliness was the whole point of the game, she went along with it. Looking around at all the other full-grown adults swigging from their bottles made her feel slightly better about it.

Within a few moments, Gage managed to empty his bottle, collapsing the thin plastic in the process. Ainsley blew a whistle to signal the end of the game. "Looks like Gage is our winner, y'all."

"Victory is mine!" Holding his empty bottle above his head, Gage grinned. "Nobody in this room can match my...suction." He and his wife exchanged a long look.

Blaine elbowed his brother, and Teagan nearly fell out of her seat laughing.

Rather than dwell too long on the implications of Gage's words, Nia asked her sister, "When is Max coming back, again?"

"Day after tomorrow." Teagan beamed at the mention of her husband, bassist Maxton McCoy. "I can't wait."

Nia felt a sigh rising within her, one of happiness tinged with a bittersweet sensation, but she held it in.

A few hours later, Nia stood by the front door. She was the last one to leave, even though she'd long since had her fill of baby-related revelry.

Eden caught hold of her hand. "Thanks again for the bassinet. I know it will come in handy."

"No problem. I saw it in the store a few days ago. One look at those precious little dancing teddy bears and I couldn't resist." She gave Eden's hand a squeeze. "Rest up, sis."

Blaine draped his arm around his wife's shoulders. "Don't worry, Nia. I'll see that she takes it easy."

"You'd better. I expect you to wait on her hand and foot." Nia pinched Blaine's arm. "I don't want Eden or the baby stressed in any way."

"Yes, ma'am." Blaine offered a mock salute.

Heading outside, she returned to her car and climbed inside. Starting the engine, she drove around the circular drive and out into traffic.

Absently scrolling through his social feed, Pierce Hamilton adjusted his position in the stiff wooden chair. He was sitting in the waiting room of Premiere Primary

Care and, having been there for the last twenty minutes, found himself growing bored. "Mother, do you think they'll call you back soon?"

Everly, seated to his left, nodded. "I'm sure they will. They aren't usually running this far behind schedule." She ran a hand over her short platinum-dyed curls, tousling them a bit with the tips of her long red nails. She wore a white silk blouse with the sash tied in a huge bow and draped over her left shoulder, a pair of tweed slacks and her favorite designer flats.

My mother always looks like she's about to step onto the runway whenever she leaves the house. Looking at her, no one can tell how tired she is.

"Chill out, Pierce," London, Pierce's twin sister, added from her seat to his right. "We haven't been here that long. Besides, what's more important than Mom's health?" London's purple jeans, fuchsia top and leopard-print pumps made for an outfit as bold as her personality.

"Nothing," he groused. "I think I'd be more patient if these chairs weren't so stiff. It's like sitting on a flat rock."

Everly laughed. "You're not wrong. I've complained to the staff plenty of times about these things."

Pierce chuckled dryly, his eyes scanning the waiting room. His gaze settled on the face of a brown-skinned woman on the opposite side of the room. Mainly because she was staring at him. Openly.

London nudged him. "Pierce, why is that lady eyeballing you?"

He shrugged. "How should I know?"

The woman stood, and he saw that she clutched something in her grasp as she slowly crossed the room. Her long braids, the ends adorned with colorful wooden beads, were reminiscent of '80s R & B singer Patrice Rushen. When she came to a stop a few feet away from him, still staring, she asked with slight hesitation in her voice, "Are you Pierce Hamilton?"

He nodded. "That's me. Do I know you from somewhere, Miss…?"

"Deja. My name is Deja." She unfurled the thing in her hand and turned it around so he could see. "I saw you in this article I was just reading in *Opulence Magazine*."

He glanced at the image, from an article on the South's most eligible Black businessmen. "Oh. Wow. Yeah, that's me. I'd forgotten about that article. It's a couple of years old now."

"I mean, you look the same." Deja grinned. "I think you're even wearing the same suit."

London stifled a laugh.

Ignoring his sister, he glanced down at his royal blue private label suit, which he'd had custom-tailored for his frame. "It's one of my favorites."

"I don't want to be too bold, but…" Deja bit her lip. "Are you still single?"

A nurse emerged from the rear of the clinic then and called out, "Everly Hamilton?"

Pierce cleared his throat, offering a kind smile. "I'm flattered, but I'm afraid I need to attend to my mother right now. If you'll excuse me."

Deja deflated a bit but nodded and returned to her

seat. Pierce and London followed the nurse escorting their mother toward the clinic's intake room.

Soon, the three of them entered a small exam room. After helping their mother up onto the table, Pierce and his sister sat in the room's two empty chairs.

At least these have a little more padding. He'd barely settled into his seat when Everly said, "Son, if you turn away every potential date, I'll never get grandbabies."

He wanted to roll his eyes but knew his mother wouldn't go for that. "Wow, you held that in for a whole five minutes, Mother."

Everly frowned, her brow furrowed. "Watch your tone, young man. I was merely making an observation."

Pierce glanced at London, who gave a brief shake of her head as indication that she had no desire to join the conversation.

"I just want you to be happy, son," Everly insisted. "I want both of you to experience the kind of love I shared with your father." Tears welled in her eyes, as they often did when she spoke of her late husband, Phillip.

Pierce felt his chest tighten.

The door to the exam room swung open, and a deep voice said, "Mrs. Hamilton, my favorite patient."

Pierce watched as his mother dashed away a fallen tear and plastered on a bright smile. "Dr. Richardson, you sly old fox. How are you?"

Darnell Richardson, MD, the tall, slender Black man who'd been Everly's primary physician for the past five years, grinned as he took a seat on his wheeled stool. "I'm well. But I am concerned about your test results from your visit last month."

Pierce leaned forward in his chair. "What's going on with Mother's health?"

Dr. Richardson's previously sunny expression sobered. "I'm not terribly pleased with your A1C, or your cholesterol, but those should level off with some diet changes." He turned his gaze to his patient. "What really concerns me, though, was your response to the stress test I gave you. Your heart is weakening, Everly."

Laying a hand over her chest, she asked, "What do I have to do? Do I need a new prescription or some such?"

Dr. Richardson shook his head. "I'd rather not add another drug to your regimen if I can help it. Your blood pressure is up. It's a slight change for now, but I think we can stop it from becoming more serious."

London appeared confused. "If you don't want to do that with meds, what are you suggesting?"

"Everly, you need to reduce your stress level. Greatly." Dr. Richardson glanced at the papers attached to his metal clipboard. "Your body simply cannot sustain the levels you have now."

In the ensuing silence, Pierce thought about what the doctor had said. *Mother does way too much at Hamilton House—I've told her that a thousand times. I wonder if hearing it from the doctor will make any difference.*

Frowning, Everly offered a curt nod. "I'll see what I can do, Dr. Richardson. I'll admit to having a lot of irons in the fire. Maybe I can take a few out."

Offering a nod and a smile, Dr. Richardson said, "That's all I ask."

Pierce sat quietly as the doctor went over Everly's

current medications and dosages with her, as well as offering advice for changes she should make to her diet.

He tried to keep his expression flat, but inside, he wondered if his mother would actually follow the doctor's orders. She was known to be stubborn and set in her ways. *At least London and I are both in the room to hear what Dr. Richardson is asking for firsthand. Maybe between the two of us, we can lean on her enough to get some follow-through.*

Later, as he held the front door open at his childhood home for his mother to enter, he asked, "What do you think about Dr. Richardson's suggestions, Mother?"

Easing into her favorite pink chintz Queen Anne chair, Everly groused, "Come now, Pierce. I already heard the lecture twice. From the doctor, and from your sister before she left. I don't need to hear it from you, too."

"I'm not lecturing. I'm just trying to see how you feel."

"Old. Tired," she sighed. "I know I'm no spring chicken, but there's still plenty of life left in me."

"Of course, there is." He walked over to where his mother sat and took her hand in his. "London and I want to see you enjoy yourself, instead of spending all your time working and worrying over things at the office."

"Hamilton House is your father's legacy. I won't see his vision squandered or carried out in the wrong fashion."

He nodded, knowing the conversation was essentially over. There was no convincing his mother to change her attitude about work, at least not now.

If I can show her I'm ready to take the lead, maybe we can finally get her to rest.

Two

Coffee in hand, Nia entered the conference room Tuesday morning and headed for the end of the table. Setting down her paper cup, her purse and her briefcase, she pulled out her chair. "Morning, everyone."

The staffers seated around the table returned her greeting.

Checking the time on her phone, Nia said, "Let's get started. Gage, you can go ahead."

Tugging the lapels of his charcoal suit, Gage stood. "Morning, everyone. My report from Operations is pretty brief. We've narrowed down the proposals on the new studio building to three companies. Nia, I've got those three proposals with me, and I'll hand them to you after the meeting."

"Do they include blueprints?" Nia asked. Gage nodded, using his remote to drop down the projection screen. "Yes, they do. Full-size, too. We folded them down to fit in the folders."

"Great. My eyes thank you." She'd recently discovered her need for reading glasses, and at thirty-eight, she wasn't interested in contributing to any further decline of her vision. After watching Gage's brief overview of the three bids, Nia spoke again. "Thanks, Gage. Tisha, what do you have from Finance?"

Tisha Lewis, Miles's longtime assistant, stood. A petite, smartly dressed bronze-skinned woman with a close trimmed natural haircut, she wore her typical pleasant smile. "Well, Ms. Woodson, Miles approved the Q4 budget before he left for his honeymoon. He also completed a draft budget for Q1, in which he's proposed an increase in funding to 404 Cares." Tisha passed a manila folder to Nia. Then, she set up and gave her own presentation, showing a few slides of the draft budget.

"Thanks, Tisha, I'll take a look at the figures. Anything else?"

With a shake of her head, Tisha retook her seat.

Nia gestured to Teagan, who stood to give her spiel. "I've had my proposal for a tech intern program for local high school graduates approved and put in the tentative Q1 budget. I'm now handing it in for your final approval." She slid Nia a glossy purple folder.

"Gotcha. Let me guess—no presentation?"

"Tech, I love. Presentations?" Teagan cringed as she sat down.

Nia chuckled. "Fair enough. I won't press you since your paperwork is usually immaculate."

"Guess it's my turn," Blaine announced, standing by his chair. He wore a pair of black jeans, a black Goodie Mob tee and a silver-studded leather jacket with a skull and crossbones on the back. His locks hung free around his face.

Nia smiled at her brother. "I love how coming back into the family business and our rather corporate environment hasn't taken the edge off your dress code."

Blaine chuckled. "You know me. Besides, I look too good in these clothes to justify switching up my style." He cleared his throat. "But, back to the matter at hand. I'm currently working with two new artists who've signed to Against the Grain in the past month, and I'm also courting a small label out of Shreveport, Louisiana, as a possible subsidiary label for us to acquire." He loaded his own presentation and gave some brief information about his new artists, as well as the label he had his eye on.

Nia grinned. "I knew I did the right thing by creating the subsidiary companies department and making you director, Blaine. You've been doing amazing work."

"Glad you see my shine, sis." Giving her a thumbs-up, he returned to his seat and handed over his documents.

"Alright. Y'all have given me quite a bit to look over." Stacking the folders she had, she continued, "That's it for today. I'll see you all for our final meeting of the year on December 5."

The small group dispersed, except for Gage, who hung back.

"I'm ready for the proposals," Nia said as she walked toward her brother.

Holding up his briefcase, he answered, "They're right here. Let's step in your office for a moment."

What is he about to say? "Okay, come on." Once they were inside the quiet confines of her office, she gestured her brother to the guest chair near her desk. "You wanna tell me what's up?"

Gage cleared his throat. "So... Dad sent me here to tell you something. But I'm gonna lead with a little personal update."

"Is that why he didn't come to the meeting?" Caleb's presence wasn't mandated since he was VP emeritus for the company, but he usually attended anyway so he could stay abreast of everything happening at 404.

"Yeah, I'm pretty sure that's why."

She frowned. "What in the world did he send you here to tell me that makes you feel you have to soften it?"

He let out a nervous chuckle. "You'll see. Anyway, I just want to say that married life is amazing. Ainsley and I are delirious with happiness. And did I mention that she loves her new job in Human Resources?"

"I know she does. I still see her around the building, and as CEO, I love having her in HR. She's a great fit for the job." Leaning back in her chair, Nia clasped her hands together. "If you're done telling me things I already know, you can hand over your paperwork and enlighten me on whatever Dad didn't want to tell me himself." *This is so ridiculous. Dad's way too old to be doing this kind of thing.*

"Alright." Gage opened his case and slid the paperwork across the surface of her desk. Drawing a deep breath, he said, "Dad has had the brilliant idea of creating something special for the gala, something he thinks will help him get back on Mom's good side."

Nia frowned. "Good grief. The only thing that's really going to work is the truth, and Mom being able to accept it, whatever it might be."

"I agree. But you know Dad—once he's decided, there's no changing his mind."

"People say I inherited that stubbornness from him," she sighed. "What is this idea, and, in the words of Nene Leakes, Why am I in it?"

"Dad asked me to give you the barest of details, because I guess he thought your curiosity might work in his favor. It's an audiovisual project that will be shown on a projection screen during the gala."

She cringed, because despite her annoyance with her father, she was curious. "That's really all you can tell me?"

"There is one more thing." He paused, appearing hesitant. "You'll have to work with a partner on this, and Dad's already set that up, too."

"Who? Teagan? She's the tech wiz here."

He shook his head slowly. "No. It's Pierce Hamilton."

Nia pushed back from her desk and stood. "No. Nope. There's no way I'm working with that guy."

"Dad told me you'd say that, but he's already—"

"Pierce is an egomaniac. He's so full of himself, there's a good chance I can't even fit in a room with him."

Gage cleared his throat. "Well… About that…"

Nia's intercom sounded, and the voice of Althea, her assistant, filled the room. "Ms. Woodson, Everly and Pierce Hamilton are waiting for you in the conference room."

Nia stared at her brother.

Gage threw up his hands. "Trust me—I didn't have anything to do with setting this up. I'm just the messenger."

Pressing the reply button, Nia said, "Tell the Hamiltons I'll be there momentarily."

I'm not a fan of being ambushed, but at the end of the day, I'm gonna keep it professional regardless. Whatever this is, I hope it doesn't monopolize too much of my day.

Pierce sat next to his mother on the right side of the long, lacquered table in the conference room of 404 Sound. *This is the last place I expected to find myself today.*

Everly's gaze swept around the space. "The last time I was in this room, the mood was very, very different."

He knew what she was referring to right away. "I still wish you'd let London and I come with you that day for support."

She shook her head. "Support? More like drama. Having the two of you here would have only complicated things, and they were already complex enough." Folding her arms over her chest, she added, "I handled things just fine on my own."

"Fair enough." He shrugged out of his jet-black suit

jacket and placed it over the back of his chair. "Yet you thought it would be a good idea to assign me to this mysterious project of yours."

Everly smoothed her palms over the lower portion of her beige sweaterdress. "I had my reasons for leaving you out last time, just as I have my reasons for asking for your help this time."

He nodded but said nothing.

Caleb Woodson entered the room and took a seat across from them. "Hello, Everly, Pierce. Thank you so much for coming."

"Anything to preserve my Phillip's legacy," Everly answered, her fingertips grazing the locket around her neck. Pierce knew his parents' wedding photo was contained within the diamond-studded gold heart.

Caleb offered a small smile. "I'm hoping more than one positive effect comes out of this project.

Pierce settled into silence then, observing his two elders. *They're up to something, but I guess I'll find out what's going on soon enough.*

Nia Woodson entered the room then, bringing with her the fresh scent of melon and gardenia. Pierce couldn't stop himself from dragging an appreciative gaze over her. Her sparkly button-down blouse provided a focal counterbalance to the black slacks that hugged her shapely hips and full thighs. With a purposeful stride, she moved into the room and around the table to sit next to her father. She looked professional, stunning. Yet her beautiful face was tightly set, indicating a certain degree of unhappiness or sour mood.

"Hello, Mrs. Hamilton." She paused and glanced at him. "Hello, Pierce."

Her terse tone wasn't lost on him, but he had no reason to match her energy. Instead, he spoke with every bit of pleasant honesty. "Always lovely to see you, Nia."

She didn't respond, instead turning to Caleb. "I'm eager to know what's going on, Dad."

"Yes, well." Caleb stood. "Everly and I have asked you two here today for a very special project. We'd like you to work together to create a short retrospective film for the anniversary gala."

"The film will give a full history of the company, from its founding till the present," Everly added.

Pierce nodded, now that he understood what was happening. "And you want me to work on it because my best friend is a filmmaker."

"Right." Everly touched his shoulder. "And I know you'll ensure your father gets the proper honor."

"Absolutely." What he lacked in memories of his father, his mother had made up for in anecdotes and stories told over meals or huddled around photo albums.

Nia spoke again. "That's lovely. But the gala is less than three weeks away. I hope your filmmaker friend is also a miracle worker."

Pierce chuckled. "He's been known to pull off some pretty impressive feats."

"Uh-huh." Then Nia addressed her father. "I don't see why you didn't ask Teagan to do this. Tech is her department."

"True," Caleb admitted. "But this is more art than tech. This is about you being the eldest daughter, and therefore having the most memories of the very early days of 404. I know I can count on you to tell our story with the proper respect."

"I'm looking forward to this. I think it will be fun." Pierce kept his gaze on Nia's face. "I'm sure the two of us can come up with something great."

Her expression was flat, unreadable. "I guess we'll see."

Everly stood. "Good. And since you two will be working together, Caleb and I are going to make ourselves scarce so you can discuss things."

Nia balked. "I don't think that's—"

Before she could finish her sentence, Caleb and Everly slipped out of the room and shut the door behind them.

Nia sat back in her chair and scoffed. "I can't believe my dad."

"My mother's no picnic either," Pierce added. It wasn't untrue, and he hoped commiserating with her might help him break through her icy exterior. "This is actually pretty light compared to the things she normally asks of me."

"Expectations are always high for me, since I run the family business." Nia's sigh was accompanied by a downturn of her deep red lips. "I'm just shocked he'd saddle me with a side project right now, when he's well aware of all the things I already have on my plate."

Pierce felt twinge in his chest at the mention of Nia's position in her family's company. It only served as a reminder of his mother's lack of trust in his abilities, but he did his best not to let it show. "You wear the position well, Nia. You exude capability. I'm sure we'll be able to meet the challenge our parents have laid out for us."

She eyed him for a long moment. "You're laying it on pretty thick, Pierce."

"Just expressing what I see."

She appeared less than convinced but offered a curt nod. "Is there something project-related you want to discuss right now? Because I have a stack of work waiting for me in my office."

He smiled, both vexed and intrigued by her apparent eagerness to get back to work and away from him. *I'm already enjoying being in her company, but she's going to make me work for it, I see.* "I'll get in contact with Hunter—he's my good friend and the filmmaker my mother referenced earlier—to see when he can meet up with me."

"I'll start by gathering up some information from the archives about the company," Nia said. "There's a lot of stuff in storage downstairs that I'll need to sort through. Once I've got some foundational notes and have a chance to gather some relevant photos and documents, I'll reach out. Does that work for you?"

He nodded. "That sounds fine." He stood, then slid his chair underneath the table. "I appreciate your willingness to do this with me."

"It's more of a favor to my father, but I'll try to be as helpful as I can." She ran a hand over her head, wrapping her fingertips around the end of her sleek ponytail for a moment before releasing the silken strands.

Pierce found the gesture intriguing, despite how innocuous it appeared. "I'll head out now so I don't take up too much of your workday. I look forward to hearing from you when you're ready."

She nodded. "I'll speak to you soon, Pierce." Her gaze lingered on his face for a moment, and a ghost of a smile tipped her lips briefly before her expression returned to its previous serious state.

Three

Nia slipped into the red leather chair at Atlanta Breakfast Club, settling into the seat directly across from her father. Eyeing his sheepish expression, she said, "Dad, what in the world made you put me on the spot like that?"

He laced his fingers together, resting his forearms on the tabletop. "I'm sorry if you feel I forced your hand, but this project is far more important that you might realize."

Their waiter approached then, with menus and glasses of iced water.

"What can I get you, ma'am?"

"I'll have the fried-chicken sandwich, with seasonal veggies on the side and unsweet tea, please." She handed her menu back.

"And you, sir?"

"I'll have the shrimp po' boy with fries and a cola..."
Caleb began.

She eyed her father, letting her eyes do the talking.

He sighed. "On second thought, I'll have the po' boy
with a side salad. And I'll be drinking water."

Once the waiter left, Nia continued to press her father for answers. "Enlighten me, Dad. Why the sudden
interest in telling our story, less than a month before
the gala? You never brought up anything like this before, and we've been planning this event for well over
a year now."

His eyes darted around the restaurant, never settling on her face.

She assumed he was searching for an answer rather
than admiring the familiar, nondescript environment.
Atlanta Breakfast Club occupied a one-story painted
brick building on Ivan Allen Jr. Boulevard, and the interior decor could easily be described as "no-frills." What
the eatery lacked in ambience, it more than made up for
in service and incredible food. "Any time now, Dad,"
she teased. "Remember, we only have an hour lunch."

"I know. I probably shouldn't have sprung it on you
like this, but you have to understand that I have important motivations behind this project."

"You can help me understand by explaining yourself."

"It's true the gala planning has been in full swing for
a long time. But it's only been recently that things have
broken down between your mother and I."

She frowned. "I'm afraid I don't see the connection.

I know you and Mom are having a hard time right now, but why does that mean I have to be stuck working on something with Pierce?"

He leaned back in his chair. "This film retrospective is about more than adding something special to the gala. It's about our family. And the foundation of our family is Addy and I." He paused. "I'm hoping that reminding her of everything we've shared, everything we've built together, will help bring her home to me."

She watched the pain playing over his face and nodded. "I understand where you're coming from."

"Good."

"I hope you have backup plan, though." She drummed her fingertips on the table. "You've given us a really tight timeline to get this done. What if it isn't finished in time for the gala? What will you do then?"

He groaned. "Honestly? I fully expect to be cleared of these false claims. Because that's exactly what they are. False. I just don't know how long that's going to take. I may as well take some kind of action in the meantime."

The waiter returned with their plates, and they spent time enjoying the well-seasoned offerings.

When he spoke again, he said, "I didn't want to bring it up in the meeting, because we were in mixed company, but I heard from my lawyer this morning."

"Really?" She leaned in. "What's going on?"

"Remember when I hired the private investigator to get to the bottom of this situation with Keegan?" His face twisted, as if that name tasted bad in his mouth. "I asked the PI to report his findings directly to my lawyer."

"Why? I'd think you would want to know what he found right away."

He shook his head. "I already know something rotten is going on, because that young man is absolutely not my son. So I asked him to go straight to Elliot for two reasons—to let Addy see the process had no interference from me, and to speed up the inevitable legal action that's going to come from this."

She quietly turned over his words in her mind. He still maintained his innocence, having never faltered from it during the course of this entire incident. *Dad is serious when he says he didn't do what he's been accused of. I have no reason not to believe him. So the real question is, what made Keegan do this?* "Well, I'm very interested to hear about the findings. It's way past time to put all this to bed."

"I can't tell you how much I agree." He shook his head. "The stress I've gone through since this man came into our lives has been unimaginable. As soon as Elliot's done a thorough examination of the findings, he'll bring them to us and explain everything."

Their plates were cleared away, but they lingered at the table as the lunch crowd began to thin out around them.

"I'm glad you told me about your motivations behind the film project, Dad." She sipped from her glass of tea. "I'm still not excited about spending time with Mr. Full of Himself."

"I actually reached out to Everly to ask if she'd allow London to help out. She was the one who insisted Pierce be the one. I suppose because he's friends with a film-maker."

That gave her pause. *I guess I can't hold Dad fully responsible for this. He isn't the one who stuck me with Pierce. Still, this isn't ideal, no matter who's responsible.* "So I have Mrs. Hamilton to thank for that. Great. At any rate, there's still a lot of work to do, between the gala and my usual duties. It won't be easy to juggle all this."

"What else is left to do for the gala?"

"Now it's mostly down to follow-up and confirmations. Making sure the RSVPs are counted and the catering finalized. Checking with the venue to be sure everything we requested is in place."

"I sympathize, honey," he said. "But can't your assistant handle those things for you?"

"She has handled most of them. But Mom asked me to do the most labor-intensive thing—celebrity guest confirmation. She thinks it's more personal if I reach out as the CEO to confirm their appearance." She paused, shaking her head. "You wouldn't believe how hard these people are to nail down."

"After decades in the business, I do believe it," he quipped. "I want you to work on this project, and I'll consider it a favor if you do. But please don't overtax yourself, okay?"

She smiled. *He's really something.* Reaching across the table, she grabbed his hand and gave it a squeeze. "Don't worry, Dad. No one juggles better than me."

Pierce drove his black Navigator into the driveway of his best friend's Spanish colonial home in Atlanta's plush Morningside neighborhood and cut the engine. It was midmorning on a Wednesday. He typically wouldn't be at Hunter's place this early on a weekday, but his mother's assignment had made the visit a necessity.

Climbing out of his car, Pierce smoothed a bit of lint off the sleeve of his white turtleneck as he headed for the front door. He rapped against the dark wood a few times before the door opened.

"Hey, P." Hunter held the door open, gesturing him inside. "Come on in." Dressed casually in a pair of khakis and a long-sleeved Clark Atlanta T-shirt, Hunter had his long locs tied up in a bun on top of his head.

"Thanks, Hunter." Slipping inside the familiar confines of the house, Pierce inhaled. "Please tell me that's coffee I smell. I'm about a liter low on caffeine, man."

Hunter laughed. "Yeah, it's fair-trade Colombian. We can both grab a cup before we head downstairs to the studio."

Strolling through the living room, past the rounded alcoves housing Hunter's impressive collection of pottery made by local Black artisans, he followed his friend into the spacious kitchen. Pierce grabbed a black ceramic mug from the wooden tree on the counter and poured himself a cup of still-hot coffee. Narrowing his eyes a bit, he asked, "Am I tripping, or did you redo your countertops?"

"You're the first person to notice," Hunter chuckled as he opened the refrigerator and handed over a carton of half-and-half. "I had them done about a month ago. Traded the old granite for this new striated quartz."

Pierce nodded, accepted the carton and added a bit of the thick liquid to his mug before handing it back. "Tell the truth. You haven't had anybody else over since you got it done, have you?"

"Nah. You know I don't bring many people to the crib."

He and Hunter had often had the conversation about not allowing people they didn't know well into their homes, so he could relate. "Anyway, I like the new counters. It looks good." He used a metal stirrer to mix his coffee and waited for his friend to finish making up his own beverage.

Mug in hand, Hunter asked, "Ready to head downstairs?"

"Yeah, let's get started." He'd promised his mother that he would return to the office before the end of lunch, so he had a little under three hours to accomplish as much as he could on the retrospective project.

They walked down the single flight of stairs near Hunter's back door and into his basement film studio. The cavernous space had a sitting area near the base of the stairs featuring a black leather sectional, and a glass-and-steel coffee table sitting atop a white fur rug.

Across from the sitting area was a long wall completely occupied by a green screen, and the floor spanning the wall was also painted the same shade. Studio track lighting directed at the wall was currently turned off.

"Let's sit down for a minute and catch up before we start filming." Hunter gestured Pierce toward the sofa.

Once they were both seated, Pierce asked, "What's

going in on your world? Haven't seen you in a couple of weeks."

"I've been in LA for the last week and a half," Hunter admitted. "I actually just got back in town last night. I was at LAX when you texted me about this project yesterday."

Pierce eyed his friend. "I don't know why you don't just use your dad's jet instead of flying commercial. I hate airports. The crowds, the lines, people who run on the moving sidewalks. It's a pain in the ass."

"I agree. But I also think flying the private jet around just because I can would be super fucking wasteful." He scratched his chin. "Besides, I was in LA with my out-west crew filming for that documentary I'm working on. You know, the one about people of color in the clean energy industry?"

He snapped his fingers. "Oh, yeah. I remember you mentioning that."

"Exactly. Now, how would it look for me to arrive there on a private jet?"

Pierce cringed. "I see your point. Did you get all the footage you needed while you were gone?"

"I think I'm good for that segment. Now it's up to my post-production folks to chop and screw it into a cohesive film." Hunter sank back into the cushions. "Now that I'm back in town, I can go back to working with the volunteers at my arts camp."

"You really enjoy that, don't you?"

"Absolutely," Hunter said. "My dad owns seven car dealerships all over the South—I can spend my time however I like. And other than filmmaking, I really enjoy influencing the next generation of artists."

Pierce sipped his coffee, enjoying the richness of the brew. "See, that's why you and I are still friends. So many of the people we went to private school with have gone on to do big things and have paid very little of it forward to the community."

Hunter shook his head. "Not just the private school crowd, either. Even some of the grads from our class at Clark Atlanta have moved away and just forgotten about A-Town."

"Not us, though," Pierce sighed. "I could never turn my back on the city that raised me. That's why the minute I had some sway in the building at Hamilton House, I instituted that fund to keep music education in schools."

They sat in congenial silence for a few moments while they finished their coffee.

Sitting his mug on the table, Hunter clapped his hands together. "Anything interesting happening with you?"

Pierce shook his head. "You know me. I've just been working and working out."

Hunter laughed, shaking his head. "I'm sure I don't have to tell you there's more to life than those two things."

"You don't. But I've been doing so much to increase profits and holdings at Hamilton House. And when I'm not doing that, my mom or my sister will inevitably draft me to participate in whatever project they have going on." He threw up his hands. "That's the whole reason I'm here right now. If Mom hadn't come up with this retrospective thing, I might be doing something that resembles having a social life."

Hunter snorted. "Sorry, man. Well, at least you know somebody who can get this thing shot and edited for you without taking up too much of your time."

"You're my one saving grace, bruh." Pierce shook his head.

"Let's go over to the green screen, and we can just start filming. I've got some questions that your mother sent over, so we'll start with you answering those."

"She didn't send over anything weird or embarrassing, did she?" He couldn't help wondering if his mother had set him up to discuss some embarrassing childhood occurrence to up the entertainment value of the piece.

"Not really, but if we come across something you don't wanna talk about, I won't press you. And remember, we're gonna edit this before anyone else sees it." Hunter activated the studio lighting, then went to the prop closet and returned with a single stool, which he set up in front of the green screen.

Seated on the stool, Pierce took a deep breath.

Hunter wheeled out a tripod with a high-tech film camera mounted to it. After playing with the positioning for a few moments, he asked, "Ready?"

Pierce nodded. "Yeah."

Hunter engaged the camera, then took a folded piece of paper from his pocket. "Today, we're here with Pierce Hamilton, director of growth and acquisitions for Hamilton House Recordings. So, Pierce, tell us about tripping over someone's skateboard and falling face-first into the punch bowl at your senior prom."

Pierce felt his jaw drop open. "Man, if you don't—"

His friend laughed. "I'm playing. Just a little ice-breaker."

Eyeing his old buddy, Pierce demanded, "Delete that footage!"

Four

Thursday morning, Nia approached a two-top table near the front of The Bodacious Bean. She placed her steaming mug of dark chocolate mint mocha and the accompanying sandwich on the table and set her Hermès clutch and attaché bag on the windowsill to her immediate left.

Settling into her seat, she took a long sip of her drink and sighed. *I live for mint-mocha season, and nobody makes them like* the staff here. Every year, as soon as the air got crisp, she got a craving for the rich, dark beverage.

She took a bite of her sandwich, and her rumbling stomach rejoiced at the crisp bacon, chewy bagel and perfectly fried egg white.

While she was savoring her breakfast, she glanced up at the tinkling of the bell over the entrance door just in time to see her sister Teagan stroll in. Teagan's long burgundy tunic, matching slacks with gold embroidery and glittery gold ballet flats were typical of what she wore to work. Nia had always lovingly referred to her sister's style as "astrologer chic."

Teagan's flowy outfit stood very much in contrast to Nia's navy slacks, red cashmere sweater and navy pumps with a red toe box. Their extreme difference in style was one of the things Nia loved about their relationship. She knew for a fact she and her little sister would never show up to a function in the same outfit.

She turned her attention back to her own food while Teagan ordered. When Teagan appeared at the table a few minutes later with her croissant and steaming cup in hand, she set the items down before settling into the empty chair. "Morning, sis."

"Hey, Teagan. What are you drinking today?"

"Honey citrus green tea. I think I overdid it on the caffeine yesterday, and I'm still a little wired." She took a tentative sip. "I don't have to ask what you're drinking. I can smell the mint already."

Nia laughed. "What can I say? I'm a creature of habit."

They munched and drank quietly for a few minutes. When Nia finished up the last of her sandwich, she tucked the ceramic plate under her mug and slid the dishes to the left. Grabbing her tablet from its case, she set it on the table. She removed her trusty fine-point stylus from its hiding spot at the base of her high bun and asked, "Ready to talk shop?"

Teagan chuckled. "Why did you have that thing in your hair?"

Nia shrugged. "So far, it's the best way I've found to keep up with it. Before I started tucking it into my hair, I'd already lost four of my custom-made ergonomic fine-tip styluses."

"Whatever works, I guess." Teagan used a paper napkin to brush away a few flaky pastry crumbs from the front of her tunic, then set her mini laptop on the table and opened it. "What's up first?"

Nia swiped over her tablet screen. "The tech intern program you brought up in the meeting. Let's talk about your proposal."

"So, you've read it already?"

She nodded. "Sure did. I really love the idea, and I think it's a great investment for two reasons. One, it looks good for 404 to be doing charity work, and this is a nice expansion on what Miles already has going on. And two, we could possibly gain some well-trained future employees for our trouble, so it could really be seen as an investment toward 404's long-term profitability."

Teagan grinned. "Awesome. I'm glad you can see the benefits. Now, are you gonna approve the funding so I can get this program started?"

"Absolutely." Nia scrolled down the document containing the notes she'd made regarding the proposal Teagan had submitted. "I can fund the program at ninety percent of what you're asking."

Teagan looked thoughtful for a few moments, then starting typing. "That seems fair. I'll do my best to get things done with what you're allocating."

"Great. If you find it insufficient, I'd suggest getting with Miles and coordinating a fundraiser to make up the difference." Nia finished the last of her mocha. "You're resourceful, though. You can probably get it done without doing too much extra."

"I appreciate your faith in me, sis." Teagan pushed a fallen curl out of her face, tucking it behind her ear. "Now, what's going on with the new studio building? I know all that preliminary stuff technically falls under Gage's domain, but since I'm the master of the studios…"

"Yes, I get it. I don't mind telling you what's going on. I know the curiosity must be bugging you by now." She navigated to another document on her tablet and turned it around for her sister to see. "I haven't made my final choice on the blueprints yet, but I'm leaning toward this one."

Teagan's eyes widened. "Wow, this is really nice. I love the setup."

"So do I. I mean, we only took bids from green and sustainable builders, but I feel like this company took that to the nth degree. See that fountain in the court-yard?"

Teagan nodded. "Yeah. Nice choice, having a bass and treble clef as a sculptural water feature."

"It's not just pretty—it's functional. The fountain is designed to catch rainwater and circulate it into an ir-rigation system for the flower beds, and it uses a nearly invisible scrim to reduce evaporation."

"That's pretty next level."

"Yeah, I agree." She turned the tablet back toward herself, then set it on the table. "I know it's off topic, but I have to ask. Did you know about Dad's little scheme?"

"The retrospective? I just found out about it yesterday. Gage told me."

She chuckled. "So Dad still has other people explaining his actions." Shaking her head, she said, "I don't necessarily think it's a bad idea. But the timing is trash. We have so little time before the gala to get it ready."

"True. He definitely could have given y'all a little more notice."

"And I can't believe he thought it would be a good idea to pair me with Pierce Hamilton." Nia rolled her eyes. "Even though our interactions have been pretty limited, I've never been fond of him."

"I'm sorry you got stuck doing a group project with somebody you're not a fan of, sis. But try not to be too ornery about it."

"Why aren't I entitled to my irritation?"

"You are, but you're gonna have to temper it just a bit," Teagan chuckled. "Remember, this is Dad we're talking about. I doubt he has any concept of your feelings about Pierce. He just hatched a plan and drafted the two people he thought most capable of carrying it out."

Nia frowned. "You're probably right." It was their father's typical way. He'd never been known to consider interpersonal relationships or their status when it came to anything to do with business. His motto was "suck it up until the job's done."

"Gage says Pierce has some filmmaker friend," Teagan remarked. "Maybe his connection will make the process quick and easy for you both."

"Let's hope so. I don't want to spend too much of my time on this little side quest." She leaned back in her chair. "There are still so many other things to do related to the gala, and with Mom out of town, that just means more work for me."

"Chin up, sis. The gala will be here before we know it, and then we can finally exhale." Teagan closed her laptop. "Plus, remember, we still have our final dress fittings coming up, and you know how much you love custom couture, girl."

Sensing the teasing in her sister's tone, Nia smiled. "You're right, sis. Me in a fly-ass dress is definitely something to look forward to."

"Hey, big head."

Pierce looked up from the papers he'd been staring at and narrowed his eyes at his twin sister, who stood in his office doorway. "London, why are you in here bothering me?"

She sidled into the room and plopped into the guest chair on the opposite side of his desk. "Stop acting like you don't love me, lil bro."

He sighed. "Seven minutes, London. You are older than me by seven minutes."

She shrugged. "Still older, though. I don't make the rules, Pierce."

He leaned back in his chair. "So, are you gonna tell me what you want, or...?"

She laughed. "Alright, I guess I've teased you enough for now." Settling into her chair and tossing one leg over the other, she said, "How's your little project with Nia Woodson going?"

He frowned. "I literally just started working on it yesterday, and already you're in my face being nosy about it?"

"Absolutely!" London grinned, swiping a hand over her mass of curls. "What else am I supposed to do for entertainment around this joint?"

"You could, I don't know, do some actual work?"

She scoffed. "Listen. As director of publicity, you best believe I work plenty hard. Anyway, just answer me. How's the project going? You and the 404 lady butting heads yet?"

He shook his head. "We haven't spent enough time together to do that. I saw her Tuesday when I went over there with Mom. That meeting lasted maybe thirty minutes. She was all too eager to get back to her office, and I haven't seen her since."

"But Mom gave you time off yesterday to work on it. So what were you doing then?" She paused, eyes wide. "Don't tell me you didn't do what Mom asked."

He stared. "London, if you must know, I was at Hunter's house. We worked on filming my confessional scenes for the film." He paused. "Which makes me think, you probably need to go over there and film some as well."

She recoiled. "No. Pierce, you know I'm camera shy."

"Come on, London. Don't you want your memories from being raised by a strong, successful Black woman to be preserved for posterity?"

She drew in a deep breath, then exhaled slowly. "I hate it when you talk sense." She burrowed her fingertips into her curls at the temple, as she often did when agitated or stressed. "Gimme a little time to get my story straight, and I'll set up something with Hunter. Tell your friend he's gotta do whatever he's gonna do in fifteen minutes or less, because after that, I'm out."

"Don't worry. He's been friends with me long enough to know how shaky you are on camera," Pierce quipped. "I'm sure he won't prolong your suffering."

"We'll see." She paused, then snapped her fingers as if remembering something. "Oh, yeah. I did come in here to tell you something. Guess who's coming to visit soon?"

He shrugged. "I don't know. Besides, I don't think it's exactly fair of you to make me guess after you spent all this time bugging me."

She laughed again. "Fine, I'll tell you. Uncle Martin is coming."

He sat forward in his chair. "Really? We haven't seen Uncle Martin in, what, two years now?"

"Yeah, that's about right. Anyway, I was with Mom when he called this morning, and I overheard his plans to visit and stay with us through the Thanksgiving holiday."

He smiled at the thought of his father's younger brother, who was easily his favorite uncle. Easygoing and funny, Martin Hamilton could always be counted on to infuse any situation with equal measures of wisdom and humor. "When is he coming?"

"I didn't hear that part, but I know he'll be here before Thanksgiving." London grinned. "You know what that means, right?"

He eyed her, letting his confusion show.

"You want the CEO slot. Everybody in the building

knows it. And if there's any outside force that can convince Mom to let you have it, it's Uncle Martin."

He stroked his chin, considering his sister's words. "That's true. He's about the only person on Earth that Mom will take advice from." Their mother was headstrong and had been that way as long as he could remember. She loved being in control, and if she ever had doubts when it came to her choices, she never let it show. He studied London's face. "Wait, why are you telling me this? Don't you want the top spot?"

She waved her hand, flashing a crystal-adorned bright yellow manicure. "Dude. We're twins, and you should know me better than that. I don't dream of labor. I have way more responsibility than I want already in publicity. You are welcome to the CEO position, honestly."

"Have you ever told Mom that?"

She shook her head. "Nah. We don't talk much about work outside the office."

He rolled his eyes. "You do know that if you told her how you feel, it might move the needle in my favor."

She appeared to consider that. "Maybe. At any rate, Uncle Martin's endorsement would hold way more weight than mine." She stood, stretched her arms above her head. "Well, I guess I'll get back to work now."

"Good. That means I can, too."

She disappeared from the room then, leaving him alone with his thoughts. He knew he needed to get back to the paperwork he'd been doing when she came in, but instead, he found himself in a contemplative mood.

Leaning back in his chair, he considered his uncle's impending visit, and his sister's declaration of disinterest in succeeding their mother as CEO of Hamilton House. *Things might finally be lining up so I can take over the company.*

His mind switched gears then, and Nia's beautiful face drifted into his thoughts. He had no idea how someone so ethereally lovely could appear so stern, or why, despite her less-than-sunny disposition, he found her so irresistible.

Is she always like that? Or does she save that energy for me? With any other woman, he'd have probably been wounded by her hasty retreat. His ego told him that at least some of that could be chalked up to her position. She was in charge and likely had a million things requiring her attention.

His phone pinged then, and he checked the screen. A reminder appeared for tomorrow's awards ceremony, hosted by the Greater Atlanta Metro Business Society or GAMBS as it was known. He was accepting an award for his charitable work and knew from the promotional material that Nia would be there to accept an award of her own as well.

I'm really looking forward to seeing her, especially all dolled up. He did his best to shake that thought away. Now that things were falling into place, he needed to put his full focus on winning the CEO position.

That meant he didn't have the time to focus on pursuing a woman, no matter how enchanting she was.

Five

Friday evening, Nia found herself frantically searching the floors of her house, seeking her other earring. Her two-story converted duplex in Inman Park had always seemed cozy to her. But now, her place suddenly seemed much larger.

Dressed in matching navy lace longline strapless bra and bikini panties, she knelt on the floor next to the chaise at the foot of her bed. "Aha!" She grabbed the sapphire-and-diamond teardrop embedded in the white carpet. Taking a seat on the chaise, she hurried to put her earrings on. She usually did that after she was dressed but thought to do it before she could misplace one or both of them again.

Blowing out a breath, she went to the closet door and took down the dress she planned to wear to the GAMBS

Stars of Charity ceremony. Normally, she would have been able to simply attend and watch as her brother accepted the award, since all charitable work at 404 Sound fell under his purview. But with Miles still away enjoying his island honeymoon, the duty of accepting the award now fell to her.

There's a difference between attending one of these events and actually having to go up onstage where everyone can see you. She lay the dress across her bed and unzipped the back so she could step into it. Once she had it on, she used the specialty long-handled zipper tool Teagan had given her a few birthdays ago to zip it up. Nia looked at her reflection in the oval mirror over her French provincial vanity.

Damn, girl. She smiled, taking in the clean lines of the cobalt-blue sheath dress. It was midi length and featured a fashionable asymmetric neckline that bared her right shoulder. A beautiful, ruffled flounce accented the left shoulder, and the soft fabric felt like butter against her skin.

Seated on the vanity's plush stool, she applied her favorite base and foundation, then added a deep blue smoky eye and a shimmery nude lip. Her hairdresser had styled her hair in an elegant high bun earlier, so now she simply removed the pins she'd used to preserve the curly tendrils left out around her temple.

Satisfied with her look, she slipped her feet into a pair of blue suede pumps accented with crystals at the toe. Grabbing her shimmery blue wrap and matching clutch, she tucked her phone and small wallet inside, then took her keys from the hook near her front door.

She exited the house just after dusk, and the briskness of the night air made her quicken her steps as she went to her black luxury sedan. The wrap protected her arms from the elements, but not her bare legs.

I'd rather freeze than be trapped in pantyhose. She'd hated the things for years and always chose a stellar leg wax and proper moisturization over those nylon torture devices.

Shutting herself inside the car, she started the engine and immediately cranked the heat in hopes of chasing away the chill in the cabin. Checking her mirrors, she backed out of the driveway and carefully merged into traffic.

The drive from her neighborhood to the Atlanta Marriot Marquis took around twenty minutes, and she was glad she'd left work early to prepare. The extra time helped her arrive fifteen minutes before the festivities were set to begin, and she knew she'd need that time to navigate the huge hotel and find her table in the ballroom.

The inside of the cavernous ballroom had been beautifully decorated for the affair. Soft lavender light illuminated dozens of round tables covered in white cloth, each seating about ten people. Tall, elegant floral arrangements of orchids and calla lilies centered each table, and gleaming china and silverware marked each place setting.

Her eyes scanned the space for the table assigned to 404. She grinned when she spotted Teagan, who was standing and flagging her toward the table with mannerisms that made her look like an extremely overdressed air traffic controller. Shaking her head, Nia wove her way through the tables and few clustered groups of attendees until she got there.

"They've got us really close to the stage, haven't they?" Nia commented as she walked up.

"Makes sense, considering you'll have to go up there." Gage stood and slid out one of the four empty chairs at the table for his older sister.

"Thanks, Gage." She sat down and placed her clutch on her lap. Glancing around the table, she greeted everyone present. There were her brothers, Gage and Blaine, and her brother-in-law Maxton, all in dark suits of varying hues. Then there was her sister Teagan, her sister-in law Ainsley and the deeply pregnant Eden, all dressed in feminine finery of their own. Seeing them all assembled there made the absence of their parents feel all the more real. "So, Blaine, I'm guessing you couldn't convince Dad to come."

He shook his head, straightening his bow tie. "I tried. But bringing up the ceremony got him started on a diatribe about how he hates these type of events—they're dull and pretentious, and a waste of money for the organization." He straightened his bow tie. "I just walked out and left him there, grousing."

Nia sighed. "He could have just said no."

"You know Dad," Teagan interjected. "He loves to give a lecture, and sometimes I think he just can't help himself."

Maxton took a sip from his champagne glass. "I just love how even after a fifteen-city tour with Jazmine Sullivan, I can still expect there to be some excitement going on when I get home."

Nia laughed. *He's not wrong. We Woodsons always seem to have some kind of drama going on.* Silence fell at the table as waiters began to serve them food. There was a salad course, then plates of herb-roasted chicken, saffron rice and garlic green beans, with a luscious red-velvet cheesecake for dessert. Conversation flowed easily between everyone at the table while they ate.

Soon, the awards portion of the evening began. A regal dark-skinned woman in a black sequined gown approached the podium, introducing herself as Dr. Grace Hutchinson, president of the GAMBS. "I'm so honored to present tonight's first award, the Bright Futures Award, to 404 Sound Recordings for their outstanding support of Atlanta's youth. CEO Nia Woodson will accept the plaque on behalf of her family's company."

Nia rose from her seat and was helped onto the stage by an usher to the sounds of applause filling the room. She accepted the large mahogany plaque, sharing a brief hug with Dr. Hutchinson before speaking into the microphone. "On behalf of my parents, Caleb and Addison Woodson, my many siblings and all the people who make 404 tick, I'd like to thank the Greater Atlanta Metro Business Society for this prestigious award. 404 will continue to honor our commitment to making life better for the young people of our city. Thank you again." More applause sounded as she returned to her seat. When she sat down and carefully placed the plaque into the empty seat next to her, she heard a musical cue that drew her attention to the onstage projection screen.

Two pictures appeared on the screen. One was of her, apparently taken from the 404 website, and the other was an image of Pierce Hamilton.

Her eyes narrowed.

The volume of the music lowered, and the voice of the emcee sounded over the images. "GAMBS is proud to announce its sponsorship of *404 Perspectives*, an innovative film retrospective on the fascinating story of the city's most storied recording studio. A collaborative effort of Nia Woodson and Pierce Hamilton, the film will debut at the thirty-fifth anniversary gala for 404 Sound, to be held later this month."

Nia frowned. *Shit.*

Any hopes she had of bailing out of her father's pet project were dashed. Because now, the entire city of Atlanta knew about it and would be expecting its results.

Every seat at the Hamilton House table was occupied. Pierce's mother sat to his right and his sister to his left. The rest of the group included Rupert and Martin from the New York office, Ravyn and Marcel from the Houston office and three shareholders to whom he'd been introduced earlier but whose names now escaped him.

When Nia had walked up to accept her award, he'd been blown away by her appearance. She looked absolutely gorgeous in her blue dress, and her upswept hair and sparkling earrings framed her face perfectly. She'd kept her speech brief before returning to her seat, and she appeared a bit overwhelmed by the applause she'd received from the assemblage.

She was barely in her seat when the video began to play onstage, and he watched it with a mixture of interest and surprise. It lasted around two minutes, and when it ended, Pierce turned to his mother. "What was that?"

"I set that up."

"The sponsorship, or the video announcing it?" London asked as she leaned in a bit.

"Both. It's great publicity for Hamilton House, and our shareholders agree with me on that." She gestured toward the three smiling men across the table from her.

Pierce could only shake his head. "Why didn't you tell me about this?"

Everly shrugged. "I figured it would just be a pleasant surprise."

Mom's nothing if not consistent. She settles on something, consults no one and just does it. "If you say so." He looked back at the 404 table and couldn't help noticing the tight, displeased expression on Nia's face. It was similar to the way she'd looked in the conference room a few days ago, but a bit more intense.

The ceremony continued, with more awards and speeches interspersed with sponsored-content videos. Pierce soon grew bored with the entire affair. Despite the money and effort invested by the organization into making the ceremony entertaining, he found the only thing in the room that really held his attention was Nia. Time and time again, his gaze returned to her. He watched her take a long sip from her champagne, admiring the graceful way her fingertips wrapped around the stem of the flute as she brought it to her glossy lips—

"Pierce!" London snapped her fingers in front of his face. "Don't you hear me talking?"

He turned her way. "No, I didn't hear you. What did you say?"

"I said, according to the program, your award should

be coming up next." She gave him a pinch on the shoulder. "Pay attention, space cadet."

He rolled his eyes at his sister's scolding, but one look in his mother's direction made him sober up. "I'm listening for my name. Trust me."

Sure enough, a few minutes later, Dr. Hutchinson began speaking about the importance of arts education. "Atlanta is a cradle and an incubator for some of the country's most talented artists, across mediums. We've produced great rap artists, singers, filmmakers, actors and so much more. So it's wonderful when our local businesses take an interest in preserving Atlanta's tradition of excellence in the arts. The Arts Advocacy Award this year goes to Hamilton House Uplift, the company's non-profit organization, for their initiative that funds music education for the youth of our city. Director of Growth and Acquisitions Pierce Hamilton will accept the award on the company's behalf."

Pierce stood, met by thunderous applause as he strode toward the stage. As he reached the podium and gave Dr. Hutchinson a hug, he accepted the heavy plaque and set it on the podium surface. Leaning into the microphone, he began the speech he'd memorized for the occasion.

"I'd like to extend my thanks to the Greater Atlanta Metro Business Society on behalf of all of us at Hamilton House. We are beyond honored to receive such a recognition." He paused for a smattering of applause. "I'd like to tell you why we're so determined to offer support and funding to our fellow ATLiens. Last week, I visited a middle school. It is one of the twenty-five schools where Hamilton House Uplift is the sole provider of funding for their music program. There, I met a seventh grader named Nathaniel. He plays drums in the school band. I sat in the classroom with him. I listened to him play. I saw the determination on his face as he tried his best to keep cadence." Pierce stepped back from the podium, the mic in his hand as he stared out over the crowd. "After practice, he told me about how difficult his home life has been, and how drumming provides an outlet for the rather complicated emotions he experiences." He paused. "And that is why I do it. If I can have a positive impact on these kids and young adults and, in turn, the city itself, then I'll do everything I can to help them. Thank you."

A few enthusiastic cheers sounded, and as they began to swell, the crowd gave Pierce a standing ovation. Standing on the stage, he pressed his hand to his heart and offered a low bow before taking the plaque and departing.

Headed down the four steps to the ballroom floor, he initially headed for his table. But instead, he tucked the plaque under his arm and made a quick turn to the 404 table. All eyes were on him as he approached and stood between Nia and her sister.

"Evening, folks." Turning his attention to Nia, he said, "Just wanted to congratulate you on your award."

She shifted her gaze up to meet his face, her eyes narrowed slightly. "Thank you. Congratulations to you, as well."

"Thanks."

Still eyeing him, she asked, "Are you the one behind that video announcing the retrospective film?"

He shook his head. "The first time I knew of it was just now, when it was played onstage. But my mother has claimed responsibility for it."

"Humph." She opened her mouth, forming an *O* and letting a rush of air escape. "I knew I'd have to be up onstage, but I wasn't expecting to be put on the spot like that."

"Neither was I," he admitted, resting his hand on the back of her chair. "At any rate, we've got to make this film amazing. The entire city of Atlanta is now waiting on the results of our little collaboration. Can't disappoint them."

She said nothing, instead picking up her flute and finishing the small amount of champagne inside. "You know, it's very bold of you to flirt with me like this, in the middle of an event and in front of my family."

He sensed the eyes of her brother on him and smiled. "I won't stay much longer. I'm sure the Woodson men won't stand to have you accosted. And that's as it should be." He took a step back and offered a bow. "I'll see you soon then, Nia."

A small smile showed on her face. "Go on back to your table, Pierce Hamilton."

He turned and walked away, well-aware of the teasing tone of her dismissal.

She's not quite as frosty as she'd like me to believe. Working with her should be very, very entertaining.

Six

Nia awoke Saturday morning and slowly raised herself to a sitting position in bed. The all-white linens practically glowed in the sunlight streaming through her window, and she stifled a yawn as she climbed from beneath the fluffy cocoon of her covers and shuffled to the bathroom.

She emerged a bit later, clean and dry. Inside her walk-in closet, she slipped into a pair of panties, an old faded T-shirt and a pair of baggy black sweatpants. Jamming her feet into fuzzy slippers, she left the closet and headed down the stairs to the kitchen.

She made herself a quick breakfast of fruity cereal and toast. When she was done, she made a cup of coffee and carried it upstairs.

Opening the door to the room across from the master,

she stepped into her art studio and inhaled. The faint scent of acrylic paint from her last session still lingered in the air. The room was sparsely furnished, save for a drafting table, a flat rectangular table with a small easel set up atop it and the seven-foot easel, which sat in the center of the room. A leather-cushioned stool on wheels rested near the large easel.

She walked across the hardwood floors, headed for the supply wall.

She'd had sixteen cube-shaped storage shelves built into the wall facing the door back when she'd purchased the duplex, and it was in these shelves that she stored all her art supplies. Tubes and tins of paints, brushes, knives and scrapers and stacks of the small canvases she used for some of her projects filled the shelves, along with a few silk plants placed here and there for aesthetic purposes.

She perused the shelves for a minute until she found the old photograph she planned on using for the art piece she would start today. She'd dropped her phone at her parents' house a few weeks back and, in retrieving it, had stumbled across the old Polaroid photograph in a dusty corner of the living room. Struck by artistic inspiration, she'd tucked it into her purse.

Odds are Mom and Dad forgot this photo ever existed. Anyway, I'll give it back to them once I finish my piece.

With the photo in hand, she began gathering her supplies. She chose a few old magazines, some newspaper shreds and a few other odds and ends for what she planned to be an ambitious mixed-media image. Then she gathered her paint and palette, brushes and scissors. Laying all her tools out on the flat table, she organized them around the photograph, which she placed carefully in the center.

She moved her large easel closer to the table, then set up the forty-inch square canvas she'd purchased. Seated on her wheeled stool, she used a pencil to roughly sketch out the lines of the image she was recreating, pausing now and again to sip her coffee.

She was nearly halfway done with her base sketch when the ringing of her phone caught her attention. Reaching into her pants pocket, she slid out the phone and answered it. "Hello?"

"Good morning, Nia. It's Mom."

She smiled at the announcement. *As if I wouldn't recognize her voice.* "Morning, Mom. How are you?" Activating the speakerphone, she set the device in her easel's tray.

"I'm fine, sweetheart. What's new with you?"

"You know me. Work, work, work." She narrowed her eyes at a small area on the canvas and flipped her pencil to erase the last short line she'd drawn. "When are you coming home? We miss you."

"I know. Don't worry, I'll be home soon." She paused. "So, there's really nothing interesting happening down there? Nothing you want to talk about?"

"Not really." She focused on redrawing a clean line to replace the one she'd erased. "I'd rather hear about you. How are things in Charlotte? How's Aunt Laurie?"

"Charlotte is gentrifying, and my sister is just fine."

Addy's tone changed. "But what's this I hear about you working on a project with Pierce Hamilton?"

She cringed. "Mom, how do you even know about that?"

"Don't be answering my question with a question, young lady," Addy admonished. "Now tell me what's going on."

Sensing that she'd better start explaining, she gave her mother a brief rundown of the retrospective film project. "This was all Dad's idea, not mine."

Addy exhaled. "That figures. It's just like Caleb to hatch a scheme like this without thinking it through from all angles."

Pausing to sharpen her graphite pencil, she asked, "What do you mean by that?"

"I mean, Pierce Hamilton is a notorious playboy. I'm sure he's already got his eye on you."

She returned to drawing on the canvas. "Maybe so, but I'm not a fan of Pierce's. He's a little too sure of himself for my tastes."

"I'm glad you feel that way, because as I heard it, he's flirting with you."

She paused, tucking her pencil into her messy bun. "Let me guess. You talked to Teagan last night?"

"Sure did, and she told me he was all in your grill."

"Yikes, Mom. Not you with the early-aughts slang."

"I'm just repeating what your sister told me," Addy laughed. "All I know is, Pierce isn't the type to just give up on something that's caught his interest. This little collaboration between you two could turn into something unexpected if you're not careful."

She took a deep breath, staring at the canvas in front of her but not really seeing the lines anymore. "Mom, trust me. I plan on spending the shortest amount of time possible with Pierce to get this film thing finished. There's so much going on with the gala, and with Miles already out and Blaine set to start paternity leave any day now, I definitely don't have time for whatever fool-ishness Pierce has in mind."

"Mmm-hmm."

Nia let her head drop back, recognizing the sound. "Come on, Mom. That's your signature 'if you say so' sound. Are you saying you don't think I can handle my-self around Pierce?"

"No, of course not. I raised you better than that." Addy paused. "All I'm saying is, be careful. It's easy to get comfortable and let your guard down when you're working with someone one-on-one. Just be mindful of that."

"I will. And now that we've had this conversation, I'll be even more vigilant." She held out her hands in front of her, flexing her fingers to relieve the tension in them. "Anything else you wanna talk about, Mom?"

"Just one more thing. I'll be taking an evening flight home on Monday. Would you mind picking me up at the airport?"

"No problem. Just text me your flight details," she said. "Why didn't you say that earlier, instead of tell-ing me you'd be home soon?"

"I wanted to get right down to the nitty-gritty, and I knew the whole airport thing could wait," Addy laughed.

Nia found herself chuckling right along with her mother. "You are something else, Mom."

"I know I am. Aren't you glad?"

"Honestly? Yes." She had many associates who lamented their broken or less-than-ideal relationships with their mothers. But the bond she shared with Addy was a balm and a respite from a world in near-constant chaos. "I'll see you soon, Mom."

"You rushing me off the phone?" Addy posed the question in a tone of mock offense.

"I sure am," she quipped. "I'm in my studio working on a piece."

"Alright, I'll let you get back to it. Love you, Nia Bear."

She smiled at the sound of her childhood nickname. "I love you, too, Mom."

Disconnecting the call, she returned to her sketching, setting aside her mother's warning about Pierce.

Just because he's handsome, wealthy and used to getting his way, doesn't mean he's gonna get his way with me. After all, there's a first time for everything.

Late Sunday morning, Pierce descended the spiral wrought iron staircase inside his two-story condo in Atlanta's artsy Cabbagetown neighborhood. The condo occupied the upper two floors of the building and had come with a hefty price tag, but since he thoroughly enjoyed his easy access to the rooftop pool and lounge area as well as the thriving neighborhood around him, he considered his home a sound investment.

He strolled into his kitchen and opened the fridge,

grabbing a cold bottle of water. Unscrewing the cap, he strode to his cream sofa and sat down, taking a swig from the bottle. The white marble fireplace directly across from the sofa supported a matching mantel, above which he'd mounted a fifty-inch flat-screen television. Grabbing the remote, he turned on the TV.

He was half listening to a sportscaster giving the latest football stats when his phone buzzed. Checking the screen, he saw the single-word text from Hunter.

Downstairs.

Shaking his head, he marveled at his good friend's brevity. *The way Hunter composes his texts, you'd think he was sending them over the telegraph wire.*

Taking a moment to finish up his water, he crushed the bottle and tossed it into the recycle bin in the kitchen. Then he grabbed his keys, tucked his wallet and phone into the back pocket of his jeans and left to meet Hunter.

When he got to the parking lot, his eyes grew wide as he spotted his friend at the curb. Dressed in a green polo and black jeans, Hunter leaned casually against a sleek black ride Pierce didn't recognize.

"Wow. New ride?"

Hunter shook his head. "I wish, man. Dad let me drive it just for the day. Wants to get my views on the finer points of this beauty to decide if he wants to sell them at our lots."

His brow rose. "Still trying to groom you to take over the family business, isn't he?"

Hunter offered a nod, his expression rueful. "Yep. No matter how many times I tell him I only want to drive cars, not sell them, he never seems to hear me." He shrugged. "Maybe one day he'll take my filmmaking seriously."

Approaching the car, Pierce admired the clean, angular lines and the slight shimmer of the paint. He whistled. "This car is immaculate."

Opening the driver's door, Hunter reached inside the car. The cloth roof began to fold until it was fully back, revealing a bright red leather interior with black piping and gold accents. "It's way too chilly out to leave the top down, but I just wanted you to see her in her full glory."

He grinned. "It's beautiful. I'd buy one myself, but I know Mother would only use that as evidence I'm not ready to be CEO."

As the roof raised and settled back in place, Hunter asked, "Why? What does a car have to do with your leadership abilities?"

"As far as I'm concerned, nothing. But my mother would see it as a frivolous purchase of a flashy toy, a sign of bad judgment and whatever other negative assumptions she can fathom."

"Damn." Hunter climbed into the car. "Hop in, bro. Let's take this thing out for a spin."

He got into the passenger seat and belted himself in moments before his friend hit the accelerator, zipping away from the curb and out of the parking lot.

As they put more distance between them and the old brick warehouse in Cabbagetown, Pierce took in the familiar urban beauty of his hometown. They traveled southeast Decatur Street, traversing the Oakland neighborhood and its historic namesake cemetery where many famous Atlantans had been laid to rest. As they continued over the bustling gridlock of I-85 and into downtown, Hunter broke the silence in the car. "I thought we'd grab lunch. You cool with Jamaican?"

He nodded. "I think I know where you're headed, and I'm absolutely cool with it." The mere mention of food had his stomach rumbling. Breakfast was now a few hours in the past.

In a short while, Hunter navigated into the small parking lot in front of the squat South Downtown building housing Dat Fire Jerk Chicken. The yellow, lime and black color scheme of the exterior replicated the Jamaican flag. And while it wasn't big or fancy, the food was among the best to be had in the city when one craved a little spice.

They left with a huge bag of food and two sodas, and Hunter drove them to his place in Morningside to enjoy the bounty. Inside his kitchen, Hunter set out their food and handed Pierce a stack of napkins and some plastic utensils.

Pierce opened the plastic lids of his foil containers and took a deep inhale, enjoying the aroma of his jerk chicken wings, rice and peas, and cabbage salad.

Hunter was already elbow deep in his jerk chicken cheese fries. "It's been way too long since I've had some of this."

"Same. Let's not make that mistake again." He grabbed a wing and dug in.

After they'd filled their stomachs and gotten rid of

their trash, they headed for the comfort of the living room sofa.

"If I sit here too long, I'm going to sleep," Pierce declared.

Hunter shook his head. "No, you're not, because you need to be awake to tell me what's going on with you and Nia Woodson."

"Do you mean, as it relates to the film?"

Hunter eyes him. "I mean, as it relates to everything. I watched some of the livestream of that awards ceremony online. I saw you stop at her table after you got your award. What were you two talking about?"

Pierce shook his head. "I forgot they were streaming it. Sheesh." With a sigh, he admitted, "There's not a whole lot to tell. I congratulated her on her award and let her know I looked forward to our collaboration... and so does the city, now that the word's out."

"And how did she react?"

"She was still a little standoffish, but I managed to get a smile out of her before I went back to my table," he chuckled. "If I'd stayed much longer, I'm pretty sure one of the Woodson men would have escorted me away."

"I don't doubt it," Hunter laughed. "Word on the street is that those guys don't play when it comes to their ladies."

"Well, I'm not trying to test that out." Pierce remembered the way they'd stared him down, a subtle nonverbal warning that they wouldn't stand to have Nia harassed or bothered in any way. "I plan on meeting up with her this week so we can get some real momentum this project."

"You should—time's ticking. I've already sent your confessional footage to be edited, and I expect it back in a day or so." Hunter tucked a fallen loc back into his ponytail. "That means I need to get some footage from her soon if we're going to wrap this up in time for the gala."

"Yeah. And it has to be done in time. If it isn't, I'll never hear the end of it."

"Listen. I'd say your best bet is to make this film the best thing ever, and really play up your family's legacy. I think that might help your case with Mrs. H." Hunter tapped his chin. "Deep down, I think she wants to pass the baton to you, bro. I think she's just looking for reassurance before she does."

"You might be right." He thought about Nia, about the brief smile that had lit her face and the warmth he'd felt inside as a result.

If I can spend time getting to know this intriguing, gorgeous woman while doing something that might work in my favor with Mother, that seems like a win to me.

Seven

As she stood in line at the counter of The Bodacious Bean, Nia stifled what felt like her hundredth yawn of the morning. Shifting her weight from her left to her right foot, she kept a tenuous hold on her patience as the older lady in front of her asked question after question about how milk came from almonds.

She sighed. *Just another manic Monday, I guess. I wish this lady would hurry up, though. I need caffeine like I need my next breath at this point.*

Last night, she'd been so caught up in a creative frenzy that she'd stayed up well past her usual bedtime to work on her mixed-media piece. Now, with the shards of sunlight penetrating the dark lenses of her sunglasses, she could clearly see the error in her decision to eschew rest in favor of her art. Mercifully, the older woman finally got sufficient answers about almond milk, as well as her nondairy latte. As she shuffled aside with her mug, Nia took one large step to approach the counter.

"Morning." The young barista, who'd been working at the coffee shop for just a few weeks, narrowed her eyes just a bit, studying her face. "Ms. Woodson. Are you okay?"

Plastering on a smile, Nia removed her sunglasses. "I'm fine, dear. But I am in desperate need of a pick-me-up. Could you please make me a dark chocolate mint mocha with a double shot? And a cinnamon raisin bagel with plain cream cheese."

"Anything else, ma'am?"

She shook her head. "That's it. And please, call me Nia. Or Ms. Woodson. Or 'hey, lady.' Just please, not ma'am."

The young woman smiled. "I got ya." Ringing up the order, she quoted a total.

Nia reached into her gray leather shoulder bag for her wallet.

A deep voice spoke behind her. "I'll take care of the lady's order. And please add on a large vanilla latte and a bacon Gorgonzola sandwich."

The worker paused, her eyes darting back to Nia, who turned slowly around. Finding Pierce Hamilton standing within five feet of her was a bit of a shock, but she swallowed the feeling. Or at least, she tried. *Damn, I should have left my shades on. My eyes are probably big as hell right now.* He smiled, showing off two rows of straight pearl-white teeth, the tiny diamonds set into his two center incisors sparkling. "Good morning, Nia."

She stared at him, unable to find her voice. Perhaps it was her sleep-deprived brain, or the early-morning sunlight streaming in to illuminate his sharply dressed figure, but the playboy of Hamilton House looked better than Nia had ever seen him look before. He wore a tailored suit in a deep shade of burgundy with a coal-black button-down. His solid tie matched the jacket and slacks perfectly, and his fashionable brown leather loafers and gold tiepin pulled the look together.

He cleared his throat. "I hope you don't mind my paying, since you were nice enough to invite me to meet you here."

I had forgotten I asked him to meet me here. Yikes, I really am tired. She gathered herself rather than alert him to her feelings. "Good morning. And no, it's not a problem." She directed the second statement to the counter clerk, who then added Pierce's requested items to the tab and quoted a new total.

As he paid for their breakfast, she scanned the space for a table. There were a few people inside enjoying their drinks and pastries, but she spotted the last empty two-top near the back. Without waiting for him, she headed for the table.

She sat down in the seat facing the front of the establishment and used the long strap to hang her purse over the back of her chair. Taking a moment to collect herself, she drew in a deep breath.

Okay, Nia. After we consume the caffeine, we can

hopefully get some blood to our brain and stop sweating this man so hard.

His walked to the table with a tray in hand, and she observed his long-legged strides with deep appreciation until he arrived at the table and set the tray down. Turning it so their food was in proper alignment, he then eased into the chair opposite her. "How are you this morning?"

She opened her mouth to speak, then slapped her hand over it when another yawn came out instead of words. "Sorry. Long night, but I'm sure this will make it all better." She grabbed her mocha and blew over the steaming surface of the beverage to cool it before taking a tentative sip.

"I can relate. Sunday always seems to go by too fast, and then it's back to the grind." He raised his own mug in salute. "If it's any consolation, you look really refreshed and put together. Very lovely."

She glanced down at her outfit. She'd tugged on the slim black trousers and white blouse because they were clean and unwrinkled, and had added the houndstooth trench and flat-soled black knee boots for warmth. "Thanks, but honestly, I go for comfort over fashion nine times out of ten."

"And the tenth time?"

"A big event, like the awards ceremony last week, or the gala." She took another sip of her drink, grateful it had cooled a bit more.

He nodded. "Well, you looked amazing at the ceremony, and I can't wait to see your look for the gala." He winked and took a bite of his sandwich.

Feeling a subtle warmth rising in her cheeks that seemed to be coming from sources other than her hot beverage, she took a nibble of the cream cheese–coated bagel.

They spent a few minutes eating in companionable quiet. When they were done with their food, he asked, "When do you think you'll have time to film your confessional segment for the film?"

"So we're doing this like a reality show?" She tilted her head to one side. "We can't dawdle too much on this since the gala is so close. Can your friend and his film people come to me?"

He nodded. "I'm sure Hunter wouldn't mind setting up wherever works for you. I'll give you his number before we leave here." He paused. "Now that I'm thinking of it, he wanted me to tell you to gather any photos you think would be significant to the story. He and his team will edit them into the final version."

She tugged the end of her ponytail, thinking. "I've already got one in my possession, but I need that one for an art piece I'm working on. I'm sure I can scare up a few, and I'll have my assistant scan and email them to your guy in the next day or so."

"Sounds great. I need to start looking for photos myself." He drank a bit more of his latte. "Listen, can I ask you something?"

"Sure."

"I've got a feeling you have some cool stories about your family, especially your siblings."

She shrugged. "I've got a few."

"Care to give me a sneak peek? I mean, since we're

in this together, I feel like I should get the inside scoop before the public."

A bit taken aback by his curiosity about her upbringing, she decided to oblige him. "Let's see. Gage, Teagan and Miles all had some kind of milestone happen at the original studio building. Gage lost his first tooth there doing some harebrained stunt in the hallway, and the twins took their first steps there."

He laughed. "Wow. That's pretty good."

"Oh, and Teagan used to love hiding in the lower cabinets under the soundboards. Sometimes, she'd get tangled in the wiring and someone would have to come rescue her." She shook her head at the memory of Teagan's tiny form, hopelessly encircled by wires of various colors. "Then she grows up to become one of the best sound engineers in the South."

"That's a good one," Pierce remarked with a grin. "You've gotta tell that story."

Caffeine was in her system by now, but even this clearheaded, she was still enjoying Pierce's company more than she ever had in the past. She could question it…but decided to just lean into it.

After all, what could the harm be? Family drama and gala madness has left my social life nonexistent. I may as well grab my fun wherever I can.

"You know, you should tell me some kind of funny story about your childhood now."

Pierce looked up from his near-empty mug, eyeing Nia across the table. "Really?"

"Yeah, really." She turned sideways in her chair, tossing one long leg over the other. "It's only fair. Don't tell me you're gonna play shy now."

He chuckled. "No, I'm just…surprised you're interested, that's all."

"The more time you spend with me," she said, lowering her gaze ever so slightly, "the more you'll see that I'm full of surprises."

He swallowed, his mind racing with all the possibilities that could lie beneath such a declaration. Clearing all that away with a mental scythe, he searched his memory for a funny story from his own childhood. "Okay. How about this—when London and I were about seven years old, our live-in babysitter got the flu and left the house to go quarantine. So, all that week, we had to go to the office with our mother."

"That must have been quite an adventure for her," Nia quipped.

"Absolutely. At that age, we had way more energy than we knew what to do with. Anyway, for the first few days, she kept saying a special visitor was coming and that we would need to be on our best behavior when they came."

She leaned forward, resting her elbow on the table, gaze locked on his face.

Her expression of interest spurring him to continue, he said, "She never mentioned a name or anything about who was coming, or why. But that Friday, it seemed like every employee in the building was hanging around the lobby, waiting for this mystery guest to show up, until finally, they did." He paused for dramatic effect. "It was Toni Braxton."

Her eyes widened. "Seriously?"

He grinned. "Yep. We heard her music all the time around the house, but at the time, none of us had any idea how huge she would become."

"Honestly, I'm jealous." She shook her head. "I love her, and after all these years in the business, I've never gotten to meet her. What was she like?"

He found her admission a little surprising but tucked it away in his memory bank. "She was really sweet, and surprisingly soft-spoken considering that amazing voice. I was playing with one of those paddleball things in the hallway, and she signed the paddle. I still have it."

She sighed aloud. "Wow. It's so cool that you got to meet her. Did you tell that story when you recorded your confessional?"

"I did. I knew it was important not just because of who she is, but because she is the first 'celebrity' I can clearly remember meeting at Hamilton House. I'm sure there were others before her, but she was so kind to me that the encounter stands out in my mind."

She nodded. "That makes a lot of sense. When you meet famous people every day, the luster wears off after a while. But when someone is genuinely nice, you remember it."

"Ever met anyone in the business like that?"

She nodded. "A few people. I'd say Jonathan stands out among then. By the time I met him, I already loved his music, and finding out he was a nice guy just made it ten times better."

Confused, he asked, "Jonathan?"

"Most people know him as Lil Jon."

Pierce grinned. "The king of crunk himself? Now I'm jealous."

"He's a really easygoing dude. Honestly, he doesn't come around as much these days, but we crossed paths a lot in the past," she laughed. "He's silly, too. Just really fun to be around, but also a consummate artist."

"Well, this is funny. I love crunk music." He thought about the extensive collection of it saved on his online music account, as well as the stacks of vintage CDs stored in his home. "This is a pleasant yet unexpected thing we have in common. Who knows what else there might be?"

She offered a coy smile as she stood. "I guess we'll find out." Grabbing her purse, she said, "I really do need to get to the office. I'll reach out to your friend, and then you and I can set up a time to meet."

"Let me text you his number. What's yours?"

She recited the digits while he entered them into his phone, then he sent the text with Hunter's contact info. He wasn't ready to leave, or to disengage from the pleasure of her company, but they both had work to do. "Sounds fine." He stood then and picked up the tray. "I'll take care of this."

"Bye, Pierce." She smiled, then turned and walked away.

He stood by the table, tray in hand, watching her departure until she climbed into her car and drove away. Then he set their mugs and the tray in the proper spot and made his own exit.

He began his drive to the Hamilton House Atlanta

headquarters just before ten. The whole way, he replayed his conversation with Nia in his mind.

Today, she'd been far more approachable than she had ever been with him in the past, even a little friendly. She'd revealed a few of the tales of her childhood, and while they weren't scandalous or terribly exciting, he still felt privileged that she'd been open with him.

A smile came over his face, despite the noisy, frustrating gauntlet known as Atlanta traffic. Being around Nia felt good. Over coffee this morning, she had felt less like a business rival and more like a friend.

And maybe…more than a friend.

He'd been treated to the beauty of her smile; he'd felt the warmth settle in his chest when she laughed; he'd watched her eyes light up. And now that he'd had a taste of her more lighthearted side, he wanted more.

We'll be working together on the retrospective for at least another week. Who knows what might happen in that amount of time?

The company's building was located in the northeastern corner of Midtown, bordering Sherwood Forest. The fifteen-story building was separated from the main road by a private service road and a huge parking lot with parking for five hundred vehicles.

He parked in his designated spot near Hamilton House's main entrance and carried his briefcase inside. He paused to speak with Jean, the lobby receptionist who'd been with the company for the past fifteen years. A quick trip across the lobby to the elevator bank took him to his office on the fourteenth floor.

As he unlocked the glass doors and let himself in,

he noticed a big box taking up most of his desktop. He frowned. *I wasn't expecting a delivery today.*

Approaching his desk, he spotted a bright yellow sticky note attached to the top. He set his briefcase on the floor and read it.

Thought these would help. Bring the box back when you're done.
Love, Mom

Lifting the lid from the box, he found it filled with photographs, brochures, magazines and all manner of glossy paper. As he sifted through the items on top, he marveled at the sheer number of items his mother had managed to stuff into the box. Its contents amounted to a time capsule of his family history, of his parents' friendship with the Woodsons and of the humble beginnings of Hamilton House.

Sitting down in his ergonomic executive chair, he hoisted the box off his desktop and sat it on the floor by his feet. *If I'm gonna make any headway going through all this, I'll need the desktop space to sort out the things I can actually use.*

Two hours later, his rumbling stomach drew his attention away from the pseudo time capsule, reminding him of his need for sustenance. He set aside the thick stack of things he'd taken out and grabbed his phone, intent on calling in a takeout order.

The phone buzzed the moment he touched it.

Reading the notification on the screen, his eyes widened. It was a text from Nia.

This may seem forward but I think you should take me out.

A broad grin spread across his face as he tapped out a quick reply.

I agree. I'll give you details by this time tomorrow.

Eight

Nia jogged into the 404 building Tuesday morning, phone in hand. It was just after eight, and though she didn't usually arrive at work until nine, she'd gotten a group text from her father calling an emergency family meeting in the conference room.

By the time she reached the conference room, she found half her family already there. All her brothers were present except Miles, and to her surprise and delight, her mother sat at one end of the long table. Addy wore a black caftan paired with matching wide-leg pants, and her hair was wrapped in gold turban that revealed little more than the salt-and-pepper strands around her hairline.

"Mom." She went straight to the end of the table.

Standing, Addy pulled her eldest child into her embrace. "Hello, my Nia Bear. I missed you."

"I missed you, too." She held on as tightly as she could, inhaling the familiar scent of her mother's signature scent, Chanel Coco. "How was your flight?" She'd been so locked into creative frenzy with her art piece, she'd dispatched Teagan to pick Addy up from the airport.

"Short," she laughed. "Charlotte to Atlanta is less than an hour. I'm just glad to be home with my babies again." Releasing her, she pecked Nia on the cheek before sitting again.

Nia glanced at her brothers, and Gage and Blaine both wore broad grins that showed they were happy to have Addy home, too. "Wait, where's Teagan? And better yet, where's Dad? This whole thing is his idea."

Blaine shrugged. "I have no idea where Teagan is, but I assume she's on the way. She replied to the group text, so we know she saw it."

"Dad said he was waiting for Elliot and that he'd be here as soon as he could," Gage added.

Nia nodded, finally understanding what this meeting was about and why their mother had shown up. Elliot Wilmont was their father's longtime lawyer. *This has to be related to this mess with Keegan Woodbine.* She placed a gentle hand on her mother's shoulder.

Addy gave her daughter a subtle nod. "It's time to get to the bottom of this and move forward."

"I couldn't agree more." The past year had been quite tumultuous for her family, and after seeing the effects, she was past ready to be done with drama. She took her seat to her mother's left, pondering on all that had happened. *Before all this, I thought Mom and Dad's marriage was impenetrable, like a fortress.* Watching the walls of that fortress crumble had been unsettling in ways she wasn't prepared for.

Teagan darted into the room, breathing heavily and looking a bit disheveled. She wore black skinny jeans and an oversized pink cashmere sweater with pink ballet flats. Only one of her arms was fully inside her sleeve, and the other sleeve dangled limply at her side. "Sorry I'm late, y'all."

Blaine laughed. "Dad's not here yet, so you're good."

Addy eyed her baby. "Teagan. Girl, why are you so out of breath?"

Righting her clothes as she spoke, she said, "I ran across the parking lot, up the stairs and straight here." Teagan dropped into the chair next to Nia, drawing a series of deep breaths. "If I'd known Dad wasn't here, I would not have done all that."

Addy laughed, reaching into her bag and sliding a small mirror across the tabletop. "Teagan, fix that lopsided ponytail."

While Teagan adjusted the rather crooked curls piled atop her head, Caleb and Elliot entered the room. As they walked to the end of the table opposite Addy, the space grew so quiet that Nia could hear the sounds of warm air being forced through the HVAC system.

Once he'd settled into his seat, Caleb's gaze searched the room before landing on his wife's face. "Thank you for coming on short notice. Especially you, Addy." He paused. "Elliot has the report back from the private investigator, and I thought it important that you all hear what was in it."

Elliot, standing behind Caleb's chair, offered a smile. "Good morning, Woodsons. We've got a lot of new information from the investigative report, and I'm happy to give you as much detail as you'd like."

"I want to know if Keegan is really Caleb's son." Addy spoke in a clear, constrained voice. "Everything else is window dressing, as far as I'm concerned."

Elliot nodded. "Understood. Then I'll start by saying, no. Keegan Woodbine is absolutely not Caleb's son."

Addy's hand flew to her mouth, and tears sprang to her eyes.

Blaine offered his mother the handkerchief from his pocket. "That's great to hear. But I'm curious about that paternity test. How did we get positive results if Dad isn't Keegan's father?"

"Simple. The results were doctored." Elliot opened his black leather case and took out a thin stack of papers. "It appears that Keegan knew someone who worked at the lab and paid them a sum of money to falsify the test results."

Nia blinked several times. "What? That seems so extreme. Why would he do that?"

"Greed. He was determined to extort your father and used particularly creative means of doing so. Keegan's so-called mother had never met him, and everything he said in his interactions with you all was fabricated." Elliot shook his head. "The man is a con artist."

"Are the authorities involved?" Gage asked.

"Absolutely," Elliot assured. "Private investigators

have a duty to report illegal activity should they discover it in the course of their work. Mr. Woodbine and his associate at the laboratory are now facing a laundry list of fraud-related charges. There may be other parties involved, but that should all come out during pretrial discovery."

"We're taking this to trial, then?" Teagan's gaze darted from her father's face to that of his lawyer.

Caleb spoke then. "Yes, that's the plan. Woodbine, and whoever else participated in this scheme that nearly tore this family apart, should be held accountable for their actions."

Addy, who'd been quietly sobbing into the handkerchief, dabbed her eyes and drew a deep breath. Without a word, she rose from her seat and made her way around the table to where her husband sat.

Caleb stood, opening his arms moments before his wife of three decades crashed into him, her turban falling off in the fray. He stroked her shimmery curls as she offered softly delivered words for his ears alone.

Nia dashed away a tear as she watched her parents, rocking and holding each other. *It's been way too long since I've seen them like this.*

Elliot offered a nod as he departed. One by one, they all filed out of the conference room, leaving Caleb and Addy to their reconciliation. Nia was the last out, and she glanced at them one more time before gently closing the conference room door.

She went to her office but found herself too overwhelmed with the events of the morning to accomplish much work. She checked the time, seeing that it was a few minutes past nine.

Hunter's supposed to meet me here at ten. I don't feel like I'm going to accomplish much before he arrives. So instead of starting any business-related tasks, knowing she'd be interrupted within the next hour, she took out the photographs she'd need to submit for the film and spent the time scanning and uploading them to email to Hunter.

By the time Hunter arrived at her office, Nia had gotten herself together. He was a good-looking, well-dressed Black man, an inch or two shorter than Pierce, with long and immaculately groomed locs. His hair was the way she imagined Blaine's might be in a few years if he kept growing it out.

As she ushered him to the sitting area of her office and settled into her favorite armchair, she watched him set up his recording equipment.

"So," Hunter began, "I know you must have some very cool memories of growing up in a world shaped by your parents' work in the music industry. Tell me about that."

She laughed. "How much time do you have?"

Pierce drove up to the front of the 404 Sound building around six on Thursday evening, easing his car into one of the empty spaces earmarked for visitors. Cutting the engine, he flipped down his visor to make use of the mirror. Giving his moustache and beard a quick grooming with the small brush he kept in his console, he returned the visor to its original position.

He tried not to watch the door in anticipation of Nia's exit but found it difficult to train his gaze elsewhere. Her offer to go out with him had been easily the most pleasant surprise of his whole week, and he'd spent time over the last couple of days making arrangements with her enjoyment in mind.

If I can pull this off, and we have a good time tonight, maybe there's a chance for something bigger, better. It seemed all the Woodsons had been against a merger with Hamilton House in the past.

Maybe they would be less leery and more open if there were a romantic liaison between Nia and me.

He remembered his sister's advice about leaning on Uncle Martin for support. While he still planned to do that, their uncle hadn't yet arrived in town. Pierce saw no harm in making his own moves toward his end goal in the meantime. There was a potential empire to be built.

She emerged from the building then, drawing his attention in the way only she could. Dressed in slim tweed trousers, an off-white turtleneck and a long black vest and knee boots, she appeared stylish and elegant. Her dark hair hung in loose waves around her shoulders, and he realized this was the first time he'd ever seen it down.

Did she wear it loose to work? Or...did she take it down for me? He liked to think it was the latter but knew better than to question her about it. He enjoyed her long, graceful strides for a moment, then remembered himself and hopped out of the vehicle so he could open the passenger door for her.

"You're right on time. I like that." She offered a soft smile as she climbed into the seat.

"Of course. I wouldn't dream of wasting your time." He closed her door and returned to his own seat. A few moments later, he started the engine and backed out of the space.

They were on the road before she spoke again. "So, what do you have planned for this evening?"

He answered while keeping his attention on the road. "I thought it would be nice to go someplace that encouraged conversation, a place that would play into a thing we both enjoy."

"Is that all you're going to tell me?"

He nodded. "Yes. But don't worry, I won't keep you in suspense too long."

As soon as they pulled up to the somewhat nondescript black-and-brown building on Travis Street NW, he heard her giggle.

"The Trap Museum?"

"Yep." He entered the lot on the side of the building and pulled into a space. There were only two other cars there, and based on the plans he'd set in motion, he assumed they belonged to staff members.

"And what gave you this idea?"

He shrugged. "When we met up, we talked about how much we both love Lil Jon. That means we both love hip-hop, so here we are." Shutting off the engine, he said, "Am I on the right track?"

She offered a soft smile. "Yeah, you are." She reached for her seat belt buckle.

He was out of the truck and at her side in a flash.

When he opened the door, she shook her head but let him help her down onto solid ground anyway.

"Not only is chivalry alive, but it might have had too much espresso today." With a laugh, she breezed past him toward the entrance.

Her invective, likely meant to poke fun at his enthusiasm, only made him more intrigued with her. *She's a whole lot of woman. Not easily impressed, either.*

He caught up with her and they entered the building together.

Just inside the entrance, they were greeted by an employee. "Mr. Hamilton. Thanks for your generous donation. If you and your companion need anything during your private tour, just let me know."

"Thank you."

"No problem. You can come to the bar whenever you're ready for champagne and strawberries."

As the employee disappeared, Nia turned to him with widened eyes. "You set all this up in two days?"

"With enough money and enough determination, you can pull off just about anything."

She laughed, shaking her head. "True enough."

He gestured ahead. "Let's begin our tour, milady."

They began in the foyer, where a unique panorama of items, including stacked tires, an electric stove and a full-size old-school sedan, were coated in a bright shade of matte pink. The interior of the building provided a thorough look into hip-hop culture, and in places, the exhibits went beyond trap to touch on other subgenres.

There were photographs and portraits of hip-hop legends both classic and current, stage costumes made famous in music videos and artifacts from heroes of the genre, including some artists tragically taken before their time.

He paused before a glass case holding a pair of blue sneakers and a portrait of late rapper and activist Nipsey Hussle. "That man was about to do something amazing. I just know it."

"I agree." Her face reflected the same sadness he felt. "Luckily, his life will have lasting impact. The marathon continues."

After a moment of somber, reflective silence, they continued on, taking in more of the museum's offerings. There were recreations of rooms one would find in an actual trap house, depicting well-worn furniture, empty liquor bottles and strewn paraphernalia. One room held an assortment of firearms and clothing belonging to the museum's owner, trap pioneer Clifford "T.I." Harris.

"Oh, snap." Nia pointed to a glass case. "Look at this. It's one of Jonathan's—I mean Lil Jon's—pimp cups."

He laughed. "Yeah, and a pair of those Oakley shades he wears all the time."

"I didn't know they had anything of his in here." She moved up for a closer look at the display. "Based on the placard, he donated it himself. That's cool of him."

"I can see why he'd donate it. It's a chance to be a part of the annals of hip-hop history."

"Those things are so tacky, and incredibly impractical to drink out of, I'd bet," Nia giggled. "But Jon and his crew made them a thing, and now they're part of the lexicon."

They finished up their tour, and he led her to the bar

near the front entrance, where the employee behind the counter served them two chilled flutes of champagne, along with a platter of ripe red strawberries and a ramekin of whipped cream.

"A toast. To a lady with excellent taste in music."

They clinked their raised glasses together and each took a sip.

"Thanks for bringing me here," she said. "I've been meaning to visit since the place opened, but I never seemed to have time."

"Gotta make time for the things you enjoy." He set his glass down. "All work and no play... Well, you know what I'm getting at."

"I do." She grabbed a strawberry and brought it to her lips.

He watched her bite into the bright, juicy flesh, and a bolt of electricity shot through him.

She chewed gracefully for a few moments before asking, "What do you think is the best subset of hip-hop? Trap? Crunk? Snap?"

He laughed. "Oh, you wanna ask the real questions, I see. This answer gonna take some time and explanation."

"I know. I fully expect you to explain your position." She rested her elbow on the bar counter. "Lucky for you, I've got some time on my hands. So tell me where you stand."

Knowing she'd probably dispute him, he took a deep breath and settled in for a lively debate.

Nine

It was well past Nia's bedtime by the time Pierce returned her to the office parking lot, but the conversation and the time she'd spent with him had been so pleasant, she didn't really mind.

As they stood on the sidewalk in front of her car, with the soft blue security light illuminating their figures, she said, "I had a great time. Thanks again."

"Thanks for spending time with me. I know you're super busy and I really appreciate you letting me take you out."

Knowing she'd be in her car and on her way home soon, she took one last visual sweep of him. It was the most casual outfit she'd seen him in yet: straight-leg dark denim jeans, a long-sleeved shirt featuring gold maple leaves on a black background and a pair of all-black sneakers. The overhead light conspired with the shadows to play up his handsome, well-groomed features.

When her gaze rose up his body and landed on his face again, she found him watching her.

He lifted his hand, bringing it slowly toward her face. "Nia, can I...?"

She knew what he was asking. And heaven help her, she wanted it. Staring into his eyes, she nodded.

A moment later, his lips pressed against hers. The kiss was soft, gentle and brief. She closed her hand around his muscled forearm and leaned in only for him to ease away from her as if he feared dragging the contact out for too long.

"Thank you for letting me kiss you. I've been wanting to do that for a while now." His voice barely broke the quiet of the night. "But I've kept you out late enough." He grazed his fingertips over her cheek "Good night, Nia."

"Good night," she whispered, still feeling the aftereffects of the kiss.

He smiled and made a slow turn, moving away from her as she took the few steps to her car and opened the driver's-side door. Then, she watched him walk back to his SUV, climb in and drive away. Releasing a pent-up breath, she got into her car and drove home.

When her alarm went off the next morning, she was jarred awake from an R-rated dream that had been quickly becoming X-rated. Opening her eyes, she grabbed her phone, swiped across the screen to cease its shrill ringing and clambered out of bed.

After a hot shower and her morning routine, she picked up her phone to check the weather. A text notification from Pierce was on her home screen, and she tapped it to see what he'd said. She could feel the grin spreading across her face as she read his message.

I really want to see you again. How do you feel about rock climbing?

She shook her head, marveling at what a difference a few days had made in her attitude toward Pierce. Up until then, she'd known him only as the playboy of Hamilton House, a man who seemed to have far more bluster than substance.

Now, though, she wasn't so sure of her predetermined notions about him. The time she'd spent with him had revealed a man possessing unexpected depth, refreshing wit, intellect and thoughtfulness.

She responded to his message with a single word of her own.

When?

He replied a few seconds later.

How about tonight?

She giggled like an excited schoolgirl, then covered her mouth, surprised she'd made such a sound. *What is this man doing to my brain? I can't recall acting like this since I've been over the age of sixteen.*

The cautious, sensible part of her brain was telling her that this whole thing between her and Pierce was nothing but a distraction, a dalliance that was wasting time better spent on something productive. Her mother's warning was there, too, singing backup. But at this moment, the tiny part of her that craved fun and something beyond the status quo won out.

She fired off another response.

Sounds awesome. Text me the details later.

With that message sent, she finally got around to checking the weather. Today's high was expected to reach only the mid-sixties, so she chose hunter green wool-blend slacks and a fitted mustard sweater. Slipping on a pair of black suede pumps, she tossed a floral scarf around her neck, added a pair of diamond studs to her ears and brushed her hair up into a high ponytail before declaring herself fit for public consumption.

Her day at work seemed to speed by, filled with meetings, phone calls and all the other things that made up a chief executive officer's massive list of daily tasks. She kept her head in the game as best she could, but her mind kept drifting off toward thoughts of Pierce and how much she was looking forward to spending time with him again. As her workday drew to a close, she changed into the clean set of clothes she kept in her gym bag: a pair of navy leggings, a yellow long-sleeved tee and white sneakers.

When she left the office around five-thirty, she stopped for a quick sandwich from a local deli before heading to The Overlook Boulder+ Fitness, a popular gym on White Street SW.

She went inside and laughed aloud when she spotted Pierce near the front desk. "Wow. That's quite an ensemble."

Glancing down and his electric-orange tracksuit and matching sneakers, he quipped, "I didn't want you to have to search for me when you got here."

"There's no way I could miss you, since you look like a traffic cone."

He chuckled. "I guess I was asking for that with the white racing stripe, huh?"

Walking toward her, he asked, "Have you been here before?"

She nodded. "Yeah, but it's been way too long. I haven't done this in ages and, considering everything going on in my life right now, I could probably use the exertion."

"We both could, I bet." He clapped his hands together. "A good workout is good for the heart. Ready to get those endorphins flowing?"

She eyed the towering matte climbing surfaces, dotted with brightly colored handholds and footholds. Because this gym emphasized bouldering, without the use of harnesses or ropes, it would be up to her to keep her body moving upward to the top. "I'm a little rusty. Here's hoping I don't bust my ass."

"Don't worry," Pierce reassured her. "They have all this soft padding to catch you if you take a tumble."

She rolled her eyes then as they began climbing adjacent surfaces.

But when Pierce came tumbling down from his perch a few minutes later, she laughed until the tears filled her eyes. She was so blinded by her watery-eyed mirth that she lost her own grip and dropped down a few feet away from him.

The two of them lay on the soft mat for a while, helpless victims to the hilarity of the moment. When their laughter finally subsided, she sat up and wiped away the tears running down her cheeks. "Wanna go again?"

"Hell yeah."

So they scrambled to their feet and began again, spending another hour and a half tackling surfaces of varying heights and inclines. Just as she'd hoped, the exertion did much to lift her mood, making her feel more carefree than she had in the past few months.

Finally, she descended and sat down on the mat, trying to settle her labored breathing.

"How are you feeling?" Pierce asked as he sauntered up next to her.

"Amazing, mentally." She blew out a breath. "But my muscles are pretty tight."

"Yeah, I'm feeling it, too. I'm sure mine will be begging for mercy by morning."

"Looks like it's time we call it a night, then."

"We probably should." He reached out a hand.

She grabbed it, using his solid strength as leverage to help her get back upright again. Once she was on her feet, she admitted, "This was a lot of fun. That makes two nights in a row that you've shown me a great time."

He leaned in and gave her a peck on the cheek. "And I'll keep doing it, just as long as you allow."

Her heart swelled, and she smiled. "Don't tempt me, Pierce."

His mouth inches from her ear, he whispered, "Tempting you is exactly what I set out to do."

Pierce held the door for Nia as they exited the gym, then let it swing shut behind them. Instead of walking back to his truck, he lingered on the sidewalk.

Nia didn't seem particularly motivated to leave, either, because she stood right there with him.

They spent a few moments just that way, standing close, watching each other beneath the star-sprinkled sky, hearing only the night breeze and the hum of passing traffic.

"I'm glad we came here," Pierce admitted. "I just hope the endorphins have a preventative effect."

Her brow creased. "What do you mean? Is there something intense going on in your world tomorrow?"

"Very. It's my father's birthday." He knew how at least part of the day would be spent, and he wasn't looking forward to it.

Her expression softened. "I see. That sounds like it might be difficult to deal with."

"It just feels like a reminder of everything I lost, you know?" He paused, thinking of his long-suffering mother and his opinionated but much-loved twin sister. "Everything my family lost."

She placed her hand on his shoulder. "I'm sorry you have to do something hard, and that your family doesn't feel whole. But I honestly believe you are equipped for whatever you need to face."

He blinked a few times. "Wow. Thank you for that."

"No problem." She gave his shoulder a squeeze. "Also, if this day causes you more strife instead of peace, you might consider changing how you spend it next year."

He nodded. "I've definitely been thinking about that." And he had. Based on everything their mother had taught them about their late father, he wasn't the type of person who would want them to experience ongoing misery on his behalf. *Convincing Mother of that may not be easy— she's very much on the "set in her ways" vibe.*

"I really should be getting home. I want to get up early and work on my art piece." She looked into his eyes. "Are you going to be okay?"

"Sure." He leaned down and gave her a quick peck on the cheek. "I'll call you, okay? Get home safely, now."

"Good night, Pierce."

He watched the sway of her shapely hips as she walked away. Only after she was safely in her car and leaving the parking lot did he climb into his SUV to make his own trip home.

Saturday, as morning waned into afternoon, Pierce stood with London in the grass at a quiet cemetery just beyond the city's borders. It was a beautiful blue-sky day, save for a few rogue clouds that appeared overhead to temporarily dampen the sunlight illuminating the rows of headstones.

A short distance away, their mother stood over their father's grave.

Pierce watched silently as his mother unfolded her

portable stool, placed it next to her husband's ornate headstone and took a seat. Once she was comfortable, she placed a bunch of flowers into the stone urn and began to speak. He could see his mother's mouth moving but was too far away to hear the words she said, and that was a purposeful choice.

He and his sister had watched this ritual play out countless times over the course of their lives. Two days every year, they came as a family to pay their respects to their fallen patriarch. Once on Father's Day, and again every November, for his birthday.

"What do you think she says to him?" London asked quietly.

He shrugged. "It's private, whatever it is."

She nodded. "I guess. She knows him so much better than us. It could be anything, really."

He adjusted his stance, shifting his weight to keep from sinking into the soil. "I wish we had known him, but in a way, I feel as though we do. Mother has done a great job keeping him alive for us." She'd been telling them stories about their father as far back as he could remember, creating a connection where there would have otherwise been a gaping void in their lives.

"And Uncle Martin was such a good male role model for us," London added, "so we never lacked in that aspect."

He nodded but remained silent. His mind traveled back to his conversation with Nia last night. What stood out for him was her kindness, the way she didn't burden him with platitudes dripping with pity or false sympathy but still showed great respect for his family's loss. She'd intrigued him from the beginning with the beauty and strength she exuded, but now he was beginning to see how special she was in other ways.

"We really need to convince her to retire." London gestured back to their mother.

He turned his head in time to see her stifling a yawn. "You're right. It's so early in the day and she's already tired. Mother isn't that old. She's not even sixty yet. It's all this overwork and stress that has landed her where she is health-wise."

"Exactly. Plus, her doctor had a laundry list of diet changes and supplements for her." London shook her head. "I know Hamilton House is important to her. But there are so many people who make the company run. She doesn't need to try to shoulder the burden alone."

"I don't know why she feels so responsible for everything. Just thinking about that is exhausting to me, and I honestly don't know how she's lasted this long." He saw his mother rocking her upper body and, recognizing her attempt to get up from the stool, began striding across the grass, his sister trailing behind him.

When they reached her, each of them gently grasped one of her arms to help her back onto her feet.

She smiled through the tears pooling in her eyes. "I'm so grateful to have you, my sweet babies. You're the best gift Phillip ever gave me."

He returned her smile, but inside, his heart was breaking.

Mother has endured so much pain and given us so much. All I want for her now is the rest and relaxation she deserves. But how can I make her see that?

Ten

Nia set down her paintbrush in the easel tray, rose from her stool and took a giant step back She'd spent the better part of her day sitting there, using her various tools and mediums to bring the image to life. Now, as afternoon melted into evening, she felt as if the work might be complete.

She made incremental movements around the large canvas, getting a look at it from various angles. Nia could feel the satisfied smile stretching her lips.

It's finally done. Wow. I really love the way it turned out.

This was her largest work, the most ambitious mixed-media piece she'd ever worked on since she'd taken up painting about six years ago. An immense sense of pride filled her as she stared at it. It wasn't exactly photorealistic, because she hadn't set out to make it so. Yet, she thought it was a great artistic representation of the old photograph she'd found.

She picked up the photo, still lying on her table, and held it up next to the canvas. Doing so solidified her confidence in the work, leaving her certain she didn't need to add anything else. "Yes. This turned out amazing."

Tapping her chin as she continued to admire her creation, she realized she wanted to share this with someone. *Who should I have come over and see this?*

She thought about calling Teagan, who usually loved to see what she was working on, but then thought better of it.

It can't be any of my sibling, because this is a surprise for Mom and Dad, and none of them can keep a secret. Addy had always possessed an uncanny skill for breaking through any barrier her children put between her curiosity and the truth.

She smiled as an image of Pierce's handsome face floated across her thoughts. *I wonder if he'd want to come over and see it.* She tugged a loose curl out of her face, sticking it back into the base of her low ponytail.

The remembered sensations of his kiss still lingered in her mind, igniting an interest that could only be satisfied by further exploration of all the things he'd made her feel.

On the surface, she'd just be asking him over for an opinion on her newly finished art. But beneath that, she knew.

I want him to come over. And not just to look at my work.

Parts of her hesitated, because this kind of thing was so far out of her usual purview. Inviting a man over knowing she planned to seduce him? She hadn't done that in a good three or four years. Did she even know how to interact with a man that way anymore?

She drew a deep breath, determined now to see how this would play out. Grabbing her phone from the table, she gave Pierce a call.

He answered on the second ring. "Hey, Nia. I was just thinking about you."

What a coincidence. "Are you busy?"

"No, I left work at four and I'm home now."

"Working on the weekend? The boss's son?" She chided.

"My grind never stops. Anyway, what's up?"

"I just finished up a really ambitious art piece. I think it turned out pretty well. But I'd love a second opinion on it."

"So you're inviting me over to your place?"

She giggled, embarrassment heating her cheeks. "I am. If…you want to come over."

"Oh, I do." His answer was immediate and declarative. "What part of the city are you in?"

"Inman Park."

"Cool. I can be there in about an hour, if you text me your address." He paused. "Is that too soon?"

"No. That's perfect. I'm sending the text now."

"I remember you saying you'd be working on your art today. Let me ask you this. Have you eaten?"

She blinked a few times, taken aback by the question. "Um... I had an apple and some string cheese this morning."

"You do realize it's almost five, right?"

She cringed. "Yikes. I guess I'd better eat."

"You guessed right. As a matter of fact, since you're letting me come over, I'll bring dinner."

"I don't know what I want."

"No problem. We're both lifelong ATLiens. I've got it covered. It may take me a little longer since I'm getting food, but I'm on my way. Just look out for me, okay?"

Enjoying this banter, and his rather caring insistence that she eat, she acquiesced. "I'll see you soon, then."

"I'm looking forward to it."

After she disconnected the call, she walked out of her studio and crossed the hall to her bedroom. A glimpse at her reflection in the vanity mirror made her cringe. She looked disheveled, as she often did when she'd spent hours in front of a canvas. Stripping off her ratty clothing, she carried herself into the bathroom and showered, careful to remove the paint streaked on her face, hands and forearms.

Clean and refreshed, she slipped into fresh undergarments, a pair of black skinny jeans and a red sweater. Freeing her hair from the ponytail, she brushed through the waves, parted it down the center and let it fall loose around her shoulders. Slippers on her feet, she headed downstairs to get out her china for two and set the table in her rarely used dining room. She added two crystal water goblets and two lit taper candles in ceramic holders to the plates and silver.

She settled in on the couch to await his arrival, entertaining herself with social media to pass the time. She was laughing at a video of a cat stuck in a pickle jar when she heard the knock at her front door. Closing the app, she pocketed her phone and answered the door.

He stood on her front porch, holding a huge bag of food in one hand and cup carrier in the other. He looked handsome as ever in a pair of blue jeans and a Clark Atlanta University sweatshirt. "Good evening. Someone order a food delivery?"

She grinned, holding open the door for him. "Come on in, you." She led him to the dining room, where he set the bag and the cup carrier down.

Eyeing the flickering candles, he said, "I see you got the elegant setup going."

"Presentation is everything," she quipped, already peering in the bag and inhaling the savory aroma. "You went to Q-Time?"

He nodded. "I ordered turkey wings, ribs and baked chicken and dressing to give you a choice of entrée." He started removing containers from the bag and lining them up on the table. "For sides, I got some mac and cheese, fried corn, turnip greens and squash. I figure, since you were raised here, there's gotta be something in this bag you're gonna like."

She laughed aloud. "You figured right. I like literally everything you brought. Except turnip greens."

He grabbed that container. "Then I'll take 'em off your hands."

They took their seats across from each other and began dipping food out of the containers and onto their plates. Nia had a small sampling of everything except the greens, while Pierce helped himself to everything except the corn. While they ate and sipped the ice cold lemonade he'd brought, they passed their phones back and forth, laughing over silly memes.

When the meal was finished, she stood and began to clear away the mess.

He stood as well. "Let me help."

"Thanks." Together, they tossed the trash and ferried the dishes to the sink for a quick rinse, after which she loaded them into her dishwasher. Drying her hands on a kitchen towel, she said, "Ready to see what I've been working on?"

"Absolutely," he said, a broad grin on his face. "The suspense is killing me."

She led him up the stairs and into her studio. Inside, she approached the canvas and gestured. "What do you think, Pierce?"

His eyes widened. "Oh, wow. This is beautiful, Nia."

"Really?" She could feel the smile tugging at her lips.

"It's amazing. Did you do this from a photograph?"

She nodded and grabbed the aged instant-camera shot from the table. "Here's the inspiration."

His gaze moved between the photo and the canvas. "Is that who I think it is?" He pointed.

"Yeah, that's them. I found this in a dusty corner of the house. Odds are pretty good my parents forgot they had it."

He was silent for a moment. When he spoke again, there was a softer quality to his tone. "Do you think you could make me a full-size print of this?"

"You like it that much?"

He nodded. "And I know someone else who would love it even more."

"Sure. I'll have one made for you."

"I'm blown away by your talent." He set the picture in the easel tray and reached out his hand. "I'm blown away by *you*."

She took it and let him draw her close to him.

A moment later, he tilted her chin and press his lips to hers.

The temperature in the small room seemed to rise twenty degrees as Pierce drew Nia's body closer to his, drawing the kiss out. The feel of her soft curves pressed against him drove him mad with desire, and the longer he kissed her, the more he could feel his blood racing to his lower half.

She eased back, looking up into his eyes. "What are we doing, Pierce?"

He buried his fingers in the dark, thick waves of her hair. "I don't think it needs to be named. It just is."

"I don't know." She swallowed. "I...don't want to be in a relationship right now. My life is already complicated enough. But..." She grazed her fingertip along his jawline. "I want this."

"So do I." Even if he didn't admit his need, the growing stiffness of his dick pressed against her would surely give him away. "I'm certainly not going to coerce you, though. What happens now is up to you."

Her gaze dropped, and she appeared somewhat conflicted. For a few moments, she was silent. Raising her gaze, she asked, "Would you make love to me tonight, with the understanding that I don't want attachments?"

"We agree on that," he admitted. "I'm not looking to stake a claim on you, Nia. But if you'll let me, I'd love to experience you."

She circled her arms around his waist. "Yes, Pierce. Just for tonight, let's see what kind of magic we can create together." She leaned in for his kiss.

This kiss was deeper, more impassioned than the last, with the promise of shared pleasure surrounding them. When she broke the kiss this time, she turned and started walking toward the door, gently tugging him along by the hand.

They crossed the hall and entered her bedroom, and he made a brief visual assessment of the space, illuminated by a chandelier-style light fixture hanging overhead. It reminded him of a suite in a high-end hotel. The king-size bed had a wealth of pillows atop the fluffy comforter. The headboard, along with the vanity and dresser, were fashioned of gray-stained wood. The decor, feminine yet understated, included wall art and various figurines in shades of soft pink and gray.

She eased him toward the bed, then turned him so she could push him back into a sitting position on its edge. Climbing into his lap, she straddled his thighs and asked in a sultry tone, "How shall we begin?"

He smiled. "I think getting out of these clothes would be a great start." Lifting her arms, he tugged the red sweater up and off, tossing it to the floor. He sucked in a breath at the sight of her pert breasts, encased in a sheer, flesh-colored bra. Leaning in, he kissed the hollow of her throat before trailing his tongue along the top of each cup. She shivered in his arms as he tugged down the gossamer fabric, freeing first one breast then the other to his appreciative eyes. A breath later, he captured one dark nipple in his mouth, and she groaned.

He took his time paying oral attention to each nipple, until she twisted and moaned. Easing away, he whispered, "Stand up for me, baby."

She did as he asked, and he soon freed her of the fitted jeans and the sheer panties. Standing there in nothing but the disheveled bra, she looked like a rich dessert, waiting to be devoured. And as he lay on his back and lifted her body above him until he lowered her open thighs over his face, devour he did. Slowly, he opened her with his fingers and savored her with his mouth, as any grown man would savor a decadent treat. He remained on his quest to taste every corner, every hidden nook, until her honeyed arousal ran down his cheeks.

When he finally released his grip, she moved away, panting and shuddering. He rested his face on his elbow and watched her. A light sheen of sweat had formed around her hairline, and her chest rose and fell in time with her labored breathing. She looked so fetching, he could barely contain his desire.

She stretched out her hand, grasping the front of his sweatshirt. "You're overdressed," she insisted.

He rose, stripping off his jeans, sweatshirt and boxers, leaving them in a pile near the foot of the bed. Taking a foil packet from his pocket, he sheathed himself with protection before returning to his place atop the soft bedding.

She rolled onto her back, parting her thighs in welcome as he moved closer to her. Her graceful fingertips wrapped around his hardness, and he sucked in a breath when she gave him a squeeze. "Ready for me, I see."

With a growl, he rocked his hips forward and slipped inside her. She was slick, hot and tight, and as he began to stroke, a low purring sound left her throat. He kept his thrusts slow and deep, reveling in the way her body gripped him and the way her fingertips dug into his waist and back, keeping him close. Being inside her exceeded any fantasies he'd had of making love to her... Reality blew his dreams out of the water. She was so soft, so responsive, he never wanted the warm, silken feel of her to end.

His pace quickened to match his rising desire, and soon he could hear her moans rising and melting with his own. She tensed, her nails digging into his hips as she called out his name, and the sound was enough to send him over the edge into the chasm of bliss.

Lying atop her in the aftermath, he listened to the beating of her heart and felt her stroking his sweat-dampened back. They lay in each other's arms for a while, and he simply enjoyed the nearness of her and the soft scent of her hair products.

He was settling into the cocoon of comfort when he heard her say, "Again."

Not one to disappoint, he raised himself up and smiled. "As you wish."

* * *

Sunlight touched Pierce's eyelids, forcing them open. He yawned and started to stretch before he realized a change of position might awaken Nia. He lay on his back, with her cuddled close to left side, his arm wrapped around her. Tucking his free hand behind his head, he contented himself with memories of their night together. They'd made love in various positions all over the bedroom before exhaustion finally claimed them and forced them to seek rest.

He recalled what she'd said to him about not wanting attachments, and how he'd agreed. But now, as he lay here with her in his arms, he realized he may have been hasty in his assumption that he could abide by her terms.

Last night, all I wanted was this. Now, I'm not so sure this will be enough.

She stirred then, murmuring as she came awake. "Good morning."

"Morning." He placed a soft kiss on her cheek.

Her eyes opened, and she looked at him. "Do you have plans today? I don't want to hold you up."

"I planned to see my barber and take care of a few errands. Nothing major."

She eased away from him and sat up. Stretching her arms above her head, she said, "Up and at 'em, then."

Already missing the warmth of her nearness, he watched as she left the bed and padded to the bathroom. The sunlight illuminated her curvaceous nudity, making her appear like a goddess to his hungry eyes. Waking up to such beauty and softness felt like a gift, one he wouldn't be opposed to opening every day of the rest of his life.

He cringed at that thought.

Yikes. This is taking on a life of its own... And if I want to keep some kind of control over this situation, I'd better get it together.

stooped and curled her fingers around the built-in handles to lift it and carry it inside.

As she walked through the kitchen into the foyer, she saw her father standing by the base of the stairs. "Where's Mom?"

Caleb, dressed in an old Georgia Tech tee and sweats that had seen better days, pointed up. "She went up to our bedroom. Says she'll supervise from there while I ferry these things up to her." He took the tote from her.

She frowned. "Dad, are you sure your back will be okay carrying this stuff upstairs?"

He grinned. "I'll be fine. She didn't take any furniture when she left." He started up the steps, calling over his shoulder as he went. "Besides, having my Addy home again makes me feel as spry as a schoolboy."

She shook her head as she watched him jog upstairs with the tote, comforted by the fact that it hadn't been very heavy. Moving through the arched doorway into the living room, she leaned against the wall and lingered for a long, silent moment.

Looking around the room, she remembered the day things had fallen apart. She could clearly picture herself and all her siblings sitting around this very room several weeks back, watching their parents' marriage dissolve before their eyes. Her place as eldest and "most level-headed" child had been used against her that day, forcing her to deliver the news. She recalled the pain she'd felt when she'd opened the envelope and read the words aloud, the words that had led to her mother moving out.

From the upper floor, she could hear the semi-distant sounds of her parents conversing, followed by her mother's loud, infectious laugh. The sound brought a smile to her face.

Being here now, and seeing things resolved, gave her a sense of peace, restoring the sense of safety she'd lost that day, when she'd been afraid her family might never be restored.

She went to the kitchen and grabbed a bottle of lemon-flavored water from the fridge. As she stood drinking it, her father entered. "Nia, your momma wants you to come upstairs and help her put things away."

She capped the bottle. "Okay, but I think she has one more bag of stuff in her trunk."

He shook his head. "If she wants to bring it inside, we can get it later. Right now, I'm on break." He strode into the living room and sat down in his easy chair.

She took the remainder of her drink up the stairs, turning left at the landing and heading for her parents' bedroom. There, she found her mother standing by the bed, taking neatly folded clothing out of the large suitcase they'd brought in earlier.

"Oh, there you are," Addy said. "I'm so glad Laurie and I spent time laundering all my clothes before I left her place. It's gonna be so much easier to put everything back since it's already clean."

"Dad said you wanted my help?"

She nodded. "I do. Go in my closet and grab about twenty or so of those velvet hangers, please."

Nia did as her mother asked, moving past her to Addy's walk-in closet. Turning on the light, she grabbed the hangers from the rack and carried them back to the bed.

Addy took them, lying them next to her pile of clothes. "Take my dresses, put them on the hangers and put them back in the closet. Remember to stick to the code."

"Gotcha." She knew her mother was talking about the color code, since she kept all her clothing arranged by hue.

"I'm gonna put up all the stuff that belongs in my dresser." Lifting more items out of the suitcase, Addy made little stacks on top of the floral comforter. "Listen, while you're here, why don't you update me on how things are going with your little project?"

She turned up the bottle, downing its entire contents, and swallowed. While she knew her mother was talking about the retrospective, her bringing it up inevitably brought her night with Pierce back to the forefront of her mind. "I think it's going pretty well. I already filmed my part and sent a boatload of pictures to be edited into it."

Addy nodded as she walked a stack of undergarments to her big mahogany dresser and tucked then into a drawer. "Okay, sounds good. When I asked you father about it, he looked so disappointed. I guess Teagan didn't know he'd planned it for me as a surprise."

Nia shook her head. "Nah, she knew. It's just that she can't keep anything from you. All of us are like that, to a degree."

"I suppose that's true." She sat down on the bed in the spot she'd just cleared. "That's why I'm going to ask you if there's anything else going on that you want to tell me about."

She sighed. "Mom, I can honestly say that there is nothing happening right now that I want to tell you about." It was the truth. This thing between her and Pierce wasn't serious. They were both in need of an outlet, a way to let off steam from their stressful work and family lives. *It's nothing more than that, and nothing worth sharing. Because the minute I do, Mom will go off the deep end.*

Addy eyed her for a moment later, then offered a brief nod, indicating her willingness to let the matter drop.

Nia picked up several of her mother's dresses and took them to the closet. As she stood, carefully slotting them in with other items of similar color, she felt the rightness of her decision.

As the oldest child, she'd had the most time with her mother. And over the course of her life, she'd learned the value of honesty in their relationship.

But she'd also learned the importance of boundaries, of having her own mind and not seeking her mother's opinion or approval on every action or decision.

And this was simply an opportunity to exercise those boundaries.

While she hung the last dress, her phone buzzed. Slipping it from her pocket, she read the text from Pierce.

Can I see you today?

She tapped out a quick reply. Sorry. My mom needs my help today, but I'll give you a call tomorrow.

Assuring the last dress was in its proper place, she put her phone away and returned to her mother's side.

Pierce spent the first half of his Sunday lounging around his condo. The entire time, thoughts of what he'd shared with Nia played in his mind, until he finally gave in and texted her.

It wasn't his way to reach out so soon after an encounter. Or at least, it hadn't been before this little entanglement with Nia. In some circles, he was known as the Playboy of Hamilton House, a nickname he wouldn't have known about if his twin sister hadn't volunteered the information. For a time, he'd worn the title like a badge of honor.

Now, as he felt the allure of everything Nia Woodson was tugging at him, he wondered if he'd made a mistake in doing that.

Her response to his message was a glorified form of "I'm busy—call you later." And it made him feel put out and pushed aside in a way he didn't like and certainly didn't want to admit to himself.

He lay on the sofa, flipping channels in search of entertainment. Nothing struck his fancy, so he gave Hunter a call to see where things were with the film.

Hunter answered after three rings. "Hey, bro. What's up?"

"Hey, Hunter. Just checking in with you. Has your editor worked his magic on the footage yet?"

There was a brief hesitation before Hunter answered. "Yeah. But it may still need a little more work."

He frowned. "What do you mean? I thought your guy was top-tier?"

"He is. This isn't a problem with editing, Pierce."

"What am I missing here?"

"Honestly, we feel like we need a little something more in order to make the final film more compelling." He paused. "I can't put my finger on it exactly, but it's missing an element that would make this film truly remarkable and memorable for the audience."

Pierce scratched his chin. "I don't know, man. Can you send me the initial cut, and I'll see if I can come up with something?"

"Sure thing. I'll email you the clip. It's about an hour long."

"Alright. I'll give it a look and do a little brainstorming."

"Sounds good," Hunter said. "In the meantime, I'll be doing some pondering of my own."

After ending the call with his friend, Pierce sat up and stretched. *I'm pretty sure Mom will have something around the house that needs doing. Let me go check on her.* He then put on a pair of sneakers, grabbed his keys and wallet, and left the condo.

A harrowing crosstown drive through city traffic took him to his family home in the ritzy Argonne Forest area. Every time he made the drive, taking him through ten miles of roadway and skirting across several neighborhoods, he wondered how long it would be before either he or London would have to move closer to their mother. As it stood now, both of them were about thirty minutes away, since London lived in a town house in North Brookhaven.

Pulling into the driveway, he noticed an unfamiliar car sitting behind his mother's luxury sedan. He frowned. *Who's here with Mother?* He hoped and prayed she wasn't entertaining a "gentleman friend." While he had no qualms about his mother enjoying herself, he just didn't want to know about it.

After parking his SUV, he headed up the steps and used his key to let himself in the front door. Inside the cavernous entryway, he called out, "Mother!"

She descended the staircase a few moments later, wearing one of the many bedazzled tracksuits she owned. "Pierce Allan Hamilton. I know I raised you better than to be hollering in my house like that."

"Sorry, Mother," he offered sheepishly. Almost afraid to ask the question, he indulged his curiosity anyway. "Do you have a visitor? I saw someone's car outside."

"As a matter of fact, she does," a deep male voice answered.

He turned his head toward the sound and watched as his Uncle Martin appeared on the landing. He wore a pair of khaki pants, a gray polo and black loafers. His tall, dark-skinned frame towered over Everly's, and a broad grin stretched his mustached lips.

Laughing, Pierce said, "Uncle Martin! When did you get here?"

Headed down the stairs behind his sister-in-law, Martin chuckled. "About an hour ago, kid. How the hell are ya?"

As they reached the bottom of the stairs, Everly pinched her houseguest. "Language, Marty."

He shook his head. "Your ears are way too delicate, sis."

"I'm good, Unc." Pierce walked up to his uncle and gave him a tight hug. "How are you?"

"I can't complain, young buck. It's good to see you." He gave him a hearty slap on the back as they broke the embrace.

"What happened to your hair?" Pierce dragged a teasing hand over his uncle's shiny head.

"Got tired of chasing a hairline and shaved it all off." He playfully tossed his nephew's hand away. "Where's my princess?"

"London? Who knows?" Everly quipped.

"It's Sunday, so she's either asleep or shopping," Pierce laughed. "Those are her two favorite pastimes."

"Ain't a thing changed since I last saw her, then." Martin grinned.

"I came over to see if you had anything for me to do," Pierce said to his mother. "But if Uncle Martin's here, whatever it is has probably already been taken care of, I'm guessing."

She nodded. "He just changed the bulbs in my bathroom, and before that, he moved a few boxes to the attic for me."

"Dang, Unc. She's had you working since you got here?"

Martin laughed. "She sure has. But you know I don't mind. Phillip would want me to take care of his pretty one." He gave Everly's shoulder a squeeze, and she smiled up at him.

Pierce smiled, watching the affection that played over their faces when they looked at each other. It reminded him what a blessing it was to have his father's little brother in their lives.

"I'm headed to the pool. You know, to recover from all the work your mama had me doing." Martin gestured toward the door. "Come on out there and catch up with me."

"Bet."

Soon, he and his uncle were on adjacent loungers, facing the heated indoor pool with beers in hand.

"So, what's going on in your world, Pierce?" Martin asked.

Eyes on the rippling surface of the water, Pierce filled his uncle in on the last couple of years but emphasized what had been happening recently between him and Nia. "She's gotten under my skin, Unc. At first, I just wanted to get with her, thinking I could win her over and convince her to merge our two businesses. But now? I don't know anymore."

Martin shook his head. "Sounds like you've got it bad."

"I guess I do. I'm usually a lot more nonchalant with women, and that gives me control over the situation. This time, I don't have control, and I really, really don't like that feeling."

He chuckled. "I don't think any man does. But since the beginning of time, women have been melting our brains, making us do things we swore we wouldn't do. It's how the human race keeps propagating."

He sighed. "Okay. But what am I supposed to do now?"

Martin shrugged. "I don't know. Depends on the outcome you're looking for."

"Right now, I just want to keep seeing her." Pierce ran a hand over his head. "Maybe I should just let go of any expectations of where this is headed and just enjoy whatever time we have together."

"That seems reasonable. Why not give it a try?" Martin took a long drink from his beer bottle. "Releasing expectations is generally a wise thing to do. Life comes at us too fast for us to try to wrestle it into submission. And when you really thing about it, that's the beauty of it."

He lay against the backrest and pondered his uncle's words.

Like it or not, I'm along for the ride. May as well enjoy it.

Twelve

When she left work on Monday, Nia headed home to change clothes. She'd arranged to meet Pierce at the dock at Lake Clara Meer in Piedmont Park, and she knew she'd need warmer clothing.

Dressed in jeans, a camisole and her favorite tour sweatshirt from the Lost Lake Festival 2017, she stepped into a pair of suede ankle books and laced them up. Running a brush through her hair, she pulled on a knit hat, then gathered her things and left.

After she parked, she walked the trail until she came to the lakeside. Streetlamps positioned at even intervals along the path illuminated the park in the fading light. She easily spotted him on the grassy area near the dock due to the bright colors of his red plaid blanket spread out on the ground. Two outdoor folding chairs were set up, and he also had a large basket as well as an array of fishing gear lying nearby.

She approached with a smile. "Hey, Pierce. This is quite the setup."

He gestured to one of the chairs. "Just wanted to make sure you'd be comfortable. Have a seat."

She went to the chair and sat down. "What's in the basket?"

"I brought a few drinks and snacks in case we get hungry." He pointed to a small covered pail. "Just don't reach into that one by mistake. That's the bait."

She laughed. "Thanks for the warning."

"Did you get things situated with your mom?" he asked.

She thought she detected a hint of sarcasm or annoyance in his voice but decided not to read too much into it. "Yeah, she's all settled in now." She didn't want to give too many more details, because not only was she unsure of how much Pierce knew about her family drama, she also didn't want to rehash it, for any reason. "What did you do yesterday?"

"Puttered around the house a bit. My uncle's in town for the holiday, so hung out with him," he chuckled. "So I did get to do something yesterday even though you were too busy to see me."

She felt a twinge when she heard that. Even though he'd delivered the phrase in a joking tone, she couldn't help feeling that he was being sardonic. It sounded as if he were pouting about yesterday.

Everything was fine as long as I said yes to whatever he wanted to do. Now he's upsetti spaghetti?

Deciding to ignore his childish remark, she said, "How long have you been fishing?"

"My uncle used to take me when I was a kid. We usually made a road trip of it. He'd drive here from his place in Savannah and take me and my sister to lakes all over the Southeast to fish." He stared out over the water as he spoke. "London never wanted to touch the fish. But Uncle Martin and I would get whatever she caught off the hook for her." He turned her way. "What about you? You agreed to do this, so I assume you've got at least a little fishing experience."

She nodded. "Yeah, we used to fish as a family every few summers, usually in conjunction with a camping trip. I haven't done it in a few years, though. I think the last time I fished was maybe eight years ago."

"So you might be a little rusty," he commented, gesturing toward the two poles he'd brought. "As long as you aren't as scary as my sister about touching the bait and the fish, we should be good."

She shook her head. "Nah. I can manage it."

He asked, "Do you wanna grab a drink or some chips?"

"Let's see what you've got."

He opened the basket, and she chose a can of orange soda and a bag of honey wheat pretzel twists, while he grabbed a cola and barbecue chips.

He sat down in the other chair, and they ate and drank for a few moments. When they'd finished, he leaned down and handed her a pole. "Ready?"

She nodded. "Let's give it a go."

They worked together to haul their chairs, the bait

bucket and their poles to the dock. Setting up a safe distance from the edge, they baited their hooks and cast them.

Darkness settled around them, making the overhead lights seem brighter. The air was cool, not cold, and the rhythmic song of insects could be heard emitting from the trees. She watched the glow play over the calm surface of the water and felt the peace of the moment wash over her. It was this communion with nature that made fishing so appealing to her.

He spoke. "Since we'll probably be sitting here awhile, let's chop it up."

"About what?"

"Hip-hop. What else?" He readjusted himself in his seat, leaning more toward her. "What do you remember about the origins of crunk and how it changed the landscape of hip-hop?"

"Wow. That's a really deep, layered question."

"I know. I'm eager to hear your perceptions."

She tugged her line a bit, then gave a little slack. "Hmm. I was in high school, probably sophomore— no, junior—year the first time I remember hearing Jon on the radio. I mean, his music. He had been an on-air personality with V-103 for a minute."

"Yeah, I remember that. He was in the clubs a lot, too, back then, I believe."

"Right. I know he had earlier music, but I really became aware of him when "Bia' Bia'" dropped. I mean, everybody was on that song. It was being played at every party, every dance, major play."

"It's a classic, for real. And it was only up from there.

So many good songs came after it, and the man is still going till this day." He sat up straight, eyeing the water.

"Did you get something?"

"I thought my bobber moved." He watched for a few more moments, then relaxed. "Anyway, do you remember what rap was like before Jon gave us crunk?"

She scoffed. "Absolutely. The nineties were great for both R & B and rap. But rap culture was so full of violence. Everybody was so focused on looking tough, on being harder than everyone else, on building so-called street cred."

"It was tense. The whole East Coast/West Coast beef, LL versus Canibus, Biggie versus Pac. The industry was just mired down in this infighting and posturing—"

"—like one massive pissing contest," she said, finishing his sentence. "When crunk came along, it was a mood shift, you know? Less talk about shooting each other, more club songs. Music we could dance to. The mood was so much lighter. It was the antithesis of what we'd just experienced in hip-hop culture."

"It was, and we needed that." He nodded his head. "You always need a release after any period of sustained tension. The cultural shift was absolutely necessary. I mean, some of the songs Jon put out, with the East Side Boyz or with other artists, still talked about fighting and mixing it up. But the tone was very different from what came before."

"That's really astute." She felt that little flicker inside, that certain kind of excitement that she could only get from truly stimulating conversation. "I didn't know anyone else had thought that deeply about this."

"We're both in the industry. I think that facilitates deeper consideration of topics like this." He sat upright again. "Okay, I definitely got something this time."

She watched, holding onto her own pole as he stood and reeled in whatever was tugging on his line. After a few minutes of tugging and pulling, he gave the crank a good spin and finally raised his catch. She smiled as the medium-sized fish broke the surface of the water, thrashing around and obviously not too keen on being caught. "He looks pretty mad," she joked.

"Good thing for our little water-dwelling homie that this lake is catch and release." He lifted the line, taking a good look at the fish. "Take a pic right quick."

She pulled out her phone and snapped the image.

Once she was done, he unhooked the fish and tossed it back into the water. "How was that?"

"Not bad." She watched him settle back into his seat and recast his line, pondering the multitudes he existed in. He was arrogant but charming. Petty and immature but could hold his own in an intellectual conversation about hip-hop culture.

What have I gotten myself into with him?

Still holding onto his fishing rod, Pierce eased his chair a bit closer to Nia's. She was quiet now and seemed content to stare out over the dark surface of the lake.

Finally, she spoke. "Have you ever thought about how crunk has stayed consistently popular, even over time? It's been around a couple of decades now."

"That's true." He thought about some of the other subsets of hip-hop that had come and gone. "Snap was good, but it was short-lived. Same with chopped and screwed. You just don't hear it as much now. Crunk just endures."

"And it evolves." She leaned forward in her seat. "I've always thought of trap as love child of gansta rap and crunk. Its violent or drug-related lyrical content with the catchy, danceable beat behind it. See what I mean?"

He felt his brow furrow. "I never thought of it that way, but hearing you say it, that checks out. It's always been odd to me seeing all the dance crazes the kids come up with to these songs, which are essentially musical storytelling about the drug trade and gang life."

"It's almost as if the beat is so catchy, the impact of the lyrics is lost." She shook her head. "At any rate, hip-hop has always been about storytelling, relating one's experiences in a culturally relevant way."

"This is one thing I think about, though." He stared rewinding his line, figuring one catch for the evening would suffice. "The words to these songs say a lot about the kinds of things these artists may or may not be actively involved in. Do you think that could ever be used against them? Like, legally?"

She tilted her head to one side, narrowing her eyes. "I guess they could. Wait, do you mean like the whole thing that went down back in the eighties, with Tipper Gore and the parental advisory label? Something large-scale like that?"

He shook his head. "No, not like that. I mean something more granular and targeted. Like, could rappers face individual negative legal consequences based on the things they speak on in their music?"

She drew a deep breath, her eyes wide. "Damn, Pierce. That's a good-ass question. I don't know if that's been done before, but I could definitely see some over-zealous officials trying to use lyrics as evidence. And if they did, and the courts actually went for it, we could be looking at an event that might potentially imprison a whole segment of the music industry."

"Absolutely. Because who's to say it would stop with artists? What about the writers, the producers, the re-cord company folks, all the people who made a profit off of an artists' lyrical descriptions of illegal activity?"

She shook her head and released a chuckle. "It's so funny to think about this. I know from my studies in music production that the whole reason Mrs. Gore started her crusade was a song by His Royal Purple-ness. That's decidedly outside the genre, yet I'd bet the majority of albums with that black-and-white sticker have probably been rap and hip-hop."

"It's really a trip, isn't it?" He started laughing.

A moment later, she joined him, and they spent a short time in the throes of shared humor.

When he finally got over his mirth, he said, "I don't think the odds are in your favor tonight, Nia."

She shook her head. "Nah. If I was gonna catch any-thing, it would have happened by now." She rewound her reel.

He stood, taking her rod. "I'll put these up. Mind bringing the chairs?"

"I got it."

They worked together to carry the chairs and the fishing gear back to the blanket he'd left on the grass. He stooped low and placed the rods inside the zippered storage bag he'd brought. Once they were closed inside, he sat down next to Nia once again.

The view of the water was slightly different here than it had been from their spot on the dock, but the glow of the park's electric lighting on the surface still elicited the same feeling of calm.

He turned his gaze skyward. He could see the distant city lights stretching for miles, the sprinkling of stars. "There's no comparison between the night sky in the city and the way it looks out at my uncle's place."

She tilted her head back. "I know what you mean. My aunt Laurie's place is outside Charlotte, far enough out to eliminate most of the light pollution. It always seems like there are a million stars when you're out in the country."

"I bought a mountain cabin in Tennessee for that very reason. I love going out there to experience that peace and quiet. Haven't been in ages, though."

She turned his way. "Is that an invitation?" Her tone was teasing.

"Maybe it is," he teased back, reaching for her. Guiding her face close to his, he placed a series of short kisses along her jawline, then pressed his lips to hers.

The kiss deepened, and he swept his tongue into her warm mouth. He continued until she rested her hand on his forearm, giving it a subtle squeeze. Sensing that she was signaling him, he eased away, whispering, "I... love you, Nia."

She stared into his eyes, looking conflicted.

He frowned. "What's wrong?"

"I...uh." Her gaze fled. "I don't really do PDA like this, usually."

Did she not hear what I said? Not wanting to dwell on the fact that she hadn't addressed it, he glanced around. "There's nobody else out here. I mean, there may be some folks still in the park, but there's nobody close enough to see us," he chuckled. "Except the Feds. We all know they be watching us through our cell phones."

The joke didn't land, and she pulled back. "It's not that. I mean, if we're supposed to just be casually enjoying each other's company, don't you think this is a little too much?"

She did hear me, then. She just...doesn't feel the same. Keeping his expression flat, he shrugged. "Not really, but if you're uncomfortable, say no more." He put a little distance between them, all the while wondering what had changed.

She stood then, stretched. "It's getting late, and we both have work tomorrow. I think I'm going to call it a night."

He nodded. "Alright. Let me gather my gear, and I'll walk you to your car." While she waited, he collapsed the chairs and put them in their bags. Tucking the folded blanket and the bait bucket into the large basket, he slung the rod and chairs over his shoulder, held the basket with one hand and offered his free hand to Nia.

They made a trek through the park, arriving shortly at the parking area where their cars were parked. She unlocked her door with the remote on her keys, and he swung it open for her.

"Thanks, Pierce. Have a good night."

"You, too." He closed her inside the car.

Waiting for her to back out of her parking spot, he then walked a few yards to his SUV, opening the lift gate and tucking all his stuff inside. Watching her taillights disappear, he thought back on their conversation.

Did I say something wrong? I just can't figure her out.

Thirteen

Tuesday, Nia left her office around ten to make it to her meeting with Pierce at Hamilton House. She stopped off for coffee on the way, her second cup of the day. Apparently, staying up past eleven on a weeknight hadn't been the best idea. While she had enjoyed her little fishing expedition with Pierce, she now thought that activity better suited to the weekends.

She arrived at the Hamilton House building forty-five minutes later, as dictated by traffic. Parking her car in a visitors' spot, she looked up at the towering structure. It was a lot larger than the 404 building, both in height and footprint. She knew that would change once 404's new studio complex was completed next year.

She entered the building a short time later and made her way across the large lobby to the gold lacquer reception desk. There were paintings hanging high on the walls, as well as concert posters and more music-related memorabilia. Everything stuck to a color scheme of silver, gold and black trim.

I can see where they were trying to go with the decor. I just don't think they got there.

The receptionist, an old woman with a salt-and-pepper bob and glasses, smiled in her direction. "Are you Miss Woodson?"

She nodded. "Yes, good morning."

"I'll let Mr. Hamilton and Mr. McClure know you're here. You can have a seat over there." She pointed to the white leather contemporary furniture grouping that sat off to one side of the space.

"Thank you." Hoping she wouldn't have to wait too long in this huge, gaudy space, she settled into the seat of a chair, setting her purse in her lap. A few minutes later, Pierce and Hunter approached. The three of them exchanged greetings, and she noticed the way Pierce seemed to be avoiding eye contact with her.

"Let's go into the media room," Pierce said, already striding toward the western end of the lobby. "It's right this way."

She followed the two men out of the lobby and down a narrow corridor, arriving at a room set up like a small theater. A group of ten deep upholstered chairs were clustered in two rows, facing a large screen occupying the wall in front of them.

"I'm all set up to cue up the film," Hunter commented. "You can sit wherever you'd like. When it's finished, we can discuss it. I'm eager to hear your thoughts on it."

She nodded and eased into a chair in the center of the front row, while Pierce and Hunter sat behind her.

The lights dimmed, and the screen came alive with images as the film began. She marveled at the sound quality emitting from hidden speakers that seemed to be positioned all around her.

She smiled during moments of nostalgia, especially when the images she'd submitted played across the screen. There were old pictures galore featuring her, her parents and all her siblings in various capacities and places related to the company's history. Seeing them all made her consider how deeply the company and her family's legacy were entwined.

When the film ended and the lights were brought back up, she took a deep breath. "Really impressive work, Hunter."

"Thank you," he said from behind her. "Although plenty of the credit goes to my buddy Steve, who does my editing."

"Can we go somewhere else to discuss it?" She turned in her seat. "It feels weird having a conversation in a space like this."

"Yeah, sure. There's a break room next door." Pierce stood and headed for the door.

A few minutes later, they were sitting at a small, round table in the room next door. The room had a wet bar and a full-size fridge along one wall, as well as a counter with a coffee maker and all the necessary accompaniments.

"Coffee? Water?" Pierce offered.

She shook her head. "Thanks, but I had some on the way over. One more cup and I'll start levitating."

Hunter chuckled. "Then that means you were super alert during the film. So, why don't you tell us what you think?"

"Have you already given your take, Pierce?"

He nodded. "I have."

"Okay. Well, again I'll start by saying I think it's amazing. Great editing, very sleek. And Hunter, you have a command of storytelling that really comes through. I feel like there may be a few small gaps in the narrative, but once we fill those in, I think it will be perfect."

Hunter reached back to regather his locs into the low ponytail they were trying to escape. "Great. What's missing?"

"I think there should be more mention of Atlanta toward the beginning. As in, using it more as a backdrop for what was going on when the company was in its infancy. When I hear my parents talk about those days, especially my mom, there's a lot of mention of the things that were happening in the city at the time."

Pierce appeared confused. "What does any of that have to do with the company, really?"

She turned her gaze in his direction. "My parents were young and impressionable. Their environment shaped their views and how they approached building the business."

"Don't you think the same thing would be true of

my parents?" Pierce's tone was sharp, bordering on accusatory.

She frowned, wondering what had brought on his attitude. "Probably so, but this story isn't about them." She turned back to Hunter. "The only other thing I think it needs is a little more focus on the vision statement my father set out with. That's another thing that's been a guiding force in the direction of the company these past three decades and change."

Pierce groused, "That wasn't Caleb's vision."

She narrowed her eyes as her gaze swung back to Pierce. "Excuse me, what?"

"That vision for the company didn't belong solely to Caleb. It belonged to my father, as well."

She drew a deep breath. They were treading in very sensitive territory, and while she didn't care at all for Pierce's tone, she didn't want to be disrespectful to Mr. Hamilton's memory, either. Maybe his father's recent birthday had brought up lingering pain for Pierce. She tried to err on the side of understanding. "That's valid."

"I know it's valid. And I'll tell you what else is valid." His tone grew more intense with each word. "404 is only half of that vision. If the vision had really been the guiding force, there wouldn't be a Hamilton House. What my father wanted was to share a business and a legacy with his best friend. He saw our two families together, conquering the music world for years to come. That's why a full merger is the only way forward."

"How did we get to that subject?" She stared at him, trying to figure out his angle. "Like, why are you even bringing that up right now?"

"Oh, would there be a more convenient time to re-mind you that this whole anniversary gala is a sham? That it dishonors my father's memory by leaving him out?"

Hunter finally interjected. "Now, hold on, Pierce. We both know you spoke at length about both your parents in your confessional segment, and I left that footage fully intact."

Pierce bolted from his chair. "It's not enough, and we all know it. It's just that I'm the only one willing to admit it." He stormed from the room.

Left sitting at the table with Hunter, Nia blinked several times.

What the hell just happened?

Hunter said, "Do you have time to film a little bit of footage, so I can add it and fix the issues? Your cri-tique is valid."

She nodded. "Sure thing. And I'm glad you can see that, since your friend has apparently gone off the deep end."

Wednesday evening, Pierce pulled up a chair to the table in the dining room of his childhood home, ready to appease his grumbling stomach. "Thanks for mak-ing your famous brisket, Uncle Martin. I haven't had it in forever."

"I don't make it often," Martin said from his seat across from his nephew. "Takes a lot of work."

"That's why I stepped in to help and made all the sides," Everly added.

"Well, I'm grateful to you both." That comment came from London, who was already chewing.

Pierce eyed his plate full of brisket, turnip greens, yams and corn muffins, and dug in. The first bit of tender, well-seasoned brisket sent his taste buds into the stratosphere. He groaned aloud.

"Good, ain't it?" Martin grinned. "You know, I brought the yams and the greens from home. Came fresh outta my garden."

"I see you, Unc." London raised her glass of iced tea in his direction. "Your green thumb and your brisket skills are undefeated."

Everly stifled a yawn between bites. "It's very good, Martin."

Pierce watched his mother, noting the drawn expression and the way her shoulders slumped ever so slightly. She wore her exhaustion just as clearly as she wore yet another spangly tracksuit.

As the meal began to wrap up, Pierce elbowed London, who sat to his immediate right.

She nodded, understanding the predetermined signal. "So, Mom. Have you given any thought to retirement?"

Everly chuckled, waving her hand. "Of course not. I am Hamilton House, and I'll be around for a long, long time running the show just like I always have."

Pierce exchanged knowing looks with his sister and his uncle. Her response had been just as rooted in stubbornness and denial as he'd expected. *She's not gonna make this easy for us. Still, it has to be done.*

London said, "Mother, you have to plan for things like this, no matter how far off you think they might be."

Everly harrumphed, rising from her seat and gathering her dishes. "I don't want to hear any of this retirement nonsense. I'm not some invalid. I know my own mind, and I won't be forced out."

Martin got to his feet, helping his sister-in-law by gathering everyone else's dishes. "Come on now, Everly. You know your babies are just looking out for you. They love you. And so do I."

"Don't you start, too, Martin," she groused.

Pierce watched his mother shuffle to the sink with the dishes and pile them inside the dishpan.

Martin added his stack of plates and silverware, then leaned against the counter, folding his big arms over his broad chest. "Let me ask you this, sis. If you had more free time on your hands, how would you spend it?"

Everly's expression softened, and she appeared to be considering the answer to the question.

Pierce was impressed; the question and the nonconfrontational manner in which it had been posed seemed to have put an end to his mother's snippiness, at least for the moment. *I see Uncle Martin's using a light touch. Nice one.*

Finally, Everly admitted, "I think I would travel more. I've been in my bridge club for twelve years now. They take a trip every quarter, someplace different, just for shopping and sightseeing. I've missed the last seven trips to do one thing or another for the company."

Placing his hand on her shoulder, Martin said quietly, "See? I bet those ladies are having tons of fun on those trips. And honestly, there's no reason you should be missing out on all that relaxation, and shopping, and time with your friends."

"He's right, Mom." London stood, possibly so her mother could see her face over the large floral centerpiece. "There are so many people at Hamilton House who care as much about its success as you do and who have the skills needed to keep it afloat."

Everly made her way back to the table, lowering herself into her seat. "You all really think it's time for me to step down?"

"It's getting close." Pierce reached for his mother's hand. "We're not rushing you. But considering your health, your energy levels and all the sacrifices you've made, how much longer are you willing to keep going at the pace you've been going?"

The room was quiet for several minutes, as Everly seemed to be considering everything she'd heard, and possibly all the experiences that had led up to this conversation. Finally, she sighed. Turning her gaze toward her brother-in-law, who was busy rinsing dishes, she said, "Martin, what's your honest opinion on this? Give me the real deal."

Turning off the water, he returned to his seat at the table. "I think you ought to listen to the kids, Everly. When Phillip left for his military training, I made him a promise. A big promise. I said I'd look after you. Even though I wasn't but a young buck, barely sixteen at the time, I meant what I said, and I've kept my promise all these years."

Tears formed in Everly's eyes as she reached for his

hand. "You have, Martin. You've been so good to me and my babies."

"As I should." He gave her hand a squeeze. "And in the spirit of that, I'm telling you it's time you ease up. Stop running yourself into the ground and let someone else step in and manage things. Can you agree to at least give it some serious thought?"

She nodded. "I will."

Pierce released a sigh of relief. "I'm so glad to hear that, Mother. You're doing the sensible thing"

She turned his way, a frown creasing her face. "Well, one of us has to, right?"

Confused, he said, "What do you mean?"

"I mean that little tantrum you threw at the office yesterday." She paused, watching his expression change. "Oh, you didn't think I knew about that, did you? Well, Jean heard you shouting all the way from that break room to the front desk. Saw you storming through the lobby like an angry bear, too." She shook her head.

Pierce cringed, as every set of eyes in the room turned on him. "I... Nia said something I didn't agree with, and I guess I reacted badly."

"Sheesh," London offered with a roll of her eyes.

Suddenly, the scrutiny was all on him, and he wasn't pleased. Still, he knew better than to act with his family the way he'd acted with Nia. "I'm sorry. I'll be sure to control my temper better next time."

"Good. Can't have you embarrassing me." Everly reached out and pinched his shoulder. "I raised you better than that, so act accordingly. First thing you need to do is call and apologize to Nia. Was anybody else there?"

He stared down at the table. "Hunter."

Martin whistled. "Your friend, too? You might need to apologize to him, as well. Depends on how much tolerance he's developed for your foolishness, I suppose."

"Point taken," he groused. He felt thoroughly chastised for his outburst, but part of him wondered how they would have reacted if they'd been there to experience Nia's dismissive words about his father, the way she'd conveniently left him out as if he hadn't played a significant role in 404's history. He wasn't going to repeat what she'd said, though, so he kept his silence and let the matter drop.

I can't be around someone who brings out that kind of behavior in me, no matter how much I might enjoy their company. And if Mother is really going to retire, then I need to be at my very best.

Fourteen

Nia held open the door to Elegance by Gladys for her mother and sister to enter the store behind her. It was Thursday afternoon, and the three of them had left the office an hour early to report to the dress shop for their final fittings. The big event was now just over a week away.

Gladys, a petite, shapely, brown-skinned woman with a mass of white, shoulder-grazing curls, lifted her wire-rimmed glasses by the string of pearls holding them around her neck. "Well, if it isn't the ladies of the house of Woodson." Gladys grinned as she walked out from behind the counter. "Good to see you, as always."

Addy embraced her old friend. "Don't tell me you forgot we have our final fitting today."

She waved her hand. "Of course not. Ruby is in the back getting your gowns ready as we speak."

Nia followed Gladys into the fitting room area in the back of the store. Two love seats and an upholstered ottoman formed a seating area to one side of the room. On the other end were the doors to the four small fitting stalls, and next to that was a round platform facing several full-length mirrors.

"You ladies can have a seat." Gladys gestured to the seating area. "Ruby and I will be back with your gowns shortly."

As Gladys disappeared, Teagan asked, "Who else is ready to be done with this gala?"

They all raised their hands.

Addy laughed. "We're racing toward the finish line, girls. In a couple of days, we can finally move on from this."

"And move right into Thanksgiving prep," Nia added with a shake of her head. "Remind me again why the gala had to be during this time of the year?"

"We opened the business in November. We're just sticking to the accurate date of that. Thankfully, the date falls on a Saturday." Addy stretched her arms above her head. "I'm tired, but excited."

Gladys returned then, with her assistant, Ruby, in tow. Ruby's arms were laden with large plastic garment bags. "Alright, ladies. Who's getting fitted first?"

"Go ahead, Mom," Teagan laughed. "I'm in no hurry to put on fancy, uncomfortable clothes."

Shaking her head, Addy stood. "I'll go first."

Gladys took Addy's gown, and Ruby handed the

other two off to their respective wearers. "Come on, Addy. I'll help you."

While her mother and the seamstress disappeared into one of the stalls, Nia peered at her dress through its plastic prison. It was a deep indigo color, and she could see a few details had been added since the last fitting. "Did Mom ask you to bedazzle my dress?"

Ruby shook her head. "No, that was me. Gladys is training me, and she asked me to add my own touch to it, so I added a few sequins around the neckline. Is it too much?"

She appeared thoughtful for a moment. "I don't think so. I'll be able to tell better once I've got it on."

"You can go ahead and try it on, if you don't mind me helping you into it," Ruby offered.

"Okay." Nia stood with her dress and followed Ruby into an empty stall. Once she was zipped up, she stepped out.

Addy was standing on the platform and could be described as no less than regal in her hunter-green A-line gown. The gown was made of satin, with matching gossamer floral lace making up the neckline and the long sleeves.

"What do you think?" Gladys asked.

"It's beautiful," Addy gushed, admiring her reflection. "I'm glad I brought in Caleb's bow tie. This fabric matches it perfectly."

Gladys grinned. "I'm so glad you love it." Turning toward Nia, she said, "And look at you. Amazing."

Ruby helped Addy down from the platform, and Nia stepped up to have her turn. She turned slowly, getting a full view of the strapless satin gown. The bodice shimmered with the added sequins, which had also been added as an accent around the high slit that revealed a portion of her left leg. The triangular floral lace inset in the back of the dress was the same type as the lace used on her mother's gown but had been dyed to match the indigo shade of Nia's. "It's gorgeous, Gladys. You've done it again."

Gladys laughed. "Of course, I have. I've been dressing this family since forever. Addy's wedding gown, both your prom dresses. You're some of my most loyal clients." She gestured for their mother. "Come, Addy. Let me get you out of yours so it doesn't get wrinkled."

Once Addy and Nia were out of their dresses, all eyes turned to Teagan.

"You can't put it off any longer," Addy said. "Go try yours on."

Teagan stood, lips pursed. "Alright."

The doorbell chimed, indicating a customer entering the shop. "Let me go help them. Ruby, could you assist Teagan, please?" Gladys was already headed to the front.

Teagan and Ruby went into the fitting room, leaving Nia and her mother sitting on the love seat.

"I really like your dress, Mom." Nia gave her mother's hand a squeeze. "You're gonna look just like a queen."

She smiled. "Thanks, sweetie. You know, I don't normally wear much green. I chose that color because it's Caleb's favorite."

"I'm glad you two have patched things up. Seeing you at odds was really disconcerting," she admitted.

"I was awful." Addy blew out a breath. "I'm glad it's over, and I'm glad my faith in your father has been restored. Part of me feels very guilty that it ever faltered in the first place."

"I think all of us had our moments of doubt, especially after those test results." Nia sighed as she remembered the feeling of that envelope in her hand. "There was no way any of us could have known they were doctored."

"Your father said the same thing, essentially. He was the only one in the room who knew it wasn't right. It pains me to think of what that felt like for him. The loneliness of that." She paused. "He's been so forgiving. He says he understands why I reacted the way I did, and he's simply happy to have me back. The fact that he's not trying to add to my suffering, even though I lost faith in him, just speaks to the kind of man he is."

Nia felt the smile tugging her lips. "You two have something special. Seeing it restored has really touched my heart."

"It's trust, Nia. Trust at the basis of it all… It makes the love come easy." Addy winked.

Nia considered what her mother had said. It made her think about Pierce, and how the more time she spent with him, the more things she discovered about him that didn't sit well with her.

We aren't in a relationship. This was supposed to be a fling. Yet I keep letting him take up my mental space, giving him energy he doesn't deserve. I need to protect myself. There's too much going on in my world. I can't let myself get caught up.

The stall door opened, and Teagan stepped out, with Ruby close behind her.

"Oh, honey." Addy squealed. "You look beautiful!"

Nia agreed as she took in her sister's outfit. It was a sky-blue satin off-the-shoulder romper, with a floral lace panel at the abdomen and a matching lace train that fell gracefully from her waistline to pool on the floor. Teagan hated dressing up, and this was the closest they could get to putting her in a fancy gown.

Teagan rolled her eyes as she stepped onto the platform. Her expression softened when she looked at her reflection. "You're not wrong, Mom. I'm still not excited about dressing up. But I do look damn good."

Nia laughed at her sister's dryly delivered words. "We're gonna slay this gala."

Pierce had a busy morning Friday, and by the time eleven rolled around, he felt like he'd spent the entire morning putting out metaphorical fires of various types and sizes. Stifling a yawn, he finally returned to his office and dropped into his executive chair, seeking a few minutes of respite from the grind.

Yikes. If I wind up in the CEO position, is this what my days will be like? He blew out a breath, knowing he'd do it anyway for a chance to have some real say in the future direction of Hamilton House.

Taking his phone from his pocket, he glanced at the screen. It had been on silent all morning, and as he looked at his notifications, he saw that there were none from Nia. He hadn't heard anything from her in the past few days. His last glimpse of her was the perplexed expression on his face when he'd strode out of the break room.

I miss talking to her, laughing with her. But maybe this is for the best.

Marisol, his assistant, poked her head through his open office door. "Mr. Hamilton. The crew from WZZT is here. They've set up in the second-floor conference room."

"Thanks. I'll head down there in a minute."

She disappeared, and he sighed. *Gotta get myself together... This is a live interview.* He leaned back in the chair and took several deep, cleansing breaths. Then he got up and left his office.

When he arrived in the conference room, he had to sidestep into the doorway to avoid a radio crew member standing nearby. The long table was occupied by a few pieces of broadcasting equipment, and two boom mics and headphones had been set up in front of two adjacent chairs.

Once of the chairs was occupied by radio personality Countess McDougald, known as Turnt Tess on the city's airwaves. Petite and dark-skinned, she wore a bright purple bob and dark sunglasses. Dressed casually in black jeans and a black tee bearing the station's logo, she stood when he entered the room. "What's up, Mr. Hamilton? Thanks for agreeing to do the interview."

"Thanks for coming out," he said, shaking her hand. "And please, call me Pierce." He slipped around the table and took a seat next to her.

"Gotcha. Now remember, we'll be live today. So the only buffer you have between what you say and what people all over the city are gonna hear is the two-second delay." She rubbed her hands together. "You ready, champ?"

He nodded. "I'm good. Like E-40 said, tell me when to go."

She grinned. "I like that, I like that. We got about five minutes before we go live, and I'll cue you in with my intro. Cool?"

He gave her a thumbs-up, slipping on his headphones.

She did the same, scooting her chair up to the boom mic.

The radio crewman raised his hand as the sound of Tess's recorded intro filled the room. Giving a silent countdown with his fingers, he then pointed to Tess.

"What's up, what's up, all my hip-hop lovers out there. It's your girl, Turnt Tess, holding it down for *Lunchtime Madness* here on WZZT, Beats 103. Today we got a special guest, a little treat for all y'all. He's live with me, in the building, right here and now. This man is responsible for some of your favorite bangers. He had a hand in launching many a hip-hop career across the South. Give it up for Mr. Pierce Hamilton of Hamilton House Recordings! Thank you so much for coming, by the way."

Leaning into the mic, Pierce smiled; his PR coach told him people could hear a smile even though they were unable to see it. "What's up, ATL. I'm happy to be here today."

"Awesome. So, like I said, you've done a lot of production work for some of the greats of hip-hop, past and present. Now, I understand there's a big event coming up tomorrow night, right here in the city, that you'll be a part of."

"Right. Tomorrow night is the thirty-fifth anniversary gala for 404 Sound, and I'll be participating in that."

"Excellent. All you real hip-hop fans know about 404. They're just as legendary as Hamilton House and have become a go-to for artists that want that boutique experience. So, Pierce, tell me what tomorrow night's gala will be about. I hear there's an exciting collab that's gonna drop. Tell us about that."

He cleared his throat. "There's a film retrospective that's going to highlight 404's history and also the wider impact of hip-hop culture on the city. I worked with Nia Woodson, 404's CEO, as well as my good friend Hunter McClure, to develop the film."

"Word. This is about to be epic. Can we expect some real behind-the-scenes information?"

He laughed. "Absolutely. That's what it's all about—letting people have a window into the inner workings of the company and of music production."

Tess nodded. "I feel you. So, this gala, and the film, all that's gonna look at the past. Tell me what you see happening for the future of music production here in Atlanta. So many artists now are doing their own recording and production. Tell me what you think is gonna keep companies like Hamilton House and 404 relevant."

"Well, it's like the old saying goes. Just because you

can do something, doesn't mean you should." He rested his elbows on the table, lacing his fingers. "Sound quality. Production value. These things matter when an artist is trying to build a fan base and a lasting career. That's where we come in. We let the artist focus on their art, while we handle the presentation and packaging."

"Tell me a little about your favorite aspects of the business."

He answered with a short speech about artist development and the discovery of talent that might otherwise go unheard.

"What do you say to up-and-coming artists who want to choose between Atlanta's top two options for recording?"

He shook his head. "I can't tell people which to choose. That's really a personal decision based on a lot of factors. What I can say is, I wish they didn't have to make a choice at all."

She frowned. "What do you mean by that?"

"Theoretically speaking, if 404 and Hamilton House were to merge, artists would have the best of all worlds. Boutique feel, corporate reach and budget."

"Whoa!" Tess eyed him. "As far as we know, there's no talk of any merger. Are you giving us tea? Is this an exclusive?

"No, nothing like that. That's why I said *theoretically speaking.* Trust me—I've spent a lot of effort, money and time looking at this from all angles. It's really the ideal situation, but if the folks at 404 don't see that, then…" He shrugged. "It is what it is."

Appearing surprised, Tess continued. "Alright, then.

Let me ask you this before I let you go. This is unrelated to what we were just talking about. But the holidays are just around the corner. What's your favorite holiday dish?"

"Oh, that's easy. Sweet potato pie, no contest."

Tess laughed. "Spoken like a true Southerner. Thank you for coming on today, Pierce. We appreciate you."

"Thanks for having me."

As Tess gave her spiel leading into a commercial break, Pierce removed his headphones and set them back on the table. When she was cleared off air, she turned his way. "Thanks again for letting us come through. We don't get a lot of industry folks to come on, at least not lately."

"No problem. I appreciate your willingness to come here."

"Sound quality is just way better if we do it in person. I hate doing the over-the-phone interviews."

He watched as Tess and her crew packed up their equipment and headed out. Alone in the conference room, he was confronted with the loud grumbling of his stomach.

Getting up from his seat, he headed out to grab lunch.

Fifteen

Nia sat in the sitting area of her office Friday, one leg tossed over the other. Her assistant had just dropped off the salad she'd ordered, and now she was parked in her comfy chair, enjoying a well-earned lunch.

Ugh, it's too quiet in here. She turned on the small radio on the end table next to her and tuned it to the local hip-hop station.

She tapped her foot in time with the beat of a new trap record, smiling when she heard her new sister-in-law's voice singing the hook. *That reminds me. Miles and Cambria got back last night. I should call him and see how he enjoyed his trip.*

After the song ended, the DJ's voice cut in. Nia listened as she carried on an interview with Pierce, one she'd had no idea he'd planned on giving. Deciding to see what he had to say, she listened to his voice answering questions over the sounds of her crunching on fresh veggies.

She finished up the salad and grabbed the plastic cup of iced lemonade. She almost choked mid-sip when she heard him say the word *merger*.

Setting her cup down, she leaned in and listened carefully to the remainder of the interview. He'd said something about a merger, making it sound like an announcement, then tried to backpedal on his statement. She took another long sip of her drink as the interview came to an end. *This man has lost his everlasting mind.*

But what really stood out to her was what he'd said about his so-called research. That he'd spent time, money and effort evaluating the pros and cons of a merger. Time and effort, she understood. But money?

How, and why, would he spend money investigating a potential merger that no one else wants?

She tossed her trash and returned to her desk. Opening her laptop, she decided to do some digging online. A series of searches related to Pierce's name and Hamilton House eventually led her to Keegan's.

She frowned. *How in the world are these two things related?* She scrolled back to the top of the page and read the headline of the piece, a newsletter from an independent contractor newsletter. The headline read "Business Consultant Lands Contract with Musical Production Firm."

She skimmed the article, but it was so short, it didn't give much detail. Left with more questions than answers, she gave her dad a quick call.

"Hey, Dad. Did you get a copy of the PI's report?"

"Yes, I have it. What's up?"

"Can you email it to me right quick?"

He sounded confused. "Sure. But…are you gonna tell me why?"

"Yes. Just not right now. I'll be waiting for your email. Love you, bye." She disconnected the call before her father could begin his questioning in earnest. Turning back to her computer screen, she opened her inbox and waited, refreshing it every few minutes. The report showed up on the second refresh, and she opened it, running a search for Pierce's name.

A single result popped up, and she felt her jaw tighten. *I can't believe this.*

Isolating the page, she printed it out, folded it in half and stuck it in her purse. Grabbing her keys, she strode from the office and headed straight for the elevator.

She passed Miles as she got off on the first floor.

He stopped, grabbing her arm gently. "Are you okay? You look like you're ready to fight."

"I am."

He narrowed his eyes. "Do you need me to rearrange someone's face, sis?"

A brief smile tugged her lips despite her burning anger. "Not right now. But if that changes, I'll give you a call.

He nodded, releasing his hold on her.

"By the way, welcome back. You look rested." She moved past him down the corridor, passing the studio suites and crossing the lobby to head outside. Nia hopped in her car and was out in traffic within the next five minutes.

She drove straight to Hamilton House, determined to confront Pierce for both his on-air bluster and his other newly discovered sin. Her single cup of coffee had long since worn off, and she arrived at the building and stalked inside, fueled by the sheer force of righteous indignation.

I was really beginning to like him, but I never got around to trusting him. Now I see why.

She offered a polite wave to the receptionist as she moved across the lobby, pausing to read the directory. Finding Pierce's name and the location of his office, Nia carried herself to the elevator bank.

His office door was ajar, but she knocked anyway. Home training wasn't going by the wayside simply because she was upset.

"Come in," he called.

She swung the door open and strode in, loaded for bear. "Pierce Hamilton. I would like you to explain yourself."

Seated behind his desk, he appeared to be reading something. He was well dressed as usual, wearing a heather-gray suit with a lime-colored shirt and a black-and-gray-striped tie. As she watched, he looked up from the open book in front of him. "Hello to you, too, Nia Woodson. Since we calling each other by our full names." He shook his head. "Mind telling me what I'm explaining, exactly?"

"I heard you on the radio."

"I don't see why that's got you upset—" He paused.

"Wait, is this about the merger thing? Because I clearly told her that was hypothetical."

"While that was problematic of you to say, that's not why I'm here." She moved closer to the desk. Taking the page she'd printed out of her purse, she unfolded it and held it out. "I'm going to need you to explain why Keegan Woodbine, the man that almost destroyed my family, was on your payroll."

Taking the piece of paper Nia handed him, Pierce brought it closer so he could read it. It appeared to be an employment-history section of some kind of dossier, with notes included. He glanced up at her, taking in her stern expression. It did nothing to diminish her beauty, or the stylishness of her jet-black skirt suit, classic white blouse and pumps. Clearing his throat, he brought his focus back to the moment at hand. "What am I looking at here?"

"That's the report from the private investigator my dad hired to look into Keegan Woodbine." She folded her arms over her chest. "There's a lot of information in it, too. But what really stood out to me, and seemed a little odd, is that he worked for you, not too long before he showed up at our offices claiming to be my father's illegitimate child."

He frowned, setting the paper on his desk. "So, why bring me the page? If you had asked me, I would have told you Keegan worked for me, albeit briefly."

She blinked several times. "Why would I need to ask? You could have just told me. You have to be aware of what's happened in my family. It was all over the gossip blogs and the city papers."

He nodded. "I know about it. But I didn't think it was a topic you'd want to discuss with anyone, least of all me."

She pressed her hand to her forehead. "Pierce. What exactly did you hire Keegan to do here?"

"I met him at a charity event last year. He came to me and pitched himself as a business consultant, specializing in data collection and analysis. I was impressed, but it was a while before I got back around to hiring him."

"To do what?"

He sighed, aware that she wouldn't be pleased with the answer. "I asked him to look into 404's finances and its general business standings. He was only supposed to use publicly available data to compile a report on… areas for improvement that Hamilton House might be able to assist with."

She narrowed her eyes. "You mean, weak points your company could use to facilitate a takeover?"

He shook his head. "It wasn't like that. You are putting words in my mouth, and besides that, you're reaching."

"How, Pierce? How is that a reach?"

"You're ascribing some kind of nefarious intent to this, when it's really just business." He leaned back in his chair, watching the anger play over her face. Her jaw was set, her brow furrowed. "As I said, it was a temporary hire. He worked on the report for about a month, turned it in and left. I never heard from him again."

"That's because he'd shifted his focus from working for your family to tearing mine apart." She shook her head slowly. "You have no idea what we've been through these past few months. It was devastating, on levels you couldn't even imagine."

He blew out a breath. "You're probably right, and it's terrible what happened to you all. I'm just trying to figure out what any of this has to do with me. As in, why are you in my office shouting at me about it?"

"You were never gonna tell me Keegan worked for you, were you?"

He shrugged. "I saw no reason to bring it up."

She swiped her tongue over her lower lip, releasing a bitter chuckle. "You know, I find it extremely interesting that you would send that man to poke around in my family's business affairs. That failed spectacularly for everyone involved, by the way."

He sighed. "Yeah, I know."

"But what really gets me is, it was only after that whole incident that you're suddenly so interested in spending time with me. I mean, you were always flirty, but word on the streets is that's how you move. You'll put the moves on anybody you think is game."

He frowned. "Hold on, now. No need to insult me."

"Oh, I think there's plenty need to tell you about yourself, Pierce. You must think I'm stupid. You don't think I can see that the only reason you've taken any interest in me is so you can finagle your way into a merger between our family companies?"

"I never said that."

She scoffed. "There's a lot you never said. The point remains." She stared at him, eyes as sharp as daggers.

"So why don't you just come out and admit it, Pierce. Admit that you pursued me, held conversation with me, made love to me, so that you could move in on 404."

He drew a deep breath and blew it out slowly. He didn't want to hurt her any further, but he knew keeping it from her now wasn't going to help. "I...may have thought that in the beginning—"

"Ha!" She cut him off. "I knew it. But let me guess. Things are different because now that you've gotten to know me, you really care about me." She held up air quotes as she said the last few words. "Spare me any more of your lies."

Her words sliced through him, and he felt the searing pain. He stood. "Nia, you have to listen to me. I really do—"

"No." She turned her back on him and walked away. Pausing at the office door, she said, "I never want to see or hear from you again, Pierce."

He took a step in her direction, softly calling her name again. "Nia, please."

"Come within ten feet of me, and I'll have my brothers put you in traction. Trust me—they'd jump at the chance to hem you up."

Sixteen

Nia ran a hand over her hair, hoping the dampness in the air wouldn't ruin her hard-won style. Fully gowned, coiffed and made-up, she was standing outside Atlanta's historic Fox Theatre, waiting for the entirety of her family to make it to the door.

She'd been first down the red carpet, keeping a quick pace. She wasn't one to enjoy being in the public eye. Now that attention had turned to her brother Miles, who'd just arrived with his gorgeous, multiplatinum wife, Cambria, on his arm, she was catching her breath beneath the comforting shadow of the stone overhang.

Teagan eased up next to her, grabbing her hand and giving it a squeeze. "How are you holding up?" Having fielded a late-night phone call, she knew what had occurred between her older sister and Pierce.

Nia sighed. "I'm okay, I guess."

"Hang in there, sis," Teagan said. "After all, the party's just getting started."

She cringed. Her sister was right. They'd finally made it to the gala, after well over a year of planning. Yet she didn't feel nearly as celebratory as the bustling crowds, bright lights and glamour all around her would suggest. She couldn't put the feeling into words, but she felt out of sorts, and decidedly out of place. Most of all, she hoped she could avoid Pierce as much as possible this evening.

As the rest of the family made it to the door, with her canoodling parents bringing up the rear, the family was escorted inside. Taking a meandering tour of the historic building, they finally arrived in the Egyptian Ballroom. The cavernous space was outfitted with tables covered in black cloth, elegant red floral centerpieces and bronze accents. Once they were all seated at the head table, Nia took in a broad view of the room. "Wow. The party planner went all out with the decor. It's really beautiful."

"With what we paid, it's as it should be," Miles quipped.

Nia shook her head. *He just can't help himself. Always thinking about the bottom line.* She supposed that was what made him such an efficient chief financial officer. "How was your trip?" she asked the couple.

"It was amazing," Cambria volunteered. In addition to the gorgeous cap-sleeved burgundy gown, upswept hair and fabulous makeup she wore, Nia's newest sister-in-law was all aglow with love. "We had the most amazing little bungalow, right on the water. The sunrises were…breathtaking."

"So were the nights," Miles quipped with a wink.

"Ew." Teagan pretended to plug her ears. "Don't even think about finishing that sentence."

Nia grabbed her water glass and took a sip, looking at everyone seated around the table. Everyone was paired off: her parents, Miles and Cambria, Blaine and the extremely pregnant Eden, Gage and Ainsley, Teagan and Maxton. The venue had given them a larger table, one that could accommodate twenty people, and she was grateful for that. If they hadn't, she'd have just been an eleventh place setting squeezed in at a table meant for ten.

Doing her best to shake that thought from her mind, she instead struck up a conversation with Eden. "How are you feeling?"

Hand on her stomach, Eden blew out a breath. "Tired. But I'm really glad this is finally happening. Your whole family has been working on it for what seems like forever."

"Tell me about it." Addy grinned. "But, seeing you all here, looking so amazing, has made it all worth it." Tears began to gather in her eyes. "I promised myself I wasn't gonna get weepy tonight." She touched Caleb's jaw with a gentle hand. "Being back home with my love…this celebration…being on the verge of becoming a grandmother… It's a lot of joy for this one little heart to contain."

"That's so sweet," Eden squeaked, fanning her face with her hands.

An amused Blaine handed his wife a white linen napkin. "She cries at the slightest thing nowadays. Yesterday, she cried because she ran out of sour pickles."

Eden elbowed her husband. "I'm making a human, for goodness' sake. Cut me some slack."

Blaine leaned in and kissed her forehead. "Yes, baby. Of course, I will."

Nia held back a sigh. All around her, she saw couples sharing gestures of affection. When she saw Teagan grab one of Maxton's ears and tug him over for a kiss on the cheek, she stood. "I'll be back. I'm going to the ladies' room." She needed to pee, yes. But more than that, she needed to escape the romantic lovefest happening at the table.

Cambria stood, too. "I'll go with you."

Surprised but not opposed to it, Nia gave her a quick nod.

They navigated through the tables and into the corridor. Greg "Captain Crusher" Alford, Cambria's longtime bodyguard, clad in a tux, was posted just outside ballroom. He nodded to them as they passed by.

"He's gonna keep coming with me to big events like this," Cambria confided as they continued down the hall toward the ladies' room. "I'm probably going to tour less, but Greg's loyal, you know?"

Nia nodded. "That's the kind of person you want to keep around." She entered the bathroom behind Cambria and ducked into an empty stall.

A few minutes later, as they stood at the sink washing their hands, Cambria asked, "Are you okay?"

Nia shrugged. "I don't know. I think I'm just…feeling the weight of the night. It's a milestone occasion, and let's just say things look very different than I expected they would at the time we started planning this."

"I'll bet. I mean, weren't all of the Woodson kids single then?"

Nia sighed. "Yep. I can't believe that in less than eighteen months, every single Woodson kid has gotten hitched…except me." Shaking her head, she checked her reflection in the mirror to ensure she didn't look like what she'd been through. "I never thought I was the type to care about this kind of thing. Turns out I was wrong."

"Do you have prospects? Like, are you seeing someone?"

"I thought I might be… But, no."

With a sidelong glance, Cambria asked, "Do I want to know what you mean by that?"

"Nah."

Cambria smiled. "I know I'm your newest sister-in-law, but I'm going to do my best to talk you off this ledge."

"I'm listening."

"I'm not religious or any of that, but I do believe in divine timing. How the Universe sends us what we need most when we need it." She grabbed Nia's hand. "Your time is coming around, and it may be sooner than you think. For right now, just try to enjoy this celebration. Your family has a beautiful legacy, and you're a big part of that."

She leaned in and gave Cambria a hug, feeling some of the tension in her chest releasing. "Thank you, Cambria. You're pretty good at this sister thing."

"Glad to hear it," she said with a laugh. "Because pretty soon, you and I are gonna have to get good at the auntie thing."

They both laughed as they headed back out into the hall.

Back at their table, Nia scanned the crowd. A lot more people had arrived in the few minutes she'd been away, and she saw many familiar faces in the crowd, some of them famous. There were singers, rappers and music industry elite, all people who'd worked with 404 in the past, who'd come out to share in a celebration of everything the company had contributed to the city of Atlanta and to hip-hop culture.

She smiled, feeling the pride that came with seeing the ripple effect of her family's work, the fruit borne by her parents' youthful dreams.

But her smile faded as she saw Pierce Hamilton crossing the room. He looked handsome in his tuxedo, and he escorted his mother on one arm and his sister on the other.

She drew a deep breath, turning away before he made eye contact.

I need to be present and focus on celebrating my family now.

Pierce had just pulled out his mother's chair when he caught a glimpse of Nia. She was at the edge of his peripheral vision, but even a sliver of her was enough to grab his attention.

"I'm sitting down, son. You can push the chair up," Everly announced.

"Sorry." He turned his attention back to his mother and gave her chair a little nudge toward the table.

He reached for London's, but she pulled out her own chair, waving him off. "I'm good, bro."

He swiveled his head, his gaze landing on Nia. She was at the head table and seemed to be holding an involved conversation with her sister. Part of him wanted to go over there, even if only to tell her how stunning she looked. He couldn't see her fully, but the view of her from the waist up was enough to send chills to his core. She was art, personified.

London cleared her throat. "You know, you could try to be less obvious, if you're going to stare at someone like that."

He sighed, bringing his attention back to his own table. Picking up the menu lying atop his place setting, he perused it. "Wow, they've pulled out all the stops on the catering."

"That's one thing I know about Addison Woodson," Everly commented. "She knows how to throw a classy affair. Always has."

Waitstaff began to move around the ballroom then, bringing with them the salad course. Salad was followed by an excellent surf-and-turf meal of lump crab cakes and sirloin tips, accompanied by huge twice baked potatoes. By the time the dessert course of red-velvet cheesecake and French vanilla ice cream was served, Pierce felt ready to loosen his pants. "Uncle Martin is going to be mad he missed out. This food is amazing."

"You know Martin would rather eat his own hat than put on a tuxedo," Everly laughed between bites of cheesecake. "But you're right about the food. Everything's been delicious."

Once the dishes were cleared away, the night's festivities began in earnest. Pierce watched as luminaries of the industry came to the stage one by one to speak about their experiences with the Woodson family. Each brought some wise perspective or funny anecdote, but all agreed that having worked with the people at 404 Sound had left an immense and indelible positive impact on their life, career or business.

A particularly moving speech came from the young artist Naiya B. "When Blaine discovered me, he took a chance on a girl from SWATS, a girl who was decidedly outside of the mainstream, a girl with a message and a mission. Being a part of Against the Grain, and a part of 404 Sound, has given me the career of my dreams. I've been able to record with artists I really admire. I've paid off my mother's mortgage. But most of all, I've been able to pour back into the community I love. And I have 404 Sound to thank for it all."

He joined in the applause filling the room, which quieted as Naiya took out her guitar and sang an original tune she'd written for the occasion. Another spirited round of clapping followed her performance, and she left the stage wearing a broad smile.

A young girl was escorted onto the stage then. Wearing a frilly pink dress and a huge matching satin bow, she appeared no more than ten. After being helped up onto a step stool in front of the podium, she leaned into the mic and said, "My name is April Oakley, and I am nine years old. I want to talk about Ms. Nia, who works at 404 Sound. This year, she came to my class to talk about what she does for work. Her job is to help people hear great music, which I think is very important. Aside from that, she was very nice to us, and she told us we can be whatever we want to be when we grow up. Because of Ms. Nia, I want to be an executive when I grow up. Thank you very much." She gave a little curtsy and was helped down from the stool.

Nia strode onto the stage a moment later, giving him a full view of the gorgeous gown she wore. Tears in her eyes, she walked straight over to little April, stooped down and said something to her. A moment later, she hugged the child, to the sounds of thunderous applause.

From the way she'd reacted to the youngster's speech, Pierce assumed April's presence had been a surprise to Nia. Either way, it was an incredibly sweet scene. Hearing a child speak on Nia's kindness tugged at his heart, because she'd showed that kindness to him as well.

The emotional scenes continued, as the film retrospective began to play once the stage was cleared. The reaction to the film was positive, with a few laughs and comments floating around the room. The final version had been trimmed down to forty minutes, and the cheers as it ended indicated the crowd's enjoyment.

Nia returned to the stage as an easel was wheeled out behind her bearing the sheet-covered artwork she'd created. Removing the mic from its stand, Nia said, "Mom and Dad, could you come up onstage, please?"

Caleb and Addison complied.

Nia then said, "And Mrs. Everly Hamilton, can you come up here, too, please?"

Everly's expression morphed, her eyes growing wide. "What on earth?"

Pierce stood, offering his arm. "Only one way to find out, Mother."

They made their way to the stage, and Pierce remained on the ballroom floor after assisting his mother onto the stage. It was as close as he could bear to be to Nia, knowing of the rift that existed between them. So he hung back, out of sight in the shadowy alcove near the stage.

"I wanted to give my parents something—a unique gift celebrating everything they've built. Because their accomplishments are what have brought us all here tonight." Nia gestured to the stagehand, who tugged the sheet away.

The huge canvas, lit by the spotlight, showed an image of four people standing outside beneath the Underground Atlanta sign. The youthful faces of Caleb, Addison, Everly and Phillip were all smiles as they posed.

"I call it *Four Dreamers*." Nia turned to Everly as another stagehand appeared from the wings with a framed, full-size reproduction. "Mrs. Hamilton, I'd like you to have this print in memory of your late husband. I thank you both for your contributions to this company, to Atlanta and to the culture."

Everly's hand flew to her mouth to cover a sob.

Addison's reaction was much the same. Even Caleb seemed to be fighting back tears.

Pierce stood in the shadows, shaking his head in amazement as they filed off the stage. *When did she have time to plan all this?* He felt like an asshole for the way he'd spoken to her. *I have to thank her for this.*

He helped his mother back to her seat and ensured that the framed print was safely in his sister's hands. As soon as the gala ended and the lights were raised again, he made his way to the head table.

He was within feet of it when a wall appeared before him, a wall fashioned of the Woodson men. Blaine, Gage, Miles and even brother-in-law Maxton all appeared, shoulder to shoulder, blocking any access to Nia.

"I just want to thank her for the print," Pierce insisted.

Gage eyed him, his disdain on full display. "We'll be sure to give her the message."

"I'd prefer to tell her myself, if you don't mind."

"Oh, we absolutely mind." Blaine cracked his knuckles.

"So, unless you want to leave here in an ambulance," Miles said, tugging his lapels, "I'd suggest you make yourself scarce, homeboy."

With a shake of his head, he glanced at Nia one last time before turning and walking away.

Seventeen

Nia rolled over in bed, roused by the sound of her ringing phone. Her bleary eyes searched the darkness until she finally located the device buried beneath her covers. She picked up the phone, saw her mother's name on the screen and immediately swiped it. Her heart thundering in her chest, she said, "Hello? Mom, what's wrong?"

"Everything's fine, honey. But Eden is in labor!"

Nia sat up in bed, stifling a yawn. "Are we sure this time? It's not a false alarm?" She looked at the time on her screen. *Sheesh, it's four in the morning.*

"No, it's the real thing. Blaine says she's gonna start pushing soon." Addy rattled the words off in quick succession, her excitement palpable. "Caleb and I are on the way to the birth center. Are you coming?"

She yawned again. "I may as well, now that I'm awake."

"Sorry, sweetie. I'm just so excited! I'll see you there."
Addy disconnected the call.

She sighed into the darkness. *I can't really be mad
at Mom. I did tell her to call me when the baby was
coming. And it's not like I was sleeping all that great,
anyway.*

As much as she hated it, she missed Pierce. Every
time she closed her eyes and tried to sleep, she saw his
face. It was a vision of him at the gala Saturday night.
That last, fleeting look of longing before her brothers
ran him off.

Nia had asked them to keep Pierce away, and they'd
obliged. She loved them and greatly appreciated the
fierce protective energy they had for her. Even Maxton had added his support, solidifying his place as a
Woodson man. Still, seeing that defeated expression
on Pierce's face as he walked away, she'd felt a twinge
of regret.

*This was supposed to be casual. I let my feelings get
involved and started thinking we could be more. And
that's where I messed up.*

Flipping on her bedside lamp, she put her phone on
her nightstand and scooted out of bed. She spent a short
time getting herself together, threw on a sweatshirt with
her fuzzy pajama pants and jammed her feet into a pair
of sneakers. Pulling up the hood of the sweatshirt, she
stepped out into the predawn chill and headed to her car.

After a quick stop off for coffee, she arrived at Atlanta Birth Center just before five. The three-story brick
building with whitewashed window trim sat on Balti-
more Place NW, in the shadow of Emory University

Midtown Hospital. Nia found the proximity of the facility to the hospital comforting, though she hoped it would prove irrelevant.

Inside the building, she found her relatives clustered in the waiting room. Gage and Caleb were stationed on a sofa, while Teagan and Miles stood nearby. Glancing around the room and taking note of who she didn't see, she asked, "Is Mom already in the birthing room?"

Teagan nodded, yawning. "Yup. You know she skated in there as soon as she arrived. Ainsley is in there, too."

Making her way to an empty chair, Nia took a seat. "Anybody know what's going on?"

Gage shook his head. "She's in active labor. That's the last update we heard."

As if summoned, Ainsley rushed out from the birthing suite. "Y'all... She's in the tub and she's pushing!"

Everyone stood except Caleb, the group clustering in the hallway as Ainsley dashed back the way she'd come.

Nia looked back over her shoulder, watching her father's expression. Concerned, she walked over to stand at his side. Giving his shoulder a squeeze, she asked, "Dad, are you alright?"

"I'm fine, just...reminiscing." He nodded. "I'm an old vet at this. I've got five babies of my own, after all."

"Can you remember all the way back to the first one?" She teased.

He laughed. "I sure can. You came into the world hollering like a banshee. Six pounds, nine ounces, twenty-one inches long."

She leaned down and kissed his forehead. "Your memory is impressive, Dad. And I'm glad you're okay."

"I'm just peacefully reflecting on my last few moments before I graduate from dad to grandpa."

She smiled at him and watched the years of memories play across his face before returning to the hall beyond the birthing suite door.

Despite the number of people huddled together, the hallway was nearly silent. Everyone seemed to be listening to the events unfolding beyond the closed door.

She could hear Eden vocalizing, and she closed her eyes against the sound and the unfathomable pain she imagined inspired it.

She wondered if she would ever experience this, the harrowing beauty of bringing another life into the world. She couldn't imagine doing that without a long-term partner but didn't know if that was in the cards for her.

There were sloshing sounds, the voices of the midwife and the doula coaching Eden through and Blaine's declarations of love and encouragement.

And then came the sound they all were anticipating. The sound of a baby's insistent wails.

Smiles spread over the faces of everyone clustered in the hall, and excited chatter began among them as they debated what the baby's name would be, or who the baby would most closely resemble.

Addy swung open the door. Her eyes filled with tears, she breathlessly announced, "She's here!"

Nia felt her heart swell. *I've got a niece. I'm going to be the most fun aunt ever.* She remained in the hall with her siblings while Addy returned to the room. After a time, Blaine appeared at the door and took a step into the hallway, with the blanket-wrapped baby in his arms. "Here's your new little niece."

Looking at her brother's face, Nia saw an expression she'd never seen before, one of such deep love and wonder that she had to hold back tears. And when she turned her gaze on the child's tiny face, gazing into her big brown eyes, she sighed aloud. "She's beautiful, Blaine."

Gage slapped him on the back. "Great job, bro."

Teagan scoffed as she jockeyed for a closer position to the baby. "Don't you think Eden deserves most of the credit?"

"Of course, she does," Miles added. "The baby looks more like Eden, anyway."

That started a whole debate, and she could only shake her head as she listened to them going back and forth.

With a chuckle, Nia leaned in a bit closer to her niece. "Buckle up, honey. Life in this family is sure to be an adventure."

Late Wednesday morning, Pierce arrived at his childhood home and climbed the stairs, seeking his mother.

He found her in her bedroom, curled up in the window seat with a book. Wearing a long housecoat and a head full of pink curlers, she looked more restful than he'd seen her in a long time. "Hey. Just letting you know I'm here."

She waved at him over her book. "Hey, sweetheart. Your uncle's outside fooling around with the smoker. Thanks for handling the food this year."

"No problem." While this hadn't been his idea, he didn't mind helping out, especially if it got his mother to relax. Returning downstairs, Pierce exited the house through the back door. On the stone patio, his uncle stood tending his trusty smoker.

"What you got in there, Unc?"

Martin looked up with a grin. "You know we do it big for turkey day. I got a pork shoulder and a whole mess of spareribs in there. They'll be right and tight by this evening." He used his long steel poker to prod the wood chips before shutting the smoker door.

Pierce took a deep inhale, enjoying the savory aroma. "What's that wood I smell? Hickory?"

"Right on. Added a little maple to it this year, to see how it's gonna come out." Martin walked over and clapped his hand against his nephew's shoulder. "You starting to come into your smoker's sense, I see."

He laughed. "I learned from the best."

Martin moved around him toward the door. "Come on back inside with me. I brought some collards that need washing and chopping." Once inside, Martin took a large bag of collard greens out of the double-door refrigerator. "You wanna handle this, Pierce?"

He took the bag and hauled it over to the sink. "We really are spoiling Mother this year, aren't we?"

"I'm guessing you're still a bit put out that I promised your mama that you and I would handle the feast this year, huh?"

Pierce turned on the cold water, stopping up one side of the deep farmhouse sink. "Um, yeah. I can't say I expected to be doing this in the middle of the week." He reached into the cabinet for the bottle of white vinegar and added a healthy splash to the water.

"Trust me—I did it for good reason." Martin walked up next to him with a bag of white potatoes. Setting the bag on the counter, he got out the cutting board and a chef's knife. "Your mama needed a break. She's in no condition to be standing in here chopping and cooking. And aside from that, you needed the distraction."

Pierce had been swirling the greens around in the vinegar solution, but when he heard his uncle's words, he paused. Lifting his hand out of the cold water, he asked, "What do you mean by that?"

"We can all tell you're upset, Pierce." Martin sidled up next to him, dumped out the bag of potatoes in the free side of the sink and used the sprayer arm to give their skins a good rinsing. "You haven't been yourself since the night of that fancy party."

"You mean, the gala where you missed an incredible dinner?"

"Yeah. I mean, I'm over missing out on the surf and turf. But you're not over whatever went down there, that's for sure." Piling the potatoes on the counter, Martin moved one to the cutting board and began dicing.

He sighed. "You're not wrong. I just…didn't know it was so obvious to everyone else."

"It is. That's why I asked your sister if she knew what the problem was."

He rolled his eyes. "And what did she say?"

"That it's got something to do with Nia Woodson." Martin grabbed a bowl from the cabinet and dumped the chopped potatoes into it. "You wanna shed some light on that?"

London was quick to dime me out, I see. He drained

the sink, then started refilling it with cold water to give the greens a second washing. While the water ran, he gave his uncle a brief rundown of things that had happened between him and Nia leading up to the night of the gala.

Martin shook his head. "Pause, rewind. You mean to tell me you didn't tell her that man worked for you? And you weren't ever gonna tell her?"

"No." He plunged his hands into the cold water again, feeling the resulting tightness in his joints. "I can see now that was wrong."

"It absolutely was. You never get anywhere with people you care about by hiding important things from them."

"I guess I just didn't consider it important."

"Whatever your thoughts on the matter, you should have known it would be important to Nia."

He swallowed. "I get it, Unc. But we were supposed to be casual. Just blowing off a little steam, you know? Once you start having deep conversations about uncomfortable topics, isn't casual off the table?"

Martin chuckled. "Kid, be honest with yourself. Casual was never really on the table for you, was it? You thought you'd swoop in there, sweep her off her feet and talk her into making a deal with you." He added more diced potatoes to the bowl. "You thought you could just do what you wanted, get the results you were after and then what? Were you gonna just walk away after the merger? Leave her high and dry?"

He cringed. "I don't know if I thought it through to that level."

"Obviously, you didn't." Martin shook his head. "I've done my best to be a positive role model for you in my brother's absence. I taught you to fish, to play basketball, how to garden and smoke a mean rack of ribs. But if my bachelor lifestyle taught you to deal with women like this, to be so cold and callous, then we got a big problem."

Pierce pulled the plug, watching the water drain away. It was too hard to look his uncle in the eye. "I'm sorry I disappointed you, Uncle Martin. But this isn't your fault. I've never had any indication that you related to women in any way other than respectful."

Martin set down his knife, folding his arms over his chest. "I ought to go upside your head, boy. But instead of that, I'm just gonna tell you this. You did something stupid. You showed your ass. But I ain't the only one you need to be apologizing to."

Pierce nodded. "I know. I'm just trying to think of a way to get her to see me so I can make things right."

"You better figure something out." Martin eyed his nephew, his tone serious. "If you think you feel bad now, just know it can get much worse. There ain't nothing like the pain of seeing the one that got away moving on with somebody that's gonna treat her like she deserves." He turned and walked to the other side of the room.

While his uncle rifled around under the cabinet for a pot, Pierce stood by the sink, wringing water from the collard leaves. His uncle's words had been harsh, but he knew they came from a place of genuine love. *It was what I needed to hear, even though it's kicking my ass.*

As he rinsed the chef's knife so he could trim and

chop the greens, he set his mind to work on a way to get Nia to listen to his apology.

She may not want anything to do with me. But I have to at least try to let her know I'm sorry. Even if I still end up having to go through life without her in it.

Eighteen

Darting around the kitchen Thursday afternoon, Nia sidestepped to avoid bumping into anyone or stepping on their feet. Thanksgiving dinner was less than an hour away, and she, Teagan and Ainsley were making last-minute preparations to ensure a smooth, enjoyable family meal.

"I'm exhausted," Teagan declared.

"Same." Nia shook her head as she pulled down her mother's favorite cut-crystal serving dishes from an upper cabinet. "Can you imagine how much work this would have been if we had to cook, too?"

Ainsley whistled as she sorted silverware. "I know some people insist on the whole 'home-cooked meal' thing, but honestly, I'm glad Addy called a caterer."

"Right. Mom never folded to any of that pressure."

Teagan stood by the sink, polishing the crystal water goblets meant to go at each place setting. "She laid it out for us years back. On holidays, we support a Black-owned business by ordering our food, and she gets to relax instead of being trapped in an apron for two days. Win-win, really."

Soon, they began carrying armloads of dishes to the dining room table. While Addy wasn't one for cooking on the holidays, she loved a properly set table and had taught her children to perform the task.

"Since this is my first holiday with y'all, I'm curious." Ainsley placed a folded linen napkin and silverware at one of the place settings. "Do your brothers ever help do this?"

Nia nodded. "We rotate. The guys did it last year, so it's our turn this year. Don't worry, they're never late for food, though."

Ainsley laughed. "I bet. I've watched Gage basically debone a chicken from across the room. He's definitely not missing out on a meal like this."

They returned to the kitchen for the second wave of items. This time, they loaded food from the caterer's foil and paper containers into Addy's crystal serving dishes. After gathering the serving utensils, the women worked together to ferry the food to the table and line all the items up along its center, careful not to disturb Addy's harvest-themed floral centerpiece.

True to form, the guys began arriving for dinner around four thirty. By then, the table was set, and Nia climbed the staircase to fetch her parents and let them know everything was ready. Approaching their bedroom door, she raised her hand to knock, but stopped when she heard the sound of her mother giggling.

Smiling, she backed away from the door. *I'm sure they'll be down soon.* Returning to the dining room, she took her seat.

Miles eyed her. "Hey, where are Mom and Dad? Didn't you tell them everything's ready?"

"They'll be down soon," she answered, turning her attention to the small tablet device positioned near Caleb's seat at the head of the table. "Did somebody set this thing up already?"

"I did." Cambria, who'd arrived with Miles, raised her hand. "That's why it took me so long to get here. When the video call comes in from Blaine, it should work fine."

"Thanks, Cambria." Setting the device down, Nia leaned back in her chair. Around her, several conversations were in progress, and she heard snippets of them all. She was comfortable, warm and surrounded by a loving family and a bountiful feast, and she was grateful for all of it.

Yet the low hum of melancholy remained with her. She hadn't been able to shake the sadness of the way things had gone down between her and Pierce, yet she couldn't bring herself to call him. *Who knows if he'll ever come around to realizing what he did was wrong? I can't put my heart at risk for someone I can't trust to be honest with me.*

A few minutes before five, Addy and Caleb appeared. Both were grinning like kids on Christmas, and Nia couldn't help smiling. Ever since Addy had moved back home, she and Caleb had rekindled a youthful passion for each other that was truly lovely to witness.

Once they were seated at opposite ends of the table, the tablet began to chime. "How do I answer this?" Caleb asked.

"Just drag your finger across the screen," Cambria instructed.

He did, and then he set the tablet in the small brass holder so everyone could see the screen. Blaine and Eden's faces appeared, and Blaine had the baby in his arms.

"Hey, everybody!" Blaine waved. "Thanks for understanding why we stayed home, Mom. And thanks for sending the food, too!"

"Of course. Why wouldn't I respect your efforts to protect my grandbaby? We need her nice and strong so she can change the world." Addy smiled and sipped from her water glass.

"We wanted to let you all know that we came up with a name for the baby," Eden added. "Her name is Helene Miriam Woodson."

"After my mother, and hers," Ainsley said, brushing away a tear.

"That's beautiful." Gage raised his glass. "A toast to little Miss Helene, the newest member of the Woodson family." Everyone raised their glasses in salute to the slumbering infant.

Caleb stood then and said grace, after which the platters of food got passed around the table. There was well-seasoned fried turkey, macaroni and cheese, mashed potatoes, green beans, broccoli and multigrain rolls.

Nia ate lightly, finding she didn't have much appetite even though the food tasted delicious.

"This food is so good!" Ainsley and Gage's preteen son, Cooper, grinned as he spooned up another helping of mac and cheese.

When dessert came around, she helped herself to a small sliver of pound cake, passing on the sweet potato pie.

"I've never seen you turn down pie, sis," Teagan remarked. "You okay?"

She nodded. "Yeah. Just trying to stave off the food coma."

Maxton laughed. "Why? That post dinner nap be hitting. It's a holiday tradition. At least, it is with my family."

"Oh, now I'm really looking forward to time with my in-laws," Teagan remarked with a laugh.

When she'd finished her dessert, Nia excused herself from the table and went into the living room. Settling onto the bench at her mother's piano, she absentmindedly picked out a few scales while gazing out the window. It was dark outside, but she could see a good portion of the grounds due to the solar lighting scattered around the property.

Teagan meandered into the room. Sitting down on the bench, she nudged her with her hips. "Scoot over."

Rolling her eyes, Nia moved over to allow her little sister more space. "What do you want, Teagan?"

"Honestly? To crash on the couch and take a nap," she chuckled. "But I can't do that with you sitting here tuning the piano, now, can I?"

"Oh, please. You've slept through worse." Nia pinched her shoulder. "When we were kids, you fell asleep at a music festival and slept through a Public Enemy set. If Flavor Flav's yelling and jumping around wasn't gonna keep you awake, you good."

"That's not what I mean, Nia. I mean, your depression music is terrible, don't get me wrong. What would really keep me awake, though, is my concern for you." She tossed an arm around Nia's shoulder. "I know this thing with Pierce was terrible, but you have to try and shake it off."

"My brain knows that. Try telling it to my heart." Nia shook her head and stopped playing.

"Seems like you miss him. Which is crazy, seeing as you couldn't stand him a month ago." Teagan sucked her lower lip. "Life is a funny thang, ain't it? Anyway, if he has any sense at all, he'll realize what a catch you are and come back begging on bended knee. Until then, try to hang in there, okay?"

Nia let her head drop onto her sister's shoulder, leaning into her embrace. "I'll try."

A flash of light came through the window, drawing her attention. "What's going on outside?"

Gage entered the room then, headed for the window. "There's somebody pulling up in front of the house. We know anybody that drives a black Navigator?"

Nia's heart jumped into her throat. "Pierce."

Gage frowned. "Oh, hell no." He marched off to the dining room and returned with Maxton and Miles. "We may be one man short, but we're still not taking any guff off this guy."

* * *

Pierce cut the engine of his truck in front of the Woodsons' house. Climbing out, he walked around to grab the huge bouquet in his passenger seat. Flowers in hand, he climbed the stairs up to the front door, taking a deep breath before he knocked.

The door swung open, and he came face-to-face with an angry-looking Gage Woodson. "What the hell are you doing here, Pierce?"

Rather than match his energy, Pierce humbled himself. "I'd like to speak with Nia, please."

Gage folded his arms over his chest. Glancing over his shoulder, he called into the house. "Sis, are you interested in talking to this guy, or do you want us to send him home?"

Pierce waited on the porch, listening.

After what seemed like an eternity spent squirming under her brother's glare, he heard her say, "Let him in."

Gage stepped back, and Pierce entered the house. Inside the living room, he was met with the stern gazes of every Woodson man. It was like the gala all over again.

He turned toward his right and saw Teagan sitting on the piano bench, her arm draped around Nia's shoulder. Nia was staring down, her gaze resting on the piano keys.

He moved toward her, aware of everyone watching him. Stopping in front of the piano, he said, "I brought you flowers. Persian buttercups are your favorite, right?"

She looked up then, first at the flowers, then at him. Clearing her throat, she said, "Can we have some privacy, please?"

Teagan gave her a squeeze, but her kept her eyes on Pierce, and got up. One by one, family members filed out of the room until Nia and Pierce were left alone.

He lay the flowers on the piano. "Thank you for letting me come in. I know you didn't have to."

"I didn't have to call off my brothers, either." She stood, moving to the sofa before sitting down again. "Don't make me regret it." Gesturing to the bouquet, she asked, "How did you know my favorite flower?"

"Read an article about you from the *Journal Constitution*." He shrugged. "It was two years old, but I had to take the shot."

"Lucky for you, I still love them." A small smile stretched her lips.

"Nia, I need to apologize to you. That's the whole reason I came here."

She nodded. "I'm listening."

Sitting down on the sofa next to her, but leaving a respectable distance between them, he looked into her eyes. "I had no idea of the kind of things Keegan was capable of when I hired him, or that he would go on to do the things he did to your family. None of that matters as much as the fact that I should have been honest to you, from the very beginning, about the fact that he worked for me."

She took a deep breath. "I'm glad you understand where I was coming from."

"As I understand it, Keegan will be facing criminal charges. I've gotten in contact with your father's lawyer. I let him know that I'm willing to testify in the case, even if it means I have to face consequences. I understand that the money I paid Keegan may have been tied up in this, but I'm willing to do whatever is necessary to set things right."

"I'll admit, I'm impressed. I appreciate you doing that."

"Not telling you was an asshole move, regardless of the level of seriousness I attributed to our relationship. I am so very sorry, and I hope you can forgive me."

"Your apology is accepted. Forgiveness may take some time."

"That's understandable, and I'm willing to wait, and to earn your trust.

She was silent for a few moments and seemed to be considering what he'd said. "I accept your apology. But I don't know if there's a way for us to move forward."

He paused, steadying himself as best he could, because he knew he was about to throw his playboy reputation right out the window. He also knew that Nia was worth it. "I brought you something. Consider it an apology gift, and a promise that, if you give me the chance, I'd like to get to know you fully. Because whether you send me away or not, you've already touched my heart." Reaching into his jeans pocket, he removed a small, oblong box.

"That better not be a ring," she said, staring.

He shook his head. "It's not." Holding the box up at eye level, he flipped the lid open, revealing a gold box-link chain necklace.

Her jaw dropped. "Oh, my... Pierce. Is that what I think it is?"

"It's a replica. I remember during your confessional,

you were talking about how proud you were to earn your Gold Award in Girl Scouts. So proud that you had the pin made into a pendant. But you lost the necklace—"

"—when I was in college," she said, finishing the sentence with tears standing in her eyes. "That footage didn't even make the final cut, and you still remembered that story?"

"Of course, I did. It seemed really important to you."

She sniffled. "Thank you so much for doing this."

"It was the least I could do." He used his thumb to brush away a fallen tear. "Do you…want me to help you put it on?"

She nodded while wiping her eyes.

Removing the necklace from the box, he stood next to the sofa. She turned slightly at her waist, lifting her hair as he draped the necklace around her neck and hooked the clasp. She let her hair fall free again and looked up at him. "You make a really good case for getting back in my good graces, Pierce Hamilton."

He offered a sheepish grin. "Does that mean I've succeeded?"

Her smile lit up the room, and the dark corners of his heart. "You're off to a great start. I'll warn you, though. It's going to be slow going. You'll have to work hard to win me."

"I'm willing to do that." He reached for her hand, gently tugging her to a standing position. "Because I know the prize will be well worth it."

She draped an arm around his waist and leaned up for his kiss.

Nineteen

December

Nia strolled down the concourse of Phipps Plaza, hand in hand with Pierce. All around her, the shops were dressed in their holiday finery, bows and wreaths. Towering, decorated trees, shimmering with lights and ornaments, seemed to occupy every available alcove.

In his free hand, Pierce held several shopping bags, procured during the last few hours of exploring the three-story mall. The bags were largely hers, save for a small bag from the Cole Haan store containing items he'd purchased.

"One last stop," she said, giving Pierce's hand a squeeze.

He blew out a breath. "You're really giving new meaning to the phrase 'shop 'til you drop,' aren't you?"

She giggled. "I just want to grab some outfits for Helene. I already got stuff for Cooper, and I can't leave out my little niece."

"Okay, so where are we headed?"

"Saks."

They went to the storied department store, and Nia headed straight for the baby section. She found herself fawning over the precious tiny outfits in various colors, as well as the little baby headbands with bows. Within the hour, they were leaving the store with another heavy bag. "Do you think I bought too much?"

He laughed. "Probably. But look on the bright side— the baby will be well-dressed until she's at least two with everything you hauled outta there."

"I know I probably got carried away, but this is my first real chance at shopping for a baby. And everything is just so damn cute!"

"Agreed, but I'm all shopped out." He gestured toward the exit. "Ready to head out?"

She nodded. "Yeah, we can go. But we're gonna have to work on your stamina."

"Now that's the first time I've ever heard that from a woman," he quipped.

She nudged him with her elbow. "You're a mess."

After leaving the mall, they headed back to her place. Surrounded by her shopping bounty, they settled in on her sofa with a plate of cookies and two steaming cups of cocoa.

Nia grabbed the remote and put a holiday music playlist on the television. Then she settled back into

Pierce's embrace, mug in hand. "This has been some hell of a year."

"You're right about that. A lot has happened. And I know my year was considerably less exciting than yours." He took a sip from his own mug.

"Absolutely. The year started out wild and only got wilder as it went on. The last few months dealing with a paternity scandal and the run-up to the gala were peak drama." She blew out a breath. "I'm exhausted. It may take me a whole 'nother year to recuperate."

"At least things have settled out now." He gave her shoulder a squeeze. "Your family's put back together, and you even got a new niece to spoil. So you could say that out of all that turmoil, something beautiful was born. Literally."

"And what about you, Pierce?" She turned to look into his eyes. "Do you feel like your loose ends are tied up for the year?"

"I do." He paused. "It wasn't easy, but I think we've settled on a solution. Mom is going to retire, effective December 31. I'm relieved, because it's time she slowed down and took better care of herself."

"And the CEO position?" She watched his face as she awaited his answer. "You promised you'd have news on that today."

"London is going to be interim CEO, while my mother's assistant, Reva, gets specialized training."

She frowned. "Are you really okay with someone else taking over?"

He shrugged. "This is probably the best solution for everyone involved. London doesn't want to be in charge.

Reva has been with my mother helping to keep all the gears turning at Hamilton House for more than twenty-two years, making her the longest-serving employee in company history, as well as the most experienced in what we do."

"I thought you wanted the CEO position. Has something changed?"

"A lot has changed." He sat his mug down and swiveled his upper body to face her. "I thought I wanted to run things, thought it would make me feel accomplished and fulfilled. I would have done anything to land the top spot. And therein lies the problem."

She nodded. "That's a really evolved thing to say."

"Once I dragged you into my games and saw how much my underhandedness hurt you, I realized I was on the wrong path. Yes, there was something missing in my life. But being CEO wasn't going to fill that void." He grabbed her hand, squeezed it. "What I really wanted was a partner. Not in business, but in life. What I needed, more than anything, was you."

She could feel the tears springing to her eyes. "Pierce."

"Listen to me, Nia. This isn't one of those cheesy speeches about how you complete me. I'm whole on my own. But I need you to know that loving you makes my life so much sweeter."

She felt her heart swell. "I love you, too, Pierce."

"I needed someone in my life who was strong enough to hold me accountable for my ways, to point out how my actions were wrong and the negative effects they had on other people's lives." He stroked her forearm. "Someone who could open my heart to compassion and love. Someone who could talk for all hours of the night about the nuances of hip-hop culture. Who could stimulate my mind, relax my body and see into my soul."

She set her mug aside, tears were coming in a stream now. "I...don't know what to say."

"I'll tell you what you could say." He reached into the back pocket of his jeans and pulled out a small box. Opening it, he revealed a three-carat marquise-cut diamond on a platinum band. "You could say you'll marry me."

Her hands few to her mouth, mainly to cover her sob.

He used his thumb to wipe away her tears.

When she finally got herself together, she nodded. "Yes, Pierce. Yes."

He moved to put the ring on her finger, but she stopped him.

"I do have a condition. I want a long engagement."

"I'm fine with that. I'm curious as to why, though."

She shook her head. "Every single one of my siblings just seemed to stumble and fall in love and immediately run off to get married." She reached out, pressed her palm against his face. "I want to savor this time, enjoy each other to the fullest. If you can be patient, I promise you I'll be the most spectacular bride you could ever ask for."

He grinned. "I'm with whatever, as long as you end up being my wife."

She held out her hand. "Then gimme my ring."

He slipped the band onto her finger.

She held it up, wriggling her fingertips and watching the lamplight play over the glittering stone. "It's beautiful, Pierce."

"Not as beautiful as you, Nia." He grabbed her hand and tugged her body close to his. "I love you."

"I love you, too."

And with the music softly playing and the lamplight casting a glow on them, she climbed into his lap to show him just how much.

* * * * *

TERRY YOUNG VA

Get 4 FREE REWARDS!

We'll send you 2 FREE Books plus 2 FREE Mystery Gifts.

FREE
Value Over
$20

Both the **Harlequin® Desire** and **Harlequin Presents®** series feature compelling novels filled with passion, sensuality and intriguing scandals.

YES! Please send me 2 FREE novels from the Harlequin Desire or Harlequin Presents series and my 2 FREE gifts (gifts are worth about $10 retail). After receiving them, if I don't wish to receive any more books, I can return the shipping statement marked "cancel." If I don't cancel, I will receive 6 brand-new Harlequin Presents Larger-Print books every month and be billed just $6.30 each in the U.S. or $6.49 each in Canada, a savings of at least 10% off the cover price, or 6 Harlequin Desire books every month and be billed just $5.05 each in the U.S. or $5.74 each in Canada, a savings of at least 12% off the cover price. It's quite a bargain! Shipping and handling is just 50¢ per book in the U.S. and $1.25 per book in Canada.* I understand that accepting the 2 free books and gifts places me under no obligation to buy anything. I can always return a shipment and cancel at any time by calling the number below. The free books and gifts are mine to keep no matter what I decide.

Choose one: ☐ **Harlequin Desire** ☐ **Harlequin Presents Larger-Print**
(225/326 HDN GRJ7) (176/376 HDN GRJ7)

Name (please print)

Address   Apt. #

City   State/Province   Zip/Postal Code

Email: Please check this box ☐ if you would like to receive newsletters and promotional emails from Harlequin Enterprises ULC and its affiliates. You can unsubscribe anytime.

Mail to the **Harlequin Reader Service:**
IN U.S.A.: P.O. Box 1341, Buffalo, NY 14240-8531
IN CANADA: P.O. Box 603, Fort Erie, Ontario L2A 5X3

Want to try 2 free books from another series! Call 1-800-873-8635 or visit www.ReaderService.com.

*Terms and prices subject to change without notice. Prices do not include sales taxes, which will be charged (if applicable) based on your state or country of residence. Canadian residents will be charged applicable taxes. Offer not valid in Quebec. This offer is limited to one order per household. Books received may not be as shown. Not valid for current subscribers to the Harlequin Presents or Harlequin Desire series. All orders subject to approval. Credit or debit balances in a customer's account(s) may be offset by any other outstanding balance owed by or to the customer. Please allow 4 to 6 weeks for delivery. Offer available while quantities last.

Your Privacy—Your information is being collected by Harlequin Enterprises ULC, operating as Harlequin Reader Service. For a complete summary of the information we collect, how we use this information and to whom it is disclosed, please visit our privacy notice located at corporate.harlequin.com/privacy-notice. From time to time we may also exchange your personal information with reputable third parties. If you wish to opt out of this sharing of your personal information, please visit readerservice.com/consumerchoice or call 1-800-873-8635. **Notice to California Residents**—Under California law, you have specific rights to control and access your data. For more information on these rights and how to exercise them, visit corporate.harlequin.com/california-privacy.

HDHP22R3